Acclaim for
Flora Thomson-DeVeaux's Translation of
The Posthumous Memoirs of Brás Cubas

"This translation . . . is a glorious gift to the world, because it sparkles, because it sings, because it's very funny and manages to capture Machado's inimitable tone, at once mordant and wistful, self-lacerating and romantic."   —Dave Eggers, from the Foreword

"Not only are the endnotes impressively accurate and useful for foreign readers, but also the translation does honor to Machado de Assis's style as it keeps an eye out for multiple layers of meaning and slippery descriptions, respecting the contours of a novel that, even as it feigns nonchalance, is in fact stunningly profound. Thomson-DeVeaux is able to preserve the elegance, humor, sincerity, and roguishness of this masterpiece of Brazilian literature."
                    —Pedro Meira Monteiro, Princeton University

"Thomson-DeVeaux's version flows better than any of the other translations and deals quite skillfully with some of the challenging nuances of the original. An obvious difference between Thomson-DeVeaux's translation and the previously published versions is the extensive apparatus of notes, which give very valuable cultural, historical, and literary information and will make the translation a valuable resource not just for those who must read the novel in English, but also for those with a reading knowledge of Portuguese."
                    —Paul Dixon, Purdue University

"Thomson-DeVeaux's translation keeps Machado de Assis's ambiguity in English and is thus much closer to his actual writing than previous translations. And it respects a 'secret' of Machado's literature—to wit, both its colloquial diction and the ability to produce virtually endless possible interpretations resorting to a disconcerting 'simplicity' in his writing manners. . . . Thomson-DeVeaux has succeeded with unparalleled elegance and precision."
                    —João Cezar de Castro Rocha, Rio de Janeiro State University

"A writer a hundred years ahead of his time . . . If Borges is the writer who made García Márquez possible, then it is no exaggeration to say that Machado de Assis is the writer who made Borges possible."
—Salman Rushdie

"A master."
—John Updike

"Machado is a miracle. The most brilliant star in the sky of nineteenth-century Iberian-American novels."
—Carlos Fuentes

"One of the few writers who not only received a state funeral, but actually deserved it."
—Louis de Bernières

"The creator of a tremendous oeuvre and an inimitable sense of humor."
—José Saramago

"A great writer who chose to use deadly humor where it would be least expected to convey his acute powers of observation and his penetrating insights into psychology. In superbly funny books he described the abnormalities of alienation, perversion, domination, cruelty, and madness. He deconstructed empire with a thoroughness and an esthetic equilibrium that place him in a class by himself."
—*The New York Times*

"One of the world's great writers."
—*The New York Review of Books*

"Machado de Assis wrote some of the most deliriously adventurous fiction of the last century."
—*Lingua Franca*

"No satirist, not even Swift, is less merciful in his exposure of the pretentiousness and the hypocrisy that lurk in the average good man and woman. Machado, in his deceptively amiable way, is terrifying."
—*The New Republic*

"Machado de Assis . . . is held by many to be not only Brazil's greatest writer but on a par with Henry James, Flaubert, and Hardy [with] his enchantingly digressive style, sly humor, and merciless exposure of hypocrisy and pretentiousness."
—*The Guardian*

PENGUIN CLASSICS

THE POSTHUMOUS MEMOIRS OF BRÁS CUBAS

JOAQUIM MARIA MACHADO DE ASSIS (1839–1908), the mixed-race grandson of freed slaves, was born in Rio de Janeiro. Orphaned young and largely self-educated, he made a living first as a printer, then as a journalist, and finally, from 1868 to his death, as a conscientious civil servant. Determined to be a writer from the age of fifteen, he published poetry, short stories, and novels, among them the brilliantly original, ironic ones for which he is best known: *The Posthumous Memoirs of Brás Cubas* (1881), *Quincas Borba* (1891), and *Dom Casmurro* (1899). He was elected the first president of the Brazilian Academy of Letters in 1897. At the time of his death he had published nine novels and more than two hundred short stories, and he was given a state funeral with full civil and military honors.

FLORA THOMSON-DeVEAUX is a translator, writer, and researcher who studied Spanish and Portuguese at Princeton University and earned a PhD in Portuguese and Brazilian studies from Brown University. She lives in Rio de Janeiro.

DAVE EGGERS is the author of many books, including *The Circle*, *The Monk of Mokha*, and *The Parade*. He is the founder of *McSweeney's*, a member of the American Academy of Arts and Letters, and a winner of the Dayton Literary Peace Prize.

THE POSTHUMOUS MEMOIRS

OF

BRÁS CUBAS

BY

MACHADO DE ASSIS

Foreword by
DAVE EGGERS

Translated with an Introduction and Notes by
FLORA THOMSON-DeVEAUX

PENGUIN BOOKS

PENGUIN BOOKS

An imprint of Penguin Random House LLC
penguinrandomhouse.com

Translation, introduction, and notes copyright © 2020 by Flora Thomson-DeVeaux
Foreword copyright © 2020 by Dave Eggers
Penguin supports copyright. Copyright fuels creativity, encourages diverse voices,
promotes free speech, and creates a vibrant culture. Thank you for buying an authorized edition
of this book and for complying with copyright laws by not reproducing, scanning, or distributing
any part of it in any form without permission. You are supporting writers and allowing
Penguin to continue to publish books for every reader.

Originally published in 1881 in Portuguese as *Memorias posthumas de Braz Cubas*
by Typographia Nacional, Rio de Janeiro

LIBRARY OF CONGRESS CATALOGING-IN-PUBLICATION DATA
Names: Machado de Assis, 1839–1908, author. | Thomson-DeVeaux, Flora, translator.
Title: The posthumous memoirs of Brás Cubas / by Machado de Assis ;
translated with an introduction and notes by Flora Thomson-DeVeaux.
Other titles: Memorias posthumas de Braz Cubas. English
Description: [New York, NY] : Penguin Books, 2020. | Includes bibliographical references.
Identifiers: LCCN 2019051790 | ISBN 9780143135036 (paperback) | ISBN 9780525506683 (ebook)
Classification: LCC PQ9697.M18 M513 2020 | DDC 869.3/3—dc23
LC record available at https://lccn.loc.gov/2019051790

Printed in the United States of America
11th Printing

Set in Sabon LT Pro

Contents

THE POSTHUMOUS MEMOIRS
OF BRÁS CUBAS

Foreword

Wit leaps centuries and hemispheres. It does not collect dust, and, when done right, it does not age. You are holding one of the wittiest, most playful, and therefore most alive and ageless books ever written. It is a love story—many love stories, really—and it's a comedy of class and manners and ego, and it's a reflection on a nation and a time, and an unflinching look at mortality, and all the while it's an intimate and ecstatic exploration of storytelling itself. It is a glittering masterwork and an unmitigated joy to read, but for no good reason at all, almost no English speakers in the twenty-first century have read it (and I first read it only recently, in 2019).

But it survives, and must be read, for the music of its prose and, more than anything else, for its formal playfulness. This translation, by Flora Thomson-DeVeaux, is a glorious gift to the world, because it sparkles, because it sings, because it's very funny and manages to capture Machado's inimitable tone, at once mordant and wistful, self-lacerating and romantic. Its narrator, Brás Cubas, is dead. He tells the story of his life from the grave, and maybe because he has nothing left to lose—being dead and all—he tells the story precisely as he wants to, convention be damned. The novel unfolds in brief, bright chapters, brightened further with endless self-referentiality and self-doubt. "I am beginning to regret that I ever took to writing this book," Brás Cubas writes in a chapter called "The Flaw in the Book." "Not that it tires me," he continues. "I have nothing else to do, and dispatching a few meager chapters into the other world is invariably a bit of a distraction from eternity."

The story, at its core, is almost conventional, a nineteenth-century aristocratic love triangle. Brás Cubas hovers at the edges of Rio de Janeiro's moneyed classes but lacks the will to marry—his sister's obsession—or the ambition to rise within the government—his father's wish. He passes on a chance to marry the beautiful Virgília and be catapulted into public life by her powerful father. Instead, an honorable man named Lobo Neves takes both Virgília's hand and her father's mentorship, and it's only then that Brás Cubas begins to feel drawn to Virgília. They begin an affair, and try—not so hard, really—to keep it hidden from Virgília's too-trusting husband. Soon everyone in Rio's society seems to know, with the danger of discovery only drawing the lovers closer.

Meanwhile, Brás Cubas contemplates the meaning of life (from the grave), aided by his friend Quincas Borba, who is trying to popularize a philosophy called Humanitism, designed, Machado/Cubas writes, "to ruin all the rest." At its core is a belief in the rightness of anything human. Brás Cubas admits that it's Panglossian but finds a certain comfort in the radical notion that humans should be allowed to do anything humans naturally do, that whatever we do we are meant to do—with special reverence for the making of more humans. "Love, for example," he writes, "is a priesthood; reproduction, a ritual. Since life is the greatest benefit the universe can bestow . . . it follows that the transmission of life, far from being an occasion for gallanting, is the supreme hour of a spiritual Mass. Hence there is truly only one misfortune in life: never being born."

Machado veers between the book's love story and its metaphysical interludes with ease, in part because though the book is about earnest things—love, life itself, the finality of death—it never takes itself seriously. In Chapter IV, "The Fixed Idea," Machado begins a grand analogy comparing lesser human endeavors to those that echo through the ages. "To offer a poor analogy, it is like the rabble, sheltered in the shadow of the feudal castle; the castle fell and the rabble remained. Indeed, they became grand in their own right, a veritable stronghold . . . No, the analogy's really no good." The chapter titles themselves are disarming. One chapter, aptly called "Sad, but Short," is followed by "Short, but Happy," which is both. There is a chapter dedicated to boots, another to the author's legs, while another is called "Not to Be Taken Seriously." Chapter CXXX is titled "To Be Inserted into Chapter CXXIX," and at the end of it, the author asks that the reader insert it between the first and second sentences of the previous chapter. There's also a long hallucination involving a hippopotamus.

Somehow none of the gags and intertextual fun does anything to diminish the power of the story. The romance between Brás Cubas and Virgília is convincing and wildly lyrical. The feeling we have for the unwitting Lobo Neves is real, and the crime that the narrator and Virgília commit on him is never punished—in life or death. And this is key. This is an atheistic book, where there is no judge but one's conscience, and where the offender lies alone, in a box permeated by worms, recounting his life and failures without any heavenly consequence. It's funny, too. It is wholly original and unlike anything other than the many books that came after it and seem to have knowingly or not borrowed from it.

Readers are an amnesiac species, and so, every few decades, we wake up to believe that an author addressing the reader directly, or playing with form, or including references to the author or the book *within* that book, is new and should be labeled post- or meta- or whatever unfortunate and confining term will come next. But the fact is that an outsize number of the classics of the world employ one or many of these so-called post/meta devices. It began with Cervantes, who allowed Don Quixote and Sancho Panza to be aware, in Book II, that they were characters in Book I. *Candide*—which Machado references many times—is endlessly self-aware, and Thackeray, in *Vanity Fair*, makes so many references to the author's presence and powers and omniscience that a reader loses count. Joyce and Austen and Nabokov and Sterne—also referenced by Machado—and Stein and Pessoa and legions more have experimented with the form of the novel, have inserted and questioned their authorial authority, and their willingness to experiment, and to have some fun with the relationship among writer, reader, and the book itself, have kept the form fresh and surprising, and so have kept it alive.

But now it is different. Now, strangely—so strangely—we live in times of profound traditionalism in literature, and it's difficult to explain why. I had the enormous pleasure a few years ago to judge a contest to name the year's best novel, and the committee I was part of had an unexpectedly good time doing the job. There were so many brilliant books. But of the four hundred or so American novels we were asked to read that year, only a few dozen could be called funny, only a few could be called playful, and I counted exactly two that were in any significant way experimental. If that's not an indication of a general fear of the new, a hesitation to take chances, and a startling and ill-advised self-seriousness about the novel, I'm not sure what is. This isn't to say that all novels, or even most, should be, or could be, as playful as this one, but it wouldn't hurt to have a few more that allow humans—characters, readers, authors even—to laugh. Denying the jokes in life, and the joke of life itself, is too sad.

DAVE EGGERS

Introduction

Fifteen pages into *Memórias Póstumas de Brás Cubas*, when the narrator, delirious and on the brink of death, is carried off by a gruff, talking hippopotamus, I remember putting the book down and staring out the window for a breath, delighted and taken aback. This was my first encounter with *Brás Cubas*. It was 2010, I was a sophomore in college with a few semesters of Portuguese under my belt, and this book was not what I had expected.

The average non-Brazilian reader might be forgiven for not expecting anything whatsoever. After all, *The Posthumous Memoirs of Brás Cubas* was Joaquim Maria Machado de Assis's first novel published in English, seventy years after its release and nearly a half-century after its author's death. "The name of Machado de Assis will probably be unknown to nine out of ten people who pick up this book," hazarded one of the early reviews of William Grossman's pioneering 1952 translation. One would be hard-pressed to alter that figure today, even after *Brás Cubas* has won over such illustrious writers as Susan Sontag, Salman Rushdie, John Barth, and Philip Roth.

In 1960, in *The Brazilian Othello of Machado de Assis*, the critic and translator Helen Caldwell spoke of the author as Brazil's "Kohinoor," the diamond plucked from India to adorn Queen Victoria's crown. Translations, needless to say, do not steal the original; English renditions of Machado de Assis's works do not deprive Brazilian readers of their jewel. Still, Machado de Assis has yet to find his place in the Anglophone canon. Each generation seems to have its "Machado moment," glimpsing the diamond of his work anew—a rediscovery by turns intimate, wondering, and "indignant," as Caldwell put it in *The Brazilian Master*. Who is this master, and why haven't we heard of him before?

For a beginning student of Brazilian literature, on the other hand, Machado de Assis seemed to be everywhere, as inescapable and imposing as the mountains of Rio de Janeiro. Born in that city in 1839, the mixed-race son of a humble family, the grandson of slaves, Machado—as he is familiarly known in Portuguese—rose from obscurity and relative poverty to become a fixture of literary life, and then a cultural patriarch. He wrote profusely, if not furiously: a largely self-educated, voracious reader, he began his career as a typographer's apprentice, then a copy editor, journalist, theater critic, and censor. He penned hundreds of newspaper columns under various pseudonyms, wrote poetry and plays, made the bookstores of the swank Rua do Ouvidor a perennial haunt, and inserted himself into a number of literary societies before cementing his reputation with a series of novels. He was the founding president of the Brazilian Academy of Letters. At his funeral, in September 1908, he was mourned by statesmen and writers alike. A legend in life, he became a monument in death.

The Posthumous Memoirs of Brás Cubas occupies an almost mythical position in Machado's trajectory. By 1880, Machado had written four well-received novels: *Resurrection* (1872), *The Hand and the Glove* (1874), *Helena* (1876), and *Iaiá Garcia* (1878), books in which marriage is either the end point or the fulcrum of the plot, and young women struggle in more or less melodramatic and scheming ways to secure their places in society.

And then came *Brás Cubas*. The novel was a long step outside the bounds of convention: the memoirs of a man, composed from his grave, dedicated to the worms gnawing at his corpse. It is full of disconcerting and playful images, mischievous mental creations brought to life. The narrator sees the idea for a grand invention somersaulting before him on a metaphysical trapeze; his thoughts take wing and nestle up against his lover's thoughts on a moonlit windowsill; he lectures readers on the importance of cross-eyed fakirs and takes them into the brain of an envious hatmaker.

For those reading the serialized narrative in the magazine *Revista Brazileira*, the story stretched from March to December 1880 and would be published in book form the following year. Over the course of 160-odd chapters,* the protagonist introduces himself, dies, is born, grows up, fails to make much of anything of himself, and complains with gusto about the task of writing and about the failings of his readers, looking down his nose at them and dismissing them from the heights of his gravebound superiority.

This peculiar work, despite the status it would come to attain, was at first received with no small perplexity. A handful of critics offered mild praise; others weren't so charitable. The reaction was so icy that Machado's brother-in-law had to give him a pep talk. "And what of it if the majority of the reading public didn't understand your latest book? There are books that are for all, and books for a few—your last is of the second sort, and I know that it was quite appreciated by those who did understand it—moreover, as you well know, the best books are not those which are the most in vogue. Do not mind or think of public opinion when you write. Justice will be done, sooner or later, you may be sure."

Indeed, this strange book would, in retrospect, be cast as the start of a new era for Machado de Assis. As a student of Brazilian literature, I became aware of the unique place it occupied in the mythology of the national canon. From certain angles, it seems that there is a before-and-after Machado de Assis—an author with whom subsequent generations have been forced to reckon—and that within Machado de Assis there is a before-and-after *Brás Cubas*. While the hard distinction between the first and second phases of his work (Romantic and conformist in the former, formally experimental and unsettling in the latter) has been rethought in recent decades as scholars have traced the roots of Machado's experimentations back to previous works, something remains of the image

*The 162 chapters of the original would gradually be combined into 160 over the course of subsequent editions.

of the dead narrator springing full-grown and grinning from the head of his creator, inexplicable and epoch-making.

What was it that made *Brás Cubas* so strange? Writing in the 1990s, the Brazilian critic Wilson Martins commented that in nineteenth-century Brazil, Machado was seen as an eighteenth-century writer; that in twentieth-century Brazil, he was seen as a nineteenth-century writer; and that outside Brazil, by the twentieth century he was starting to be seen as a twenty-first-century writer. The eighteenth-century tag comes courtesy of the book's evident debt to Laurence Sterne; the list of striking commonalities between the *Posthumous Memoirs* and Sterne's *The Life and Opinions of Tristram Shandy, Gentleman* (1759–1767) includes both works' digressiveness and formal experimentation. On the first score: in trying to tell the story of his life, Tristram famously gets so distracted that he gets around to narrating his birth in only the third volume; whereas Brás takes only ten chapters to do the same, he is given to wandering down all sorts of tangents and chastising readers when they fail to follow his zigzagging train of thought. On the second score, both books have daringly short chapters, some of which are composed entirely with punctuation, or less still: Tristram decides to cut ten pages from his *Life and Opinions*, for example, leaving a gap in the numbering, while Brás's chapter "Of How I Did Not Become a Minister of State" is one long, disappointed ellipsis.

Even for those who had followed Machado's increasingly whimsical *crônicas* (newspaper columns in which he, under a variety of pseudonyms, recounted and reflected on current events), it was jarring to find him plunging into the disagreeable head of a ghost with memoiristic ambitions. Perhaps the least unsettling thing in the book is its prose, which is masterfully elegant and largely law-abiding, though it conceals many a pitfall for the translator.

We may get a clearer sense of how odd the book seemed by looking at the company it kept. Machado's contemporaries and immediate predecessors could mostly be found writing urban society dramas or origin stories that dwelled on the fusion of the nation's "three races"—the Portuguese, Native peoples, and African slaves. (This was the sort of weighty narrative I think I expected to find when I sat down to read Brazil's greatest novelist.) Their prose, for the most part, has aged, while Machado's remains eerily fresh. "Death does not age one," as Brás reminds us, exasperated, in Chapter CXXXVIII; a skeleton's smile is eternal, and Machado's style, while intricate, is anything but overly fleshy. When held against paeans to the lush Atlantic forest and self-sacrificing indigenous heroes, Machado's novels seemed to many of his contemporaries rather lacking in national spirit, a grave defect for a country still working to define its culture and identity in relation to its former imperial power. As Machado would write in a famous 1873 essay: "One sometimes hears an opinion regarding this topic that I consider erroneous. This is that the only works of true national spirit are those that describe local subjects, a belief that if correct, would greatly limit the resources available to our literature." If Shakespeare could lift plots from Italy and Spain, why couldn't Machado dip his pen into a Sternean inkwell?

John Gledson, a Machado scholar and translator, wrote that his attempts to read the master had been frustrated until he read a series of analyses by the literary critic Roberto Schwarz that gave him the key to interpret him. Gledson sums up one of the major arguments as follows: the seemingly arbitrary, disconcerting structure of *The Posthumous Memoirs of Brás Cubas*, "narrated by a frivolous, blithely inconsistent member of the ruling class, is itself socially inspired—there could hardly be a tighter connection between form and content." In other words, Brás is far more than a reheated Tristram Shandy: his disconcerting freedom as a narrator is rooted in his disproportionate perch in a highly arbitrary Brazilian society. Machado's appropriation of the Sternean form becomes a critique of his country's relationship to power, albeit one so finely executed and so unwilling to be didactic that it would be perceived as such only belatedly. (In the case of one of his other masterpieces, *Dom Casmurro*, it took over a half-century for critics to grasp that the central fact of the narrative may be all in the narrator's imagination. Their eyes were opened by none other than a Machadian translator, Helen Caldwell, who suggested that the protagonist, Bento Santiago, might not be an embittered, betrayed husband, but rather a cruel "Brazilian Othello.")

Beyond the structural characteristics that refer back to the power dynamics of Brazilian society, the reader looking to appreciate the brilliance of *Brás Cubas* is faced with more hurdles—namely, issues of historical memory. Slavery haunts the novel in ways that might have been immediately present and uncomfortable for Machado's contemporaries, but whose subtleties lie in contextual knowledge not readily accessible to modern readers. Brás's perplexity at the cruelty of the yellow fever epidemic that swept through Rio in 1850, for example, is comprehensible on its face, but it takes on a different light entirely when we read that the plague had a distinctly racial bent. The city's African population was largely spared, thanks to inherited immunity to the virus that caused the disease, while European immigrants and the white population were hardest hit. The disparity was so stark that some attributed the disease to revenge by Benedict, the black saint, after white churchgoers' refusal to carry his statue on their shoulders during an 1849 religious procession. When another character fantasizes about mustering a half-dozen good men to throw all the English out of Rio de Janeiro, the sentiment becomes both slightly more understandable and more sinister when we know that the English government was working to strangle the Atlantic slave trade and had recently affirmed its right to stop Brazilian ships and search them for suspect cargo. The novel's meanings far overspill its historical context, of course, but a fuller understanding of these time-bound elements—remote for Brazilian high school students today and downright otherworldly for the English-speaking reader with little knowledge of Brazil—enriches it immeasurably.

Take the opening to Chapter LXVIII. In the first sentence, Brás lets us know that he was strolling through a place called Valongo. What he does not tell us—in part because he doesn't need to, given the dark familiarity of the name for Rio natives, and in part because he has no inclination to make his reflections on the subject anything but glancing—is that the Valongo was the city's old slave market. By the time of the scene in the novel, the Americas' largest slaving port, which alone may have received as many as a million enslaved Africans (more than double the total number brought to the United States), had been officially deactivated; but Machado would recall smuggled slaves being sold in broad daylight, years after the ban. Shortly after Brás's stroll, in 1843, the Valongo wharf was chosen as the site to welcome Emperor Pedro II's bride and renamed the "Empress's Landing," its irregular cobblestones covered over with even flagstones. After the monarchy fell, the area was used as a landfill. Only in the first decades of this century, thanks to the excavations prompted by the World Cup and the Olympics, did parts of the old slave wharf see the light again. Not too far off is the site of the Cemitério dos Pretos Novos, the common grave of tens of thousands of newly arrived Africans who succumbed even before they could be sold.

The sentence reads, *Tais eram as reflexões que eu vinha fazendo, por aquele Valongo fora, logo depois de ver e ajustar a casa*; "Such were my reflections as I strolled through Valongo, just having visited the house and made the necessary arrangements." Brás's reflections are shortly interrupted by the spectacle of a black man, his former slave, brutally whipping his own slave, a sight that he finds first bothersome, then philosophical, then rather funny. This notorious chapter is so short and so dense with meaning that any attempt by a translator to contextualize within the narration itself would bloat the prose and blunt its wickedness. And yet to leave the sentence as such, without any context, would be to impoverish it immeasurably.

The politely bemused initial reaction to this tour de force of a book is partially captured in the prologue to the fourth edition, as reproduced here: in January of 1881, the historian Capistrano de Abreu wrote to Machado, wondering whether *Brás Cubas* might properly be considered a novel at all. Elsewhere in the letter, he described the reading experience as *deliciosa— e triste também*, delightful and sad at the same time.

My first reading was pure delight: I thrilled at the narrator thumbing his nose at readers and critics alike, leaping around the events of his life, crafting and discarding metaphors in the same breath, existing in blithe contradiction. But as I revisited the book in undergraduate and graduate seminars over the years, the hilarity of that first encounter seemed to fade away. More and more, what I saw was Brás's bleak disregard for his fellow man in both life and death, which is as plain on the book's face as its absurd humor. In the end, it was the process of translating the *Posthumous Memoirs* that unveiled the darkest parts of its history—and also helped me to laugh at its jokes again.

In part, getting to know the book better has been an exercise in dismantling my initial wonderment. By this I don't mean ruining the book's bitter fun—far from it. But to regard the novel as wonderfully inexplicable is to accept a blinkered view that cuts out the very real world from which it emerged; that became untenable as the process of parsing the text thrust me ever deeper into its time and place. While almost entirely shorn of jungles and beaches (as one contemporary of Machado's would complain, *"Não há uma árvore!"*—there's not so much as a tree in his urban, people-focused landscapes), the novel bears deep and abiding marks of its Brazilian origin. Many readers—including me—are swept off their feet by Chapter VII, "The Delirium," in which Brás, hallucinating in his last days, is able to contemplate the frenzied march of humanity from his deathbed. The chapter is a remarkable, unhinged jaunt through time, narrated by a man who, "on the verge of leaving the world, felt a devilish pleasure in jeering at it." Prepossessing as the scene is, what the translation process and the exercise of historical contextualization reveal is the brilliant, cruel absurdity behind seemingly tamer or more elliptical passages in the novel, such as the chapter silently set in the city's old slave market.

If *Brás Cubas* already seems like an anomaly in Portuguese, the strangeness is doubled, or squared, when it is appraised outside the Brazilian context. Looking to insert Machado into their literary constellations, both Carlos Fuentes and Harold

Bloom called him a miracle: the heir of Cervantes or Sterne, shooting up unexpectedly from poor tropical soil. And then there's the nickname that stuck to him, bestowed by the great Brazilian poet Carlos Drummond de Andrade: *o Bruxo do Cosme Velho*, the Wizard of Cosme Velho, a reference to the Rio neighborhood where he spent most of his adult life.

Not a miracle, not a mage: my Machado de Assis is an illusionist. There's magic in the final effect, to be sure. But behind it are pure craft and skill, as well as the manipulation of human behavior—misdirection, playing with our assumptions, our vanity, our foolishness. These past few years translating his work have been an apprenticeship, spent staring at a deft-fingered master and doing my best to replicate his tricks for a new audience.

FLORA THOMSON-DeVEAUX

A Note on the Translation

My route to translating *The Posthumous Memoirs of Brás Cubas* was a circuitous one, as must be any path snaking up the side of a mountain. I had become acquainted with (and charmed by) Machado de Assis as an undergraduate student of Brazilian literature, the same period in which I discovered and fell in love with translation, but it never crossed my mind to combine the two. Then, in 2014, having become a professional translator and about to enter graduate school, I agreed to translate a book by João Cezar de Castro Rocha titled *Machado de Assis: Toward a Poetics of Emulation*. I thought of it as translating the author's analysis of Machado de Assis's works; that was a part of it, of course, but I had signed up for something much bigger than I could have imagined.

You may have realized what I hadn't when I took on the book: that, of course, not everything that Castro Rocha quoted had been translated into English before. While my mental library of Brazilian literature had swelled considerably since my first reading of *Brás Cubas*, and while I had found my footing as a translator, the thought of laying hands on Machado made me quake.

O que não tem remédio, remediado está—what can't be cured must be endured. Or surreptitiously enjoyed, in this case. Whenever I could find an existing translation, I dutifully plugged it into the book as I went along. Whenever I couldn't, I translated the snippets being quoted with a slight thrill of irresponsibility and something else. It was exhilarating to plunge into Machado's sentences—read them, reread them, threeread them, disjoint the words, take out one syllable and then another, examine them inside and out, from all sides, against the light, dust them off, wipe them on my knee (the translator bears an unfortunate resemblance to the hapless bibliomaniac from Chapter LXXII of the *Posthumous Memoirs*), and try to put them back together again.

At first I was translating only brief excerpts from shorter pieces—*crônicas*, short stories, critical essays—and quoting from existing translations for the novels. Soon, however, it became clear that many of those published translations didn't function when bracketed by Castro Rocha's analysis, with its keen attention to etymology and structure. It seemed as if the author's close reading were referring to another text entirely. There was nothing for it but to retranslate.

The experience left me with the impression that there was room for a new rendering of many a Machadian text; what's more, my experiments with translating excerpts left me with a sense of unfinished business. In for a penny, in for a pound (or in for a *tostão*, in for a *meia-dobra*—more on translating currencies in the endnotes). I devoted the next four years, over the course of my PhD program, to the research, preparation, and process of retranslating Machado's masterpiece. In this I was aided by many, including my Brown committee—Nelson Vieira, Luiz Fernando Valente, and Leonor Simas Almeida—and scholars at other institutions, such as João Cezar de Castro Rocha, Pedro Meira Monteiro, and Bruno Carvalho, as well as a motley crew of readers who ranged from my high school English teacher Mike Evans and childhood friend Daniel Brinkerhoff Young to onetime professor João Moreira Salles and fellow translator Branca Vianna. My parents, stepparents, and sisters have been supportive ever since they let me fly off to South America at age nineteen; and I am eternally grateful to my wife, Paula Scarpin, for her love and support over this yearslong process—and for her tolerance of teetering stacks of nineteenth-century dictionaries.

I have been preceded in this task by William Grossman, with his *Epitaph of a Small Winner* (1952); E. Percy Ellis, with *Posthumous Reminiscences of Braz Cubas* (1955); and Gregory Rabassa, with *The Posthumous Memoirs of Brás Cubas* (1997). For their assistance during the research process, I would like to thank the families of Grossman and Ellis, as well as the staff at the Howard Gotlieb Archival Research Center, where Rabassa's papers are held. After completing an initial draft, I set the other translations side by side and took to examining them—not against the original, as in a fact-checking exercise, but rather *with* it and with one another, as interpretations of a slippery text caught in amber for the bilingual reader's perusal. Cervantes famously compared reading a work in translation to looking at the back of a Flemish tapestry, where one can make out the main figures but finds them covered by threads and knots. While I have yet to see a Flemish tapestry from behind, I found the metaphor useful, although not in Cervantes's sense. This view is not obstructed, but illuminating: by looking at the back of the fabric, one can get a sense of how the figures are woven, which images pose the greatest difficulty, and what the artist's intent may have been. The points at which the translators fail to converge are like thick clusters of thread on the tapestry's reverse, concepts or passages that present unexpected difficulty and thus point to the central ambiguities and cultural baggage at the heart of any work—perhaps that which is most essential. Where other divergences or dissatisfactions with the translated text rear their heads, I can only hope that readers will be drawn back to the fathomless original and come to contemplate its depths.

A Note on the Endnotes

The practice of translation is an idiosyncratic genre of research, and this particular translation thrust me down countless paths: the history of pyrotechnics, and of the categorization of mental disorders; the finer points of nineteenth-century fashion, ceramics, and house-painting; shifts in terminology related to mealtimes; and colloquial expressions involving feet and ears, to name just a few. The invisible results of these journeys are to be found in my translation choices, informed as much by this haphazard research as by my instincts and a battery of nineteenth-century dictionaries. The visible results are to be found in my endnotes—and it is here that I half-proudly, half-abashedly announce that this is the first annotated English-language translation of *The Posthumous Memoirs of Brás Cubas*.* Abashedly, because notes are often portrayed by authors and translators alike as a mark of shame—the text dragging a chain like Jacob Marley's, each link a failure of linguistic ingenuity. Proudly, because I have come to feel that to ignore certain elements in the text is to rob it of crucial historical and

---

*Mine are endnotes, however, not footnotes like this one, because the *Posthumous Memoirs*—as befits the creation of an ex-typographer—is exquisitely aware of its existence as a book, commenting on bindings, capitalization, and so on, and nowhere does Brás indicate that his grave-composed masterpiece has anything marring its lower margins. E. Percy Ellis's translation, titled *Posthumous Reminiscences of Braz Cubas,* includes a handful of footnotes, but they are few and far from systematic.

cultural ballast, whereas to shoehorn information into Machado's prose would be to deprive it of its deliberate obliqueness.

The notes, then, are a testament to the book's malevolent grace and depth, and an attempt to restore it in its fullness. The book is dotted with winking references, jokes half-buried in the sands of time—such as the fact that Brás's schoolteacher, whose surname is Barata (meaning Cockroach), lives on Rua do Piolho (Louse Street), a very real thoroughfare whose name has since been substituted by the more palatable Rua da Carioca (Carioca being the name of a river flowing through the city, which later became the demonym for Rio natives). Other details give us a sense of nineteenth-century Rio that is often lost on even contemporary Brazilian readers. When it came to the sums of money tossed around by the upper crust of which Brás is a scion, I turned to an economic historian for help, thinking that my calculations based on contemporary exchange rates were absurdly high—only to conclude that the fortunes of imperial Brazil's 1 percent were indeed obscene.

This translation also takes a cue from the layout of the editions published during Machado's lifetime—apparently a minor note, but less so if we recall that the author himself once worked as a typographer and the text itself makes reference to different elements of the printing process (Brás is quite keen to let us in on his "Theory of Human Editions"). Accordingly, inspired by the work of the scholar Raquel Castedo, this edition preserves the page breaks after each chapter and distinctive epitaph-like formatting of the title, dedication, and Chapter CXXV.

Another novelty that this edition presents, in the endnotes, is the translation of selected excerpts from the novel that were cut or altered between the first printing, in serial form in the *Revista Brazileira*, and its subsequent book editions. Why weigh down the work, one might fairly ask, with snippets pared from it some 130 years ago? In the absence of manuscript drafts, this is our best hope to see how Machado's thought process worked, the final stages of refining his prose. The types of alterations that we see him make repeatedly— leaving the language more terse and less emphatic, cutting ostentatious allusions—are also the sorts of modifications that guide the translation. Moreover, since even Machadian cast-offs have their charm, it is my pleasure to provide English-speaking readers with an additional smattering of the off-kilter wit that has charmed generations of readers.

Suggestions for Further Reading

NOVELS

All of Joaquim Maria Machado de Assis's novels, listed here in chronological order by original publication date, have been translated into English, some multiple times. *Memórias Póstumas de Brás Cubas*, as noted in the introduction, was first brought into English in its entirety in 1952 by Noonday, in a translation by William L. Grossman with the title *Epitaph of a Small Winner*; *Posthumous Reminiscences of Braz Cubas*,* by E. Percy Ellis, was published in 1955 by Brazil's Instituto Nacional do Livro and has since gone out of print; and *The Posthumous Memoirs of Brás Cubas,* by Gregory Rabassa, was published in 1997 by Oxford University Press. The list that follows does not include Robert Scott-Buccleuch's translation of *Dom Casmurro* as *Lord Taciturn*, given the elimination of multiple chapters from the original text.

Ressurreição (1872)
  Resurrection. Translated by Karen Sherwood Sotelino. Pittsburgh: Latin American Literary Review Press, 2013.

---

*The Portuguese language underwent a major reform in 1946, with multiple consequences for punctuation and spelling. The most visible ramifications for Machado's work are the names Brás Cubas (which during the author's lifetime was spelled Braz Cubas), Iaiá Garcia (spelled then as Yayá Garcia), and Conselheiro Aires (then spelled Ayres). Translators working with older editions tended to preserve the pre-1946 convention.

A Mão e a Luva (1874)
> *The Hand and the Glove*. Translated by Albert I. Bagby Jr. Lexington: University Press of Kentucky, 1970.

Helena (1876)
> *Helena*. Translated by Helen Caldwell. Berkeley: University of California Press, 1984.

Iaiá Garcia (1878)
> *Yayá Garcia: A Novel*. Translated by Robert Scott-Buccleuch. London: Peter Owen, 1976. Reprinted as *Iaiá Garcia*.

> *Yayá Garcia*. Translated by Albert I. Bagby Jr. Lexington: University Press of Kentucky, 1977.

Casa Velha (1885)
> *The Old House*. Translated by Mark Carlyon. Rio de Janeiro: Cidade Viva, 2010.

Quincas Borba (1886/1891)*
> *Philosopher or Dog?* Translated by Clotilde Wilson. New York: Noonday, 1954. Also published as *The Heritage of Quincas Borba*. London: W. H. Allen, 1954.

> *Quincas Borba*. Translated by Gregory Rabassa. New York: Oxford University Press, 1998.

Dom Casmurro (1899/1900)
> *Dom Casmurro*. Translated by Helen Caldwell. New York: Noonday, 1953.

> *Dom Casmurro*. Translated by John Gledson. New York: Oxford University Press, 1997.

---

*A handful of Machado's novels were published in installments in various periodicals before their definitive book forms, and thus they have multiple publication dates.

Esaú e Jacó (1904)
> *Esau and Jacob*. Translated by Helen Caldwell. Berkeley: University of California Press, 1965.

> *Esau and Jacob*. Translated by Elizabeth Lowe. New York: Oxford University Press, 2000.

Memorial de Aires (1908)
> *Counselor Ayres' Memorial*. Translated by Helen Caldwell. Berkeley: University of California Press, 1972.

> *The Wager: Aires' Journal*. Translated by Robert Scott-Buccleuch. London: Owen, 1990.

SHORT STORIES

Machado de Assis's short stories were the first of his works to be brought into English, by the Harvard professor Isaac Goldberg, who published three of them in the 1920 collection *Brazilian Tales*. The list that follows includes a few of the many short story collections that came in its wake. There is significant overlap among them, the exception being Margaret Jull Costa and Robin Patterson's recent *Collected Stories*, which presents all of the stories published in book form during Machado's lifetime. Around a hundred short stories, originally published in newspapers and other periodicals and not included in subsequent collections, await English translations.

> *The Psychiatrist and Other Stories*. Translated by William L. Grossman and Helen Caldwell. Berkeley: University of California Press, 1963.*
> *A Chapter of Hats and Other Stories*. Translated by John Gledson. London: Bloomsbury, 2008.

*Grossman's translation of the novella *O Alienista*, originally published under the title "The Psychiatrist," was lightly edited and reissued as *The Alienist* by Melville House in 2012.

The Alienist and Other Stories of Nineteenth-Century Brazil. Edited and translated by John Chasteen. Cambridge: Hackett, 2013.

The Collected Stories of Machado de Assis. Translated by Margaret Jull Costa and Robin Patterson. New York: Liveright, 2018.

OTHER WRITINGS

Machado's poetry, plays, and *crônicas* (hundreds of playful, critical newspaper pieces) are only patchily available in English as of yet. His 1873 essay on the state of Brazilian literature, "Reflections on Brazilian Literature at the Present Moment: The National Instinct," referred to in the introduction, was translated by Robert Patrick Newcomb and published in 2013 in the journal *Brasil/Brazil*.

SELECTED CRITICAL WORKS

There follows a list of English-language studies and essays on the works of Machado de Assis, a handful authored by some of his translators. Among the readings that informed this translation and may be of interest to readers of Machado are Mary Karasch's *Slave Life in Rio de Janeiro, 1808–1850* (Princeton, NJ: Princeton University Press, 1987) and Lilia Moritz Schwarcz and Heloisa M. Starling's *Brazil: A Biography* (New York: Farrar, Straus & Giroux, 2018).

Aidoo, Lamonte, and Daniel F. Silva, eds. *Emerging Dialogues on Machado de Assis.* New York: Palgrave Macmillan, 2016.

Caldwell, Helen. *The Brazilian Othello of Machado de Assis: A Study of* Dom Casmurro. Berkeley: University of California Press, 1960.

———. *Machado de Assis: The Brazilian Master and His Novels.* Berkeley: University of California Press, 1970.

Candido, Antonio. "An Outline of Machado de Assis." In *On Literature and Society*, trans. Howard Becker. Princeton, NJ: Princeton University Press, 1995, 104–18.

Castro Rocha, João Cezar de, ed. *The Author as Plagiarist: The Case of Machado de Assis*. North Dartmouth, MA: Tagus Press (University of Massachusetts Dartmouth), 2005.

———. *Machado de Assis: Toward a Poetics of Emulation*. Translated by Flora Thomson-DeVeaux. East Lansing: Michigan State University Press, 2015.

Daniel, G. Reginald. *Machado de Assis: Multiracial Identity and the Brazilian Novelist*. University Park: Pennsylvania State University Press, 2012.

Fitz, Earl E. *Machado de Assis*. Boston: Twayne, 1989.

Gledson, John. *The Deceptive Realism of Machado de Assis*. Liverpool: Cairns, 1984.

——— and Luana Ferreira de Freitas, trans. "Translating Machado de Assis / Traduzindo Machado de Assis." *Scientia Traductionis*, no. 14 (2013): 6–63.

Graham, Richard, ed. *Machado de Assis: Reflections on a Brazilian Master Writer*. Austin: University of Texas Press, 1999.

Jackson, K. David. *Machado de Assis: A Literary Life*. New Haven: Yale University Press, 2015.

Maia Neto, José Raimundo. *Machado, the Brazilian Pyrrhonian*. West Lafayette, IN: Purdue University Press, 1984.

Nunes, Maria Luisa. *The Craft of an Absolute Winner*. Westport, CT: Greenwood, 1983.

Schwarz, Roberto. *A Master on the Periphery of Capitalism*. Translated by John Gledson. Durham, NC: Duke University Press, 2001.

———. *Misplaced Ideas: Essays on Brazilian Culture*. Translated by John Gledson. London: Verso, 1992.

Sontag, Susan. "Afterlives: The Case of Machado de Assis." *New Yorker*, May 7, 1990: 102–8.

Wood, Michael. "Master Among the Ruins," *New York Review of Books*, July 18, 2002.

TO THE WORM

THAT

FIRST GNAWED AT THE COLD FLESH

OF MY CADAVER

I DEDICATE

AS A FOND REMEMBRANCE

THESE

POSTHUMOUS MEMOIRS

Prologue to the Fourth Edition

The first edition of these *Posthumous Memoirs of Brás Cubas*[1] came out in installments in the *Revista Brazileira*, around 1880. When it was published as a book, I corrected the text in a number of places. Being obliged to look over it again for the third edition,[2] I have made a few more amendments and taken out two or three dozen lines. In this form, the work, which seems to have inspired some benevolence on the part of the public, now comes to light once more.

Capistrano de Abreu,[3] when commenting on the book's publication, had asked: "Is *The Posthumous Memoirs of Brás Cubas* a novel?" Macedo Soares,[4] in a letter to me around the same time, made friendly reference to Almeida Garrett's *Travels in My Homeland*.[5] To the former, the late Brás Cubas himself would answer (as readers have seen and shall see in his prologue, which follows) both yes and no, that it was a novel for some and not so for others. As for the latter, the dead man explained himself as follows: "This is a diffuse work, in which I, Brás Cubas, if I have adopted the free form of a Sterne[6] or a Xavier de Maistre,[7] may have added a few grumbles of pessimism." All of them traveled: Xavier de Maistre around his room, Garrett in his own land, Sterne in the lands of others. Of Brás Cubas, one might perhaps say that he traveled around life itself.

What makes my Brás Cubas an author all his own is what he calls his "grumbles of pessimism." There is in the soul of this book, as smiling as it may seem, a bitter and harsh edge that is a far cry from its models. The glass may be the work of the same school, but it bears another wine. I shall say no more so as not to begin criticizing a dead man, since he painted both himself and others as he saw fit and best.

MACHADO DE ASSIS

THE POSTHUMOUS MEMOIRS

OF

BRÁS CUBAS

TO THE READER

That Stendhal should have confessed to writing one of his books for only a hundred readers[1] is a source of surprise and consternation. What comes as no surprise, nor will likely provoke any consternation, is if this book fails to garner even Stendhal's hundred readers, nor fifty, nor twenty, nor even ten, if that. Ten? Perhaps five. This is, it's true, a diffuse work, in which I, Brás Cubas, if I have adopted the free form of a Sterne[2] or a Xavier de Maistre, may have added a few grumbles of pessimism. That may well be. The work of a deceased man. I wrote it with the pen of mirth and the ink of melancholy, and it is not difficult to predict what may come of such a union. Add to which the fact that serious people will find in the book some likeness to an out-and-out novel, while frivolous people will not find their usual novel here; it will thus be deprived of the esteem of the serious and the love of the frivolous, which are the two chief pillars of public opinion.

But I still harbor hopes of winning the sympathies of that opinion, and the first remedy is to avoid a drawn-out, exhaustive prologue. The best prologues have the fewest things, or say them in an abrupt, obscure manner. Accordingly, I will refrain from relaying the extraordinary process that I employed in composing these *Memoirs*, crafted here in the otherworld. It would be of interest, but tediously lengthy, and superfluous to one's understanding of the work. The work in itself is all: if it should please you, my fine reader, I am paid for my labors; if it should not please you, I will pay you with a flick of a finger,[3] and farewell.

BRÁS CUBAS

CHAPTER I

THE DEMISE
OF THE AUTHOR[1]

I debated for a time as to whether I ought to open these memoirs at the beginning or at the end—that is, if I would start out with my birth or with my death. Granting that the common practice may be to begin with one's birth, two considerations led me to adopt a different method: the first is that I am not exactly an author recently deceased, but a deceased man recently an author,[2] for whom the tomb was another cradle; the second is that this would make the writing wittier and more novel. Moses, who also recounted his own death, did not put it at the commencement but at the finish: a radical difference between this book and the Pentateuch.[3]

That being said, I expired at two o'clock in the afternoon on a Friday in the month of August, 1869, at my handsome country home in Catumbi.[4] I had seen some sixty-four robust and prosperous years, I was a bachelor, I had around three hundred thousand milréis[5] to my name, and I was accompanied to the cemetery by eleven friends. Eleven! True, there had been neither letters nor announcements. What's more, it was raining—drizzling—a fine, doleful, steady patter, so steady and so doleful that it led one of those faithful at the last to insert this inspired idea into the speech that he delivered at the edge of my grave:

> You who knew him, gentlemen, you may join me in saying that nature herself seems to be weeping for the irreparable loss of one of the finest figures to have ever honored humanity. This gloom, these drops from on high, those dark clouds veiling the blue like a mourning band, all this is the raw, wicked pain

tearing nature to the quick; all this is a sublime paean to our illustrious deceased.

Good, faithful friend! No, I don't regret the twenty bonds I left him. And it was thus that I came to the close of my days; it was thus that I set off for Hamlet's undiscovered country,[6] without the young prince's anguish or doubts, but slowly and falteringly, like one leaving the stage far too late. Late and weary. Some nine or ten people saw me go, among them three ladies: my sister Sabina, married to Cotrim; her daughter, a fair lily of the valley; and . . . —A little patience, please! I'll soon tell you who the third lady was. Content yourselves for the moment with the knowledge that this anonymous woman, though no relation of mine, suffered more than those who were. It's true, she suffered more. I won't say that she tore her hair with grief or that she rolled across the floor in convulsions. Nor, for that matter, was there anything terribly dramatic about my death . . . A bachelor breathing his last at age sixty-four is hardly the classic tragedy. And even if it were, the least appropriate thing for this anonymous woman to do would have been to reveal her sentiments.[7] Standing beside my bed, her eyes glassy, mouth half-open, this pitiful lady could barely credit my extinction.

"Dead! dead!" she repeated to herself.

And her imagination, like the storks that an illustrious traveler once saw take flight from the Ilissos, bound for the shores of Africa, heedless of the ruins and the ages[8]—the lady's imagination also soared over the wreckage of the present to the shores of a youthful Africa . . . Let her go; we shall go later; we shall go when I restore myself to those early years. For now I want to die peacefully, methodically, hearing the sobbing of the ladies, the low murmuring of the men, the rain drumming on the caladium leaves in the garden, and the piercing sound of a razor being sharpened by a knife grinder, out by the door to a currier's shop. I swear to you all that this orchestra of death was much less sorrowful than it might seem. After a point, it became positively delightful. Life floundered in my chest like the surging of an ocean swell, my consciousness melted away, I was drifting down into physical and moral immobility, my body becoming a plant, a stone, loam, nothing at all.

I died of pneumonia; if I should say that it was less pneumonia than a grand and useful idea that caused my death, my reader may not believe me, and yet this is the truth. I will lay out the case for you in brief. Judge for yourself.

CHAPTER II

THE PLASTER[1]

The fact is, one morning when I was out for a walk in the garden, an idea hopped up onto the trapeze in my head. Once hanging there, it began to wave its arms, swing its legs, and perform such daring tumbler's somersaults as one could scarcely believe. I let myself contemplate it. Suddenly, it took a flying leap and stretched out its legs and arms, forming an X: decipher me or I devour thee.[2]

This idea was nothing less than the invention of a sublime remedy, an anti-hypochondriacal[3] plaster destined to alleviate our melancholy humanity. In the patent application that I subsequently drew up, I called the government's attention to this genuinely Christian aim. To my friends, I did not deny the pecuniary advantages that were sure to result from the distribution of a product with such sweeping and profound effects. Now, however, that I am on the other side of life, I can confess it all: what drove me most of all was the gratification it would give me to see in newsprint, showcases, pamphlets, on street corners, and finally on the medicine boxes, those four words: *The Brás Cubas Plaster*. Why deny it? I had a weakness for hubbub, banners, pyrotechnics. Modest sorts may reprove this defect in me; I would wager, however, that the clever will grant me this talent. My idea had two faces, like a medal, with one turned toward the public and one toward me. On one side, philanthropy and profit; on the other, a thirst for fame. Let us call it a love of glory.

An uncle of mine, a canon receiving a full prebend, used to say that the love of temporal glory was the ruin of the soul, which ought to covet only the eternal sort. To which another uncle, an officer in one of the old *terço* infantry regiments, replied that the love of glory was the most authentically human thing in man, and hence his most genuine feature.[4]

Let the reader decide between the military man and the priest; I will return to the plaster.

CHAPTER III

GENEALOGY

But, now that I've spoken of my two uncles, allow me to draw up a brief sketch of my genealogy.

The founder of my family was one Damião Cubas, who flourished in the first half of the eighteenth century. He was a cooper by trade, hailing from Rio de Janeiro, where he would have died in penury and obscurity if he had limited himself to making the *cubas*, or barrels, that gave him his name. But no; he became a farmer, planted, reaped, and exchanged his products for a pretty and honest penny until he died, leaving a substantial fortune to a son, Luís Cubas. This young man is truly the start of my forebears—of the forebears that my family would own to—since Damião Cubas was, after all, a cooper, and perhaps even a bad one at that, whereas Luís Cubas studied at Coimbra,[1] became a distinguished statesman, and was a personal friend of the viceroy, Count da Cunha.[2]

Since the name Cubas wafted of cooperage, my father, Damião's great-grandson, alleged that the cognomen had been given to a knight, a hero of the African campaigns, in recognition of a feat in which he captured three hundred barrels from the Moors. My father was a man of great imagination; he escaped from the cooper's shop on the wings of wordplay. He was a good man, my father, worthy and loyal like few others. He had a way of putting on airs, it's true, but who in this world hasn't wrapped himself in an air or two? It may be appropriate to note that he resorted to invention only after having tried out falsification; he had initially grafted himself onto the family of my famous namesake, Captain-Major Brás Cubas, who founded the town of São Vicente and died there in 1592, and it was for that reason that he gave me the name Brás.³ The family of the captain-major objected, however, and it was then that my father conjured up the three hundred Moorish barrels.

A few members of my family are still alive—my niece Venância, for example, the lily of the valley, the flower of the ladies of her time; and her father, Cotrim, a fellow who . . . well, let's not anticipate events; let's be done with our plaster once and for all.

CHAPTER IV

THE FIXED IDEA

My idea, after all its somersaults, had become a fixed idea. God save you, reader, from a fixed idea; better a mote in your eye, or even a beam. Look at Cavour;[1] it was the fixed idea of Italian unity that killed him. It's true that Bismarck hasn't died;[2] but it must be said that Nature is a fickle maid and History is an inveterate flirt. For example, Suetonius gave us a Claudius who was a simpleton, or a "pumpkinhead," as Seneca called him, and a Titus who was deservedly the delight of Rome. Recently, a professor has come along and found a way to show that of the two Caesars, the truly delightful one was Seneca's "pumpkinhead."[3] And you, Madame Lucrezia, the flower of the Borgias, while a poet painted you as a Catholic Messalina, along came a skeptical Gregorovius to wash away a great deal of that depiction,[4] and while you may not have come out as a lily, neither were you left a swamp. I shall let myself stand somewhere between the poet and the scholar.

Long live history, then, voluble history, which can go every which way; and, returning to fixed ideas, I shall say that they are what make strong men and madmen; wandering, vague, or shimmering ideas make for Claudiuses—in Suetonius's version, that is.

My idea was fixed, as fixed as . . . Nothing comes to mind that is quite so fixed in this world: perhaps the moon, perhaps the pyramids of Egypt, perhaps the late German Diet. The reader may pick the analogy that suits him the best; go on, pick one, and don't get your nose out of joint just because we still haven't arrived at the narrative part of these memoirs. That is where we are headed. I do believe that you prefer anecdotes to meditations, like all the other readers, your comrades, and I believe you do well to prefer them. Well, that is where we are headed. Nevertheless, it should be said that this book is written unhurriedly, at the pace of a man no longer burdened by the brevity of the age; it is a supinely philosophical work, but of an inconstant philosophy, first austere and just as quickly playful, one that neither edifies nor destroys, neither inflames nor chills, and is nevertheless more than a pastime and less than an apostolate.

All right; straighten out your nose, and let us get back to the plaster. We shall leave history, with her elegant lady's whims. None of us ever waged the Battle of Salamis[5] or wrote the Augsburg Confession;[6] for my part, if Cromwell ever comes to mind, it is only to think that His Highness, with the same hand that locked the doors of Parliament, might have forced the Brás Cubas Plaster on the English.[7] Do not laugh at the joint triumph of pharmacy and Puritanism. Who does not know that at the foot of every large, public, prominent flag, there are often a number of other, more modestly proportioned flags, which are hoisted and flutter in the shadow of their larger counterpart, and which quite often survive it? To offer a poor analogy, it is like the rabble, sheltered in the shadow of the feudal castle; the castle fell and the rabble remained. Indeed, they became grand in their own right, a veritable stronghold . . . No, the analogy's really no good.

CHAPTER V

IN WHICH A LADY BETRAYS HERSELF[1]

And then, just as I was occupied with preparing and perfecting my invention, I was struck squarely by a draft; I fell ill straightaway and took no steps to cure myself. I had the plaster on the brain; I bore within me the fixed idea of the mad and the strong. I beheld myself from afar, rising up from the mob-thronged ground and ascending into the heavens like an immortal eagle, and when faced with such a stupendous spectacle, no man can feel the pain that pricks at him. The following day, I was worse; I finally treated myself, but only partially, with no method, care, or persistence; such was the origin of the ill that brought me to eternity. You already know that I died on a Friday, an unlucky day, and I believe to have proven that it was my invention that killed me. Some demonstrations are less lucid, and no less triumphant for it.

It would not have been impossible for me to step over the threshold of a century and appear in the papers, in the company of other Macrobians.[2] I was healthy and robust. Suppose that, instead of laying the foundations for a pharmaceutical invention, I had been attempting to piece together the elements of a political institution or a religious reform. The breeze would come along all the same, with far greater efficacy than the human faculty of calculation, and all would be done for.[3] Thus goes the lot of men.

With this reflection, I bade farewell to the woman—I won't call her the most discreet, but certainly the loveliest among her contemporaries—the anonymous woman from the first chapter, the very same, whose imagination, like the storks of the Ilissos . . . She was then fifty-four years old, and she was a ruin, an imposing ruin. Just imagine, reader, that we had loved each other, she and I, many years before, and that one day, having taken ill, I see her appear at my bedroom door . . .

CHAPTER VI

CHIMÈNE, QUI L'EÛT DIT? RODRIGUE, QUI L'EÛT CRU?[1]

I see her appear at my bedroom door, pale, shaken, all in black, and pause there for a minute, without the heart to enter, or stayed there by the presence of a man who was with me. From the bed where I lay, I contemplated her for that span of time, forgetting that I said nothing, nor made any sign to her. It had been two years since we had seen each other last, and I saw her now not as she was but as she had been, as we both had been, for some mysterious Hezekiah[2] had turned back the sun to our youthful days. The sun turned back, I shook off all my miseries, and this handful of dust, which death was ready to scatter to the eternity of nothingness, triumphed over time, which is the minister of death. Here, no Hebe's cup[3] could rival simple nostalgia.

Believe me, remembrance is the lesser evil; let none place their faith in present happiness; there's a bitter drop of Cain's drool in it. Once time has worn on and the rapture has ceased, then, perhaps only then, may one truly take pleasure in what has passed; when given a choice between two illusions, the better is that which may be enjoyed without pain.

The vision didn't last long; reality soon asserted itself; the present cast out the past. Perhaps I'll expound to the reader, in some corner of this book, my theory of human editions. What should be imparted now is that Virgília—her name was Virgília—entered the bedroom, steadfast, with the gravity lent her by her clothes and her years, and came over to my bed. The stranger got up and left. He was a fellow who visited me every day to speak about rates of exchange, colonization, and the need to develop the railways: nothing more enthralling for a dying man. He left; Virgília stood there; for some time we gazed at each other without uttering a word. Whoever would have thought it? Two great lovers, two unbridled passions, and nothing was left twenty years later; only two withered hearts, devastated by life and sated of it, whether in equal measure I can't say, but sated all the same. Virgília now possessed the beauty of old age, an austere and maternal air; she was less slender than when I had seen her last, in Tijuca, at a celebration for the Feast of St. John;[4] and because she was one of those who hold out to the last, her dark hair was only just beginning to yield to a few silver strands.

"Visiting dead men, are you?" I said to her.

"Dead men, come now!" replied Virgília with a tut. And then, after giving my hands a squeeze: "I'm putting slugabeds out on the street."

The tearful caresses of yesteryear were gone, but her voice was friendly and sweet. She sat down. I was alone, at home, with only a sick nurse; we could speak to each other without danger. Virgília gave me a drawn-out report of the latest goings-on, narrating them charmingly and seasoning them with a tart dash of gossip; I, on the verge of leaving the world, felt a devilish pleasure in jeering at it, persuading myself that I left nothing behind.

"What ideas you've got in your head!" Virgília interrupted, rather put out. "I won't come back at this rate. Die! All of us must die; that's what comes of being alive."

And, looking at the clock:

"Goodness! It's three. I must go."

"So soon?"

"Yes; I'll come by tomorrow or after."

"That may not be wise," I retorted. "The invalid is a bachelor, and there are no ladies living in the house . . ."

"What about your sister?"

"She'll come by to spend a few days, but not before Saturday."

Virgília reflected for a moment, shrugged, and said gravely:

"I've grown old! No one takes any notice of me anymore. But to leave no room for suspicion, I'll come with Nhonhô."[5]

Nhonhô was a university graduate,[6] the only child of her

marriage, who, at the age of five, had been an unconscious accomplice to our love affair. They came together two days later,
and I must confess that upon seeing them there in my bedroom,
I was taken by a bashfulness that kept me from immediately
repaying the young man's kind words. Virgília guessed me out
and said to her son:

"Nhonhô, pay no mind to this sly old fox here; he's not talking so he can make you believe he's at death's door."

Her son smiled. I believe I smiled as well, and it all ended in
pure fun. Virgília was calm and cheerful, with the air of one
who had led an immaculate life. No suspicious gaze, no gesture
that might betray a thing; she displayed an equanimity of word
and spirit and a mastery of herself that struck me as unusual,
and perhaps were. When we touched, innocently enough, on the
subject of an illicit love affair that was somewhere between secret and public, I saw her speak with disdain and a bit of indignation of the woman in question, who happened to be a friend of
hers. Her son felt satisfied, hearing those dignified and forceful
words, while I wondered to myself what the sparrowhawks
might say of us, if Buffon[7] had been born a sparrowhawk . . .

My delirium was beginning.

CHAPTER VII

THE DELIRIUM

As far as I am aware, no one has ever narrated his own delirium; I shall do so now, and science will thank me for it. If you, my reader, should not be given to the contemplation of such mental phenomena, you may skip the chapter; go straight to the narration. But, incurious as you may be, I can certainly say that it is interesting to know what went on in my head during some twenty or thirty minutes.

First of all, I took on the figure of a Chinese barber, potbellied and nimble-fingered, giving a close shave to a mandarin, who paid me for my trouble with pinches and candies: such are the whims of a mandarin.

Shortly thereafter, I felt myself transformed into St. Thomas Aquinas's *Summa Theologica*, a volume bound in Moroccan leather, with silver clasps and illustrations; this idea impressed upon my body the most complete immobility; and I still remember that my hands were the clasps of the book, I had crossed them over my stomach, and someone uncrossed them (Virgília, undoubtedly) because the position made me look like a corpse.

Finally, restored to human form, I saw a hippopotamus come up and carry me off. I let myself go, fallen quiet, whether out of fear or trust I cannot say; but presently the gallop became so headlong that I dared to speak, and tactfully remarked that we seemed to be bound for nowhere in particular.

"You're mistaken," replied the animal. "We are going to the origin of the ages."

I hinted that it must be terribly far off; but the hippopotamus either did not understand me or did not hear me, or perhaps feigned one or the other; and when I asked it, seeing that it could speak, whether it was descended from Achilles' horse or Balaam's ass,[1] it retorted with a gesture peculiar to those two sorts of quadrupeds: it twitched its ears. For my part, I closed my eyes and let myself go where chance would take me. Now I have no compunctions about confessing that I felt a tickling of curiosity to know where the origin of the ages lay, if it was as mysterious as the origin of the Nile, and principally if it was more or less worth my while than the consummation of those selfsame ages: all these, the reflections of a sick brain. As I kept my eyes closed, I saw nothing of the route; I can recall only that the cold grew keener as the journey proceeded, and that after a time it seemed to me that we were entering the region of eternal ice. Indeed, I opened my eyes and saw that my animal was galloping across a plain white with snow, with a few snow mountains, snow vegetation, and a number of large snow animals. All snow; we were even chilled by the rays of a snowy sun. I tried to speak, but could only grunt out the following question:

"Where are we?"

"We've already passed Eden."

"All right, then, let's stop at Abraham's tent."

"And turn around?" scoffed my steed by way of an answer.

This was both vexing and confounding. The journey came to strike me as tiresome and outlandish, the cold disagreeable, the means of transport jolting, and the result far from clear. And—a sick man's musings—even if we should arrive at the destination in question, mightn't the ages, irritated at having their origin so exposed, crush me between their equally age-old nails? As these thoughts passed through my mind, we swallowed up the ground and the plain flew past beneath our feet, until the animal came to a halt and I could look around me more calmly. Look, that was all; I saw nothing but the vast whiteness that had now overtaken even the sky itself, which had been blue until then. Here and there was to be seen an enormous, brutish plant, wagging its long leaves in the wind. The silence of that place was like that of the tomb: one might have said that the life in things had fallen stunned in the presence of man.

Did it fall from the sky? Did it rise from the earth? I do not know; I know only that an immense shape, the figure of a woman, appeared to me then, fixing me with eyes as brilliant as the sun. Everything about the figure bore the vastness of the wilds and surpassed the comprehension of the human gaze, as its edges bled away into its surroundings and that which appeared dense was often diaphanous. Stupefied, I said nothing, not even crying out; but after a time, which was brief enough, I asked who she was and what she was called: such was the curiosity born of delirium.

"Call me Nature or Pandora; I am your mother and your enemy."

Upon hearing this last word, I drew back, gripped with fear. The figure let out a peal of laughter, which had the effect of a typhoon around us; the plants writhed and a long moan broke through the hush of the surroundings.

"Do not be frightened," said she, "my enmity does not kill; it affirms itself through life. You are alive: I desire no other torment."

"I'm alive?" I asked, digging my nails into my palms as if to certify myself of my existence.

"Yes, worm, you are alive. You must not fear losing the tattered rags that are your pride; for a few hours yet you shall still taste the bread of pain and the wine of misery. You are alive: now, even in your madness, you are alive; and should your mind retrieve an instant of sense, you will say that you wish to live."

Thus saying, the vision extended an arm, seized me by the hair, and lifted me up as if I were a feather. Only then could I behold her face, which was immense. Nothing could be stiller; no violent grimace, no expression of hate or ferocity; its sole expression, general and all-pervasive, was that of a selfish impassivity, an everlasting deafness, an immovable will. Wrath, if she had any, was locked away in her heart. At the same time, in that face, with its glacial expression, there was an air of youth, a mixture of strength and vigor before which I felt myself the feeblest and most decrepit of all beings.

"Do you understand me?" she said after a time of mutual contemplation.

"No," I answered, "nor do I wish to understand you; you're absurd, you're a fable. I'm dreaming, surely, or, if it should be true that I've gone mad, you're nothing more than a lunatic's fancy, a vain thing that an absent mind can neither govern nor touch. You, Nature? The Nature I know is only a mother, no enemy; she does not make life a torment, nor is her face as indifferent as the tomb. And why Pandora?"

"Because I carry in my bag all good and evil, and the greatest thing of all, hope, the comfort of men. Do you tremble?"

"Yes; your gaze is mesmerizing."

"Indeed; for I am not only life, I am also death, and you are about to return what I have lent you. For you, great hedonist, there await all the sensual pleasures of nothingness."

As that last word rolled like a thunderclap across the immense valley, it struck me that this was the last sound that would ever reach my ears; I seemed to feel myself suddenly disintegrating. I faced her with a pleading gaze and asked for a few more years.

"Wretched minute!" she exclaimed. "Why would you want a few more moments of life? To devour and then be devoured? Have you not tired of the spectacle, of the struggle? You have had your fill of all of the least vile and least grievous things I have to offer: the breaking of day, the melancholy of dusk, the quiet of night, the face of the earth, and, last of all, sleep, the greatest benefit my hands can bestow. What more can you want, sublime idiot?"

"Just to live. I ask nothing more. Who but you put this love of life in my heart? And if I love life, why must you do yourself injury by killing me?"

"Because I have no more need of you. Time cares not for the passing minute, only that which is to come. The minute ahead is strong, merry, believes it is the bearer of eternity, and it, too, bears death and perishes like the one before it—but time remains. Selfishness, you say? Yes, selfishness, I know no other law. Selfishness, preservation. A jaguar kills a calf because the jaguar reasons that she must live, and if the calf's flesh is tender, so much the better: this is the statute that governs the universe. Come up and see."

So saying, she swept me up and bore me to the top of a mountain. I turned my eyes down one of its slopes and contemplated at length, far off and through a mist, an incomparable thing. Imagine, reader, all the ages of time in miniature, and in an unending procession; all the races, all the passions, the tumult of empires, the war of appetite against appetite and hatred against hatred, the reciprocal destruction of beings and things. Such was the spectacle, a cruel and curious one. The history of man and the earth was of an intensity of which neither imagination nor science could conceive, for science is too slow and imagination too vague, and what I beheld then was the living condensation of all time. To describe it, one would have to make the lightning stand still. The ages marched along in a whirlwind, and, nevertheless, as delirium lends one different eyes, I could see everything that passed before me, torments and delights, from that thing called glory to that other thing called misery, and I saw love multiplying misery, and misery aggravating weakness. There came all-consuming greed, maddening wrath, slavering envy, the hoe and the pen, both damp with sweat, and ambition, hunger, vanity, melancholy, riches, love, and they all shook man like a rattle until they destroyed him like a rag. These were the various forms of a single ailment, which would gnaw at the entrails at times and the mind at others, all the while parading its harlequin's garb around the human species. Pain gave way here and there, but only to indifference, which was a dreamless sleep, or to pleasure, which was a bastard pain. And then man, tormented and unyielding, would run ahead of the fatality of things after a nebulous, elusive figure cobbled together out of scraps, a scrap of the intangible, another of the improbable, another of the invisible, all sewn with flimsy stitches by the needle of the imagination; and this figure—nothing less than the chimera of happiness—either fled constantly or allowed itself to be caught by its train, upon which man would clasp it to his breast, and then the figure would give a scornful laugh and vanish like an illusion.

Upon contemplating this calamity, I could not stifle a cry of anguish, which Nature or Pandora heard with neither protest nor laughter; and, driven by some principle of cerebral disturbances, it was I who then set to laughing—a braying, idiotic laugh.

"You're right," I said, "this all is amusing, and worth the while—monotonous, perhaps, but worth the while. When Job cursed the day he was conceived,[2] it was only because he wanted to watch the spectacle from up here. Let's go, Pandora, open up your maw[3] and digest me; this all is amusing, but be done with it and digest me."

Her response was to force me to look downward and watch the swift and turbulent ages as they kept on passing by, generations overtaking generations, some sorrowful, like the Hebrews in captivity, others joyful, like the libertines under Commodus, and all arriving punctually at the grave. I wanted to flee, but a mysterious force held my feet; and so I said to myself: "Well, if the centuries are passing by, mine will arrive, and it will pass as well, and then the last of all will give me the key to the riddle of eternity." And I fixed my gaze and continued to watch the ages as they came and went; now I was tranquil and resolute, if not even happy. Perhaps even happy. Each age bore its portion of shadow and light, of apathy and combat, of truth and error, with their processions of systems, new ideas, and new illusions; in each of them there burst forth the green of spring, which would yellow, only to bloom again. While life obeyed the regularity of a calendar, history and civilization were made, and man, naked and unarmed, armed and dressed himself, built huts and palaces, humble villages and Thebes of the hundred gates, created science, which scrutinizes, and art, which enraptures, became an orator, a mechanical, a philosopher, girdling the globe, descending to the bowels of the earth, and rising to the sphere of the clouds, thus contributing to the mysterious work with which he staved off the needs of life and the melancholy of abandonment. My eyes, wearied and distracted, at last beheld the present age, and the ages to come behind it. As it came, the former was agile, cunning, vibrant, and self-assured, a bit scattered, bold and learned, but in the end as miserable as the first, and so it passed like all the rest, with the same swiftness and like monotony. I redoubled my attention; I fixed my gaze; I would finally see the end—the end! But by then the speed of the procession was such that it escaped all comprehension; compared to it, a lightning bolt would last a century. Perhaps that was why things set to changing; some grew, others dwindled, others vanished into the air; a fog covered everything—except the hippopotamus that had brought me, and it, for that matter, began to shrink, shrink, and shrink, until it was the size of a cat. It was, in fact, a cat. I looked at it more closely; it was my cat Sultan, playing with a ball of paper by my bedroom door . . .

CHAPTER VIII

REASON VERSUS FOLLY

My reader has no doubt understood that this was Reason, who had returned home and invited Folly to leave, crying out the words of Tartuffe, and with better reason than he:

"*La maison est à moi, c'est à vous d'en sortir.*"[1]

But Folly has an old habit of becoming accustomed to houses that are not her own; once she has made herself at home, it is no easy task to expel her. Force of habit; she won't be removed; she grew hardened to shame long ago. Now, if we look to the immense number of houses that she occupies, some for good, others only during the summertime, we may conclude that this charming wanderer is the veritable bane of householders. In our case, there was nearly a scuffle at the door to my brain: the intruder refused to turn over the house, while the owner stood determined to take back what was hers. In the end, Folly declared she would settle for a corner of the attic.

"No, madam," countered Reason, "I am tired of surrendering attics to you, tired and tried. What you want is to creep from the attic to the dining room, and from there to the drawing room and the rest."

"All right, just let me stay a bit longer. I'm on the trail of a mystery . . ."

"What mystery?"

"Two of them," Folly corrected herself, "the mysteries of life and death. Just give me ten more minutes."

Reason began to laugh.

"With you it's always the same . . . always the same . . . always the same . . ."

And so saying, she grabbed Folly by the wrists and dragged her outside; then she went in and locked the door. Folly whined a few pleas, snarled a few curses; but she soon resigned herself, stuck out her tongue, and went on her way . . .

CHAPTER IX

TRANSITION

Now, behold the dexterity and skill with which I shall carry out the most important transition in the book. To wit: my delirium began in the presence of Virgília; Virgília was the great sin of my youth; there can be no youth without childhood; childhood presupposes birth; and thus we have arrived, with no effort at all, at the 20th of October, 1805, the day of my birth. You see? No visible joints, nothing to upset the reader's calm attention—not a thing. The book is given all the advantages of method without its inflexibility. And it was about time, for that matter.[1] This business of a method, indispensable as it may be, works better sans cravat and sans suspenders, lightly and loosely dressed, taking no mind of the lady who lives across the street or the watchman on the block. It is like eloquence; there is the genuine, vibrant variety, with a natural, enchanting art, and another sort, which is stiff, pressed, and altogether hollow. Let us go to the 20th of October.

CHAPTER X

ON THAT DAY

On that day, the tree of the Cubas family brought forth a fair flower. I was born; I was received in the arms of Pascoela, the illustrious midwife from Minho who boasted that she had opened the door to the world for a whole generation of noblemen. It's certainly not impossible that my father might have heard this exclamation; I believe, nevertheless, that it was his fatherly feeling that drove him to gratify her with two half-dobras.[1] Once washed and swaddled, I became at once the hero of our house. Each predicted my future as best fit his fancy. My uncle João, the old infantry officer, saw a Bonapartean look in me, an observation that made my father nauseated; but my uncle Ildefonso, then a simple priest, sniffed out a canon in me.

"He's to be a canon, and I won't go any further so as to not seem prideful; but I shouldn't wonder a bit if God has destined him for a bishopric . . . Yes, a bishopric; it's not impossible. What say you, brother Bento?"

My father replied to everyone that I would be whatever God willed; and he raised me up into the air, as if to show me to the city and the world; he asked everyone if I looked like him, if I was intelligent, handsome . . .

I say these things rather in passing, as I heard them told years later; I was not privy to most of the particulars of that famous day. I do know that all the neighborhood came to greet the newborn, or sent compliments, and that during the first weeks our house was paid many visits. No sedan chair was left idle; many a frock coat and many fine breeches were aired out for the occasion. If I refrain from narrating the endearments, the kisses, the admiration, the blessings, it is because, should I do so, the chapter would never end, and end it must.

Item, I can say nothing of my baptism, as nothing of it was related to me, except that it was one of the grandest celebrations of the following year, 1806; I was baptized in the church of São Domingos on a Tuesday in March, a clear day, bright and pure, my godparents being Colonel Rodrigues de Matos and his wife. Both descended from old Northern families and truly honored the blood that ran through their veins, blood spilled once upon a time in the war against the Dutch.[2] I believe that their names were among the first things I learned; and I certainly reeled them off charmingly, or revealed some precocious talent in doing so, as I was unfailingly called upon to recite them for every visitor.

"Young master, tell them your godfather's name."

"My godfather? Why, he's the Most Excellent Senhor Colonel Paulo Vaz Lobo César de Andrade e Sousa Rodrigues de Matos; my godmother is the Most Excellent Senhora Dona Maria Luísa de Macedo Resende e Sousa Rodrigues de Matos."

"What a clever boy you have!" those listening would exclaim.

"Very clever," my father would agree; and his eyes would well up with pride, and he would lay a hand on my head and gaze on me at length, enamored, bursting with satisfaction.

Item, I began to walk—I don't know precisely when, but ahead of time. Perhaps to hasten nature along, I was forced to hang on to chairs, hoisted up by the diaper, given pushcarts.

"That's it, young master, on your own now," my mother's slave would say to me.

And I, drawn to the tin rattle that my mother shook before me, would go on ahead, falling here and there; and I walked, probably not too well, but I walked, and so I kept on walking.

CHAPTER XI

THE CHILD IS FATHER
OF THE MAN

I grew up; this the family had no part in; I grew naturally, the way magnolias or cats do. Cats may be less shrewd, and magnolias are certainly less restless than I was as a child. A poet once said that the child is father of the man.[1] If that is true, then let us observe a few of the features of the child.

From age five I had earned the nickname "devil child," and it was truly fitting; I was one of the wickedest of my time, cunning, bold, troublesome, and headstrong. For example, one day I broke the head of a slave because she had refused to give me a spoonful of the coconut sweet she was making, and, not content with the deed, I threw a handful of ashes in the pot, and, not satisfied with that mischief, I went and told my mother that the slave had ruined the sweet "out of spite"; and this at age six. Prudêncio, one of our slave boys, was the horse I rode around on; with his hands on the ground and a length of string between his teeth by way of a bit, I would climb astride his back with a little switch in hand, whipping him, riding up and down and around, and he would obey, moaning at times, but obeying without a word, or at most an "Ow, little master!" to which I would retort, "Shut your mouth, beast!" Hiding visitors' hats, pinning paper tails on dignified people, pulling the pigtails of their wigs, pinching matrons' arms, and many other feats of the same sort were signs of an unruly temperament, but I must be sure that they were also expressions of a robust spirit, as my father esteemed me greatly; if he ever reprehended me in the sight of others, it was out of pure formality: in private, he would cover me with kisses.

One should not conclude that I spent the rest of my life

breaking heads and hiding hats; but stubborn, selfish, and somewhat contemptuous of mankind, that I was; and while I didn't pass my time hiding hats, I did pull a few wig-tails on occasion.

Besides, I took a fancy to the contemplation of human injustice; I was inclined to minimize it, explain it away, classify it by parts, and understand it, not through a rigid model, but in keeping with each place and circumstance. My mother instructed me in her own fashion, having me memorize a few precepts and prayers; but I felt that I was governed less by prayers and more by my nerves and blood; and good rules lost their spirit, which is what gives them life, to become vain formulas. In the morning before my porridge, and at night before bed, I asked God to forgive me my debts, as I forgave my debtors; between morning and night I would work terrible mischief, and my father, once the tumult had died down, would pat me on the cheek and exclaim, laughing, "Ah, you rascal! Ah, you rascal!"

Yes, my father did adore me.[2] My mother was a weak woman, of little brains but great heart, exceedingly credulous, sincerely pious—homespun though pretty, and modest though wealthy, fearful of thunderclaps and of her husband. He was her god on earth. The collaboration of these two creatures produced my education, which, if possessed of certain virtues, was largely unsound, incomplete, and altogether negative on some scores. Now and then my uncle the canon would take his brother to task; he said that I was given more freedom than instruction, and more affection than correction; but my father replied that he was applying to my education a system wholly superior to the one in general use; and while failing to deceive his brother, he thus deluded himself.[3]

Along with my extraction and education was the example set by the rest of the domestic environment. We have seen my parents; let us turn to my uncles. One of them, João, was a man with a loose tongue, a merry life, and an endless supply of roguish conversation. From age eleven on I was granted admittance to the stories he told, some true, some not, but all shot through with obscenity or filth. He had no care for my youth, just as he had no care for his brother's cassock; the difference was that the priest fled whenever he started in on some scabrous subject. I never did; I would let myself listen, understanding nothing at first, then understanding, and finally finding the fun in it. After a while, I was the one seeking him out; and he liked me very much, and would give me sweets and take me out with him. At home, when he happened to spend a few days with us, I found him more than a few times behind the house, in the laundry, chatting with the slave women as they beat at the clothes; then there would come a string of jokes, japes, questions, and bursts of laughter that nobody could hear, since the laundry was quite far from the house. The slave women, their dresses tucked into the tanga-cloths[4] round their waists, some wading in the laundry tank, others outside it, leaning over the clothes as they beat, soaped, and wrung them, would take in and snap back at Uncle João's witticisms, punctuating them now and again with the following exclamation:

"Lord help us! Massa João here is the devil himself!"

My uncle the canon was altogether different. He was possessed of great austerity and purity; these gifts, however, rather than heightening the splendor of a superior spirit, only served to compensate for a mediocre one. He was not one to see the substance of the Church; he saw its exterior, the hierarchy, the preferments, the surplices, the genuflections. More a man of the sacristy than of the altar. A lapse in ritual offended him more grievously than a violation of the Commandments. Now, at a distance of so many years, I can't say whether he might easily understand a passage from Tertullian or expound the history of the Nicene Creed without hesitation; but no one knew better than he the number and style of reverences due to the officiant at high mass.[5] To be a canon was his only ambition in life; and he would say wholeheartedly that it was the highest honor to which a man could aspire. Pious, severe in his habits, a painstaking observer of rules, weak-willed, timorous, and subordinate, he possessed a few virtues, in which he was exemplary—but he was entirely lacking in the strength to impose them on or instill them in others.

I shall say nothing of my maternal aunt, Dona Emerenciana, who was, as it happens, the person who held the greatest authority over me; this set her apart from the rest, but she lived only a short while in our company, two years or so. Other relatives and a few friends of the family fail to merit mention; we lived together only intermittently, with long spans of separation. What matters is a general view of the domestic sphere, which is hereby set out—vulgar characters, a love of hubbub and ostentatious appearances, a weakness of will, the unchallenged reign of whims and fancies, and all the rest. From that earth and that manure was this flower born.

CHAPTER XII

AN EPISODE FROM 1814

But I don't wish to move on without summarily recounting a merry episode from 1814, when I was nine years old.

At the time of my birth, Napoleon was reveling in the splendor of his glory and power; he was emperor and had utterly conquered the admiration of men.[1] My father, who by dint of persuading others of our nobility had come to persuade himself, nursed a purely mental hatred of him. This was the cause of vicious squabbles in our house; my uncle João, whether out of an esprit de corps or professional sympathy, was given to pardoning in the despot what he admired in the general, while my uncle the priest stood inflexibly against the Corsican, and other relatives were divided; hence the controversies and quarrels.

When the news arrived in Rio of Napoleon's first fall,[2] our house was naturally shaken, but there were no gibes or taunts. The defeated, in face of the public rejoicing, judged it more decorous to remain silent; some went so far as to join in the applause. The population was heartily pleased and did not stint on demonstrations of affection toward the royal family; the streets were lit, there were volleys of gunfire, a *Te Deum*, a procession, and acclamations. Around those days, I could be found sporting a new smallsword that my godfather had given me on St. Anthony's Day; and, frankly, the sword interested me far more than Bonaparte's fall. Never did I forget that phenomenon. Never did I cease to ponder that our smallsword always looms larger than Napoleon's blade. And note that I heard many a speech when I was alive, I read many a sensational page of great ideas and greater words; but, I know not why, deep down behind the praise falling from my lips, there often echoed that voice of experience:

"Come, now, all you care about is your smallsword."

My family, not content to have an anonymous part in the public rejoicing, found it both opportune and indispensable to celebrate the toppling of the emperor with a dinner, and such a dinner that the roar of the acclamations might reach the ears of His Highness, or at least those of his ministers. No sooner said than done. All the old silverware inherited from my grandfather Luís Cubas was brought down; out came the Flanders linens, the great jars from the Indies; a barrow pig was slaughtered; compotes and marmalades were ordered from the nuns of the Ajuda Convent; drawing rooms, staircases, candlesticks, sconces, the immense lamp chimneys, all the trappings of classical luxury were washed, scoured, and polished.

The appointed hour was met by a select gathering: the king's magistrate, three or four military officers, a few merchants and lawyers, several government officials, some with their wives and daughters, others without them, but all united by the desire to bury Bonaparte's memory down a turkey's gullet. This was not a dinner but a *Te Deum*; those were more or less the words of one of the lawyers present, Dr. Vilaça, the renowned improvisatore, who complemented the dishes put out by the house with the delicacies of the Muses. I remember, as if it were yesterday, I remember seeing him rise, his long-tailed wig, silk dress coat, an emerald on his finger, asking my priest uncle to repeat the theme, and, once it had been repeated, fixing his eyes for a moment on the forehead of a lady, and then coughing, raising his right hand—clenched but for the index finger, which pointed ceilingward—and, thus composed, delivering an improvisation on the theme. He glossed it not once, but three times; then he swore to his gods to never cease. He asked for a theme, was given it, and improvised on it straightaway, and soon asked for another and yet another; at length one of the ladies present was unable to stifle her great admiration.

"You say that, madam," Vilaça responded modestly, "because you never heard Bocage, as I did, at the end of the century, in Lisbon. Now, that was a sight! What ease! And what verses! We sparred for an hour, two hours, in Nicola's Tavern, improvising amidst cheers and bravos.[3] What an immense talent Bocage had! I heard precisely the same thing a few days ago from the Duchess of Cadaval . . ."[4]

And these last three words, spoken with considerable emphasis, sent a quiver of admiration and astonishment through all assembled. This affable, artless man not only sparred with poets, but also discoursed with duchesses! A Bocage and a Cadaval! At coming into contact with such a man, the ladies felt themselves superbly refined; the men looked on him with respect, some with envy, not a few with incredulity. He, all the while, sailed along, piling adjective upon adjective, adverb upon adverb, running through all of the rhymes for *tyrant* and *usurper*. Dessert had come; nobody thought of eating. In between glosses, there came a cheerful murmur, the chatter of satisfied stomachs; languid and moist eyes, or lively and bright ones, sprawled out or darted up and down the table, which was crowded with sweets and fruits: here slices of pineapple, there cuts of melon, the glass serving dishes revealing the finely grated coconut sweet, gleaming yolk-yellow; farther along, the dark, thick molasses, not far from the cheese and the sweet yams. Now and then a jovial, hearty, unselfconscious laugh, the way one laughs when among family, would come to break through the political solemnity of the banquet. Alongside the grand common interest, smaller, personal matters stirred as well. The young ladies spoke of the songs they would sing at the harpsichord, of minuets and English solo dancing; and there was, of course, a matron who swore she'd dance a measure or two, just to show how she'd made merry in her girlhood. A fellow next to me was telling another the latest about the new blacks that were coming in, according to letters he'd received from Luanda, one letter in which his nephew reported he'd already acquired around forty, and another letter in which . . . He was carrying them right there in his pocket, but couldn't read them out just yet. What he did hazard is that this journey alone would bring us some hundred and twenty blacks at the very least.

Clap! Clap! Clap! Vilaça called the room to attention. The

clamor ceased all at once, like an orchestra cutting off a note, and all eyes turned to the improvisatore. Those farther away cupped a hand behind an ear so as not to miss a word, and most, even before hearing the gloss, already had an easy, frank half-smile on their faces.

As for me, there I was, lonely and unremembered, casting a wistful and loving eye on one of the compotes. At the end of each improvisation I brightened, hoping it was the last, but it never was, and the dessert remained untouched. Nobody thought to speak up. My father, at the head of the table, drank it all in deeply, savoring his guests' joy; he saw himself reflected in the gleeful faces, the dishes, the flowers, delighting in the familiarity struck up between the most dissimilar souls under the sway of a fine dinner. I saw all this as I dragged my gaze from the compote to him, and from him to the compote, as if begging him to serve it to me; but I did so in vain. He saw nothing; he saw only himself. And the improvisations came one after the other, washing over me in torrents, forcing me to check my desire and my pleas. I bore it as long as I could; and that wasn't long. First I asked for the sweet quietly; then finally I bellowed, bawled, and stamped my feet. My father, who would give me the sun if I asked for it, called a slave over to serve me the dessert; but it was too late. Aunt Emerenciana had wrenched me from my chair and turned me over to a slave girl, despite my shouting and thrashing.

Such was the improvisatore's crime: he had delayed the compote and caused my banishment. This was enough for me to plot vengeance; and it had to be grand and exemplary, something that would make him look ridiculous. After all, he was a dignified man, Dr. Vilaça, measured and sedate, forty-seven years old, married and with children. I wouldn't be satisfied with a paper tail or a yanked wig; I needed something worse. I spent the rest of the afternoon watching him, then following him around the grounds as the guests embarked on a postprandial stroll. I saw him talking with Dona Eusébia, the sister of Sergeant-Major Domingues, a robust spinster, who, though not pretty, was hardly homely.

"I'm very angry with you," she said.

"Why?"

"Because . . . I don't know why . . . it seems to be my fate . . . at times I feel I'd rather die."

They had ducked into a small thicket; it was twilight; I followed them in. Vilaça's eyes glimmered with the sparks of wine and the weakness of the flesh.

"Let me be!" she said.

"Nobody can see us. Die, my angel? What's gotten into you? You know that I would die, too . . . What am I saying? I die every day of passion, of longing . . ."

Dona Eusébia dabbed her eyes with her handkerchief. The improvisatore scoured his memory for some scrap of literature and came up with this, which I later found to be from one of Judeu's operas.

"Weep not, my dear, lest the day break with two dawns."[5]

This he said; he pulled her toward him; she resisted somewhat, but let herself go; their faces came together, and I heard the light smack of a kiss, the most timorous of kisses.

"Dr. Vilaça kissed Dona Eusébia!" I bellowed, running out across the grounds.

My words were like a thunderclap; everyone froze in stupefaction; eyes cast here and there; furtive smiles and secrets were exchanged as mothers carried off their daughters, claiming that they might catch cold. My father was truly vexed by my indiscretion and made a show of boxing my ears; but the next day at breakfast, as he recalled the incident, he simply tweaked my nose and laughed:

"Ah, you rascal! Ah, you rascal!"

CHAPTER XIII

A LEAP

Let us put our feet together and take a flying leap over the school, that tedious school, where I learned to read, write, count, deliver punches and take them, and to make mischief in the hills or on the beaches, wherever proved more inviting to the idle.

That time had its torments, it's true; there were the reprimands, the punishments, and the arduous, interminable lessons, but scant more: very little and very light at that. Only the paddlings came down hard, and even so . . . O paddle, terror of my boyhood, you were the *compelle intrare*[1] with which an old schoolmaster, a bald and bony man, impressed into my brain the alphabet, prosody, syntax, and whatever else he knew. Blessed paddle, so heartily cursed in the modern age, if I could have only remained under your yoke, with my callow soul, my ignorance, and my smallsword, that little sword from 1814, so superior to Napoleon's! What was it that you wanted, after all, teacher of my first letters? Lessons learned by heart and good behavior in class; nothing more, nothing less, than is demanded of us by life itself, which teaches us our last letters; the difference being that while you did make me fear you, you never made me angry. Even now I can see you enter the classroom in your cloak and white-leather slippers, handkerchief in hand, bald pate shining, chin clean-shaven; I see you sit down, sigh, grunt, take a first pinch of snuff, and then begin the lesson. And so you did for twenty-three years, quiet, unsung, and punctual, tucked away in a little house on the Rua do Piolho,[2] never troubling the world with your mediocrity, until one day you took that great leap into the darkness, and no one wept

for you, save one old negro—no one, not even I, who owe you
the rudiments of writing.

The schoolmaster's name was Ludgero. I want to write out
his whole name on this page: it was Ludgero Barata, which
means cockroach, an unfortunate surname that was the eternal butt of the boys' jokes. One of us, Quincas Borba, was
downright cruel to the poor man. Two or three times a week,
he would leave a dead cockroach in the pocket of the schoolmaster's trousers—which were conveniently loose-fitting—or
in the desk drawer, or next to the inkwell. If the schoolmaster
came across it during class, he would start, turn a pair of flaming eyes on us, and call us the worst names he could muster:
we were vermin, scoundrels, blackguards, urchins. Some trembled, while others muttered; Quincas Borba, however, kept
quiet, his eyes fixed on nothing in particular.

A flower, Quincas Borba. Never in my childhood, never in
all my life, did I find such a charming, inventive, mischievous
boy. He was the flower not only of the school, but also of all
the city. His mother, a widow of some means, adored her son
and kept him pampered, neat, and prettily adorned, with a
handsomely dressed servant boy who let us shirk school, go off
and hunt for birds' nests, run after lizards on Livramento or
Conceição Hill, or simply roam at our leisure like two idle
dandies. And as an emperor! It was a delight to see Quincas
Borba play the emperor at the feast of the Holy Spirit. In our
childish games, for that matter, he would always choose the
part of king, minister, general, whatever might place him
above the rest. He had a grace about him, that troublemaker,
and a grave air, with something magnificent in his attitudes
and gestures. Who would have thought that . . . Halt the pen
there, lest we reveal coming events.[3] Let us leap ahead to 1822,
the date of our political independence and of my own first captivity.[4]

CHAPTER XIV

THE FIRST KISS

I was seventeen; my lip was afflicted with down that I was making every endeavor to coax into a moustache. My eyes, lively and resolute, were my only truly masculine feature. As I exuded a certain arrogance, it was difficult to discern whether I was a child putting on manly airs or a man with the look of a boy. On the whole, I was a handsome lad, handsome and daring, striding into life in boots and spurs, whip in hand and blood in my veins, atop a sinewy, swift charger in fine fettle, like the charger from the old ballads that the Romantics went looking for in medieval castles, only to light upon it along the streets of our century. The worst is that they overworked the poor beast so terribly that it had to be left by the side of the road; the Realists found it there, leprous and worm-eaten, and, out of compassion, took the animal into their books.

Yes, I was that handsome, graceful, wealthy lad; and one may easily imagine that more than one lady inclined a pensive brow in my direction, or raised a pair of covetous eyes to meet mine. But of all of them, the one who captivated me straightaway was a . . . a . . . I'm not sure I should say; this book is chaste, at least in its intentions; in its intentions it is supremely chaste. But let's have at it, and say all or nothing. My capturer was a Spanish lady, Marcela, "lovely Marcela," as the young men of the day called her. And they were right. She was the daughter of a gardener from Asturias; she told me so herself, on a sincere day, because the accepted version had it that she was born to a lawyer from Madrid, a victim of the French invasion who was wounded, imprisoned, and shot when she was just twelve years old. *Cosas de España.* Whoever he might have been, her father, lawyer or gardener, the truth is that Marcela lacked any rustic innocence, and barely understood the morality of the law at that. She was pretty, agreeable, sans scruples, and somewhat hampered by the austerity of the time, which kept her from parading her fancies and fine carriages down the streets; luxurious, impatient, fond of money and of young men. That year, she was fairly dying for love of a certain Xavier, a wealthy fellow, and consumptive to boot—a gem.

I saw her for the first time at the Rossio Grande, on the night the houses were all lit just after the declaration of independence; a festival of spring, the dawning of the public soul. We were two youths, the nation's people and I; we were scarce out of childhood, with all the ardor of adolescence. I saw her emerge from a sedan chair, graceful and gaudy, her body slender and undulating, bold in a way I'd never seen in chaste women. "Follow me," she said to her servant. And I followed her, just as much a servant as he, as if the order had been directed at me; I let myself go, enamored, quivering, brimming over with the dawn of life. Along the way, someone called her "lovely Marcela," reminding me that I'd heard that name from my uncle João, and, I'll confess it, I was left giddy.

Three days later, my uncle asked me in secret whether I would like to go to a supper in Cajueiros, where "young ladies" would be in attendance. We went; it was at Marcela's house. Xavier, though consumed by his consumption, presided over the nocturnal banquet. I ate little or nothing, as I had eyes only for the hostess. How charming the Spanish girl was! There were another half-dozen ladies—all of the night—and they were pretty, enchanting in their own right, but next to the Spaniard . . . Enthusiasm, a few swallows of wine, and my imperious, rash temperament all led me to do one single thing; as we were leaving, at the door to the street, I told my uncle to wait a moment and went up the stairs again.

"Did you forget something?" Marcela asked, standing at the head of the stairs.

"My handkerchief."

She moved to let me through to the drawing room; I took her hands, pulled her toward me, and gave her a kiss. I don't know whether she said anything at all, if she shouted, if she called out to anyone; I know nothing; I know only that I went down the stairs again, swift as a whirlwind and unsteady as a drunk.

CHAPTER XV

MARCELA

It took me thirty days to get from the Rossio Grande to Marcela's heart, no longer astride the charger of blind desire, but riding the wily, stubborn ass of patience. There are, in truth, two methods for winning over a woman: through violence, as with Europa and the bull, or through insinuation, as with Leda and the swan and Danae and the shower of gold: three of Father Zeus's inventions, which, having fallen out of fashion, are replaced here by the horse and the ass. I'll not speak of the plots I devised, nor of the bribes, nor the alternating of confidence and fear, nor the waiting in vain, nor any of these other preliminaries. I will declare to you that the ass was worthy of the charger—a Sancho Panza of an ass, a true philosopher, who led me to her house at the end of the period in question; I dismounted, gave it a slap on the flank, and sent it off to graze.

First frenzy of my youth, how sweet you seemed! At the Creation, such must have been the effect of the first sunlight. Imagine for yourself the effect of that first sunlight, beating down on the face of a fresh-formed world. Well, this was the same thing, friend reader, and if you were ever eighteen, you must remember that it was just like that.

There were two phases to our passion, or our liaison, or whatever name you wish to call it by, for I take no mind of names; there was the consular phase and the imperial phase. During the first, which was short-lived, Xavier and I reigned together, though he never knew that he was sharing the government of Rome with me; but when credulity could no longer withstand evidence, Xavier laid down his insignia and I held all power in my hands; this was the Caesarean phase. The universe was mine; but, alas! it didn't come free of charge. I had to scrape together money, multiply it, and then invent it. First I tested my father's largesse; he would give me everything I asked without rebuke, without delay, without a cold word; he would tell everyone that I was a young man, and he too had been one. But it reached such extremes that he came to restrict his liberality somewhat, and then more, then still more. Then I turned to my mother and persuaded her to lay aside some of her household allowance, which she gave me in secret. It was too little; and I took to a last resort: I began taking credit on the inheritance I expected from my father, signing promissory notes to be paid off with interest.

"Really," Marcela would say to me when I brought her some jewel or some silks, "I do believe you want us to quarrel . . . This just isn't right . . . such an expensive gift . . ."

And if it was a piece of jewelry, she would say this as she contemplated it between her fingers, holding it up to the light, trying it on, and laughing, and kissing me again and again, impetuous and sincere; even as she protested, her happiness poured forth from her eyes, and I felt happy to see her so. She took a liking to old dobras, and I brought her as many of the gold coins as I could come by; Marcela collected them all in a little iron coffer, and no one knew where she kept the key; she hid it for fear of the slaves. The house where she lived in Cajueiros was her own. The furniture, of carved jacaranda wood, was sturdy and well made, as were all the other effects, mirrors, vases, and the crockery—a beautiful set from the East India Company, which had been given to her by a judge. Accursed crockery, you dealt my nerves many a blow. I said so to the owner of the crockery many a time; I never disguised how these and other spoils of her past loves exasperated me. She would listen to me and laugh, with a frank expression—it was frank and something else, which I didn't quite understand at the time; now, as I think back on it, I believe it was a hybrid smile, such as might come from the creature born of, say, one of Shakespeare's witches and one of Klopstock's seraphim. I may not be making myself clear. Precisely because she had taken note of my belated jealousy, she seemed to like to spur it on. So it was that one day, when I was unable to give her a necklace she'd seen in a jeweler's, she retorted that it was just a joke and that our love needed no such vulgar inducements.

"I'll never forgive you if you get such wretched ideas of me," she concluded, threatening me with a finger.

And then, as quickly as a little bird, she put out her hands, clasped my face in them, drew me to her, and pulled a charming, childish face. Then, leaning back on her divan, she went on simply and straightforwardly, saying that she would never let her affections be bought. She had often sold her appearances, but reserved her inner self for a scant few. Duarte, for example, the sub-lieutenant, whom she had truly loved two years before, could only rarely manage to give her something of value, as I could; she would unreservedly accept only meagerly priced gifts, such as the gold cross he had once given her on a feast day.

"This cross . . ."

As she said this, she put her hand to her breast and held up a delicate gold cross, held round her neck by a blue ribbon.

"But that cross," I observed, "didn't you say it was your father . . ."

Marcela wagged her head with an air of pity.

"Didn't you see that it was a lie, that I told you so as not to upset you? Come now, *chiquito*, don't mistrust me so . . . I loved another; what does it matter, if it's passed? One day, when we part . . ."

"Don't say that!" I cried.

"Everything comes to an end! One day . . ."

She couldn't finish; a sob choked her voice; she stretched out her hands, took mine, nestled me to her breast, and whispered in my ear:

"Never, never, my love!"

I thanked her with damp eyes. The next day I brought her the necklace she had rejected.

"For you to remember me by when we part," I said.

Marcela at first responded with an indignant silence; then she made a magnificent gesture, and moved to throw the necklace out the window. I caught her arm and begged her not to affront me so, begged her to keep the gift. She smiled and kept it.

Meanwhile, she paid me amply for my sacrifices; she guessed at my most furtive thoughts; there was no desire that she did not hasten to fulfill, sincerely and simply, obeying a sort of law of conscience and the necessities of the heart. These were never reasonable desires, but pure childish willfulness, a fancy to see her dressed a certain way, with such and such adornments, in this dress and not that one, to go on outings, or something of that sort, and she gave in to everything, smiling and chattering.

"You're an Arabian-night sort of fellow,"[1] she'd say.

And she'd go to put on the dress, lace, or earrings with enchanting obedience.[2]

CHAPTER XVI

AN IMMORAL REFLECTION

I'm struck by an immoral reflection, which is also a rectification of my style. I believe I said in Chapter XIV that Marcela was dying of love for Xavier. She wasn't dying, she was living. Living is not the same thing as dying; all the jewelers in the world will tell you that, and they are quite well versed in grammar. Good jewelers, what would be left of love were you not there to offer up baubles and credit? A third, perhaps a fifth, of the universal trade in hearts. This is the immoral reflection I had planned on making, which is even more obscure than it is immoral, because what I mean to say is not entirely clear. What I mean to say is that the loveliest brow in the world is left no less lovely when girded with a diadem of precious stones; no less lovely, no less beloved. Marcela, for example, who was quite beautiful, Marcela loved me . . .

CHAPTER XVII

CONCERNING THE TRAPEZE
AND OTHER MATTERS

. . . Marcela loved me for fifteen months and eleven thousand milréis;[1] nothing less. My father, once he got wind of the eleven thousand milréis, was truly alarmed; he felt that the matter had overstepped the bounds of youthful caprice.

"This time," he said, "you'll go to Europe; you'll study at a university, most likely Coimbra; I want you to be a serious man, not a gadabout and a thief."

And when I looked astonished:

"A thief, yes, sir, there's no other word for a son who does what you've done . . ."

He produced from a pocket my promissory notes, which he had already paid off, and shook them in my face.

"See this, you dandy? Is this how a young man should care for the family name? Do you think my grandfathers and I earned our money in gambling houses or roaming the streets? You miserable beggar! This time you'll come to your senses or you'll be left with nothing."

He was furious, but his fury was tempered and brief. I listened to him in silence and mounted no objections to the journey, as I had on other occasions; I was mulling over the idea of taking Marcela with me. I went to see her, laid out the crisis, and put the proposal to her. Marcela listened to me blankly, without responding right away; when I insisted, she said that she would stay, that she couldn't go to Europe.

"Why not?"

"I can't," she said with a mournful look, "I simply can't breathe that air while I'm still haunted by the memory of my poor father, slain by Napoleon . . ."

"Which one of them, the gardener or the lawyer?"

Marcela furrowed her brow and hummed a seguidilla through her teeth; then she complained of the heat and called for a cup of aluá. The slave brought it over on a silver tray, which was part of my eleven thousand milréis. Marcela politely offered me the sweet wine; my response was to slap the cup and the tray, whereupon the liquid spilled into her lap, the negress shrieked, and I bellowed at her to get out. Once we were alone, I poured out all the despair in my heart; I said she was a monster, that she'd never loved me, that she'd brought me this low without even the excuse of sincerity; I called her many an ugly name, to which I added wild gesticulation. Marcela let herself sit there, tapping a nail on her teeth, cold as a slab of marble. I felt the impulse to strangle her, or at least to humiliate her and see her grovel at my feet. I might have done so; but somehow the act become another; it was I who threw myself at her feet, contrite and beseeching; I kissed them, recalled the months of our private happiness, repeated the sweet names of old, sitting on the floor with my head between her knees, pressing her hands in mine; breathless, beside myself, I pled tearfully that she not forsake me . . . Marcela gazed at me for a moment or two, both of us silent, until she lightly turned me aside and said, with a weary air:

"Stop pestering me."

She rose, shook out her wet dress, and walked into her bed-chamber.

"No!" I bellowed. "You mustn't go . . . I won't have it . . ."

I was ready to fall on her; it came too late; she had gone in and closed the door.

I went out, beside myself; I spent two deadly hours wandering round the most far-flung and deserted neighborhoods, where I wouldn't easily be found. I gnawed at my despair with a sort of morbid gluttony; I evoked every day, hour, and instant of rapture, first heartening myself with the thought that they were eternal and that all this was nothing more than a nightmare, and then deceiving myself, trying to shrug them off as a useless burden. Then I would resolve to set off at once, to cleave my life in two, and I delighted in the idea that Marcela would be consumed with longing and remorse when she heard of my departure. After all, she had loved me madly, so she must feel something, be left with some memory, like that of the sub-lieutenant . . . At that, jealousy buried a barb in my heart; my whole nature bellowed that I had to take Marcela with me.

"I must . . . I must . . ." I repeated, wounding the air with a blow.

At last, I had a providential idea . . . Ah! Trapeze of my sins, trapeze of all my abstruse conceptions! The providential idea swung from it like the idea of the plaster (Chapter II). It was simply to enthrall her, enthrall her beyond measure, dazzle her, sweep her away; and it occurred to me to use a method more concrete than supplication. I didn't consider the consequences; I took out one last loan, went to the Rua dos Ourives, bought the finest piece of jewelry in the city, three large diamonds set in an ivory comb; and I ran to Marcela's house.

Marcela was reclining in a hammock, her features slack and tired, a dangling leg revealing a foot in a silk stocking, hair loose, her gaze calm and drowsy.

"Come with me," I said, "I'll find the means . . . we have a great fortune, you'll have everything you wish . . . Look, this is for you."

And I showed her the comb with the diamonds . . . Marcela started slightly, raised up halfway,[2] and, leaning on an elbow, gazed at the comb for a few brief moments; then she turned her gaze away; she had mastered herself. Then I laid hands on her hair, heaped it up, hastily arranged it into an impromptu coiffure, a crooked one at that, and finished it off with the diamond comb; I leaned back, drew close again, correcting a few stray tresses, evening out one side, searching for some symmetry in the disorder before me, all with the painstaking affection of a mother.

"There we are," I said.

"Silly!" was her first reply.

Her second was to pull me to her and pay me for my sacrifice with a kiss, the most ardent yet. Then she took out the comb and admired the material and the workmanship at length, looking at me from time to time and wagging her head as if to re-buke me:

"Oh, you . . ." she sighed from time to time.

"Will you go with me?"

Marcela reflected for a moment. I disliked the expression with which she slid her eyes from me to the wall and from the wall to the gems; but my misgivings vanished when she answered resolutely:

"I'll go. When do you set off?"

"In two or three days."

"I'll go."

I thanked her on my knees. I had found my Marcela of the early days again, and I told her so; she smiled and went to put the comb away as I headed down the stairs.

CHAPTER XVIII

A VISION IN THE HALLWAY

At the foot of the stairs, at the end of the dark hallway, I stopped for a few moments to breathe, come to myself, call my scattered thoughts to order, compose myself after so many profound and contrary sentiments. I found that I was happy. The diamonds tainted that happiness somewhat, it's true; but it is no less true that a pretty woman may well love both the Greeks and their presents. And I trusted my sweet Marcela; she might have flaws, but she loved me . . .

"An angel!" I murmured, gazing at the ceiling in the hallway.

And there, as if to mock me, I saw Marcela's gaze, that gaze that had just given me a shadow of mistrust, eyes sparkling above a nose that was at once Bakbarah's nose and my own. Poor lover of the *Thousand and One Nights*![1] I saw you right there, running after the vizier's wife, along the gallery, she waving to you with the promise of her hand, and you running, running, running, down the long passage, whereupon you emerged onto the street and all the curriers[2] jeered at you and beat you. Then it seemed to me that Marcela's hallway was the passage, and that the street was the street in Baghdad. Indeed, as I looked at the door, I saw three of the curriers there, one in a cassock, one in livery, and one in civilian dress, upon which all three came into the hallway, took me by the arms, and marched me into a coach, my father on the right, my uncle the priest on the left, and the one in livery at the head of the coach, whereupon they took me to the house of the police intendant and from there to a ship bound for Lisbon. You may imagine the resistance I mounted; but all resistance was useless.

Three days later I left the harbor behind, disheartened and speechless. I didn't even cry; I had a fixed idea ... Damn those fixed ideas! Just then, all I could think to do was plunge into the ocean, repeating Marcela's name.

CHAPTER XIX

ON BOARD

We were eleven passengers: a madman accompanied by his wife, two young men out on a trip, four merchants, and two servants. My father entrusted me to all of them, starting with the ship's captain, who had plenty on his hands already; in addition to everything else, he was traveling with his deathly consumptive wife.

I don't know whether the captain suspected something of my macabre plans, or whether my father had warned him; I know that he never took his eyes off me, and called me after him wherever he went. When he couldn't be with me, he took me to see his wife. She was nearly always in a low bed, coughing constantly and promising to show me the countryside around Lisbon. She wasn't thin, she was transparent; it seemed impossible that she wouldn't die from one hour to the next. The captain pretended not to believe in her impending death, perhaps attempting to deceive himself. I knew nothing and I thought nothing. What did it matter to me what befell a consumptive woman in the middle of the ocean? The world, for me, was Marcela.

One night after a week had passed, I found a promising opportunity to die. I went cautiously up on deck, but there I found the captain, his eyes fixed on the horizon.

"A storm?" I asked.

"No," he said with a shudder, "no, I'm admiring the splendor of the night. Look; it's simply celestial!"

The style was at odds with the man, a rather rustic type who would have seemed unacquainted with refined turns of phrase. I turned to look at him; he seemed to savor my astonishment. After a few seconds, he took me by the hand and pointed at the moon, asking me why I didn't compose an ode to the night; I responded that I was no poet. The captain muttered something, took two steps, stuck a hand in his pocket, and took out a heavily creased piece of paper; then, by the light of a lantern, he read a Horatian ode about the freedom of maritime life. He had written it himself.

"What d'you say?"

I can't recall what I said; I do recall that he shook my hand with great vigor and many thanks; soon thereafter he recited two sonnets and was about to recite another when word came that his wife wanted him.

"I'll be right there," he said, and recited the third sonnet to me, lingeringly and lovingly.

I was left alone; but the captain's muse had swept the evil thoughts from my spirit; I preferred to sleep, which is a provisional form of dying. We awoke the next day amidst a terrible storm that frightened us all, except the madman, who began leaping around and saying that his daughter was coming to fetch him in a fine carriage; the death of his daughter had been the cause of his madness. No, I shall never forget the dreadful vision of that poor man, amidst the din of the passengers and the howls of the hurricane, singing and dancing with his eyes starting out of his head, his face pale, his hair unkempt and long. At times he would stop, raise his bony hands, and make crosses with his fingers, then crisscrosses, then rings, as he laughed long and desperately. His wife could no longer care for him; given over to her terror of death, she prayed for her own salvation to all the saints in heaven. At last the tempest relented. I confess that it was an excellent diversion from the tempest in my heart. I, who had pondered seeking out death, didn't dare meet its gaze when it sought me out.

The captain wanted to know if I'd been afraid, if I'd been in any danger, if I hadn't found the spectacle sublime, all this with friendly interest. The conversation naturally turned to life at sea; the captain asked me if I liked piscatorial idylls, to which I responded innocently that I didn't know what they were.

"You'll see," he responded.

And he recited a little poem to me, then another—an

eclogue[1]—and then finally five sonnets, with which he finished off his literary confidences for the day. On the following day, before reciting anything, the captain explained to me that he had taken to the maritime profession only for compelling reasons; his grandmother had wanted him for the priesthood, and he had some Latin; he never came to be a priest, but he never ceased to be a poet, which was his natural vocation. To prove it, he recited some hundred verses right then and there. I observed a phenomenon: his gesticulation was such that on one occasion I laughed; but it so happened that as the captain recited, he turned his gaze so far inward that he neither saw nor heard anything.

The days passed away, and the waters, and the verses, and with them the life of the captain's wife. She was near the end. One day, just after lunch, the captain said to me that she might not see the end of the week.

"So soon!" I exclaimed.

"She had a very bad night."

I went to see her; to my eyes she was on the brink of the grave, but still going on about resting in Lisbon for a few days before going with me to Coimbra, as she planned to accompany me to the University. I left her side, distraught; I found her husband watching the waves break and die against the ship, and tried to console him; he thanked me, recounted the story of their love, praised his wife's fidelity and dedication, recalled the verses he'd written for her, and recited them to me. At this point he was called to her side; we both ran to her; she was in the throes of a fit. This and the next day were cruel; the third day brought her death; I fled from the spectacle, finding it repugnant. Half an hour later I found the captain sitting on a coil of rope, his head in his hands; I gave him a word of comfort.

"She died like a saint," he replied; and, lest these words be ascribed to weakness, he straightened up at once, shook his head, and fixed his gaze long and deeply on the horizon. "Now," he went on, "let us deliver her to the grave that is never to be opened."

Indeed, a few hours later, the cadaver was cast into the sea with the customary ceremony. Sadness had withered every face;

the widower's bore the expression of a mountaintop cleaved by a lightning bolt. A great silence. The wave opened its maw, received the remains, closed once more—a slight wrinkle—and the ship moved on. I let myself remain there for a few minutes, at the stern, my eyes resting on that unknown point of the sea where one of us had been left . . . From there I sought out the captain, looking to distract him.

"Thank you," he said, understanding my intent; "you may be sure that I will never forget your kindness. God bless you for it. Poor Leocádia! You'll think of us in heaven."

He wiped a troublesome tear away with his sleeve; I cast around for a diversion in poetry, his passion. I spoke to him of the verses he'd read to me and offered to have them printed. The captain's eyes livened a bit.

"I might accept," he said, "but then again, the verses are quite weak."

I swore to him that they weren't; I asked him to gather them together and give them to me before we docked.

"Poor Leocádia!" he murmured without responding to my request. "A cadaver . . . the sea . . . the sky . . . the ship . . ."

The next day he read me a freshly composed dirge recalling the circumstances of his wife's death and burial; as he read, his voice was truly moved, his hands trembling; at the end he asked me if the verses were worthy of the treasure he had lost.

"They are," I said.

"They may not be inspired," he pondered after a moment, "but no one will deny me their feeling—if the feeling itself hasn't compromised their perfection, that is . . ."

"I wouldn't say so; the verses are perfect."

"Yes, well . . . The verses of a seaman."

"Of a seaman and a poet."

He shrugged, looked at the paper, and recited the composition again, but this time with no tremors at all, accentuating the literary flourishes, underscoring the images and the melody of the verses. At the end, he confessed that it was his best-wrought work yet; I agreed; he shook my hand and predicted a great future for me.

CHAPTER XX

I TAKE MY DEGREE

A great future! As the words echoed in my ears, I returned my eyes to that mysterious, uncertain horizon off in the distance. One idea drove out another, and ambition unseated Marcela. A great future? Perhaps a naturalist, a man of letters, an archaeologist, a banker, a politician, or even a bishop—even that would do—as long as it meant rank, preeminence, a great reputation, a superior position. If ambition were an eagle, just then it had pecked through its shell and unveiled a tawny, penetrating eye. Farewell, loves! Farewell, Marcela! Days of delirium, jewels without price, life without order, farewell! Here go I on to toil and glory; I leave you with my knee breeches.

And it was thus that I disembarked in Lisbon and headed for Coimbra. The University awaited me with its arduous subjects; I studied them in quite a mediocre fashion, but not even that deprived me of my law degree; it was awarded with the customary solemnity, after the stipulated number of years, in a fine celebration that filled me with pride and wistfulness—mostly wistfulness. In Coimbra I had made quite a name for myself as a merrymaker; I was a wastrel, a superficial, troublemaking, and petulant student, given to adventures, following romanticism in practice and liberalism in theory, living with a pure faith in dark eyes and written constitutions. On the day the University certified on sheepskin that I had acquired knowledge that was, in truth, far from rooted in my brain, I confess that I found myself to some extent cheated, albeit proud. Let me explain: the diploma was a letter of emancipation; while it gave me freedom, it also gave me responsibility. I stowed it away, left the banks of the Mondego, and headed off, rather crestfallen, but already feeling an urge, a curiosity, a desire to rub elbows, to influence, to enjoy, to live—to prolong the University throughout my life . . .

CHAPTER XXI

THE MULETEER

And just then, the donkey I was riding on balked; I whipped it, and it bucked twice, then thrice, then once again, this last time throwing me from the saddle, but at such an unfortunate angle that my left foot remained caught in the stirrup; I tried to hang on to the animal's belly, but it, now frightened, set off flying down the road. Rather, I should say: it tried to set off, and indeed took a couple of bounds, but a muleteer who happened to be nearby rushed over in time to seize the reins and detain the donkey, not without considerable effort and danger to himself. With the brute subdued, I disentangled myself from the stirrup and righted myself.

"Just look what an escape you had, sir," said the muleteer.

And it was true; if the donkey had run off, I would have been gravely injured, and death might await me at the end of my calamity; a split head, a congestion, any sort of disturbance within, and that would be the end of all my blossoming knowledge. The muleteer might well have saved my life; that seemed certain; I felt it in the blood surging through my heart. Blessed muleteer! As I gathered myself, he took to fixing the donkey's harness, carefully and skillfully. I resolved to give him three gold coins of the five I had with me; not because this was the price of my life—which was beyond measure—but because it was a reward worthy of the selflessness with which he had saved me. It's settled; I'll give him the three coins.

"There you are," he said, handing me the reins.

"Just a moment," I replied. "Let me be, I'm not myself yet . . ."

"Bah!"

"Well, wasn't I nearly killed?"

"If the donkey'd run off, p'rhaps; but with the Lord's help, sir, none of that came to pass."

I went to the saddlebags and took out the old waistcoat with the five gold coins in the pocket; and during that time I pondered whether the payment wasn't excessive, and if two coins wouldn't do. Perhaps one. Indeed, one coin would suffice to make him quake with joy. I examined his clothing; he was a poor devil who'd never seen a gold coin in his life. One coin, then. I took it out and saw it shine in the sunlight; the muleteer didn't see it, as I had turned my back to him; but he may have surmised it, for he began talking to the donkey in meaningful tones; he gave it advice, telling it to behave, saying that "the gentleman" might punish it: a paternal monologue. For heaven's sake! I even heard the smack of a kiss; the muleteer had kissed it on the forehead.

"Well!" I exclaimed.

"Forgive me, sir, but I'll be damned if the beast isn't giv'n' us such a charming look . . ."

I laughed, hesitated, placed a silver cruzado[1] in his hand, mounted the donkey, and went off at a brisk trot, somewhat discomfited, or rather, somewhat uncertain of the coin's effect. But at some yards' distance, I looked back; the muleteer was bowing and scraping, with evident signs of contentment. And he must have been; I had paid him handsomely, perhaps too well at that. I put my hand into the pocket of the waistcoat I had on and felt a few copper coins; these were the vinténs I ought to have given the muleteer, instead of the silver cruzado. After all, he had not sought any reward or virtue, he had given in to a natural impulse, to the temperament and the habit of his profession; moreover, the circumstance of his being neither farther ahead nor behind, but at precisely the point where the accident occurred, would seem to indicate that he had been a simple instrument of Providence; and in either case, the merit of the act was positively naught. This reflection distressed me; I called myself a spendthrift and credited the cruzado to my old extravagances; I felt (why not say it all?), I felt remorse.

CHAPTER XXII

RETURN TO RIO

You blasted donkey, you've snapped the thread of my thoughts. Now I'll not say what I thought of from there to Lisbon, nor what I did in Lisbon, on the peninsula and in other places in Europe—old Europe, which just then seemed to be growing young again. No, I'll not say that I gazed on the dawn of Romanticism or that I, too, went to live out a few romantic poems in the bosom of Italy; I'll say nothing at all. For that I would have to write a travel diary, and not memoirs such as these, in which only the substance of life may enter.

After some years of peregrinations, I heeded my father's pleas. "Come," he had written in the last letter; "if you do not come quickly, you will find your mother dead!" This last word was a blow to me. I loved my mother; I could still see the last time she had given me her blessing, on board the ship. "My poor son, I shall never see you again," the wretched lady had wept, pressing me to her breast. And those words now rang to my ear as a prophecy fulfilled.

Note that I was in Venice, still wafting of the verses of Lord Byron; there I was, steeped in a dream, reliving the past tense, seeing myself back in the Most Serene Republic. It's true; once I happened to ask the innkeeper if there would be a procession of the doge that day. "What doge, *signor mio*?" I came to my senses, but I didn't confess my fancy; I said that my question was a sort of American riddle; he gave signs of understanding, and added that he liked American riddles very much. He was, after all, an innkeeper. Well, I left all that, the innkeeper, the doge, the Bridge of Sighs, the gondola, the verses of the lord, the ladies of the Rialto. I left everything and set off like a bullet in the direction of Rio de Janeiro.

I came . . . But no, let's not prolong this chapter. At times I forget myself as I write, and the pen sets to devouring paper, at great cost to me, the author. Long chapters are better suited for ponderous readers; and we are not much for folios, but rather duodecimos,[1] with little text, broad margins, an elegant type, gilt edges, and illustrations . . . especially illustrations . . . No, let's not prolong the chapter.

CHAPTER XXIII

SAD, BUT SHORT

I came. I'll not deny that, upon sighting the city of my birth, I felt a new sensation. This was not the effect of my political homeland; it was that of the place of my childhood. This street, that tower, the fountain on the corner, women in mantillas, hired-out slaves working odd jobs, the things and scenes of boyhood, engraved into memory. Nothing less than a rebirth. My spirit, like a bird, paid no mind to the current of the years, turned the course of its flight toward the primordial font and went to drink of its fresh, pure water, which was yet to mingle with the torrent of life.

Upon further consideration, there's a commonplace there. Another commonplace, sadly common, was my family's affliction. My father embraced me in tears.

"Your mother can live no longer," he said.

Indeed, it was no longer rheumatism that was killing her, but a cancer of the stomach. The poor thing was suffering cruelly, for cancer is indifferent to virtue; when it gnaws, it gnaws; to gnaw is its profession. My sister Sabina, by then married to Cotrim, was staggering with fatigue. Poor girl! She slept three hours a night, nothing more. Uncle João himself was downcast and sad. Dona Eusébia and a few other ladies were there as well, no less sad and no less devoted.

"My son!"

The pain withdrew its claws for a short while; a smile shone from the invalid's face, upon which death was beating its eternal wing. It was less a face than a skull: beauty had passed, like a bright day, and left only bones, which never grow thin. I could barely recognize her; it had been eight or nine years since we had seen each other last. Kneeling by the bed with her hands between mine, I stayed mute and still, not daring to speak; each word would be a sob, and we feared forewarning her of the end. A vain fear! She knew how near it was; she told me so; we saw it for ourselves the next morning.

Long was the agony, long and cruel, a painstaking, cold, unrelenting cruelty that filled me with pain and stupefaction. This was the first time that I had seen someone die. I knew death by hearsay; at most I had seen it petrified on the face of some cadaver that I accompanied to the cemetery, or had my idea of it wrapped up in the rhetorical amplifications of professors of ancient things—Caesar's treacherous death; Socrates' austere death; Cato's proud death. But this duel between to be and not to be, death in action, aching, doubled up, convulsing, with no political or philosophical trappings, the death of a loved one, this was the first time I had looked full at it. I didn't cry; I remember that I didn't cry during the spectacle: my eyes were vacant, my throat choked, my mind agape. What? Such a docile, sweet, saintly creature who had never caused a single tear to be shed, a tender mother and immaculate spouse—did she have to die this way, racked with pain, pierced by the dogged tooth of a merciless disease? I confess that all this struck me as opaque, incongruous, insane . . .

A sad chapter; let us pass to another, happier one.

CHAPTER XXIV

SHORT, BUT HAPPY

I was left prostrate. And yet I was, at that time, a faithful compendium of triviality and presumption. The problem of life and death had never weighed on my brain; never, until that day, had I gazed into the abyss of the Inexplicable; I lacked that essential thing, that impulse, that vertigo . . .

To tell you the whole truth, I reflected the opinions of a hairdresser I met in Modena, who distinguished himself by having none whatsoever. He was the flower of the hairdressers; as long as the hairdressing process might be, it was never tiresome; he alternated strokes of the brush with jokes and banter, full of wit and flavor . . . He had no other philosophy. Nor did I. I won't say that the University taught me none whatsoever; but I had only memorized the formulas, the vocabulary, the skeleton. I dealt with it as I did Latin; I pocketed three lines of Virgil, two of Horace, and a dozen moral and political maxims, to be dispensed in conversation. I dealt with them as I did history and jurisprudence. I plucked from all things the phraseology, the shell, the ornamentation . . .[1]

The reader may be taken aback by the frankness with which I expose and emphasize my own mediocrity; he should recall that frankness is the primary virtue of a late man. In life, the gaze of public opinion, the clash of interests, the struggle between rival greeds oblige us to hide our old rags, to disguise splits and stitches, to not extend to the world that which we reveal to our conscience; and the best of this obligation is when, by dint of deluding others, a man deludes himself, because in this case he is spared humiliation, which is a painful sensation, and hypocrisy, which is a ghastly vice. But in death, what a difference! What an unburdening! What freedom! How we can shake off our cloaks, toss our spangles into the gutter, unbutton ourselves, unpaint ourselves, unadorn ourselves, confess plainly what we were and what we failed to be! Because, after all, there are no more neighbors, nor friends, nor enemies, nor acquaintances, nor strangers; there is no audience. The gaze of opinion, that piercing, judicial gaze, loses all its power as soon as we set foot in the territory of death; this is not to say that it doesn't reach this far, examining and judging us; but it is we who have no compunctions about the examination or the judgment. My good living sirs and madams, there is nothing so incommensurable as the disdain of the deceased.

CHAPTER XXV

IN TIJUCA

Oh! There goes my pen, slipping over into the emphatic. Let us be simple, simple as the life I led in Tijuca[1] during the first weeks after my mother's death.

On the seventh day, after the Mass, I gathered up a gun, a few books, clothes, cigars, a slave boy—Prudêncio, from Chapter XI—and sought refuge in an old house we owned. My father strove to dissuade me, but I could not have obeyed him, even if I had wanted to. Sabina wanted me to live with her for a time, two weeks at the least, and my brother-in-law was on the verge of bringing me by force. A good fellow, Cotrim had gone from extravagance to prudence. Now he dealt in imported goods and worked from morning to night, fervently and doggedly. At night, sitting by the window and twisting his side whiskers, he thought of nothing but work. He loved his wife and the son they had then, who died a few years later. People said he was avaricious.

I renounced everything; my spirit was stunned. I believe that this is when hypochondria began to unfurl within me, that yellow flower, a solitary and morbid bloom with an intoxicating, subtle scent. "'Tis good to be sad and say nothing!"[2] When these words of Shakespeare drew my attention, I confess that I felt them echo within me, a delightful echo. I recall that I was sitting under a tamarind tree with the poet's book open in my hands, my spirit even more downcast than my figure—crestfallen, or *jururu*, as we say of sulking chickens. I clasped my taciturn grief to my breast with a unique sensation, something I might call the voluptuousness of woe. The voluptuousness of woe: learn that phrase by heart, reader; keep it for yourself, study it, and if you never do come to understand it, you may conclude that you are ignorant of one of the subtlest sensations of this world and that time.

At times I hunted, at others I slept, at others I read—I read a great deal—and at others I did nothing at all; I let myself drift from idea to idea, from fancy to fancy, like a wandering or famished butterfly. The hours dripped one by one, the sun sank, the shadows of night veiled the mountain and the city. No one came to visit me; I had recommended expressly that I be left alone. One day, two, three, an entire week spent without saying a word would be enough to dislodge me from Tijuca and restore me to the busy throng. Indeed, after seven days I was sick of solitude; the pain had subsided; my soul was no longer satisfied with shooting and books, nor with the sight of the trees and the sky. Youth stirred; I had to live. I stowed the problems of life and death, the poet's melancholy, my shirts, my meditations, and my cravats away in my trunk and was about to close it when Prudêncio the slave boy came to say that a person of my acquaintance had moved to a red house[3] just two hundred paces from ours.

"Who?"

"You might not remember Dona Eusébia, master . . ."

"I do . . . Is it she?"

"And her daughter. They came yesterday morning."

I immediately thought of the incident from 1814, and felt chagrined; but I saw that events had proved me right. In fact, it had been impossible to turn a deaf ear or a blind eye to the intimate relations between Vilaça and the sergeant-major's sister; even before my departure, there were mysterious mutterings about the birth of a baby girl. My uncle João sent word later that when Vilaça died, he left a sizable bequest to Dona Eusébia, which set the entire neighborhood talking. Uncle João, a glutton for scandals, spoke of nothing else in the letter, which was many pages long at that. Events had proved me right. And even if they hadn't, 1814 was off in the distance, and with it my mischief, and Vilaça, and the kiss in the thicket; lastly, I had no close relations with her. I reflected thusly to myself and proceeded to close the trunk.

"Won't you visit Missus Eusébia?" Prudêncio asked. "She was the one who dressed my late mistress's body."

I remembered having seen her among other ladies on the occasion of my mother's death and funeral; I hadn't known, however, that she had paid my mother this final kindness. The slave boy's point was reasonable; I owed her a visit; I resolved to do so immediately and then go down to the city.

CHAPTER XXVI

THE AUTHOR HESITATES

Suddenly, I hear a voice:

"Now, my boy, this is no life!"

It was my father, with two proposals in his pocket. I sat down on my trunk and greeted him listlessly. He stood there for a few moments, looking at me; then he stretched out his hand in a heartfelt gesture:

"Resign yourself to the will of God, my son."

"I already have," was my answer, and I kissed his hand.

He hadn't lunched; we ate together. Neither of us alluded to the unhappy reason for my seclusion. We spoke of it only once, in passing, when my father brought the conversation back to the Regency; that was when he alluded to the letter of condolence that one of the regents had sent him. He had the letter with him; it was quite creased by that point, perhaps from having been read to many other people. I believe I've said that it was from one of the regents. He read it to me twice.

"I've already seen him to thank him for the mark of consideration," my father concluded, "and I believe you ought to as well . . ."

"I?"

"Yes, you; he's a prominent man, he stands in the emperor's place. Moreover, I've brought you an idea, a plan . . . or, yes, I'll tell you everything; I've got two plans, a seat in the Chamber of Deputies and a marriage."

My father pronounced these words slowly, and each in a different tone, lending them a form and disposition as if to impress them onto my spirit. The proposal, however, clashed so forcibly with my recent feelings that I could barely understand it at first. My father, unflinching, repeated it; this time he gilded both the seat and the bride-to-be.

"Agreed?"

"I don't know anything about politics," I said after a moment; "as for the bride . . . let me live like the bear that I am."

"But bears marry," he replied.

"Well, then, bring me a she-bear. Look, there's the Ursa Major . . ."

My father laughed, and, after laughing, he began to speak in earnest again. I needed a political career, he went on, for twenty-odd reasons, which he deduced with singular volubility, illustrating them with examples of people we knew. As for the bride-to-be, I had only to see her; once I did, I would ask her father for her hand before the day was out. He tried charm, then persuasion, then exhortation; I kept quiet, sharpening the point of a toothpick or rolling balls out of soft bits of bread, smiling or reflecting; and, to be honest, neither yielding to nor rebelling at the proposal. I felt dazed. A part of me said yes, that a pretty wife and a political position were goods worthy of consideration; another said no; and my mother's death stood as an example of the fragility of things, of affections, of family . . .

"I won't leave without a definite answer," my father said. "Definite!" he repeated, beating out the syllables with his finger.

He drank the last of his coffee, settled into his chair, and began to hold forth on everything: the Senate, the Chamber of Deputies, the Regency, the Restoration, Evaristo, a coach he planned to buy, our house on the Rua de Mata-cavalos . . . I stayed where I was at the corner of the table, writing absentmindedly on a piece of paper with a bit of pencil; I scrawled a word, a phrase, a verse, a nose, a triangle, and repeated them again and again in no particular order, at random:

arma virumque cano

A

Arma virumque cano

    arma virumque cano

    arma virumque

        arma virumque cano

    virumque[1]

Mechanically, all of this; and, nevertheless, there was a certain logic, a certain sequence; for example, the *virumque* led me to the name of the poet himself, on account of the first syllable; I was going to write *virumque*, and it came out *Virgil*, and so I went on:

Vir   *Virgil*
    Virgil   *Virgil*
        Virgil
                            Virgil

My father, a bit ruffled at my indifference, rose, came over to me, cast his eyes over the paper . . .

"Virgil!" he exclaimed. "That's you, my boy; the name of your bride-to-be is Virgília."

CHAPTER XXVII

VIRGÍLIA?

Virgília? Then it was the same lady who, some years later . . . ?
The very same; it was precisely the lady who would witness
my last days in 1869 and who had played a great part in my
most intimate sensations long before then. She was only fifteen
or sixteen at the time; she was possibly the sauciest creature to
ever grace our land, and certainly the most willful. I won't say
that she was first in beauty among the young ladies of the age,
as this is not a novel, in which the author may gild reality and
close his eyes to freckles and spots; but nor, for that matter,
will I say that any freckle or spot marred her countenance. She
was pretty, fresh-faced, come from the hands of nature, brimming with that fragile and eternal enchantment that one individual gives off to another for the secret designs of creation. This
was Virgília, and she was fair, very fair, coquettish, ignorant,
childish, brimming with mysterious impulses, a great deal of la-
ziness and some measure of piety—piety or perhaps fear; I believe it was fear.

There, reader, in a few lines you have the physical and moral
portrait of the person who was to later shape my life, and was
all that at age sixteen. As you read me, if you are still alive
when these pages come to light—as you read me, beloved Virgília, don't you see the difference between the language of
today and that which I used when first I knew you? You may
believe that I was as sincere then as I am now; death has not
made me bitter, nor unjust.

"But," you'll say, "how is it that you can make out the truth
of that time, and express it after so many years?"

Ah, how indiscreet! Ah, how ignorant! This is precisely what makes us lords of the earth, the power to restore the past, so that we might reveal how fleeting our impressions are, and how vain our affections. Let Pascal say that man is a thinking reed. No; he is a thinking erratum, that's what he is. Each season of life is an edition that corrects the last and that will be corrected in turn until the definitive edition, which the editor delivers to the worms, free of charge.

CHAPTER XXVIII

PROVIDED THAT . . .

"Virgília?" I interrupted.

"Yes, sir; that's the name of the bride. An angel, my silly goose, an angel without wings. Imagine a girl about this tall, live as quicksilver, and quite the pair of eyes . . . Dutra's daughter . . ."

"Which Dutra?"

"Counselor Dutra, you don't know him; he's quite the political influence. Well, then, do you accept?"

I didn't respond straightaway; I stared for a few seconds at the tip of my boot; then I declared that I was willing to consider both things, the candidacy and the match, provided that . . .

"Provided that what?"

"Provided that I won't be obliged to accept both; I believe that I can be either a married man or a public man—"

"Every public man ought to be married," my father interrupted sententiously. "But do what you will; I shall stand for whatever you see fit; and I'm sure that seeing will be believing! Moreover, the bride and the Parliament are all the same thing . . . that is, well . . . you'll see later . . . Bah! I accept the delay, provided that—"

"Provided that what?" I interrupted, imitating his voice.

"Ah, you rascal! Provided that you don't just sit around and become useless, obscure, and melancholy. I didn't dole out money, cares, and efforts not to see you shine. It befits you, it befits all of us; our name must be carried on, carried on and made even more illustrious. Why, I'm sixty years old, but if I had to start a new life, I wouldn't hesitate for a moment. Fear obscurity, Brás; flee from petty things. Men may show their worth in a number of ways, you know, and the surest of all is to be found worthy in the opinion of other men. Don't waste the advantages of your position, of your means . . ."

And the magician had only to shake a rattle before me, just as they had when I was a baby, to make me walk; the flower of hypochondria shrank back into its bud to make way for another flower, this one less yellow and not morbid in the slightest—the love of fame, the Brás Cubas Plaster.

CHAPTER XXIX

THE VISIT

My father had won; I was ready to accept the candidacy and the marriage, Virgília and the Chamber of Deputies.

"The two Virgílias," said he, in a flush of political tenderness.

I accepted them; my father gave me two hearty embraces. Finally, he could recognize his own blood.[1]

"Are you coming down to the city with me?"

"I'll go tomorrow. First I'll pay a visit to Dona Eusébia . . ."

My father looked down his nose but said nothing; he bade me farewell and went down to the city. As for me, that afternoon I went to visit Dona Eusébia. I found her scolding a negro gardener, but she stopped immediately to greet me with such excitement and such sincere pleasure that I was soon put at ease. I believe she went so far as to wrap her robust arms around me. She had me sit by her side on the veranda, among many exclamations of contentment:

"Well, now, Brasinho! A grown man! Who would say, so many years ago . . . Such a strapping young man! And handsome! I never! I'm sure you won't remember me . . ."

I assured her that I did, that I could never forget such a close friend of the family. Dona Eusébia began to speak of my mother with such longing in her voice that I was soon captivated, although saddened. She saw it in my eyes and steered the conversation in another direction; she asked me to tell of my travels, my studies, and my loves . . . Yes, yes, the loves as well; she confessed that she was a saucy old woman. At this I recalled the incident from 1814—her, Vilaça, the thicket, the kiss, my shout—and as I recalled it, I heard the creaking of a door, the rustling of skirts, and:

"Mama . . . Mama . . ."

CHAPTER XXX

THE FLOWER
OF THE THICKET

The voice and the skirts belonged to a dark young girl, who stopped short in the doorway for a moment or two upon seeing unfamiliar faces. A brief and embarrassed silence. Dona Eusébia broke it, in the end, resolutely and frankly.

"Come here, Eugênia," she said. "This is Dr. Brás Cubas, Mr. Cubas's son, come from Europe."

And, turning to me:

"My daughter Eugênia."

Eugênia, the flower of the thicket, hardly responded when I bowed to her; she looked at me, bashful and bewildered, and slowly moved over to her mother's chair. Her mother fixed one of her braids, the end of which had come undone.

"Ah! Naughty!" she said. "You can't imagine, Dr. Cubas, what she gets up to . . ."

And she kissed her daughter with such expansive affection that I was rather moved; my mother came to mind, and—I'll say it all—I felt an itch to be a father.

"Naughty?" I said. "It would seem she's past the age."

"How old would you say she is?"

"Seventeen."

"Minus one."

"Sixteen. There you have it! She's a young lady."

Eugênia couldn't conceal the satisfaction that my words brought her, but she soon recovered herself and became straight-backed, cold, and silent once more. Indeed, she seemed to be even more of a woman than she was in fact; she might be a child when left to her youthful devices, but once quiet and impassive, she had the composure of a married woman. This may have diminished her virginal charm somewhat. We shortly became familiar; her mother praised her to no end, I listened to the praise readily, and the girl smiled, her eyes shining, as if a butterfly were flitting around inside her head with wings of gold and diamond eyes . . .

I say inside her head, because on the outside what came fluttering up was a black butterfly, which suddenly invaded the veranda and began batting its wings around Dona Eusébia. She gave a shriek, stood up, and let out a few stray imprecations:

"Out with you! Get away, you devil! By the Virgin!"

"Don't be afraid," I said; and, taking out my handkerchief, I expelled the butterfly.

Dona Eusébia sat down again, breathing heavily, somewhat embarrassed; her daughter, perhaps pale with fear, hid her feelings with great strength of will. I shook their hands and left, chuckling to myself at the two women's superstition; it was a philosophical chuckle, aloof and superior. That afternoon I saw Dona Eusébia's daughter riding by on horseback, with a slave following after; she flicked her whip by way of a greeting. I'll confess that I flattered myself with the notion that after a few paces she would look back; but she did not.

CHAPTER XXXI

THE BLACK BUTTERFLY

The next day, as I was preparing to go down to the city, a butterfly came into my room, just as black as the other one and much larger. I recalled the incident of the day before and laughed; I soon thought of Dona Eusébia's daughter, the fright she'd taken, and the dignity she had nonetheless been able to preserve. The butterfly, after fluttering around me for some time, landed on my forehead. I brushed it away; it landed on the windowpane; and, when I brushed it away again, it flew off and landed atop an old portrait of my father. It was black as night. The gentle way in which it began moving its wings, once settled, had a sneering air[1] that greatly displeased me. I shrugged and left the room; but when I returned, minutes later, to find it in the same place, I felt a sudden urge, snatched up a towel, struck it, and it fell.

It wasn't dead; its body still twitched, and its feelers still moved. I felt sorry for it, placed it in the palm of my hand and went to put it on the windowsill. Too late; the unfortunate creature expired after a few seconds. This left me somewhat bothered, put out.

"Why the devil couldn't it have been blue?" I said to myself.

And this reflection—one of the most profound to be produced since the invention of butterflies—consoled me for my misdeed, and I made peace with myself. I let myself contemplate the cadaver with some affection, I confess. I imagined that it had left the forest, content and having breakfasted. The morning was lovely. It had wandered out, modest and black, reveling in its butterflydom, below the vast dome of a blue sky—the sky which is always blue, no matter the color of one's wings. It went in through my window and happened upon me. I presume it had never seen a man; therefore, it could not know what a man was; it traced countless circles around my body and saw that I moved, that I had eyes, arms, legs, a divine air, colossal stature. Then it said to itself: "This is probably the inventor of butterflies." The idea overpowered it, cowed it; but fear, which may also be persuasive, insinuated to the butterfly that the best way to thank its maker would be to kiss him on the forehead, and so it kissed me on the forehead. When I brushed it away, it landed on the windowpane, and from there it spotted the portrait of my father. It may well have hit upon a half-truth—that this was the father of the inventor of butterflies—and, accordingly, it flew over to beg his mercy.[2]

Then a towel-blow brought its adventure to an end. Not the blue vastness, nor the joy of the flowers, nor the splendor of the green leaves could avail it against a hand-towel, two spans of raw linen. See how good it is to be superior to butterflies! It must be said: if it were blue or orange, its life would have been no safer; it was not impossible that I might have run it through with a pin, the better to admire it. Indeed, it was not. This latter idea restored my consolation; I put my middle finger to my thumb, dispatched a flick, and the cadaver fell into the garden. Just the right time; there came the provident ants . . . No, back to the first idea; I believe it would have been better for it to have been born blue.

CHAPTER XXXII

BORN LAME

From there, I went to finish preparing for the journey. No more dawdling. I'm going down right away; and go down I will, even if some circumspect reader should stop me to ask if the last chapter was merely insipid or if his leg is being pulled . . . Alas, I hadn't reckoned with Dona Eusébia. I was all ready to leave when she appeared at the house. She had come to invite me to put off my descent and dine with them that day. I went so far as to refuse; but she pressed, pressed, and pressed until I was forced to accept; after all, I owed her as much; and so I went.

Eugênia disadorned herself that day on my account. I believe it was on my account, but she might have gone about that way quite often. Not even the gold earrings she had worn the day before hung from her ears now, two finely shaped ears on the head of a nymph. A simple white muslin dress; no brooch at the neck, but a mother-of-pearl button, with another button at the wrist to fasten the cuffs, and not a bracelet in sight.

That was the body; as for the spirit, it was hardly different. Clear ideas, simple manners, a certain natural grace, the air of a lady, and perhaps something else; yes, her mouth, exactly the same as her mother's, which reminded me of the incident of 1814 and inspired an urge to improvise on the same theme with the daughter . . .

"Now I'll show you the grounds," said the mother, as soon as we had drunk the last drop of coffee.

We went out onto the veranda, from there to the grounds, and it was then that I noticed something. Eugênia limped slightly, so slightly that I even asked if she'd hurt her foot. Her mother fell silent; but she responded without hesitation:

"No, sir, I was born lame."

I cursed myself heartily; I called myself an ass and a lout. Of course the very possibility of her being lame would have sufficed for me to not ask anything. Then I recalled that the first time I had seen her—the day before—she had come over to her mother's chair slowly, and that later I had found her already seated at the supper table. Perhaps that was to conceal the defect; but why then would she confess it now? I looked at her and found her downcast.

I worked to erase the vestiges of my blunder; this did not prove difficult, for her mother was, in her own words, a saucy old woman, and promptly struck up a conversation with me. We saw all there was to see on the grounds—trees, flowers, the duck pond, the laundry, countless things that Dona Eusébia showed to me and remarked on, as I, all the while, stealthily perused Eugênia's gaze . . .

I swear to you that Eugênia's gaze was not lame but straight, perfectly sound; it came from a pair of calm, black eyes. I believe that on two or three occasions they looked down, slightly clouded; but only two or three times; in general they stared at me frankly, neither bold nor prim.

CHAPTER XXXIII

BLESSED ARE THEY
THAT GO NOT DOWN

The pity was that she was lame. Such clear eyes, such a sweet mouth, such a stately bearing; and lame! The contrast might imply that nature is, at times, a tremendous joke at our expense. Why pretty, if lame? Why lame, if pretty? This was the question I posed to myself as I returned home that night, without lighting on the solution to the enigma. The best thing to do when one can't resolve an enigma is to throw it out the window; and that was what I did; I snatched up a towel and shooed away this, the other black butterfly flapping around my brain. Thus relieved, I went to sleep. But dreams, which are a cranny leading to the soul, let the little creature in again, and I spent the whole night poring over the mystery, finding no explanation.

The morning brought rain, and I put off my return; but on the next day the morning was clear and blue, and in spite of that I stayed, as I did on the third day, and the fourth, and through the end of the week. Lovely, fresh, inviting mornings; down below was my family calling me, and my bride-to-be, and Parliament; I was deaf to it all, enraptured at the feet of my crippled Venus. *Enraptured* is merely a rhetorical flourish; there was no rapture, but rather pleasure, a certain physical and moral satisfaction. I liked her, it's true; next to such a simple creature, a lame and bastard daughter, formed of love and disgrace, next to her I felt good, and as for her, I believe she felt even better next to me. And all this in Tijuca. A veritable eclogue. Dona Eusébia kept watch over us, but it was far from rigorous; she tempered necessity with convenience. Her daughter, in this first flourishing of nature, gave unto me her soul in bloom.

"Will you go down tomorrow?" she asked me on Saturday.

"I intend to."

"Don't."

I didn't, and I added a new verse to the Gospels: Blessed are they that go not down, for theirs is the young ladies' first kiss. And indeed, Sunday brought Eugênia's first kiss—the first any man had taken from her, and not stolen or seized, but given up artlessly, as an honest debtor pays a debt. Poor Eugênia! If you only knew what ideas were wandering through my mind on that occasion! You, trembling with emotion, your arms on my shoulders, contemplating me as your heaven-sent spouse, and I with my eyes on 1814, the thicket, Vilaça, suspecting that you could not flee from your blood, your origin . . .

Dona Eusébia came in unexpectedly, but not so suddenly as to catch us together. I went over to the window; Eugênia sat down, fixing one of her braids. What delightful dissembling! What a boundless, delicate art! What profound Tartuffism![1] And it was all so natural, so vibrant and unaffected, as natural as eating or sleeping. So much the better! Dona Eusébia suspected nothing.

CHAPTER XXXIV

TO A SENSITIVE SOUL

Among the five or ten people reading me, there is a sensitive soul who is doubtless a bit distressed by the previous chapter, has begun to quake for Eugênia's fate, and perhaps . . . yes, perhaps, deep down, may be calling me a cynic. I, a cynic, sensitive soul? By Diana's thigh![1] That insult ought to be washed away with blood, if blood ever washed away anything in this world. No, sensitive soul, I am no cynic, I was a man; my brain was a theater in which plays of all genres were staged, sacred plays, austere dramas, sentimental works, gay comedies, topsy-turvy farces, morality plays, burlesque—pure pandemonium, sensitive soul, a tumult of things and people in which you might see everything, from the rose of Smyrna to the rue growing in your own backyard, from Cleopatra's magnificent couch to the corner of the beach where a beggar shivers away the night. It was host to thoughts of the most various castes and complexions. Nor was it the sole province of the eagle and the hummingbird; the slug's and the toad's habitats were represented there as well. Take back those words, then, sensitive soul, give your nerves a shake, clean off your eyeglasses—sometimes it's all in the eyeglasses—and let us do away with this thicket flower once and for all.

CHAPTER XXXV

THE ROAD TO DAMASCUS

Now it so happened that, a week later, as if I were on the road to Damascus, I heard a mysterious voice whispering the words of the Scripture (Acts 9:6): "Arise, and go into the city." The voice came from me, and it sprang from two things: pity, which disarmed me before the girl's innocence, and the dread of coming to truly love her and wed her. A crippled wife! As for the second motive for my departure, there is no doubt that she perceived it, and told me so. It was on the veranda, on a Monday afternoon, after I had announced that I would go down to the city the next morning.

"Goodbye," she sighed, holding out her hand with a natural air. "You're doing the right thing." And as I said nothing, she went on: "You're doing the right thing, running away from the laughable idea of marrying me."

I was going to deny it; she retired slowly, choking back her tears. I overtook her in a few steps and swore by all the saints in heaven that I had to go, but that I still cared for her, very much so; all listless hyperboles, which she listened to without saying a word.

"Do you believe me?" I asked her at the end.

"No. And I say that you're doing the right thing."

I moved to hold her back; but the gaze she directed at me was no longer entreating, but commanding. I came down from Tijuca the following morning, a bit aggrieved, but another bit satisfied. As I came, I repeated to myself that it was right to obey my father, that it was only proper to embrace a political career . . . that the Constitution . . . that my bride-to-be . . . that my horse . . .

CHAPTER XXXVI

ON THE SUBJECT OF BOOTS

My father, who hadn't been expecting me, embraced me with affection and gratitude.

"Is it really true?" he asked. "May I at last . . . ?"

I left him in his ellipsis and went to take off my boots, which were tight. Once relieved, I breathed deeply and stretched out while my feet, and all the rest of myself after them, entered into relative bliss. Then I pondered that tight boots are one of the greatest blessings on earth, for by causing one's feet to hurt, they make way for the pleasure of taking them off. Mortify your feet, wretch, then unmortify them, and there you have cheap happiness, befitting both shoemakers and Epicurus. As this idea worked away on my famous trapeze, I cast my eyes to Tijuca, saw the little crippled girl vanish away on the horizon of the past tense, and felt that my heart would not be long in taking off its own boots. And take them off it did, the wanton thing. Four or five days later, it would savor that swift, ineffable, irrepressible moment of pleasure that follows a racking pain, a worry, a discomfort . . . From this I inferred that life is the most ingenious of all phenomena, as it sharpens hunger only for the purpose of providing occasion to eat, and it invented corns only because they work to perfect earthly happiness. Verily I say unto you that the sum total of human wisdom isn't worth a pair of tight boots.

As for you, my Eugênia, you never took your boots off; you went off along the road of life, limping from your leg and from love, sad as a pauper's burial, solitary, quiet, unflagging, until you, too, arrived at this other shore . . . What I cannot say is whether your existence was quite necessary to the age. Who knows? One fewer supernumerary and the whole human tragedy might have been booed off the stage.[1]

CHAPTER XXXVII

AT LAST!

At last! Here we have Virgília. Before going to Counselor Dutra's house, I asked my father if there was any prior arrangement about the marriage.

"No arrangement whatsoever. Some time ago, when I was
speaking with him about you, I confessed my desire to see you
in the Chamber of Deputies; I said it in such a way that he
promised to do something, and I believe he will. As for the
bride, that's just my word for a little creature who's a gem, a
flower, a star, a rare thing indeed . . . She's his daughter; I
imagined that if you married her, you would find yourself a
deputy more quickly."

"Is that all?"

"That's all."

From there we went to Dutra's house. The man was a
pearl—smiling, jovial, patriotic, somewhat out of sorts about
society's ills, but not yet despairing of mending them quickly.
He judged my candidacy solid; it would be best, however, to
wait a few months. In short order he introduced me to his
wife—an estimable lady—and his daughter, who did not belie
my father's panegyric in the slightest. I swear to you, not in the
slightest. Reread Chapter XXVII. I, who had my ideas about
the girl, gazed at her in a certain way; she, who may have had
ideas of her own, returned the gaze in kind; and our first look
was purely and simply conjugal. After a month's time we were
on intimate terms.

CHAPTER XXXVIII

THE FOURTH EDITION

"Come dine with us tomorrow," Dutra said to me one night.

I accepted the invitation. The following day, I had my coach wait for me at the Largo de São Francisco de Paula, and I went out for a stroll. Do you still recall my theory of human editions? Well, know, then, that at that time I was in my fourth edition, revised and amended, but still infested with lapses and barbarisms, a defect that found some compensation in the type, which was elegant, and the binding, which was luxurious. Having strolled far and wide, I took out my watch as I went down the Rua dos Ourives, and the glass fell onto the sidewalk. I went into the first shop at hand; it was little more than a dark, dusty box.

At the back, behind the counter, there sat a woman whose yellow, pockmarked face could not be made out at first glance; but once it came into view, it was a curious spectacle. She could not have been ugly; on the contrary, it was clear that she had been pretty, and not a little; but the disease and a precocious old age had destroyed the flower of her charms. The smallpox had been ruinous; the marks, which were large and numerous, had left protuberances and furrows, slopes and ruts, giving the impression of sandpaper, terribly rough sandpaper. Her eyes were the better part of her figure, but they bore a singular and repugnant expression, which changed, however, as soon as I began to speak. As for her hair, it was gray and nearly as grimy as the shop front. On one of the fingers of her left hand there gleamed a diamond. Will you believe it, posterity? That woman was Marcela.

I didn't recognize her straightaway; it was difficult; but she recognized me as soon as I addressed her. Her eyes sparkled and their ordinary expression was replaced by another, somewhere between sweet and sad. I saw her move as if to hide or flee; this was the instinct of vanity, which lasted no more than an instant. Marcela settled back and smiled.

"Would you like to buy something?" she asked, holding out a hand.

I said nothing. Marcela understood the cause of my silence (it was not difficult), and only hesitated, I believe, in deciding which was foremost, the astonishment of the present or the memory of the past. She offered me a chair, and, with the counter between us, she told me at length of herself, the life she had lived, the tears I had made her shed, the longing, the misfortunes, and finally the pox, which had blighted her face, and time, which had helped the malady along in accelerating her decay. The truth is that her very soul was decrepit. She had sold everything, nearly everything; a man who had once loved her and died in her arms had left her the jeweler's; but as if to crown her ill fortune, the shop was now little frequented—perhaps for the singular fact of its being run by a woman. Then she asked me to tell of my life. I spent very little time in doing so; the story was neither long nor interesting.

"Are you married?" Marcela asked at the end of my narrative.

"Not yet," I replied tersely.

Marcela turned her gaze to the street, with the blank look of one caught in reflection or recollection; I also let myself drift to the past, and, amidst the memories and nostalgia, I wondered why I had gone to such foolish lengths. This was certainly not the Marcela of 1822; but was her former beauty worth even a third of my sacrifices? That was what I sought to glean from Marcela's face. The face told me no; at the same time, the eyes told me that then, as now, the flame of greed burned bright within them. Mine had been unable to see it; they were first-edition eyes.

"But why did you come in? Did you see me from the street?" she asked, coming out of her torpor.

"No, I thought it was a watchmaker's; I wanted to buy a

glass for this watch. I'll go somewhere else; forgive me, I'm in a hurry."

Marcela sighed mournfully. The truth is that I felt both distressed and vexed, and yearned to be free of the place. Marcela, however, called a slave boy, gave him the watch, and, over my protests, sent him to a nearby shop to buy the glass. There was nothing to be done; I sat down again. She then said that she would be glad of the patronage of her old acquaintances; she surmised that sooner or later I would, of course, marry, and guaranteed that she would find me fine jewels for cheap prices. She didn't say *cheap prices*, but rather used a delicate, transparent metaphor. I began to suspect that she had suffered no great misfortune (save the disease), that her money was safe and sound, and that she negotiated with the sole aim of feeding her passion for profit, which was the gnawing worm at the heart of her existence. That was precisely what I was told later on.

CHAPTER XXXIX

THE NEIGHBOR

As I reflected thusly, a short, hatless fellow came into the shop, holding a girl of four by the hand.

"Have you had a good morning?"

"So-so. Come here, Maricota."

The fellow picked the child up by her arms and set her on the other side of the counter.

"Come now," he said, "ask Dona Marcela if she had a good night. She was eager to come here, but her mother hadn't been able to get her dressed . . . Well, Maricota? Go on, kiss her hand . . . You don't want a switching, do you? That's the way . . . You can't imagine her at home; she speaks of you all the live-long day, and now she sits here like a lump. Just yesterday . . . Shall I tell her, Maricota?"

"Don't, Papa."

"Was it something bad, then?" Marcela asked, patting the girl on the cheek.

"I'll tell you; her mother taught her to say the Lord's Prayer and the Hail Mary every night to Our Lady; but yesterday the little one came to ask me, very meekly . . . can you imagine what? She wanted to offer her prayers to Saint Marcela."

"Poor thing!" said Marcela, giving her a kiss.

"She's infatuated, head over heels, there's no describing it . . . Her mother says she's been bewitched . . ."

The fellow told a few more anecdotes, all quite pleasant, before leaving with the girl, but not without casting a questioning look, or perhaps a suspicious one, in my direction. I asked Marcela who he was.

"He's a watchmaker in the neighborhood, a good man; so is

his wife; and the daughter is delightful, isn't she? They seem to have taken a liking to me . . . they are good people."

As she uttered these words, there was a quaver of joy in Marcela's voice; and it was as if a wave of happiness swept across her face . . .

CHAPTER XL

IN THE COACH

At this the slave boy came in bearing the watch, now with a new glass. It was high time, for being there was an ordeal; I gave the boy a silver coin, told Marcela that I would come back another day, and strode out. If the truth be told, I must confess that my heart was pounding a little; but it was a sort of death knell. My spirit was caught between clashing impressions. Note that the day had begun joyfully for me. Over breakfast my father had recited the first speech that I was to give in the Chamber of Deputies; we laughed heartily, and the sun laughed with us, shining just as on the most beautiful days the world has ever seen—and Virgília would laugh brightly, too, when I told her of our breakfast-table fantasies. And then the glass falls from my watch, I go into the first shop at hand, and the past emerges before me, lacerating me and kissing me, interrogating me, its face disfigured by nostalgia and pockmarks . . .

There I left it; I got hastily into the coach, which was waiting for me at the square, and ordered the coachman to set off. He whipped up the beasts, the coach began to jolt me around, the springs groaned, the wheels quickly plowed through the mud left by the recent rain, and yet everything seemed to stand still. Doesn't there sometimes come a certain warm wind, not strong or harsh, but stifling, which neither snatches our hats away nor sets women's skirts whirling, and yet it is worse, or may seem to be worse, than if it did one or the other, since it casts down, enfeebles, and practically dissolves one's spirit? Well, that wind blew around me then; and, convinced that it was because I found myself in a narrow pass between the past and the present, I ached to burst out onto the plain of the future. The worst of it was, the coach wasn't moving.

"João!" I bellowed at the coachman. "Is this coach going to move, or not?"

"But master, we're already stopped outside the Counselor's."

CHAPTER XLI

THE HALLUCINATION

It was true. I rushed in; I found Virgília anxious and out of sorts, her brow clouded. Her mother, who was deaf, was in the drawing room with her. After an exchange of greetings, the younger woman said curtly:

"We expected you earlier."

I defended myself as best I could; I spoke of a balky horse and a friend who'd kept me. Suddenly my voice died on my lips as I was paralyzed by astonishment. Virgília . . . was this young lady Virgília? I stared at her at length, and the sensation was so painful that I took a step back and turned my gaze away. I looked again. Pockmarks had eaten away at her face; her skin, only recently so fine, rosy, and pure, now looked yellowed, afflicted with the same malady that had devastated the Spanish lady's face. Her eyes, once mischievous, had gone dull; her mouth was dejected, her air weary. I looked at her closely; I took her by the hand and drew her gently to me. I wasn't mistaken; there were the pockmarks. I think I showed some sign of disgust.

Virgília moved away and went to sit on the sofa. I contemplated my feet for a while. Should I leave or stay? I rejected the first device, which was simply absurd, and went over to Virgília, who was sitting there quietly. Good Lord! There, once again, was the fair, young, flowering Virgília. I sought in vain for any sign of the disease on her face; there was none; only the same fine, white skin as always.

"Haven't you ever seen me before?" asked Virgília, seeing that I was staring intently at her.

"Never so lovely."

I sat down as Virgília clicked her fingernails, not saying a word. There was a pause of a few seconds. I spoke of things unrelated to the incident; but she gave no answer, nor would she look at me. Except for the clicking, she was Silence on a monument. Only once did she let her eyes fall on me, superciliously, as she raised the left corner of her lip and furrowed her brows until they met; this lent her face an expression halfway between comic and tragic.

There was a measure of affectation in that disdain; there were airs in the gesture. Inside she was suffering, and not a little, whether it was pure distress or only spite; and since dissembled pains hurt all the worse, it is quite probable that Virgília was actually suffering twice as much as she really should have been. I believe that is metaphysical.

CHAPTER XLII

WHICH ESCAPED ARISTOTLE

Another thing that also strikes me as metaphysical is this: a ball is put in motion, for example; it rolls, comes up against another ball, transmits the driving force, and here we have the second ball rolling just as the first did. Let us suppose that the first ball is called . . . Marcela—a mere supposition—while the second ball is called Brás Cubas, and the third, Virgília. Thus we have it that Marcela, receiving a flick from the past, rolled until it touched Brás Cubas, which, ceding to that propulsive force, set off rolling until it ran into Virgília, which had nothing to do with the first ball; this is how, through the simple transmission of force, social extremes may touch one another, creating what we may call the solidarity of human disgruntlement. How on earth did this chapter escape Aristotle?

CHAPTER XLIII

A MARCHIONESS, FOR I'LL BE A MARQUIS

She was positively a little devil, Virgília, an angelic devil, if you like, but she was one all the same, and then . . .

Then there came Lobo Neves, a man who was not more svelte than I was, nor more elegant, nor more educated, nor more winning, and nonetheless it was he who took both Virgília and the candidacy from me in a matter of weeks, in a truly Caesarean stroke. There was no precipitating incident; there was no violence between houses. Dutra simply came one day to tell me that I was to wait for more favorable winds, since Lobo Neves's candidacy was backed by influential figures. I gave in; this was the beginning of my defeat. A week later, Virgília asked Lobo Neves with a smile when he would become a minister.

"If I have my way, now; if others have theirs, in a year's time."
Virgília replied:
"Promise to make me a baroness one day?"
"A marchioness, for I'll be a marquis."

From there on out, I was lost. Virgília compared the eagle and the peacock and chose the eagle, leaving the peacock with his astonishment, his resentment, and three or four kisses she had given him. Perhaps five kisses; but had they been ten, it would have been all the same. A man's lip is not like the hoof of Attila's horse, which left the soil it struck barren; it is precisely the opposite.

CHAPTER XLIV

A CUBAS!

My father was aghast at the outcome, and I do believe that he died of it. He had erected so many castles, dreamt so many sundry dreams, that he could not see them crumble without suffering a considerable shock to his organism. At first he refused to believe it. A Cubas! A branch of the illustrious tree of the Cubases! And he said this with such conviction that I, having already been informed of our ancestor the cooper, forgot my fickle lady for a moment and simply contemplated this phenomenon, which, while not rare, was nonetheless curious: a figment of imagination promoted to the rank of fact.

"A Cubas!" he repeated to me the following morning, over breakfast.

This breakfast was not a happy affair; for my part, I was exhausted. I had lain awake for much of the night. Out of love? Impossible; one can't love the same woman twice, and I, who would come to love her some time later, was not then tied by any bond other than a passing fantasy, a measure of obedience, and a great deal of vanity. That was enough to explain my sleepless night; it was resentment, a needle-sharp little resentment that was dissipated through cigars, pounding fists, and truncated bouts of reading until the break of dawn, the calmest of dawns.

But I was young, and I bore my remedy in myself. It was my father who could not take the blow so easily. Upon further reflection, the disaster may not have been the precise cause of his death, but it certainly compounded his final pains. He died four months later, disconsolate and forlorn, with an intense, incessant preoccupation, something like remorse, a fatal dis-

illusionment that took the place of his rheumatism and coughing fits. He was to have one final half-hour of happiness; that
was when one of the ministers visited him. I saw on him—I
can remember it well—I saw on him the grateful smile of former times, with a concentration of light in his eyes that was, in
a way, the last spark of his expiring soul.

But sorrow returned soon thereafter, the sorrow of dying
without seeing me placed in some high place, as befitted me.

"A Cubas!"

He died a few days after the minister's visit, on a May morning, between his two children, Sabina and me, as well as Uncle
Ildefonso and my brother-in-law. He died, finding no succor in
the doctors' science, nor our love, nor all the cares taken,
which were many; he could not but die, and so he died.

"A Cubas!"

CHAPTER XLV

NOTES

Sobs, tears, the house in funeral array, black velvet over the entryways, a man who came to dress the corpse, another to measure for the coffin, the coffin, the catafalque, tall candles, invitations, the visitors who came in slowly, stepping softly, and pressed the hands of the family, some sorrowful, all serious and silent, priest and sacristan, prayers, sprinkling of holy water, the coffin hammered shut, six people who take it from the catafalque, raise it up, and make their way laboriously down the stairs, over the cries, sobs, and fresh tears of the family, and go to the hearse, where they set it down, lash it in place, and fasten the straps, the hearse rolling off, the carriages rolling off, one by one . . . These, apparently items in a simple inventory, were notes that I had taken for a sad and banal chapter that I will not write.[1]

CHAPTER XLVI

THE INHERITANCE

Behold us, reader, a week after my father's death: my sister sitting on a sofa, Cotrim before her, leaning on a console table with his arms crossed, worrying at his moustache, and I pacing up and down, my eyes on the floor. Deep mourning. A great silence.

"But, after all," said Cotrim, "this house can't be worth much more than thirty thousand milréis; let us say that it's worth thirty-five . . ."

"It's worth fifty," I maintained. "Sabina knows that it cost fifty-eight . . ."

"It might have cost sixty," Cotrim replied, "but that doesn't mean that it was worth it, much less that it's worth that today. You know that the houses around here have gone down in price over the years. Look here, if this one is worth fifty thousand milréis, how much would the one you want for yourself, out at the Campo, be worth?"

"For goodness' sake! That's an old house."

"Old!" exclaimed Sabina, throwing her hands up.

"It seems new to you, I take it?"

"Come now, brother, let's have none of this," said Sabina, rising from the sofa. "We can settle things civilly, and be plain with one another. For example, Cotrim won't take the slaves, he only wants Papa's coachman and Paulo . . ."

"Not the coachman," I objected. "The coach is going to me, and I won't go out and buy another coachman."

"All right; I'll take Paulo and Prudêncio."

"Prudêncio is free."

"Free?"

"It's been two years now."

"Free? How your father dealt with these things around here, without telling anyone! Very well. As for the silver . . . he didn't free that, did he?"

We had already spoken of the silver, the old silverware from the time of King José I, the dearest part of the estate, whether by virtue of its craftsmanship, its antiquity, or its history; my father used to say that Count da Cunha, when he was viceroy of Brazil, had given it to my great-grandfather Luís Cubas as a present.

"As for the silver," Cotrim went on, "I wouldn't insist in the slightest if your sister didn't want it; but I believe she is entitled. Sabina is married and needs a decent, presentable set of silver plate. You're a bachelor, you don't entertain, you don't . . ."

"But I may get married."

"What for?" interrupted Sabina.

This question was so sublime that it made me forget my own interests for a few moments. I smiled; I took Sabina's hand and patted it lightly, all with such a benevolent air that Cotrim interpreted the gesture as one of acquiescence, and thanked me.

"What now?" I rejoined. "I haven't given up anything, nor do I intend to."

"Don't you?"

I shook my head.

"Never mind, Cotrim," said my sister to her husband. "See if he wants the clothes off our backs; that's all he's missing."

"There's nothing missing. He wants the coach, he wants the coachman, he wants the silver, he wants everything. Look here, it'd be much quicker to call us to court and bring witnesses to prove that Sabina isn't your sister, I'm not your brother-in-law, and God isn't God. Do that and you won't lose a thing, not even a teaspoon. Come now, try another one!"

He was so irate, and I no less, that I thought to offer a means of conciliation: dividing up the silver. He laughed and asked who would take the teapot and who would take the sugar bowl; and after this question, he declared that we'd be able to settle the claim in court, at least. Meanwhile, Sabina had gone over to the window overlooking the grounds, and after a moment she came back and suggested giving me Paulo and another slave on the condition that she keep the silver; I was about to say that this didn't suit me, but Cotrim answered the same thing before I could.

"Never! I'm no almsgiver!" he said.

We had a melancholy supper. My uncle the priest showed up at dessert, in time to witness a minor altercation.

"My children," he said, "remember that my brother left a loaf large enough to be shared with all."

To which Cotrim replied:

"Certainly. The matter, however, is not the bread, but the butter. I won't be made to swallow dry bread."

The apportionments were made, in the end, but we had fallen out. And I tell you all that, even so, it pained me greatly to quarrel with Sabina. We had been such friends! The games and quarrels of childhood, the laughter and sorrows of our adult years; we had often broken the bread of joy and misery, fraternally, like the good brother and sister that we were. But we had fallen out. Just as Marcela's beauty had fallen away with the pox.

CHAPTER XLVII

THE RECLUSE

Marcela, Sabina, Virgília . . . here I am, blending together all the contrasts, as if these names and people were nothing more than the various manifestations of my innermost affections. Ill-mannered pen of mine, tie a proper cravat around your style and find yourself a slightly less filthy waistcoat; and then you may come with me, come into the house and stretch out in this hammock, where I swayed away the better part of the years between the inventory of my father's estate and 1842. Come: if you should detect a waft of dressing-table perfume, do not imagine that I had it scented for my own pleasure; that is a vestige of the lovely N. or Z. or U.—for all those capital letters swayed here as well, in their elegant abjection. But if you should want something besides the aroma, you'll be left wanting; I kept neither portraits, nor letters, nor memories; even the emotion faded away, and I was left only with the initials.

I became somewhat of a recluse, going now and then to some ball or the theater or a lecture, but spending most of the time by myself. I lived; I let myself drift in the wax and wane of events and days, restive one moment, listless the next, between ambition and dejection. I wrote politics and practiced literature. I sent articles and verses to the papers, and gained a reputation as something of a polemicist and a poet. When I recalled Lobo Neves, who had already become a deputy, and Virgília, the future marchioness, I asked myself why I wouldn't be a better deputy and a better marquis than Lobo Neves—I, who was so very superior to him—and I pondered this as I stared at the tip of my nose . . .

CHAPTER XLVIII

A COUSIN OF VIRGÍLIA'S

"Do you know who arrived yesterday from São Paulo?" Luís Dutra asked me one evening.

Luís Dutra was a cousin of Virgília's, who also communed with the Muses. His verses were better than mine, and better liked; but he craved the approval of some to confirm the praise he received from others. His bashfulness meant that he never asked anyone outright, but he would delight in hearing an admiring word; then he would muster fresh strength and assail the task with youthful zeal.

Poor Luís Dutra! As soon as he published anything at all, he would run to my house and begin circling me, lying in wait for a judgment, a word, a gesture approving of his latest production; and I would speak of a thousand different things—the latest Catete ball, the debates in the legislature, carriages and horses—anything but his verses or prose. He would reply eagerly at first, then more weakly, then steer the conversation toward his concern, opening a book and asking me if I had anything new written, and I would tell him yes or no, but steer the conversation elsewhere, and there he would follow me until he finally balked and went away downcast. My aim was to make him doubt himself, dispirit him, eliminate him. And all the while, I stared at the tip of my nose . . .

CHAPTER XLIX

THE TIP OF THE NOSE

Nose, conscience sans remorse, you served me greatly in life . . . Have you ever meditated on the purpose of the nose, beloved reader? Dr. Pangloss's explanation[1] is that the nose was created so we might use eyeglasses, and I'll confess I found it definitive for a certain time; but there came a day when, in ruminating on these and other obscure philosophical matters, I hit upon the sole, true, definitive explanation.

Indeed, I had only to attend to the habits of the fakir. The reader will know that a fakir spends hours upon hours staring at the tip of his nose with the sole aim of beholding the celestial light. When he trains his eyes on the tip of his nose, he loses all sense of the outside world, becomes enraptured in the invisible, grasps the impalpable, unlashes himself from the earth, dissolves, becomes one with the ether. This sublimation of one's being via the tip of the nose is the loftiest phenomenon of the spirit, and its obtainment is not the sole province of the fakir: it is universal. Every man has both the need and the power to contemplate his own nose so as to behold the celestial light, and such contemplation, the effect of which is the subordination of the universe to nothing more than a nose, ensures the equilibrium of societies. If noses only contemplated one another, the human race would never have lasted two centuries: it would have extinguished itself during the first tribes.

At this, I hear an objection from the reader. "How can that be," he says, "if nobody has ever, never, not once seen men contemplating their own noses?"

Obtuse reader, this merely proves that you have never entered the brain of a hatmaker. A hatmaker passes by a hat shop; this is a rival's shop, opened two years ago. Back then it had two doors, today it has four; it promises to grow to six, then eight. The rival's hats flaunt themselves in the windows; the rival's customers walk in through the doors; the hatmaker compares this shop with his, which is older and still has only two doors, and these hats with his, which are less sought-after, though equally priced. He is distressed, of course; but he keeps on walking, concentrated, his eyes cast down or staring straight ahead, poring over the causes of the other's prosperity and his own hardship, when he as a hatmaker is a much better hatmaker than the other hatmaker . . . At this instant, his eyes fix on the tip of his nose.

The conclusion here is that there are two capital forces in this world: love, which multiplies the species, and the nose, which subordinates it to the individual. Procreation, equilibrium.

CHAPTER L

VIRGÍLIA, MARRIED

"My cousin Virgília, married to Lobo Neves. That's who arrived from São Paulo," Luís Dutra went on.

"Ah!"

"And I only found out something today, you rogue."

"What's that?"

"That you wanted to marry her."

"My father's idea. Who told you that?"

"She did. I said a good bit about you, and then she told me everything."

The next day, as I stood on the Rua do Ouvidor at the door of Plancher's printing office, I saw a splendid woman come into view at a distance. It was she; I only recognized her at a few paces, such was the transformation, so greatly had nature and art refined their work. We greeted one another; she went on her way; she and her husband entered their carriage, which was waiting for them just ahead; I was left stunned.

A week later, I saw her at a ball; I believe we exchanged two or three words. But at another ball, a month later, at the home of a lady who had graced the salons of the First Reign and did not disgrace those of the Second,[1] our encounter was closer and lingered longer, for this time we both spoke and waltzed. The waltz is a delightful thing. We waltzed; and I won't deny that as I held that supple, magnificent body next to mine, I had a singular sensation, that of a man who has been robbed.

"It's quite hot," she said as soon as we had finished. "Shall we go out on the terrace?"

"No; you might catch cold. Let's go into the other room."

In the other room was Lobo Neves, who praised my political writings highly, adding that he would say nothing of my literary work, as he understood nothing of it; but the political writings were excellent, well thought out and well written. I responded in kind, with hearty praise, and we parted quite pleased with one another.

Around three weeks later, I received an invitation for a small gathering at his home. I went; Virgília greeted me with this charming welcome:

"You really must waltz with me again tonight."

It's true, I was known as a master waltzer; it was no wonder she preferred me. We waltzed once, and once again. A book was Francesca's undoing; here, the waltz was ours.[2] I believe that on that night I took her hand in mine, and she left it in my grasp as if she had forgotten it, while I embraced her and all eyes looked on us and on the others who were also embracing one another and waltzing round and round . . . Pure delirium.

CHAPTER LI

MINE!

"Mine!" I said to myself, as soon as I passed her on to another gentleman; and I confess that over the rest of the evening the idea began burying itself in my spirit, not with the force of a hammer, but rather that of a gimlet, which is a more insinuative tool.

"Mine!" I said as I arrived at my door.

And then, as if fate or destiny, or whatever it might have been, should have wished to feed my possessive raptures, something round and yellow shone at me from the ground. I bent down; it was a gold coin, a half-dobra.

"Mine!" I repeated, chuckling, and put it in my pocket.

That night I thought no more of the coin; but on the following day, as I recalled the incident, I felt my conscience twitch, and heard a voice asking me why on earth a coin that I had neither inherited nor earned, but simply found on the street, should be mine. Evidently it was not mine; it belonged to another, to whoever had lost it, be he rich or poor, and perhaps he was poor, some worker who no longer had the means to feed his wife and children; even if he were rich, my duty would remain the same. It was only proper to return the coin, and the best way, the only way, was with the help of a notice or the police. I wrote a letter to the chief of police, sending my find along with it and begging him to use the means at his disposal to return it to the hands of its true owner.

I sent the letter and breakfasted at ease, even jubilantly. My conscience had waltzed so much the previous evening that it had been stifled, left breathless; but the restitution of the half-dobra was a window opening up onto the other side of morality; a wave of pure air wafted in, and my conscience, that poor lady, was able to breathe deeply. Ventilate your consciences! I shall say nothing more. All other circumstances aside, my act was a fine one, as it expressed an honorable concern, the sentiment of a delicate soul. That was what my inner lady said to me, at once austere and mild; that was what she said to me as she leaned on the sill of the open window.

"Very good, Cubas; you've behaved perfectly. This air is more than pure, it's a balsam, a breath from the everlasting gardens. Would you like to see what you've done, Cubas?"

And the good lady took out a mirror and held it before my eyes. There I saw, and clearly saw,[1] the half-dobra of the previous evening, round, bright, multiplying itself—becoming ten—then thirty—then five hundred—thus expressing the benefits that the simple act of restitution would bring me in life as in death. And as the whole of my being luxuriated in the contemplation of the act, I saw myself in it again and I found myself good, perhaps even great. A simple coin, eh? Just see what a few more turns of the waltz can do.

And so it was that I, Brás Cubas, discovered a sublime law, the law of the equivalence of windows, and determined that the way to compensate for one closed window is to open another, so that morality may continually air out one's conscience. You may not have understood this; perhaps you would prefer something more concrete—a parcel, for example, a mysterious parcel. Well, here you have a mysterious parcel.

CHAPTER LII

THE MYSTERIOUS PARCEL

So it was that, a few days later, as I was on my way to Botafogo, I stumbled across a parcel on the beach. That's not quite
right; it was less of a stumble than a kick. Seeing a parcel, not
large, but clean and well tied with thick twine, a thing that
looked like it was something, I decided to give it a kick, just to
see what would happen, and so I did, and the parcel held up. I
cast my eyes around me; the beach was deserted; off in the
distance—a few boys playing—a fisherman mending his nets
even farther off—nobody who might see what I was up to; I
bent over, picked up the parcel, and went on.

I went on, but not without apprehensions. This might be
some boys' prank. I thought of returning my find to the beach,
but I felt the parcel and rejected the idea. A bit farther along, I
changed course and headed home.

"Let's have a look," I said as I entered my study.

And I hesitated for a moment, I believe out of shame; I was
overtaken once more by apprehensions of a prank. Of course
there were no external witnesses; but inside of me I had a boy
who was certain to whistle, squeal, grunt, stamp, sneer, cackle,
and raise hell if he saw me open up the parcel and find a dozen
soiled handkerchiefs or two dozen rotten guavas.[1] It was too
late; my curiosity had been piqued, as must be the reader's; I
untied the parcel and saw . . . found . . . counted . . . counted
again . . . nothing less than five thousand milréis.[2] Nothing
less. Perhaps ten milréis more. Five thousand milréis in fine
bills and coins, all clean and neat, an extraordinary find. I tied
up the parcel again. At supper, it seemed to me that one of the
slave boys had said something to another with his eyes. Might
they have spied on me? I interrogated them discreetly and

concluded that they had not. Just after supper I went back to my study, examined the money, and laughed at my dispensing maternal cares to five thousand milréis—I, a wealthy man.

To think no more of it, that night I went to the house of Lobo Neves, who had insisted greatly that I continue attending his wife's social gatherings. There I saw the chief of police, and was introduced to him; at once he recalled the letter and the half-dobra that I had sent him a few days earlier. He recounted the story; Virgília seemed to savor my actions, and each of those present hastened to tell a similar anecdote, which I listened to with all the impatience of a hysterical woman.

That night, the following day, and for the rest of that week, I thought as little as possible about the five thousand milréis, and I will confess that I left them to their own devices in my desk drawer. I would happily speak of anything except money, much less found money; not that it was a crime to find money, it was a boon, good fortune, perhaps an act of Providence. It could be nothing else. One doesn't lose five thousand milréis the way one loses a snuff handkerchief.[3] One carries five thousand milréis around with thirty thousand senses all alight, feeling them from time to time, never taking one's eyes off them, nor one's hands, nor one's thoughts, and for them to be lost so foolishly, on a beach, there must have been . . . It couldn't have been a crime, my find; neither a crime, nor dishonorable, nor anything that might tarnish a man's character. It was just a find, happy chance, like winning the lottery or a bet on a horse, like the gains of an honest game, and I will go so far as to say that my good fortune was well deserved, for I did not feel myself to be wicked, nor undeserving of the benefits of Providence.

"Those five thousand milréis," I pondered to myself three weeks later, "I'll put them to some good end, perhaps as the dowry for a poor girl, or something of the sort . . . I'll see . . ."

That same day, I took them to the Bank of Brazil. There I was met with many warm allusions to the half-dobra, the news having already spread among those who knew me; I responded vexedly that the incident hardly merited such fanfare; upon which they praised my modesty—and when this exasperated me, they replied that it was simply extraordinary.

CHAPTER LIII

. . . .

Virgília, meanwhile, thought no more of the half-dobra; all her being was concentrated on me, on my eyes, my life, my thoughts; that was what she said, and it was true.

Some plants take root and grow quickly; others are slow and stunted. Our love was one of the former; it shot up with such force and sap that it was soon the most colossal, leafy, and exuberant creature in all the forests. I cannot tell you with any certainty how many days it took to grow. I do recall that on a certain night there bloomed a flower, or a kiss, if you wish to call it that, a kiss that she gave me, trembling—poor thing—trembling with fear, since it came by the garden gate.[1] We were united by that single kiss—brief as the occasion, ardent as our love, the prologue to a life of delights, terrors, remorses, pleasures that came to pain, troubles that blossomed into joy—a patient, systematic hypocrisy, the only check on an unchecked passion—a life of agitation, fury, despair, and jealousy, which a single moment paid for handsomely; but then another moment came and swallowed the first, and all with it, leaving only the agitations and the rest, the remainder of the remainder, which is tedium and satiety: such was the book that followed that prologue.

CHAPTER LIV

THE PENDULUM CLOCK

I left, savoring the kiss. I couldn't get to sleep that night; I did lie down in bed, but it was as good as nothing. I heard all the hours strike that night. Ordinarily, when I found myself unable to sleep, the sound of the pendulum clock tormented me; that somber, bone-dry, sluggish *tick-tock* seemed to say with each stroke that I now had one fewer moment of life. Then I would envision an old devil seated between two sacks, one of life and one of death, and taking the coins from life and passing them over to death, counting them out:

"Another one gone . . ."

"Another one gone . . ."

"Another one gone . . ."

"Another one gone . . ."

The most peculiar thing is that if the clock stopped, I would wind it up, so that it would never stop striking and I could count every one of my lost moments. Some inventions are transformed or fade away; institutions themselves come to grief; but the clock is definitive and everlasting. The last man on earth, as he bids farewell to the cold, sapped sun, will have a watch in his pocket so as to know the exact hour of his death.

On that night I was not visited by that terrible ennui, but by another sensation, a delightful one. Fantasies were aflutter within me, one tumbling after the other, like pious ladies jostling to see the singing angel in a religious procession. I heard not the moments lost, but the minutes gained. At some point hence I heard nothing at all, for my thoughts, cunning and restless as they were, leaped out the window and flew over to

Virgília's house. There they found Virgília's thoughts on a windowsill, where they greeted one another and struck up a conversation. There we were, tossing and turning in our beds, perhaps feeling cold, deprived of rest, as those two vagabonds echoed the age-old dialogue of Adam and Eve.

CHAPTER LV

THE AGE-OLD DIALOGUE OF ADAM AND EVE

BRÁS CUBAS

. . . . ?

VIRGÍLIA

. . . .

BRÁS CUBAS

. . . .
. . . .

VIRGÍLIA

. . . . . !

BRÁS CUBAS

. . . . .

VIRGÍLIA

. . . .
. . . . . ? . . . . . .
. . . .

BRÁS CUBAS

. . . .

VIRGÍLIA

.　　.　　.　　.　　.

BRÁS CUBAS

.　.　.　.　.　.　.　.　.　.

.　.　.　.　.　.　.　.　.　.

.　.　.　.　.　,　.　.　.　.

.　.　.　.　.　.　.　.　!　.

.　.　.　!　.　.　.　.　.　.

.　.　.　.　.　.　.　.　.　!

VIRGÍLIA

.　.　.　.　.　.　.　.　?

BRÁS CUBAS

.　.　.　!　.　.　.　.　.

VIRGÍLIA

.　.　.　!　.　.　.　.

CHAPTER LVI

THE OPPORTUNE MOMENT

And yet—dash it all! Who can explain the reason for this change? One day we saw one another, arranged a marriage, undid it, and separated, coldly, painlessly, for there had been no passion whatsoever; I was stung by some resentment, nothing more. Years pass, I see her again, we waltz three or four times, and here we are, deliriously in love. Virgília's beauty had reached a great degree of refinement, to be sure, but we were largely the same; and I, for my part, had become neither handsomer nor more elegant. Who can explain the reason for this change?

The reason could be none other than the opportune moment. The first moment had not been opportune; while neither of us was unready for love, we were both unready for *our* love: a fundamental distinction. There can be no love unless the time is opportune for both parties. I hit upon this explanation myself, two years after the kiss, on a day when Virgília was complaining to me of some dandy who was doggedly courting her.

"How importunate!" she said, scowling.

I started, looked at her, and saw that her indignation was sincere; then it occurred to me that I might have once provoked the same scowl, and I understood then just how great my evolution had been. I had come all the way from importunate to opportune.

CHAPTER LVII

FATE[1]

Yes, sir, we were in love. Now that all the laws of society barred it, now we were truly in love. We found ourselves yoked together, like the two souls that the poet found in Purgatory:

Di pari, come buoi, che vanno a giogo[2]

but I shouldn't compare us to oxen, for we were another species of animal altogether, less plodding, more shameless and lascivious. There we went, not knowing how far we might go, nor down which devious byways; this problem haunted me for a few weeks, but I left its solution in the hands of fate. Poor Fate![3] Where are you now, great solicitor of human affairs? Perhaps off creating a new skin, another face, other manners, a different name, and perhaps . . . Now I can't remember where I was . . . Ah! Down the devious byways. I said to myself that things were in God's hands. We were meant to love one another; otherwise, how could one explain the waltz and the rest? Virgília thought the same. One day, after confessing to me that she had moments of remorse, and when I said that if she felt remorse, it was because she didn't love me, Virgília enfolded me in her magnificent arms, murmuring:

"I love you, for Heaven wills it."

She didn't say so lightly; Virgília was somewhat religious. She didn't attend Mass on Sundays, it's true, and I believe that she went to church only on festival days, or when there was a spare seat in a reserved pew. But she prayed every night, fervently, or at least drowsily. Thunderclaps frightened her; when she heard them, she would cover her ears and mumble all the prayers in the catechism. In her bedroom there was a little altar in carved jacaranda wood, three spans high, with three statues on it; but she never spoke of it to her friends. On the contrary, she called the religious ones sanctimonious. For some time I suspected that she was somewhat ashamed at believing, that her religion was a sort of flannel undershirt, a furtive safeguard; but evidently I was mistaken.

CHAPTER LVIII

TRUST

At first, Lobo Neves frightened me greatly. Pure imagination! He adored his wife, and never tired of telling me so; he thought that Virgília was perfection itself, a combination of fine, staunch qualities, doting, elegant, austere, a paragon. Nor did his trust stop there. It began as a chink and became a wide-open door. One day he confessed to me that he had something eating away at his existence; it was the lack of public glory. I cheered him; I offered him many a pretty word, which he absorbed with the religious zeal of a desire seeking to rise from its deathbed; then I understood that his ambition was weary of beating its wings without ever taking flight. Some days later, he told me of all his tediums and failings, the gall he had stifled, the rage he had smothered; he said that political life was woven of envies, grudges, intrigues, betrayals, interests, and vanities. Evidently this was a crisis of melancholy; I tried to beat it back.

"I know very well what I'm saying," he replied sadly. "You can't imagine what I've gone through. I entered politics out of a taste for it, my family, my ambition, and in part out of vanity. As you can see, I have all the motives that lead a man to public life; I only lacked an interest of another nature. I had seen the play from the audience, and by God, it was beautiful! The scenery was magnificent, and there was life, movement, and grace in the acting. I signed on; they gave me a role that . . . But why am I tiring you with this? I'll keep my troubles to myself. I swear, I've spent hours and days . . . There is no constancy, no gratitude, nothing . . . nothing . . . nothing . . ."

He fell silent, profoundly despondent, his eyes staring, seeming to hear nothing but the echo of his own thoughts. After a few moments, he rose and held out a hand:

"You'll surely laugh at me," he said, "but pardon me for the outburst; I had something eating at my spirit."

And he laughed, a somber, sad laugh; then he asked me that I not tell anyone what had occurred between us; I argued that nothing, strictly speaking, had occurred. Two deputies and a local political boss came in. Lobo Neves received them with an air of joy that was slightly forced at first, but then became natural. After half an hour's time, no one would say that he was not the most fortunate of men; he chatted, joked, and laughed, and they all laughed together.

CHAPTER LIX

AN ENCOUNTER

"Politics must be a restorative wine," I said to myself as I left Lobo Neves's house; and I went on walking and walking until, on the Rua dos Barbonos, I saw a carriage, and inside it one of the ministers, an old schoolmate. We greeted one another affectionately, the carriage went on, and I went on walking . . . walking . . . walking . . .

"Why can't I be a minister?"

This idea, resplendent and imposing—clad in bizarre garb, as Father Bernardes might say[1]—this idea began a whirling of somersaults, and I let my eyes rest on it, finding it entertaining. I thought no more of Lobo Neves's sorrow; I felt the pull of the abyss. I recalled that companion of my school days, of our running up and down the hills, our joys and high jinks, and I compared the boy with the man, and asked myself why I couldn't be in his place. Then I went into the Passeio Público, and everything in the park seemed to pose the same question: "Why don't you become a minister, Cubas?" "Cubas, why don't you become a minister of state?" Upon hearing this, my being was flooded with a delicious sensation. I went and sat on a bench, mulling over the idea. And then there was Virgília; how she'd like it! A few minutes later I saw a face that was not unfamiliar come over in my direction. I knew it, but I couldn't recall where I'd seen it.

Imagine a man of between thirty-eight and forty, tall, gaunt, and pale. His clothes, save their style, seemed to have escaped the Babylonian Captivity;[2] the hat was a contemporary of Gessler's.[3] Now imagine an overcoat far more capacious than would have been required by the flesh—or, to be literal, the bones—of the person; the black of the garment was giving way to a dull yellow; the nap was gradually vanishing; of the original eight buttons, three were left. The brown canvas trousers had two great holes at the knees, and the hems had been gnawed away by the heels of boots lacking in both pity and polish. At his neck there floated the ends of a cravat of two colors, both faded, tied around a week-old shirt collar. I believe that he was also wearing a dark silk waistcoat, torn here and there and hanging unbuttoned.

"I'll wager you don't remember me, Dr. Cubas," he said.

"I can't recall . . ."

"I'm Borba, Quincas Borba."

I shrank back, astonished.[4] Had I only the solemn oratory of Bossuet or Vieira, the better to narrate such desolation! It was Quincas Borba, the charming boy of yesteryear, my school companion, so intelligent and well-to-do. Quincas Borba! No; impossible; it can't be. I could not believe that this squalid figure, this white-spattered beard, this aged tatterdemalion, this ruin of a man, was Quincas Borba. But it was. His eyes bore a remnant of their old expression, and his smile had not lost a certain distinctive mocking air. All the while, he bore up manfully under my astonishment. After some time, I dragged my gaze away; while the sight repelled me, the comparison grieved me.

"I need not tell you anything," he said at last. "You've guessed it all. A life of misery, tribulations, and struggles. Do you remember how I always played the king? What a fall! I've become a beggar . . ."

And, as he raised both his right hand and his shoulders with an air of indifference, he seemed resigned to the blows of fortune, perhaps even content. Certainly impassive. There was no Christian resignation in him, nor philosophical acceptance. It seemed that poverty had hardened his soul so that he could no longer feel the mire. He wore his tatters as he had once worn the royal purple: with a certain indolent grace.

"Come see me," I said. "I may be able to find something for you."

A magnificent smile came across his lips.

"You're not the first to promise me something," he replied,

"and you may not be the last who will do nothing for me. And why would you? I want nothing of you but money; money, yes, because I must eat, and taverns give no credit. Nor do the peddlers. A scrap, two pennies' worth of porridge, the damned peddlers won't even give credit for that. It's hell, my . . . I was about to say 'my friend' . . . Hell! Devil take it! All the devils! Look here, I haven't had any breakfast today."

"No?"

"No; I left home quite early. D'you know where I live? On the third step of the stairs to the church of São Francisco;[5] on the left as you're going up; there's no need to knock at the door. An airy house, extremely airy. Well, I left early, and I still haven't eaten . . ."

I took out my wallet, chose a five-milréis bill[6]—the least clean of the lot—and gave it to him. He took it from me, eyes glittering with greed, and raised the bill into the air, brandishing it with glee.

"*In hoc signo vinces!*"[7] he cried out.

Then he kissed it with many a tender gesture, and with such noisy affection that I felt something between disgust and pity. He was clever, and understood my reaction; he grew serious, grotesquely so, and begged my pardon for his joy, saying that it was the joy of a poor man who had not seen a five-milréis bill in many years.

"Well, you have in your hands the chance to see many more," I said.

"Is that so?" he said, lunging toward me.

"By working," I concluded.

He looked scornful, fell silent for a few moments, then told me determinedly that he did not want to work. I had grown sick of this tragicomic abjection, and made as if to leave.

"Don't go before I've taught you my philosophy of misery," he said, planting himself squarely in front of me.

CHAPTER LX

THE EMBRACE

I thought that the poor devil was mad, and was going to move away when he took me by the wrist and stared for a moment or two at the diamond ring I was wearing. I felt a few quivers of greed, itchings of ownership, tremble in his hand.

"Magnificent!" he said.

Then he began to walk around me and examine me minutely.

"You take good care of yourself," he said. "Jewelry, fine and elegant clothing, and . . . Compare these shoes to mine; what a difference! No wonder! I'll say, you do take good care. And how about ladies? Are you married?"

"No . . ."

"Neither am I."

"I live at—"

"I don't want to know where you live," Quincas Borba interrupted. "If we meet again, give me another five milréis; but allow me to refrain from going to your house to fetch them. It's a sort of pride . . . Goodbye, now; I see you're impatient."

"Goodbye!"

"And thank you. Will you allow me to thank you closer up?"

And as he said this, he embraced me so forcefully that I could not avoid it. We finally separated and I strode off, my shirtfront wrinkled from the embrace, vexed and sad. Now my pity had given way to disgust. I wished he had been dignified in his poverty. And yet I couldn't help comparing the man of today to the figure of yesteryear, growing sad, and contemplating the abyss that separates the hopes of one time from the reality of another . . .

"Good riddance to that! Let's have supper," I said to myself.

I put my hand into my vest pocket and failed to find my watch. The final disillusion! Borba had stolen it from me during the embrace.

CHAPTER LXI

A PLAN

I had a melancholy supper. It was not the loss of the pocket watch that pained me, but the image of he who had stolen it, and the memories of childhood, and once again the comparison, and the conclusion . . . Starting at the soup course, the yellow and morbid flower from Chapter XXV began to bloom within me, and I dined quickly so as to run to Virgília's house. Virgília was the present, and I wanted to take refuge in it to escape the oppressions of the past; the encounter with Quincas Borba had turned my gaze to the past, not as it had been, but a tattered, abject, beggarly, thieving past.

I left home, but it was still early; I would find them at the supper table. I thought again of Quincas Borba, and then I felt a desire to return to the Passeio Público in hopes of finding him; the idea of rehabilitating him swelled into a powerful need. I went, but didn't find him. I asked the guard, who told me that, indeed, "that fellow" came around sometimes.

"What time of day?"

"No regular time."

It wasn't unlikely that I might find him again; I promised myself that I would come back. The need to rehabilitate him, bring him back to work and self-respect, filled my heart; I began to feel a peace of mind, loftiness, admiration for myself . . . By then, night was falling; I went to see Virgília.

CHAPTER LXII

THE PILLOW

I went to see Virgília; and I quickly forgot Quincas Borba. Virgília was the pillow for my spirit, a soft, warm, aromatic pillow wrapped in cambric and Brussels lace. It was there that my spirit went to rest from any bad, simply tedious, or even painful sensations. And, all things considered, there was no other reason for Virgília's existence; there could be no other. Five minutes were enough for me to forget Quincas Borba completely; five minutes of mutual contemplation with our hands clasped; five minutes and a kiss. And there went the memory of Quincas Borba . . . Scrofula of life, rag of the past, what do I care if you exist and offend the eyes of others if I have two spans of a divine pillow upon which to close my eyes and sleep?

CHAPTER LXIII

LET'S RUN AWAY!

Alas! Not always to sleep. Three weeks later, upon going to Virgília's house—it was four o'clock in the afternoon—I found her sad and downcast. She wouldn't tell me what it was; but when I pressed her:

"I believe Damião suspects something. I've noticed some strange signs in him . . . I don't know. He treats me well, to be sure; but it seems his gaze is no longer the same. I haven't slept; last night I woke up, terrified, dreaming that he was going to kill me. It may be my imagination, but I think he suspects . . ."

I calmed her as best I could; I said that it might be political worries. Virgília agreed, but remained quite excitable and agitated. We were in the drawing room, which looked out onto the grounds where we had exchanged our first kiss. An open window let in the breeze, making the curtains sway gently; I stared at the curtains without seeing them. I had taken up the binoculars of imagination; I could glimpse, off in the distance, a house of our own, a life of our own, a world of our own, in which there was no Lobo Neves, no marriage, no morality, nor any other bond that might hinder the free expansion of our will. This idea intoxicated me; with the world, morality, and the husband eliminated, all that was left was to enter that angelic abode.

"Virgília," I said, "let me propose something."

"What is it?"

"Do you love me?"

"Oh!" she sighed, putting her arms around my neck.

Virgília loved me furiously; that answer was the manifest truth. With her arms round my neck, quiet and breathing heavily, she gazed upon me with her large, beautiful eyes, which conferred a singular sensation of dewy light; I let myself simply behold them, coveting her mouth, fresh as dawn and as insatiable as death. Virgília's beauty now bore a glorious air that it had not possessed before marriage. She was like a figure carved in Pentelic marble, finely made, open and pure; she had the tranquil beauty of a statue, but was neither indifferent nor cold. On the contrary, she seemed possessed of an ardent nature, and one might say that, in truth, she epitomized love itself. This was particularly true on that occasion, in which she mutely expressed everything that a human pupil is capable of conveying. But time was pressing; I unclasped her hands, took her by the wrists, and, with my gaze fixed on her, I asked if she had the courage.

"To do what?"

"To run away. We'll go wherever is most comfortable for us, a large house or a small one, whatever you like, in the countryside or in the city, or in Europe, wherever you like, where no one will disturb us, there'll be no danger for you, and we can live for one another . . . What do you say? Let's run away. Sooner or later, he'll discover something, and you'll be lost . . . do you hear me? Lost . . . dead . . . and so will he, because I'll kill him, I swear to you."

I broke off; Virgília had gone very pale, let her arms fall by her sides, and sat down on the sofa. She remained that way for a few moments without saying a word, either hesitating over her choice or terrified by the idea of being found out and killed. I went to her, insisted on my proposition, stating all the advantages of a life all our own, with no jealousies, fears, or suffering. Virgília heard me out in silence; then she said:

"We might not escape; he'd come and kill me just the same."

I showed her that this was not the case. The world was vast, and I had the means to live wherever there was fresh air and plentiful sunlight; he would never make it that far; only great passions drive great acts, and he did not love her so passionately that he would seek her out if she were far away. Virgília looked taken aback, almost indignant; she murmured that her husband was very fond of her.

"Maybe," I replied, "maybe so . . ."

I went to the window and began drumming my fingers on the sill. Virgília called me; I remained there, mulling over my jealousy, yearning to strangle the husband, were he there at hand . . . Just then, Lobo Neves appeared at the gate. Don't tremble so, my pale reader; rest assured, madam, not a drop of blood shall stain this page. As soon as he came in view, I greeted him amicably, with a word of welcome; Virgília hastened to leave the drawing room, which he entered three minutes later.

"Have you been here long?" he asked.

"No."

He had come in with a serious, strained air, casting about distractedly as he was wont to do, which was overtaken by pure joviality when he saw his son, Nhonhô, the future university graduate of Chapter VI; he took the boy in his arms, raised him up in the air, and kissed him many times. I, who hated the boy, moved away from the both of them. Virgília returned to the drawing room.

"Ah!" sighed Lobo Neves, sinking down onto the sofa.

"Tired?" I asked.

"Quite; I endured two supremely tiresome bores, one in the Chamber and one on the street. And there's a third awaiting us," he added, looking at his wife.

"What is it?"

"It's . . . guess!"

Virgília had sat down beside him; she took one of his hands, straightened his cravat, and asked again what it was.

"Nothing less than box seats."

"To hear Candiani?"[1]

"To hear Candiani."

Virgília clapped her hands, stood up, and gave her son a kiss with a childish glee unbefitting her; then she asked if it was a stage box or a center box and consulted her husband in a whisper about her toilette, the opera to be sung, and any number of other things.

"You'll dine with us, good sir," said Lobo Neves.

"That's just why he came," confirmed his wife; "he says you have the best wine in Rio de Janeiro."

"And yet he barely drinks."

At supper, I proved him wrong; I drank more than I was wont to, and yet less than would have deprived me of my senses. I was already agitated, and became a bit more so. This was the first time I had felt furious at Virgília. I didn't look at her once during supper; I spoke of politics, the press, the administration, and I believe I would have spoken of theology if I had known or remembered anything on the subject. Lobo Neves followed along with me, ever placid and dignified, with an air of superior benevolence; and all of that irritated me as well, and made the supper even bitterer and longer for me. I bade them good night as soon as we had risen from the table.

"We'll see you shortly, won't we?" asked Lobo Neves.

"Maybe."

And I left.

CHAPTER LXIV

THE TRANSACTION

I wandered through the streets and retired at nine o'clock. Unable to sleep, I took to reading and writing. By eleven I regretted not having gone to the theater, looked at the clock, and felt moved to dress myself and go out. I realized, however, that I would arrive too late; moreover, it would be a sign of weakness. Evidently Virgília was beginning to tire of me, I thought. And this idea made me alternately despairing and cold, ready to forget her and kill her. I could see her there, reclining in the box, her magnificent arms bare—the arms that were mine, and mine alone—and transfixing the eyes of all, with the sumptuous dress she was bound to be wearing, her milky bosom, her hair parted in the fashion of the day, and her jewels, less luminous than her eyes . . . I saw her so, and it pained me that others should as well. Then I began to undress her, setting aside her jewels and silks, tousling her hair with my eager, wanton hands, and leaving her—if not more beautiful, if not more natural—leaving her mine, mine alone, only mine.

The next day, I couldn't contain myself; I went early to Virgília's house, and found her eyes red from crying.

"What happened?" I asked.

"You don't love me," was her reply, "and you never had the slightest bit of love for me. You treated me yesterday as if you hated me. If I only knew what it was that I did! But I don't. Won't you tell me?"

"What? I don't believe you did a thing."

"Not a thing? You treated me worse than you'd treat a dog . . ."

At these words, I seized her hands and kissed them, and two tears sprang from her eyes.

"It's all over, it's all over," I said.

I hadn't the heart to accuse her—and, for that matter, accuse her of what? It wasn't her fault if her husband loved her. I said to her that she hadn't done anything to me, that I was bound to be jealous of the other man and that I couldn't always bear it smilingly; I added that he might be hiding his true feelings, and that the best way to put an end to our fears and squabbles was to accept my idea from the day before.

"I've thought about it," Virgília said readily, "a little house just for us, out of the way, tucked away in a garden on some hidden street, isn't that it? The idea is a good one; but why run away?"

She said this with the naive, casual tone of one who means no evil, and the smile that bent the corners of her mouth bore the same frank expression. At this, drawing back, I responded:

"You've never loved me."

"I?"

"You're selfish, that's what you are! You'd prefer to see me suffer every single day . . . you're unspeakably selfish!"

Virgília burst out crying; so as not to attract attention, she bit her handkerchief to stifle her sobs, in an explosion that disconcerted me. If anyone heard her, all would be lost. I leaned toward her, took hold of her wrists, and whispered our sweetest pet names; I reminded her of the danger we were in, and fear calmed her.

"I can't," she said after a few moments, "I won't leave my son; if I take him, I'm sure that *he* will seek me out at the ends of the earth. I can't; kill me yourself, if you want, or let me die . . . Oh God! God!"

"Calm down; they might hear you."

"Let them hear! I don't care."

She was still agitated; I begged her to forget everything, forgive me, saying that I had lost my mind, but that my insanity began with her and would end with her. Virgília dried her eyes and held out her hand. We both smiled; minutes later, we returned to the topic of the solitary little house, on some out-of-the-way street . . .

CHAPTER LXV

EYES AND EARS

We were interrupted by the sound of a coach on the grounds. A slave came to say that it was Baroness X.

Virgília consulted me with her eyes.

"If you've got such a terrible headache," I said, "it would seem best not to receive her."

"Has she already gotten out?" Virgília asked the slave.

"Yes, and she says she needs to speak to Missus right away!"

"Well, let her in."

The baroness came in shortly. I don't know if she expected to find me in the drawing room; but it would be impossible to have made a greater fuss.

"A sight for sore eyes!" she exclaimed. "Where have you been hiding? Why, just last night I was surprised not to see you at the theater. Candiani was delightful. What a woman! Do you like her? Of course you do. You men are all the same. The baron was just saying last night in our box that one Italian woman is worth five Brazilians. What cheek! And from an old man, which is worse. But why weren't you there last night?"

"A headache."

"Nonsense! Some rendezvous; don't you think, Virgília? Well, hurry up, my friend, because you must be forty . . . or near that . . . Aren't you forty?"

"I can't say for certain," I responded, "but if you'll allow me, I'll go consult my baptismal certificate."

"Go on . . ." she said, holding out a hand. "When shall we see you? On Saturday we'll be in; the baron has missed you so . . ."

As I stepped out onto the street, I regretted having left. The baroness was one of the people who most suspected us. She was fifty-five but looked forty, with a soft figure, an easy smile, vestiges of beauty, an elegant bearing, and fine manners. She didn't speak often, nor did she say very much at all. She possessed that great talent for listening to others, keeping watch over them; she would recline in her chair, unsheathe a long, sharpened gaze, and let herself be. Others, not knowing what she was, would speak, look, and gesticulate, and all the while she would simply watch, motionless at times, lively at others, guileful enough as to cast her eyes down and let her lids fall; but with her eyelashes as a lattice, the gaze kept up its work, raking through the souls and lives of others.

The second person was a relative of Virgília's, Viegas, a withered, yellow relic some seventy winters old who suffered from a stubborn rheumatism, a no less stubborn asthma, and a damaged heart; he was a walking infirmary. His eyes, however, radiated life and health. During the first weeks, Virgília had no fear of him; she said that when Viegas seemed to fix a person with a prying gaze, he was just counting money to himself. Indeed, he was a great miser.

And then there was Virgília's cousin, Luís Dutra, whom I now took to disarming by way of speaking of his verses and prose and introducing him to those in my circle. When they, connecting the name to the person, were visibly glad to have met him, Luís Dutra clearly thrilled with happiness; but I cured myself of his happiness with the hope that he would never expose us. Finally, there were two or three ladies, several dandies, and the help, who naturally avenged themselves of their servile condition by keeping close watch over us, and all this constituted a veritable forest of eyes and ears, among which we had to glide as strategically and softly as snakes.

CHAPTER LXVI

LEGS

Now, as I contemplated those people, my legs carried me down the streets, and before I knew it I found myself at the door of the Hotel Pharoux. I ordinarily dined there; but, not having walked deliberately, I can take no credit for the act, and all must go to the legs that executed it. Blessed legs! And to think that some treat you with disdain or indifference. I myself had thought ill of you until then and would become cross when you tired or when you could go no farther, leaving me longing to flutter off, like a chicken tied by its feet.

This incident, however, was an illumination. Yes, dear legs, you left to my head the task of thinking about Virgília, and said to one another: "He needs to eat, it's suppertime, let's take him to the Pharoux; let's divide up his conscience, leave a part with the lady, and we will take the rest, so that he can walk in a straight line, not crash into people and carts, tip his hat to acquaintances, and make it to the hotel safe and sound." And you fulfilled your aim to perfection, kind legs, obliging me to immortalize you on this page.

CHAPTER LXVII

THE LITTLE HOUSE

I dined and went home. There I found a box of cigars from Lobo Neves, wrapped in tissue paper and tied with pink ribbons. I understood, opened up the box, and took out this note:

> My B . . .
> They suspect us; all is lost; forget me forever.
> We will never see one another again. Farewell;
> think no more of poor
>
> V . . . a

The letter was a blow; and yet as soon as night fell, I ran to Virgília's house. Just in time; she had changed her mind. Through an open window, she told me what had happened with the baroness. The woman had told her frankly that my absence from Lobo Neves's box had been the subject of much comment at the theater the night before; people had spoken of my relations with their house; in short, we had come under public suspicion. She concluded by saying that she didn't know what to do.

"The thing for us to do is run away," I suggested.

"Never," she replied, shaking her head.

I saw that it would be impossible to separate two things that were entirely connected in her soul: our love and public esteem. Virgília was capable of great and equal sacrifices to preserve both advantages, and running away left her with only one. I may have felt something similar to resentment; but the commotions of those two days had been considerable, and the resentment was quick to die. Well, then, let's see to the little house.

Indeed, I found it just days later, made to order in a corner of Gamboa. A gem! New, freshly whitewashed, with four windows in front and two on each side, brick-red shutters, creepers climbing up the corners, a garden out front; mystery and solitude. A gem!

We agreed that a woman whom Virgília knew would live there, one who had been a seamstress and dependent in her house, and over whom Virgília exerted a genuine fascination. She would not be told of everything; she could easily accept the rest.

For me, this was a new state of affairs for our love, one with all the trappings of exclusive ownership and absolute dominion, something that might lull my conscience and preserve decorum. I had grown tired of the other man's curtains, his chairs, his carpet, his couch, all those things that constantly reminded me of our duplicity. Now I could avoid the frequent suppers, the evening teas, and the presence of their son, my accomplice and my enemy. The house rescued me from all that; the ordinary world ceased at the door; inside was infinity, an eternal, superior, exceptional world, ours and ours alone, without laws, institutions, baronesses, eyes, or ears—one world, one couple, one life, one desire, one affection—the moral unity of all things, by way of the exclusion of all those which went against me.

CHAPTER LXVIII

THE WHIP

Such were my reflections as I strolled through Valongo,[1] just having visited the house and made the necessary arrangements. My reflections were interrupted by a throng; a negro was whipping another in the square. The other did not dare flee; he simply moaned these words: "No, forgive me, master; master, forgive me!" But the first paid no mind, and at each plea he responded with a new lash of the whip.

"Here, you devil!" he said. "Here's your forgiveness, you drunk!"

"Master!" moaned the other.

"Shut your mouth, beast!" retorted the whipper.

I stopped and looked . . . Gracious heavens! Who was the one with the whip? None other than my slave boy Prudêncio, whom my father had freed some years earlier. I went over; he stopped right away and kissed my hand; I asked if the negro was his slave.

"Yes, master."

"Has he done anything to you?"

"He's an idler and a drunkard. Today I left him at the stall while I went into town, and he went off to go drink."

"Well, forgive him, go on," I said.

"Of course, master. Master's word is an order. Get on home, you drunk!"

I left the crowd, which looked at me in astonishment and muttered conjectures. I went on my way, unfurling countless reflections, which I'm afraid I have forgotten entirely; they would have made for a good chapter, perhaps a cheerful one. I like cheerful chapters; I have a weakness for them. On the outside, the Valongo incident was dreadful; but only on the outside. As soon as I slid the knife of reasoning farther in, I found a marrow that was mischievous, refined, even profound. This was Prudêncio's way of freeing himself from the blows he had received—by passing them on to another. I, as a child, had ridden on him, put a bit in his mouth, and thrashed him mercilessly as he groaned and suffered. Now that he was free, however, the master of his own arms and legs, able to work, rest, and sleep, unshackled from his former condition, now he had surpassed himself: he had bought a slave and was paying back, with steep interest, the sums he had received from me. See how clever the rascal was![2]

CHAPTER LXIX

A DASH OF LUNACY

This incident reminds me of a madman I once knew. His name was Romualdo, and he claimed to be Tamerlane.[1] This was his sole, great mania, and he had a peculiar way of explaining it.

"I am the great Tamerlane," he would say. "Once I was Romualdo, but I fell ill and took so much tartar, so much tartar, so much tartar, that I became a Tartar, and then the king of the Tartars. Tartar has the virtue of making Tartars."

Poor Romualdo! People laughed at his reply, but the reader is likely not to, and rightly so; I don't find it funny in the slightest. When heard, it had some wit to it; but written out on paper, and on the score of a lashing received and transferred, one must admit that it is far better to return to the little house in Gamboa; let us leave the Romualdos and Prudêncios aside.

CHAPTER LXX

DONA PLÁCIDA

Let us return to the little house. You wouldn't be able to enter it today, curious reader; it grew old, and begrimed, and was left to rot, and the owner knocked it down to replace it with another, three times its size—but I swear to you that it is far smaller than the original. The world was too narrow for Alexander; a hollow under the eaves is boundless for a swallow.

Behold the neutrality of this globe, which carries us through space like a boat of castaways heading for shore: today a virtuous couple sleeps on the same bit of ground that once suffered a sinning couple. Tomorrow a clergyman may sleep there, then a murderer, then a blacksmith, then a poet, and all will bless that corner of the earth, which gave them a few fleeting dreams.

Virgília made the place a delight; she chose the most fitting furnishings and arranged them with her elegant lady's eye; I brought over a few books, and everything was left to the cares of Dona Plácida, the ostensible and, in some respects, the true lady of the house.

She struggled greatly to accept the house; she had sniffed out its purpose, and the charge pained her; but at last she gave in. I believe she wept, at first: she was disgusted with herself. At least she didn't raise her eyes to me during the first two months; she looked down when she spoke to me, seeming serious and sullen, and at times sad. I wanted to win her over, and so I took no offense; I treated her with care and respect and strove to obtain her benevolence, and then her trust. Once I had obtained her trust, I imagined up a heartrending story of my and Virgília's love, a courtship before her marriage, how her father had resisted, how harsh her husband was, and other novelistic touches. Dona Plácida did not spurn a single page of the novelette; she accepted them all. Her conscience demanded it. After six months' time, anyone seeing the three of us together would have said that Dona Plácida was my mother-in-law.

I was not ungrateful; I made her a gift of five thousand milréis—the five thousand I had found in Botafogo—as a sum for her old age. Dona Plácida thanked me with tears in her eyes and never failed to pray for me every night before a statue of the Virgin in her bedroom. That was how her disgust died away.

CHAPTER LXXI

THE FLAW IN THE BOOK

I am beginning to regret that I ever took to writing this book. Not that it tires me; I have nothing else to do, and dispatching a few meager chapters into the other world is invariably a bit of a distraction from eternity. But the book is tedious, it reeks of the grave, it bears a cadaveric grimace; this is a grave defect, and yet a minor one on the whole, for this book's greatest flaw is you, reader. You are in a hurry to grow old, and the book moves slowly; you love direct, robust narration and a smooth and regular style, and this book and my style are like drunkards, they veer right and left, stop and go, grumble, bellow, cackle, threaten the skies, slip, and fall . . .

And they fall! Wretched leaves of my cypress tree, you, too, must fall, like all others so beautiful and splendid; and, had I eyes, I would shed a tear of remembrance for you. This is the great advantage of death: while it leaves no mouth to laugh, nor does it leave eyes to weep . . . You, too, must fall.[1]

CHAPTER LXXII

THE BIBLIOMANIAC

I may do away with the previous chapter; among other reasons, in the last few lines there is a phrase that verges on nonsense, and I have no intention of providing fodder for future critics.

Look: seventy years from now, a scrawny, sallow, grayheaded fellow who loves nothing but books will lean over the previous page to see if he can find the nonsense; he reads it, rereads it, threereads it, disjoints the words, takes out one syllable, then another, yet another and the rest, examines them inside and out, from all sides, against the light, dusts them off, wipes them on his knee, washes them, and to no avail; he cannot find the nonsense.

He is a bibliomaniac. He hasn't heard of the author; this name Brás Cubas is nowhere to be found in his biographical dictionaries. He found the volume by chance in a filthy, rundown secondhand bookstore and bought it for just two hundred réis. He inquired, investigated, rummaged around, and came to find that it was the only copy in existence . . . the only copy! Thou who not only lovest books, but also sufferest from a mania for them, thou knowest full well the weight of the word, and may thus envisage the delight of my bibliomaniac. He would spurn the crown of the Indies, the papacy, all the museums of Italy and Holland, if he had to give over this single volume in exchange; and not because it was a copy of my *Memoirs*; he would do the same for Laemmert's *Almanack*, were there only one copy of it.

It's a pity about the nonsense. The man is still leaning over the page with a glass in his right eye, entirely devoted to the noble and grim undertaking of deciphering the nonsensical element. He has promised himself that he will write a brief article in which he recounts finding the book and discovering the sublime meaning, if there is any, behind that obscure phrase. In the end he discovers nothing of the sort and contents himself with possession. He closes the book, examines it, reexamines it, goes over to the window, and shows it to the sun. The only copy! Just then, a Caesar or a Cromwell passes by beneath his window, on the road to power. He shrugs, closes the window, stretches out in his hammock, and leafs through the book slowly, lovingly, sip by sip . . . The only copy!

CHAPTER LXXIII

REFRESHMENTS[1]

The nonsense has made me waste another chapter. How much better it would be to say things smoothly, without all this jolting! I've already compared my style to a drunkard's walk. If the idea strikes you as indecorous, I will say that it was precisely what my meals with Virgília were at the little house in Gamboa, where we often had our feasts, our refreshments. Wine, fruit, compotes. We ate, it's true, but the eating was punctuated with the commas of sweet words, tender gazes, childish moments, an endless stream of these asides of the heart which are the true, uninterrupted discourse of love. At times a lover's quarrel would come to temper the surfeit of sweetness. She would leave me and take refuge in a corner of the sofa, or go inside to hear Dona Plácida's cooing. Five or ten minutes later, we would resume the thread of our conversation again, as I resume the thread of narration, only to abandon it yet again. Note that not only did we not flee from method, we also habitually invited it, in the form of Dona Plácida, to join us at the table; but Dona Plácida never said yes.

"It seems you don't care for me anymore," Virgília said to her one day.

"Saints preserve us!" the good lady exclaimed, throwing her hands up. "If I don't care for Missus, then who do I care for in this world?"

And taking hold of her hands, she looked at Virgília fixedly, fixedly, fixedly, until her eyes began to water, so fixed was her gaze. Virgília covered her in caresses; I slipped a silver coin into the pocket of her dress.

CHAPTER LXXIV

THE STORY
OF DONA PLÁCIDA

Never regret your generosity; the silver coin won me Dona Plácida's trust, and hence this chapter. Days later, when I found her alone in the house, we struck up a conversation and she told me her story in a few words. She was the illegitimate child of a sacristan at the See and a woman who made sweets from her home. She had lost her father at age ten. By then she had already been set to grating coconut and whatever other sweetmaker's tasks were compatible with her age. At fifteen or sixteen she married a tailor who died of consumption some time later, leaving her with a daughter. A young widow, she was left with her daughter, then age two, and her mother, exhausted from a lifetime of work. She had to support the three of them. She made sweets, which was her profession, but she also sewed doggedly, day and night, for three or four shops, and taught some children in the neighborhood for a few coins[1] a month. The years slipped away, but not her beauty, for she had never had any to begin with. A few courtships, proposals, and seductions presented themselves, but she resisted them all.

"If I could've found another husband," she told me, "I would have married, believe me; but nobody wanted to marry me."

One of the suitors managed to win acceptance; but since he proved no nobler than the rest, Dona Plácida sent him away in turn, and, having done so, wept a great deal. She continued sewing and keeping the sugar pots at a boil. Her mother was surly by virtue of temperament, age, and want; she bedeviled her daughter to accept one of the proposals put to her by borrowed husbands or chance lovers. And she would bawl:

"D'you want to be better than me? I don't know where you

got these rich lady's airs. Life won't just see to itself, my dear, we can't eat air. Bah! Fellows as fine as Policarpo from the shop . . . You're waiting for some nobleman, aren't you?"

Dona Plácida swore to me that she wasn't waiting for a nobleman. It was her temperament. She wanted to be married. She knew very well that her mother had never married, and knew a few women who had simply taken up with their fellows; but her temperament demanded that she be married. Nor did she want anything else for her daughter. She worked hard, burning her fingers on the stove and her eyes at the lamp, to be able to eat and keep her footing. She grew thin, fell ill, lost her mother, buried her with the help of charity, and continued to work. Her daughter was fourteen; but she was a feeble little thing and did nothing but flirt with the ne'er-do-wells who hung around her window. Dona Plácida took exceptional care, bringing the girl along with her when she went to deliver her sewing. People in the shops stared and winked, convinced that she was looking to find a husband for the girl, or something else entirely. Some cracked jokes or accosted her; the mother even received offers of money . . .

She broke off for a moment, and then went on:

"My daughter ran away; she went off with some man, and I'll hear no more of it . . . She left me alone, and so awful sad I thought of dying. I had nobody else in the world, and I was nearly an old woman, and sickly. It was around then that I met Missus's family: good folk, who kept me busy and even took me in. I was there for many months, a year, more than a year, under their protection, sewing. I left when Missus got married. Then I lived at God's mercy. Look at my fingers, look at these hands . . ." And she showed me her callused, creviced hands, her needle-pricked fingers. "These aren't made by chance, sir; God knows they aren't . . . Thank goodness Missus took me in, and you, too, sir . . . I was afraid I might end up on the streets, begging . . ."

As she let out these last words, Dona Plácida shivered. Then, as if coming to her senses, she seemed to realize how unseemly it was to make such a confession to the lover of a married woman and began to laugh, go back on what she'd said, calling herself a fool, "full of airs," as her mother said; finally, tiring of my silence, she withdrew from the room. I was left staring at the tip of my boot.

CHAPTER LXXV

TO MYSELF

As some of my readers may have skipped the previous chapter, I will observe that it must be read in order to understand what I said to myself just after Dona Plácida had left the room. What I said was this:

"And so the sacristan at the See, helping to say Mass one day, saw the lady come in who was to be his collaborator in creating Dona Plácida. He saw her on other days, for weeks on end, liked what he saw, and made some winning remark or nudged her foot as he was lighting the altars on feast days. She took a liking to him, they grew closer, and they loved one another. Of this conjunction of idle lustings, there sprouted Dona Plácida. One assumes that Dona Plácida did not yet speak when she was born, but if she could, she might have said to the authors of her days: 'Here I am. Why have you called me?' And the sacristan and the sacristine would naturally reply: 'We called you to burn your fingers on pots and your eyes at sewing, to eat poorly or not at all, to plod up and down in endless drudgery, ailing and mending, only to ail and mend once again, now sorrowful, soon desperate, tomorrow resigned, but always with your hands at the pot and your eyes on your sewing, until you end your days in the gutter or in the hospital; this is why we called you, in a moment of good feeling.'"

CHAPTER LXXVI

MANURE

My conscience suddenly twitched and accused me of having forced Dona Plácida's integrity to give in, obliging her to take on a shameful role after a long life of work and want. A go-between was no better than a concubine, and I had lowered her to this profession by means of favors and monies. That was what my conscience said; for ten minutes, I could find no reply. It added that I had taken advantage of Virgília's influence over the ex-seamstress, the woman's gratitude, and her need. It noted Dona Plácida's resistance, her tears in the early days, her scowls, her silences, her lowered eyes, and how I skillfully bore up under it all until I won her over. And it tugged at me again, seeming irritated and agitated.

I agreed that this was so, but I alleged that Dona Plácida was now safe from beggary in her old age, and that this was ample compensation. Were it not for my love, she would probably share the fate of so many other human creatures; from which one may deduce that vice is quite often the manure for virtue. None of which prevents virtue from being a fragrant, healthy flower. My conscience agreed, and I went to open the door for Virgília.

CHAPTER LXXVII

RENDEZVOUS

Virgília entered, smiling and at ease. Time had carried away our frights and mortifications. How sweet it had been to see her arrive during those first days, trembling and ashamed! She would come in a coach, her face veiled, wrapped in a sort of manteau that concealed her undulating figure. The first time, she collapsed onto the sofa, breathless, scarlet, her eyes on the floor; and—I swear to you!—on no other occasion had I found her so beautiful, perhaps because I had never felt more flattered.

Now, however, as I was saying, the frights and mortifications had ended; we saw each other with chronometric regularity. The intensity of our love was the same; the difference was that the flame had lost the furor of the first days to become a simple radiant beam, calm and constant, as in marriages.

"I'm quite cross with you," she said as she sat down.

"Why?"

"Because you didn't come yesterday, as you'd said you would. Damião asked several times if you wouldn't at least come for tea. Why didn't you?"

Indeed, I had broken my promise, and it was all Virgília's fault. A matter of jealousy. That splendid woman knew perfectly well that it was, but she liked to hear it said, whether shouted or in a murmur. Two evenings earlier at the baroness's house, she had waltzed twice with the same dandy after having listened to his affected courtesies over by a window. She was so joyful! So expansive! So self-assured! When she spied an interrogative and threatening wrinkle between my eyebrows, she was not startled, nor did she grow suddenly serious; but she threw the dandy and his affected courtesies overboard. She came over to me, took my arm, and guided me to another, less populated room, where she complained of fatigue and said many other things with the childish air that she normally had on such occasions, as I listened while making almost no reply.

Even now it was a struggle to reply at all, but I finally told her of the reason for my absence at tea . . . No, eternal stars, I never saw eyes more astonished. Her mouth half-open, her eyebrows arched, a visible, tangible, undeniable stupefaction: this was Virgília's first rebuttal. She shook her head with a pitying, tender smile that confounded me entirely.

"Oh, you!"

And she went to take off her hat, lively and good-humored as a girl coming back from school; then she came over to where I was seated and tapped me on the forehead with a finger, saying: "You, you, you"; until I had no remedy but to laugh as well, and it all ended in fun. It was clear I'd been deceived.[1]

CHAPTER LXXVIII

THE PRESIDENCY

One day, months later, Lobo Neves came home saying that he might take on the presidency of a province.[1] I looked at Virgília, who went pale; he, seeing her pale, asked:

"I gather you aren't pleased, Virgília?"

Virgília shook her head.

"It's not much to my liking," was her answer.

Nothing more was said; but at night Lobo Neves made the case for the plan a bit more resolutely than he had that afternoon; two days later he declared to his wife that the presidency was a fait accompli. Virgília was unable to disguise her distaste of it. Her husband's answer to everything was "political necessity."

"I can't refuse their requests; and it's good for us, our future, your titles, my love. I promised that I'd make you a marchioness, and you're not even a baroness yet. You may call me ambitious, and truly I am, but you mustn't weigh down the wings of my ambition."

Virgília was disoriented. On the following day I found her at the Gamboa house, sorrowfully awaiting me; she had told everything to Dona Plácida, who consoled her as best she could. I was no less stricken.

"You must go with us," Virgília said.

"Are you mad? It would be foolhardy."

"What, then . . . ?"

"Then we've got to undo the plan."

"Impossible."

"Has he already accepted?"

"I believe so."

I rose, threw my hat onto a chair, and began pacing up and down, unsure as to what I would do. I cogitated at length and hit upon nothing. Finally I went to Virgília, who was sitting down, and took her hand; Dona Plácida went over to the window.

"In this little hand lies the whole of my existence," I said. "You are responsible for it; do with it what you may."

Virgília made a distressing face; and I went to lean on the console table opposite her. A few moments of silence followed; all we heard was the barking of a dog and perhaps the murmur of waves breaking on the beach. She said nothing, and so I looked at her. Virgília had her eyes on the floor, immobile and dull, her clasped hands resting on her lap in an attitude of supreme despair. Were it another occasion, were it a different reason, I would certainly fall at her feet and comfort her with all my reason and tenderness; now, however, she had to be compelled to act for herself, to make sacrifices, to attend to the responsibility of the life we shared, and hence I had to forsake her, leave her, and go off; which was what I did.

"I repeat, my happiness is in your hands," I said.

Virgília moved to hold me back, but I was already out the door. I heard a burst of weeping, and I tell you that I was on the verge of going back to dry the tears with a kiss; but I mastered myself and left.

CHAPTER LXXIX

COMPROMISE

If I were to recount in minute detail what I suffered in those first hours, I should never finish. I wavered between wanting and not wanting, between the pity thrusting me toward Virgília's house and another sentiment—selfishness, let's say—which said: "Stay where you are; leave her alone with the problem, and she'll decide on the side of love." I believe that these two forces were equally powerful, assailing and resisting at the same time, ardent and tenacious, and neither would give way entirely. At times I felt a pang of remorse; it seemed that I was taking advantage of the weakness of a woman in love and in the wrong, while I neither sacrificed nor risked anything of my own; but just as I was about to capitulate, love would come again, repeating its selfish counsel, and I was left irresolute and restless, yearning to see her and fearing that the sight of her might lead me to share the responsibility for the solution.

Finally, there came a compromise between selfishness and pity; I would go see her at her home, only there, in the presence of her husband, say nothing to her, and await the effect of my intimation. That way I could reconcile the two forces. Now that I write this, it strikes me that the compromise was a farce, that the pity was still a form of selfishness, and that the decision to go console Virgília was merely prompted by my own suffering.[1]

CHAPTER LXXX

AS A SECRETARY

On the following night, I did go to Lobo Neves's house; both were there, Virgília quite downcast, he quite jovial. I could swear that she felt a measure of relief when our eyes met, full of curiosity and tenderness. Lobo Neves told me of his plans for the presidency, the local difficulties, his hopes, his resolutions; he was so content! So confident! Sitting by the table, Virgília made as if to read a book, but looked at me over the page from time to time, inquisitive and anxious.

"The trouble," Lobo Neves said suddenly, "is that I still haven't found a secretary."

"No?"

"No, and I have an idea."

"Ah!"

"An idea . . . how would you like to take a trip to the North?"

I don't know what I said to him.

"You're wealthy," he went on, "and you have no need of the meager salary; but if you wished to oblige me, you might go with me as a secretary."

My spirit leaped back as if it had spotted a snake. I looked hard at Lobo Neves to see if I could make out any hidden reflection . . . Not a shadow; his gaze was direct and frank, his features naturally serene and peaceable, a serenity dotted with satisfaction. I took a breath, but couldn't bring myself to look at Virgília; I felt her gaze over the book, asking me the same question, and I said yes, I would go. Indeed, to have a president, a presidentess, and a secretary was a fine administrative solution.

CHAPTER LXXXI

RECONCILIATION

As I left, however, I felt a shadow of doubt; I pondered if it wouldn't mean foolishly risking Virgília's reputation, if there wasn't another reasonable way to square the government with Gamboa. I could find none. The next day, when I rose from bed, I had made up my mind to accept the nomination. At noon, a servant came to say that a lady wearing a veil was in the drawing room. I hastened to her; it was my sister Sabina.

"Things can't go on this way," she said, "we must make peace once and for all. Our family is coming apart; we mustn't behave like two enemies."

"That's all I could ever want, sister!" I cried, holding out my arms.

I sat her by my side, and we spoke of her husband, her daughter, their affairs, everything. All was well; her daughter was as beautiful as the day. Her husband would bring her to see me, if I agreed.

"But of course! I'll go visit her myself."

"Will you?"

"You have my word."

"So much the better!" sighed Sabina. "It's time to be done with this."

I found her plumper, and perhaps more youthful. She looked twenty, though she was over thirty. Charming, affable, not a shred of bashfulness or resentment. We stared at one another with our hands clasped, speaking of everything and nothing, like two sweethearts. My childhood itself was reviving, fresh-faced, boisterous, and fair; the years tumbled away like the castles of cards I used to play with as a boy, allowing me to glimpse our house, our family, our celebrations. I bore up under the memory with some effort; but a barber in the neighborhood took it upon himself to begin scratching away at an old fiddle, and that voice—the memory had been mute until then—that voice from the past, twanging and nostalgic, moved me so greatly that . . .

Her eyes were dry. Sabina had not inherited the morbid yellow flower. What did it matter? She was my sister, my blood, a piece of my mother, and I told her so, tenderly and sincerely . . . Just then, I heard a knock at the drawing-room door; I went to open it; there stood a five-year-old angel.

"Come in, Sara," said Sabina.

It was my niece. I snatched her up and kissed her again and again; the girl, startled, pushed at my shoulder with a little hand and squirmed to get down . . . Just then, a hat emerged in the doorway, and then a man, Cotrim, none other than Cotrim. I was so moved that I set the daughter down and threw myself into the arms of the father. This effusiveness may have disconcerted him somewhat; he certainly seemed reserved. A mere prologue. Soon we were speaking like old friends. No allusions to the past, many plans for the future, a promise to dine at each other's houses. I made sure to say that these alternating suppers might undergo a brief interruption, as I had a notion to travel to the North. Sabina looked at Cotrim, and Cotrim at Sabina; they agreed that my notion made no sense. What on earth was there for me in the North? Wasn't it at the Court, at the heart of the Court, that I was meant to shine and outdo all the young fellows? There was truly none other to rival me; he, Cotrim, had been observing me from a distance, and despite our ridiculous quarrel, he had always taken an interest, pride, and satisfaction in my triumphs. He had heard what was being said about me, on the streets and in the salons; it was a concert of praise and admiration. And leave all that to spend a few months in the provinces when there was no need, no serious reason? Unless it were political . . .

"That's precisely what it is," I said.

"Even so," he replied after a moment. And then, after another silence: "In any case, come dine with us tonight."

"Of course I will; but tomorrow or the night after, you must come dine with me."

"I don't know, I don't know," objected Sabina, "yours is a bachelor's house . . . You've got to get married, brother. I want a niece of my own, you hear?"

Cotrim checked her with a gesture that I did not entirely understand. No matter; the reconciliation of a family is well worth an enigmatic gesture.

CHAPTER LXXXII

A MATTER OF BOTANY

Let the hypochondriacs say what they will: life is sweet. That was what I thought to myself as I watched Sabina, her husband, and her daughter bundle down the stairs, calling up many affectionate things to where I stood—at the top—calling down in turn. I kept on thinking that, in truth, I was happy. I had the love of a woman, the trust of her husband, I would go as secretary to both, and I had reconciled with my family. What more could I ask for in twenty-four hours?

On that very day, trying to pave the way in the public sentiment, I started to make it known that I might go to the North as provincial secretary so as to carry out certain political designs of a personal nature. I said so on the Rua do Ouvidor, and repeated it the following day at the Pharoux and at the theater. Some, connecting my nomination to that of Lobo Neves, which was already rumored, smiled mischievously; others clapped me on the shoulder. At the theater, a lady commented to me that I was taking my love of sculpture to inordinate lengths. She was referring to Virgília's magnificent figure.

But the most barefaced allusion came at Sabina's house, three days later. It was made by one Garcez, an elderly surgeon, a trivial, blathering fellow of the sort who might reach seventy, eighty, or ninety years of age without ever acquiring that austere composure that is the grace of the aged. A ridiculous old age may be the last, saddest surprise that human nature reserves for us.

"I know—this time you'll be reading Cicero," he said to me, upon hearing of the trip.

"Cicero!" exclaimed Sabina.

"What of it? Your brother is a great Latinist. He can translate Virgil at a glance. Virgil, mind, not Virgília . . . don't confuse the two . . ."

And he laughed, a coarse, contemptible, frivolous laugh. Sabina looked at me, fearing some retort; but when she saw me smile, she smiled as well, then turned away to hide it. The others looked at me with an air of curiosity, indulgence, and sympathy; it was clear that they had heard nothing new. My affair was more public than I could have imagined. Nevertheless, I smiled, a brief, fleeting, greedy smile—as garrulous as the gossiping magpies of Sintra.[1] Virgília was a beautiful transgression, and it is so easy to confess a beautiful transgression! At first I grew surly when I heard allusions to our love; but—I swear to you!—I felt a soft, flattering sensation inside. Once it so happened that I smiled, and I kept on doing so on subsequent occasions. I do not know whether anyone can explain this phenomenon. My explanation is as follows: my contentment, for as long as it remained within me, was itself a smile, but a smile in the bud. As time went on, it bloomed into flower and appeared to the eyes of others. A simple matter of botany.

CHAPTER LXXXIII

13

Cotrim removed me from my rapture by taking me over to the window.

"May I tell you something?" he asked. "Don't take this journey; it's foolish and dangerous."

"Why?"

"You know very well why," he replied. "It's dangerous, above all, very dangerous. Here at the Court, an affair like this fades into a multitude of people and interests, but in the provinces things are different; and when it comes to political figures, things become pure madness. As soon as they sniff it out, the opposition papers will put it in the headlines, and next will be the sallies, the insinuations, the nicknames . . ."

"But I don't understand . . ."

"Yes, you do. As a matter of fact, you would hardly be a friend to us if you denied what everyone knows. I've known of it for many months. I repeat, do not take this journey; endure the absence, which is preferable, and you may avoid a great scandal and even greater grief . . ."

This he said, and went back in. I remained there with my eyes on the street lamp at the corner—an old oil lamp—sorrowful, dim, and curved like a question mark. What was I to do? It was the challenge put to Hamlet: either suffer fortune, or take up arms against it and bend it to my will. In other words: to embark or not to embark. That was the question. The street lamp told me nothing. Cotrim's words echoed in the ears of my memory, and with a very different ring from Garcez's. Perhaps Cotrim was right; but could I part from Virgília?

Sabina came to me and asked what I was thinking. I replied that I wasn't thinking about anything, that I was tired and would be going home. Sabina fell quiet for a moment.

"I know what you need; it's a wife. Leave it to me, and I'll find one for you."

I left feeling downtrodden and disoriented. I had been ready to set off, heart and soul, and now the doorkeeper of propriety had popped up and was demanding that I present my ticket. To hell with propriety, and the same for the constitution, the legislature, the ministry, and all the rest.

The next day, I opened up a political paper and read the news that by a decree of the 13th, Lobo Neves and I had been named president and secretary of the province of ***. I wrote to Virgília immediately, and two hours later I went to Gamboa. Poor Dona Plácida! She was growing ever more distressed; she asked if we might forget our old woman, if we would be away very long, whether the province was very far away. Though I consoled her, I needed consoling myself; Cotrim's objections were distressing me. Virgília arrived shortly thereafter, lively as a swallow; but upon seeing me sad, she grew quite serious.

"What's happened?"

"I'm wavering," I said. "I don't know if I should accept . . ."

Virgília let herself fall back on the sofa, laughing.

"Why?" she asked.

"It's not sensible, it'll draw too much attention . . ."

"But we're not going anymore."

"What do you mean?"

She told me that her husband was going to refuse the nomination, and for a reason that he had confided only to her, swearing her to the greatest secrecy; he could confess it to no one else.

"It's childish," he observed, "it's ridiculous; but, in short, it is a powerful motive for me."

He informed her that the decree was dated the 13th, and that this number was shrouded in death for him. His father had died on a 13th, thirteen days after a supper attended by thirteen people. The house in which his mother had died was number 13. Et cetera. It was an ill-fated figure. He could never claim as much to the minister; he would have to allege that he had personal motives to refuse the nomination. I was left much as the reader must be, somewhat astonished by this sacrifice to a number; but since he was an ambitious man, the sacrifice must have been heartfelt . . .[1]

CHAPTER LXXXIV

THE CONFLICT

Fateful number, do you recall how many times I blessed you? Thus the red-headed virgins of Thebes must have blessed the red-maned mare that stood in for them in Pelopidas's sacrifice—a lovely mare who died there, covered with flowers, with no one to give her a word of remembrance.[1] Well, I will give you one, piteous mare, and not only for your pious death, but also because, among the spared maidens, there may very well have been a grandmother of the Cubas line . . . Fateful number, you were our salvation. Her husband never confessed to me why he had refused the nomination; he also told me that he had private matters to attend to, and the serious, persuaded look with which I listened to him was a tribute to humanity's capacity for dissembling. He, on the other hand, could barely disguise the profound sorrow eating away at him; he spoke very little, became withdrawn, and took to retiring to his home and reading. At other times he would receive guests, and then he conversed and laughed a great deal, loudly and affectedly. He was oppressed by two things—ambition, whose wings had been clipped by a worry, and then doubt, hard on its heels—and perhaps regret as well, but a regret that would come again if the scenario were to repeat itself, for the superstitious foundation remained. He doubted his superstition without coming to reject it. The persistence of a sentiment in an individual who finds it loathsome was a phenomenon worthy of some attention. But I preferred the pure naiveté of Dona Plácida when she confessed that she couldn't bear to see an upturned shoe.

"What's the matter with it?" I would ask.

"'Tain't good," was her only reply.

That alone, that only reply, bore for her the same weight as the book of the seven seals. 'Tain't good. She had been told that as a child, with no other explanation, and she was content with the general certainty of its being bad. The same was not true, however, of pointing at a star with one's finger; in that case, she knew perfectly well that it would cause a wart to grow.

A wart, or whatever it might be, what was that compared with losing a provincial presidency? A free or cheap superstition may be tolerated; one that carries off a part of one's life is unbearable. This was the case of Lobo Neves, added to which was his doubt and his dread of having behaved ridiculously. And what was more, the minister was unconvinced by his personal motives and attributed Lobo Neves's refusal to political maneuverings, a perception aggravated by appearances; the minister treated him poorly, made his distrust known to colleagues; incidents came to pass; eventually, after some time, the resigning president went over to the opposition.

CHAPTER LXXXV

THE MOUNTAINTOP

Those who escape a danger love life with a different sort of intensity. Having been on the verge of losing her, I came to love Virgília much more ardently, and the same was true for her. The presidency thus merely revived our initial affections, in the end; it was the drug that we used to savor our love all the more, and prize it more greatly as well. In the first days after the incident, we delighted in imagining the pain of our separation, if it had come to pass, and the growing sadness of each as the sea expanded between us like an elastic sheet; and, like children who run to their mothers' laps to flee from a pulled face, we fled from the imagined danger, holding each other tight.

"My sweet Virgília!"

"My love!"

"You're mine, aren't you?"

"Yours, yours . . ."

And so we resumed the thread of adventure, just as the sultaness Scheherazade resumed the thread of her stories.[1] This was, I believe, the crowning point of our love, the mountaintop from which, for some time, we gazed upon the valleys to our east and west, and above us the calm blue sky. Having rested for that time, we began to go down the slope, our hands clasped at times, unclasped at others, but always going down, down . . .

CHAPTER LXXXVI

THE MYSTERY

On our way down, seeing her somewhat changed, whether disheartened or something else, I asked her what was wrong; she fell silent and gestured as if to indicate weariness, or an indisposition, or exhaustion; I persisted, and she told me that . . . A subtle fluid swam through my whole body: a powerful, swift, singular sensation that I shall never be able to fix on paper. I clasped her hands, drew her gently toward me, and kissed her on the forehead with the delicacy of a zephyr and the gravity of an Abraham. She trembled, took my head between her palms, stared into my eyes, and then caressed me with a maternal gesture . . . There's a mystery here; let us leave the reader time to decipher it.

CHAPTER LXXXVII

GEOLOGY

Around this time there came a misfortune: the death of Viegas. Viegas passed by here a while back, from atop his seventy years, stifled by asthma and disjointed by rheumatism, and with a damaged heart to boot. He was among the keen-eyed observers of our adventure. Virgília harbored great hopes that this old relative of hers, a man as grasping as the grave, would see to her son's future with some inheritance; if her husband thought similarly, he concealed or strangled those reflections. The truth must be told: Lobo Neves bore a measure of fundamental dignity, a layer of rock that stood firm against the dealings of men. The upper layers of loose soil and sand were carried away by life, which is a perpetual torrent. If the reader still recalls Chapter XXIII, he will observe that this is now the second time that I have compared life to a torrent; but he will also note that this time I have added an adjective: perpetual. And God knows the power of an adjective, principally in new and balmy countries.

What is new in this book is the moral geology of Lobo Neves, and probably that of the gentleman who is reading me. Yes, those layers of character that life alters, preserves, or dissolves, according to their resistance, those layers would merit a chapter, which I will not write so as to not draw out the story. I shall only say that the most righteous man I ever met in my life was one Jacó Medeiros or Jacó Valadares, I can't remember his name precisely. Perhaps it was Jacó Rodrigues; in any case, Jacó. He was righteousness in the flesh; he could have become a rich man by violating a tiny scruple, and refused to do so; he let no less than four hundred thousand milréis slip through his hands; and he was so exemplary in his righteousness that it became petty and wearisome. One day, when we found ourselves alone at his house in lively conversation, we received word that Dr. B., a tiresome fellow, had come to call. Jacó asked to say that he wasn't at home.

"That won't work," bellowed a voice from the hallway. "Here I am."

Jacó went to greet him, claiming that he'd believed the caller to be someone else, and adding that he was quite pleased at the visit. This earned us an hour and a half of mortal tedium, and only that because Jacó took out his watch and Dr. B. asked him if he was going out.

"With my wife," said Jacó.

Dr. B. departed, and we began to breathe again. Once we had breathed, I said to Jacó that he had just lied four times in less than two hours: the first, by denying his presence; the second, by rejoicing at the unwanted visitor; the third, by saying that he was going out; and the fourth, by adding that he was going with his wife. Jacó reflected for a moment and then confessed to the accuracy of my observation, but excused himself by saying that absolute veracity was incompatible with an advanced state of society, and that the peace and prosperity of cities might be maintained only through reciprocal deceit . . . Ah! now I remember: his name was Jacó Tavares.

CHAPTER LXXXVIII

THE INVALID

Naturally I refuted this pernicious doctrine with the most elementary arguments; but he was so flustered by my rebuke that he resisted to the very end, showing a certain feigned indignation, perhaps to cloud his conscience.

Virgília's case was slightly more serious. She was less scrupulous than her husband: she manifested her hopes of an inheritance quite clearly, heaping upon her relative enough courtesies, cares, and caresses to earn her at least a codicil. She fawned over him, to put it plainly; but I observed that women's fawning is not the same as men's. The latter lists toward servility; the former may be taken for affection. A charmingly curving figure, a sweet word, and even physical fragility lend women's flattery a dash of local color, an air of legitimacy. No matter the age of the fawned over; the woman will always strike him as motherly or sisterly—or as a nurse, another feminine profession for which even the ablest of men will always lack some *quid*, some fluid, something else entirely.

That was what I thought to myself when Virgília became all sweetness and light around her old relative. She would greet him at the door, chatting and laughing, take his hat and cane, offer her arm, and take him to a chair, or, rather, to *the* chair, "Viegas's chair," a special, comfortable construction made for the elderly or infirm. She would hasten to close a nearby window if it was windy or open the window if the day was hot, but doing so such that he should not catch a draft.

"Well? You're looking heartier today . . ."

"Bah! I spent a dreadful night; this damned asthma won't let up."

And he would wheeze, slowly recovering from the effort of coming up the stairs, not from the journey over, for he always came in his coach. Just beside and slightly in front sat Virgília, on a low stool, her hands on the sick man's knees. Meanwhile, Nhonhô would come into the drawing room, not skipping about as he normally did, but discreet, meek, and serious. Viegas liked him very much.

"Come here, Nhonhô," he would say; and with great difficulty he would insert a hand into his ample pocket, take out a box of lozenges, place one in his mouth and give the boy another. Anti-asthma lozenges. The boy said that they were quite good.

All this repeated itself, with variations. Since Viegas liked to play checkers, Virgília would indulge him, abiding at length as he moved the pieces with a slack, faltering grip. On other occasions they would go down to stroll around the grounds, she offering him her arm, which he spurned at times, saying that he was hale enough to walk a league. They would walk, sit, and walk again, speaking of many things: a family matter, a bit of drawing-room gossip, and finally of a house he had it in mind to build for himself, one with a modern make, as his was an old place, a contemporary of King João VI's, like those that (I believe) may still be found in the neighborhood of São Cristóvão, with their sturdy columns out front. He felt that the manse in which he lived might be replaced, and he had already ordered a plan from a renowned mason. Ah! Then Virgília would really see what an old man with good taste could get up to.

He spoke, as one might imagine, slowly and laboriously, intercut with gasping that was uncomfortable for both him and others. From time to time there came a coughing fit; doubled over and moaning, he would bring his handkerchief to his mouth and then investigate its contents; once the fit had passed, he would return to the plan for the house, which was to have so many bedrooms, a terrace, a coach house—a thing of beauty.

CHAPTER LXXXIX

IN EXTREMIS

"Tomorrow I'll spend the day at Viegas's house," she said to me once. "Poor thing! He's got no one . . ."

Viegas had taken to bed once and for all; his daughter, who was married, had fallen ill just then and couldn't keep him company. Virgília would go from time to time, and I took advantage of the situation to spend the day at her side. It was two o'clock in the afternoon when I arrived. Viegas was coughing so violently that I felt my own chest burn; in between fits, he was haggling over the price of a house with a thin fellow. The fellow was offering thirty thousand milréis. Viegas demanded forty. The buyer insisted, with the air of a man afraid of missing a railway train, but Viegas would not give in; he first refused the thirty thousand milréis, then two more, then three more, and finally had a violent fit that kept him from speaking for fifteen minutes. The buyer was most solicitous, plumped his pillows, and offered him thirty-six thousand milréis.

"Never!" groaned the invalid.

He asked that a heap of papers be brought from the desk; having no strength to remove the elastic band holding them together, he asked me to take it off, which I did. These were his accounts of the expenses on the construction of the house: bills for the stonemason, the carpenter, the painter, bills for the wallpaper in the drawing room and the dining room, the bedrooms, the studies; bills for the ironwork; the cost of the land. He opened them up one by one, with a trembling hand, and asked me to read them, and I did so.

"Look here; twelve hundred, paper at twelve hundred a roll.

French hinges . . . See, you'll have it for nothing," he concluded, once the last bill had been read.

"That may be . . . but . . ."

"Forty thousand; I'll give it to you for no less. The interest alone . . . calculate the interest . . ."

His words were coughed out, gulp by gulp, syllable by syllable, as if they were the shreds of a crumbling lung. His flashing eyes rolled in their deep sockets, reminding me of a midnight lamp. The sheets revealed the outline of his skeleton, peaking at the knees and the feet; his skin was yellowed, limp, and wrinkled, merely enwrapping the skull of an expressionless face: a cap of white cotton rested upon a cranium shorn by time.

"Well, then?" the thin fellow said.

I motioned for him not to press his case, and he fell silent for a few moments. The sick man stared at the ceiling, quiet, breathing heavily; Virgília went pale, stood up, and went over to the window. She suspected that death was nigh, and she was afraid. I tried to speak of other things. The thin fellow told an anecdote and then returned to the matter of the house, raising his offer.

"Thirty-eight," he said.

"Eh . . . ?" the invalid groaned.

The thin fellow went over to the bed, took his hand, and found it cold. I came over to the sick man, asked if he was in any pain, and if he would like a cup of wine.

"No . . . no . . . f . . . for . . . f . . . f . . ."

He sank into a coughing fit, which was his last; shortly thereafter he expired, to the great consternation of the thin fellow, who later confessed to me that he was willing to offer forty thousand; but it was too late.

CHAPTER XC

THE AGE-OLD COLLOQUY
OF ADAM AND CAIN

Nothing. No remembrance in the will, not even a lozenge so that he might not seem utterly ungrateful or forgetful. Nothing. Virgília swallowed her frustration bitterly, and told me so with some caution, not for the thing in itself, but because it had to do with her son, of whom she knew I was not greatly fond, nor even slightly so. I insinuated that she ought to think no more of it. Best to forget the dead man, that mean old dolt of a skinflint, and turn to happier things; our child, for example . . .

There I've let slip the key to the mystery, that sweet mystery of a few weeks earlier, when Virgília struck me as being somewhat different than she had been. A child! A being wrought of my being! That became my sole concern. The eyes of the world, the jealousy of her husband, the death of Viegas, nothing interested me then, neither political conflicts nor revolutions, earthquakes, or anything else. I thought only of that anonymous embryo of doubtful paternity, and a secret voice said to me: It is your child. My child! And I repeated those two words with a certain indefinable pleasure and unspeakable paroxysms of pride. I felt I was a man.

The best of it was that the two of us conversed, the embryo and I, we spoke of present and future things. The scamp loved me, he was a charming little rascal, and he would pat me on the face with his chubby hands, or then, resplendent in his lawyer's robes—as he would undoubtedly take a degree—he would give a speech in the Chamber of Deputies. And his father would listen from the gallery, eyes gleaming with tears. From the university he would become a little schoolboy again, slate and books under his arm, or he might sink back into his cradle to rise once more as a man. I sought in vain to fix his spirit in a single age or attitude: to my eyes, the embryo was all sizes and complexions: he suckled, he wrote, he waltzed, he was the infinite in the space of a quarter hour—baby and legislator, student and dandy. At times, next to Virgília, I forgot her and everything else; Virgília would give me a shake and reproach me for my silence, saying that I no longer cared for her. The truth is that I was in dialogue with the embryo; this was the age-old colloquy of Adam and Cain, a wordless conversation between life and life, between mystery and mystery.

CHAPTER XCI

AN EXTRAORDINARY LETTER

Around this time I received an extraordinary letter, accompanied by a no less extraordinary object. Here is what the letter said:

My dear Brás Cubas,

Some time ago, in the Passeio Público, I borrowed a watch from you. I have the satisfaction of restoring it to you with this letter. The difference is that it is not the same watch, but another, which is, if not superior, then equal to the first. *Que voulez-vous, monseigneur?* as Figaro said—*c'est la misère.*[1] Many things came to pass after our encounter; I will recount them precisely, if you should not close the door on me. Know that I no longer wear those decaying boots, nor the famous overcoat whose tails were lost in the mists of time. I have given up my step outside the church of São Francisco; at long last, I eat breakfast.

Having said this, I beg your leisure to present to you an undertaking, the fruit of great study, a new system of philosophy that not only explains and describes the origin and consummation of things, but also takes a great stride beyond Zeno and Seneca, whose stoicism was truly a child's toy next to my moral prescription. My system is singularly astonishing; it rectifies the human spirit, eliminates pain, ensures happiness, and brings tremendous glory to our land. I call it Humanitism, from *Humanitas*, the principle behind all things. My first idea was manifestly conceited; it was to call it Borbism, from Borba—a vain denomination, and a homely and burdensome one at that. And certainly less eloquent. You shall see, my dear Brás Cubas, you shall see that it is truly monumental; and if there is anything that can make me forget the sorrows of life, it is the joy of having finally seized on truth and happiness. Behold them in my hand, these elusive two; after so many centuries of struggle, study, discoveries, systems, and downfalls, behold them in the hands of man. Goodbye for the present, my dear Brás Cubas. Regards from

Your old friend

JOAQUIM BORBA DOS SANTOS.

I read the letter without understanding it. It was accompanied by a purse containing a handsome watch with my initials engraved on it, along with the following words: *A keepsake from old Quincas.* I returned to the letter and reread it slowly and attentively. The restitution of the watch excluded any possibility of its being a joke; the lucidity, the serenity, the conviction—a touch immodest, it's true—seemed to exclude any suspicion of derangement. It seemed that Quincas Borba had come into an inheritance from one of his relatives in Minas, and abundance had restored his old dignity. I'll not go so far; certain things may never be recovered in full; but some recuperation was not impossible. I put aside the letter and the watch, and awaited the philosophy.

CHAPTER XCII

AN EXTRAORDINARY MAN

I'll have done with the last of the extraordinary things now. I had just put aside the letter and the watch when a thin, middling man came by with a note from Cotrim, inviting me to supper. The bearer was married to a sister of Cotrim's, had arrived just a few days earlier from the North, was named Damasceno, and had taken part in the revolution of 1831.[1] He told me so himself in the space of five minutes. He had left Rio de Janeiro after a disagreement with the Regent, who was an ass, only slightly less of an ass than the ministers who served under him. For that matter, revolution was nigh yet again. On this point, while his political ideas were somewhat scrambled, I managed to organize and formulate the government of his preference: it was despotism, tempered, not by songs—as they say in other parts—but by the plumes of the National Guard.[2] I only failed to grasp whether he favored the despotic rule of one man, three, thirty, or three hundred. He spoke in favor of several matters, among them the development of the trade in Africans and the expulsion of the English.[3] He was quite fond of theater; as soon as he arrived, he had gone to the São Pedro Theater, where he saw a magnificent drama, *Maria Joana*, and a very interesting comedy, *Kettly, or the Return to Switzerland*. He had also been very taken by Deperini, in *Sappho*, or in *Anne Boleyn*, he couldn't quite remember which. But Candiani! Yes, sir, she was sumptuous. Now he wanted to hear *Ernani*, which his daughter sang at home, on the piano: "Ernani, Ernani, involami . . ." At this, he rose and sang a quiet little strain. In the North, all these things arrived as echoes. His daughter was dying to hear all the operas. She had quite a darling voice, his daughter. And taste, good taste. Ah! He'd been eager to return to Rio de Janeiro. He had already roved around the whole city, satisfying his nostalgia . . . He swore that in a few places he almost came to tears. But he would never sail again. He had gotten quite sick on board, like all the other passengers, except an Englishman . . . The devil take them, those English! Things wouldn't be right until they'd all been sent seaward. What could England do to us? If he were to find a few willing people, it'd be a night's work to expel those *god-damners* . . . Thank God, he was a patriot—at this he thumped his chest—which was no wonder, as it ran in the family, he was descended from an old provincial governor who was a great patriot. Yes, he was no drudge. If the time came, he'd show just what sort of wood his canoe was made of . . . But it was growing late, and he was about to say that he'd be there at the supper, where he would await me for more conversation. I took him over to the drawing-room door; there he stopped, saying that he was quite fond of me. When he had married, I was in Europe. He knew my father, an upright man, and they'd danced together[4] at a famous ball at Praia Grande . . [5] Things! Things! He'd speak later, it was growing late, and he had to take my reply to Cotrim. He left; I closed the door after him . . .

CHAPTER XCIII

THE SUPPER

What an ordeal the supper was! Happily, Sabina seated me by Damasceno's daughter, one Dona Eulália, or, more familiarly, Nhã-loló, a charming young lady, somewhat timid at first, but only at first. She lacked in elegance, but made up for it with her eyes, which were magnificent and whose sole defect was that they never left me, except when they sank to her plate; but Nhã-loló ate so little that she hardly looked at her plate. She sang that night; her voice was, as her father had said, "quite darling." Even so, I made my escape. Sabina came to the doorway and asked how I had found Damasceno's daughter.

"So-so."

"Very sweet, isn't she?" Sabina cut in. "Still a bit lacking in refinement. But what a heart! She's a pearl. An excellent bride for you."

"I'm not fond of pearls."

"You curmudgeon! How long will you save yourself? Until you're so ripe you're almost falling off the branch, I'm sure. Well, my good man, like it or not, you'll marry Nhã-loló."

And as she said this she patted me on the cheek, gentle as a dove, and yet commanding and resolute. Good Lord! Was this the reason behind our reconciliation? I was somewhat shaken by the idea, but a mysterious voice was calling me to the Lobo Neves house; I bade farewell to Sabina and her threats.

CHAPTER XCIV

THE SECRET CAUSE

"How's my darling mother tonight?"

At this word, Virgília's face fell, as it always did. She was alone by a window, gazing at the moon, and greeted me happily; but when I spoke of our child, her face fell. She disliked these remarks, and she shrank from my premature paternal caresses. I, for whom she had already become a sacred person, a divine ampulla, let her be. I had supposed at first that the embryo, that emblem of the unknown making its way into our adventure, had restored her awareness of our sins. I was mistaken. Virgília had never seemed more expansive, more unreserved, less concerned about others or about her husband. There was no remorse. I also came to imagine that the pregnancy might be pure invention, a way to tie me to her, a device of no abiding efficacy and which might have begun to weigh on her. The hypothesis was not absurd; my sweet Virgília sometimes lied so charmingly!

On that night, I discovered the true cause. It was her fear of childbirth and the indignity of pregnancy. She had suffered greatly when her first child was born; and at the very thought of that hour, made up of minutes of life and minutes of death, her imagination gave her the chills of the gallows. As for the indignity, it was rendered even more onerous by the forcible privation of social pleasures. This was certainly it; I made as much known to her and delivered a reprimand, partly in the name of my rights as a father. Virgília stared at me; then she looked away and smiled incredulously.

CHAPTER XCV

THE FLOWERS
OF YESTERYEAR

Where are they now, the flowers of yesteryear?[1] One afternoon, after a few weeks of gestation, the edifice of my paternal fantasies was reduced to rubble. The embryo departed at that stage when one can barely tell Laplace from a turtle. I received the news from Lobo Neves, who left me in the drawing room and followed the doctor to the bedroom of the frustrated mother. I leaned on the windowsill, looking out over the grounds, at the greening of the flowerless orange trees. Where had they gone, the flowers of yesteryear?

CHAPTER XCVI

THE ANONYMOUS LETTER

I felt a hand on my shoulder; it was Lobo Neves. We faced each other for a few moments, mute and inconsolable. I asked after Virgília, and then we spoke for about half an hour. At the end of that time, a letter arrived for him; he read it, went very pale, and folded it with trembling fingers. I believe that I saw him move as if to fall on me; but I can't recall. What I do recall clearly is that during the days that followed, he was cold and taciturn in my presence. Days later, in Gamboa, Virgília finally told me everything.

Her husband had shown her the letter as soon as she recovered. It was anonymous, and it denounced us. It did not tell everything; it said nothing, for example, of our encounters outside her home; it merely warned him of my familiarity and added that the suspicions were public. Virgília read the letter and said indignantly that it was the most abominable slander.

"Slander?" asked Lobo Neves.

"Abominable slander."

The husband was able to breathe again; but when he returned to the missive, it seemed that each word wagged a finger, each letter cried out against his wife's indignation. This man, this intrepid man, had now become the most fragile of creatures. Perhaps his imagination showed him the famous eye of opinion, off in the distance, staring at him with a sarcastic and mocking air; perhaps an invisible mouth whispered into his ear all of the coarse jokes he had ever heard or proffered. He pressed his wife to confess everything, saying that all would be forgiven. Virgília understood that she was safe; she made her irritation at his insistence clear and swore that she had only ever heard courteous and witty remarks from me. The letter had to be from some luckless suitor. And she mentioned a few—one who had courted her openly for three weeks, another who had written her a letter, and more, and still more. She mentioned them by name, providing details, studying her husband's eyes, and concluded by saying that, so as to give the slander no foothold, she would treat me in such a way that I would not return.

I absorbed all of this somewhat troubled, not because of the additional deception that would be required from here on out, going so far as to distance myself entirely from Lobo Neves's house, but because of Virgília's moral serenity, the lack of commotion, fright, longing, or even remorse. Virgília noted my concern, lifted my chin, for I had been looking at the floor, and said somewhat bitterly:

"You're not worth the sacrifices I make."

I said nothing; there would be no use in reflecting to her that a bit of despair and terror would lend our situation the biting tang of its early days; and if I did say so, it was not impossible that she might build up that hint of despair and terror slowly and cunningly. I said nothing. She was tapping her toe nervously; I leaned over and kissed her on the forehead. Virgília recoiled as if it had been the kiss of a dead man.

CHAPTER XCVII

BETWEEN LIPS AND FOREHEAD

I feel that the reader has shuddered—or ought to have shuddered. Naturally, those last words have suggested three or four reflections. Regard the picture well: in a little house in Gamboa, two people who have loved one another for a long time, one leaning over the other and kissing the other's forehead, and the other recoiling as if at the touch of a cadaver's mouth. There in the brief span between lips and forehead, before the kiss and after the kiss, there is an ample space that may be inhabited by many a thing: a grimace of resentment, a wrinkle of distrust, or the pale, drowsy nose of satiety . . .

CHAPTER XCVIII

TAKEN OUT

We parted in good spirits. I went to supper, at peace with the situation. The anonymous letter had restored the salt of mystery and the pepper of danger to our adventure; and in the end it was well and good that Virgília hadn't lost her self-possession during the crisis. That night I went to the São Pedro Theater; a great play was being performed, and Estela was wrenching tears from the audience. I went in; I ran my eyes across the boxes; in one of them I saw Damasceno and his family. The daughter was dressed with uncommon elegance and a surprising measure of refinement, as her father earned only enough to go into debt; for that matter, perhaps this was the reason.

At intermission, I went to visit them. Damasceno greeted me with many words, his wife with many smiles. As for Nhã-loló, she never took her eyes off me. She now seemed prettier than on the day of the supper. I saw in her a certain ethereal softness wedded to the refinement of earthly forms: that is a vague turn of phrase, worthy of a chapter in which all must be vague. Truly, I know not how to express to you that I felt quite fine next to that young lady, who was smartly dressed in an exquisite gown, a gown that gave me Tartuffian ticklings. As I contemplated the gown, which was chastely and wholly covering its wearer's knees, I made a subtle discovery: to wit, that nature foresaw human vesture as a necessary condition for the development of our species. Habitual nudity, in light of the multiplication of individuals' works and cares, would tend to dull the senses and hold back the sexes, while clothing, by provoking nature, whets and entices desires, activates them, reproduces them, and thus moves civilization forward. Blessed be the habit that has given us *Othello* and transatlantic steamers!

I have a mind to take out this chapter. This downward slope is a dangerous one. But after all, I am writing my memoirs and not yours, mild reader. Next to that charming damsel, I felt myself overtaken by a twofold, indefinable sensation. It wholly expressed Pascal's duality, *l'ange et la bête*, the difference being that the Jansenist would not stand for the simultaneity of both natures, while here they were quite nicely joined—*l'ange*, which spoke a few heavenly words—and *la bête*, which . . .[1] No; decidedly, I'll take this chapter out.

IN THE ORCHESTRA SEATS

In the orchestra seats I found Lobo Neves talking with a few friends. We spoke briefly and coldly, equally uneasy. But at the next intermission, just as the curtain was about to go up, we met in one of the hallways with no one else around. He came over to me, quite affable and smiling, pulled me over to an oculus, and we spoke at length, principally he, who seemed to be the calmest of men. I even asked after his wife; he replied that she was well, but soon turned the conversation toward general affairs, speaking expansively and almost gaily. Whoever would like to guess at the cause of this change may do so; as for me, I'll flee from Damasceno, who is watching me from the door of his box.

I heard nothing of the second act, neither the words of the actors nor the applause of the audience. Reclining in my chair, I plucked the shreds of the conversation with Lobo Neves from memory, reconstructed his behavior, and concluded that this new situation was far preferable. Gamboa was enough for us. Frequenting the other house would only sharpen jealousies. Really, we could go without speaking every day; this was even better, for it introduced a note of longing into our love. As for the rest, I was past forty and I had become nothing, not even a parish elector. I had to do something, if only for love of Virgília, who would swell with pride when she saw my name shine . . . I believe that just then there was a great round of applause, but I can't swear to it; I was thinking of something else.

O multitude, whose love I coveted unto death, this was how I avenged myself on you at times; I let humanity thrum around my body without hearing it, as Aeschylus's Prometheus did to his tormentors. Ah! You thought you had chained me to the rock of your frivolity, your indifference, your agitation? Fragile chains, my dear friend; I shattered them with a Gulliverian gesture. It is only too common to go contemplate in the wilderness. What is truly sensuous and exquisite is for a man to insulate himself in the midst of a sea of gestures and words, nerves and passions, to declare himself lost in thought, inaccessible, absent. The most that one can say of him, when he returns to himself—that is, when he returns to the company of others—is that he has come down from the moon; but the moon, that luminous, discreet garret of the brain, what is it if not the disdainful affirmation of our spiritual freedom? By God! There you have a good ending to a chapter.

CHAPTER C

PROBABLY THE CASE

If this world were not a realm of inattentive souls, there would be no need to remind the reader that I affirm certain laws only when I am entirely sure of them; as for the rest, I limit myself to admitting their probability. An example of the second class may be found in the present chapter, the reading of which I recommend to all those who appreciate the study of social phenomena. It would seem, and this is not improbable, that between the events of public life and those of private life there is a sort of reciprocal, regular, and perhaps periodical interaction at work—or, to make use of an image, something similar to the tides on Flamengo Beach and on other, equally surf-beaten shores. Indeed, as each wave falls upon the beach, it flows far across the sand; and yet that same water returns to the sea, whether with equal strength or less, and goes to join the wave yet to come, which will flow back in turn like the first. This is the image; let us see its application.

I said on another page that Lobo Neves, having been named provincial president, refused the nomination on the grounds of the date of the decree, which was the 13th: a grave act, the consequence of which was to separate Virgília's husband from the administration. Thus, the private fact of aversion toward a number gave rise to the phenomenon of a political breach. We have only to see how, some time later, a political act was to decree the cessation of movement in private life. Since it would not suit the method of this book to immediately describe that other phenomenon, I will simply say for now that Lobo Neves, four months after our encounter at the theater, reconciled with the administration: a fact that the reader should not lose from sight should he wish to penetrate the subtlety of my thought.

CHAPTER CI

THE DALMATIAN REVOLUTION

It was Virgília who gave me the news of her husband's political volte-face, one October morning, between eleven and noon; she spoke of meetings, conversations, a speech . . .

"So you'll be a baroness at last," I interrupted.

She let the corners of her mouth sag, and shook her head; but this gesture of indifference was belied by something less definable, less clear, an expression of pleasure and expectation. I can't say why, but I imagined that the imperial letter of nomination might draw her back to virtue, not for virtue's sake but out of gratitude to her husband. She had a sincere love of nobility. One of the greatest afflictions to ever buffet our life together had been the appearance of a fop from the legation of—from the legation of Dalmatia, let's say—one Count B.V., who flirted with her for three months. This man, a true nobleman by blood, turned Virgília's head somewhat; on top of it all, she had a talent for diplomacy. I can't say what might have become of me if a revolution hadn't broken out in Dalmatia, toppling the government and purging the embassies. It was a bloody revolution, harrowing and formidable; at each ship that arrived from Europe, the newspapers transcribed the fresh horrors, measured the blood spilt, counted the severed heads; all groaned with indignation and pity . . . Not I; inside I blessed the tragedy, which had removed a pebble from my shoe. And after all, Dalmatia was so far away!

CHAPTER CII

A RESPITE

But that same man who rejoiced at the departure of his rival was soon to commit . . . No, I won't recount it on this page; let this chapter serve as a respite for my vexation. A callous, low act, with no possible explanation . . . I repeat, I won't speak of it on this page.

CHAPTER CIII

DISTRACTION

"No, sir, that just isn't done. You'll pardon me, but that just isn't done."

Dona Plácida was right. No gentleman arrives a full hour late to the place where his lady is waiting. I came in out of breath; Virgília had gone. Dona Plácida told me that she had waited a long time, grown irritated, cried, and swore to never see me again, among other things that our housekeeper related with a catch in her voice, begging me not to forsake her missus, saying that it would be so unfair after she'd sacrificed everything for me. I explained that it had been a mistake, and so on . . . But it wasn't, I believe it was pure distraction. A pleasantry, a conversation, a joke, something of the sort had kept me; it had been pure distraction.

Poor Dona Plácida! She was truly distraught. She was pacing back and forth, wagging her head, sighing clamorously, glancing out the window from time to time. Poor Dona Plácida! With what skill she had tucked in the linens, caressed the cheeks, and lulled the tantrums of our love! What a fertile imagination in making the hours more pleasurable and fleeting! Flowers, sweets—the delightful sweets of old—all wreathed in smiles and endearments, smiles and endearments that only increased over time, as if she wished to fix our adventure as it was, or restore its first bloom. Our confidante and housekeeper would stop at nothing; nothing, not even lies, for she recounted sighs and longings to each of us that she had manifestly not witnessed; nothing, not even slander, for she once accused me of having found a new love. "You know I could never care for another woman," was my reply when Virgília spoke of it to me.

And those words alone, with no protest or reproof, were enough to dissolve Dona Plácida's slanders, to her distress.

"Very well," I said to her after a quarter of an hour. "Virgília must see that it was no fault of mine . . . Would you like to take her a letter now?"

"She must be so very sad, poor thing! Look here, sir, I wouldn't wish for anyone's death, but if one day you come to marry Missus, then you'll see what an angel she truly is!"

I remember that I turned my face away and lowered my eyes to the floor. I recommend this gesture to people who have no ready response, or to those who fear to face the pupils of other eyes. Under such circumstances, some prefer to recite a stanza from the *Lusiads*, while others turn to the recourse of whistling *Norma*. I am partial to the gesture I mentioned; it is simpler and calls for less effort.

Three days later, all was explained. I suppose that Virgília was a little startled when I begged her forgiveness for the tears I'd made her shed on that sad occasion. I can't recall whether, deep down, I suspected that the tears had been Dona Plácida's. Indeed, it might have been the case that Dona Plácida had wept upon seeing her disappointed, and through some visual phenomenon, the tears in her own eyes seemed to be falling from Virgília's. Be that as it may, all was explained, but not forgiven, much less forgotten. Virgília had no few harsh words for me, threatened me with separation, and praised her husband. He was a worthy man, far superior to me, a paragon of courtesy and affection; that's what she said as I sat with my elbows planted on my knees, looking at the floor, where a fly was dragging along an ant that had bitten its leg. Poor fly! Poor ant!

"Won't you say anything at all?" Virgília asked, stopping short in front of me.

"What can I say? I've explained everything; you insist on taking offense; what can I say? Do you know what I think? I think you've had enough, that you're tired, that you want to be done with this . . ."

"Exactly!"

And she went to put on her hat, her hands trembling with anger . . .

"Goodbye, Dona Plácida," she shouted.

She went to the door, unlocked it, and was about to go out; I caught her around the waist.

"All right, all right," I said.

Virgília kept struggling to leave. I held her back, asking her to stay and forget everything; she moved away from the door and sank onto the sofa. I sat down by her and said many a tender thing, some humble things and a few charming ones. I can't declare whether our lips came as close as the breadth of a cambric thread, or even closer; that is a matter of controversy. What I do recall is that in the excitement, one of Virgília's earrings fell off; I leaned over to pick it up, and the fly I had seen climbed onto the earring, still dragging the ant along on its leg. Then I, with the delicacy innate to a man of our century, placed the tormented couple on the palm of my hand; I calculated the distance between my palm and the planet Saturn, and I wondered what interest there might be in such a wretched little episode. If you happen to conclude from this that I was a barbarian, you are roundly mistaken, for I asked Virgília for a hairpin so as to separate the two insects; but the fly sniffed out my intention, opened its wings, and flew off. Poor fly! Poor ant! And God saw that it was good, as the Scriptures say.

CHAPTER CIV

IT WAS HE!

I returned the hairpin to Virgília, who replaced it in her hair and prepared to leave. It was late; the clock had struck three. All was forgiven and forgotten. Dona Plácida, who was watching for an opportune moment to leave, suddenly shut the window and exclaimed:

"Holy Mother of God! Here comes Missus's husband!"

The moment of terror was brief, but complete. Virgília turned the color of the lace on her dress and ran to the bedroom door; Dona Plácida, who had closed the blind, fumbled to shut the inner door as well; I readied myself to await Lobo Neves. That brief moment passed. Virgília returned to her senses, pushed me into the bedroom, and told Dona Plácida to go back to the window; our confidante obeyed.

It was he. Dona Plácida opened the door with many exclamations of surprise:

"You around here, sir! Honoring this old woman's house! Come in, come in. Just guess who's here . . . You don't have to guess, that's why you came . . . Come here, Missus."

Virgília, who was off in a corner, ran over to her husband. I watched them through the keyhole. Lobo Neves came in slowly, pale, cold, and quiet, showing no signs of rashness or fury, and cast his gaze around the room.

"What's this?" Virgília exclaimed. "What brought you around here?"

"I was passing by, I saw Dona Plácida in the window, and I came to say hello."

"I'm much obliged," the latter added. "And people say that nobody cares for old women . . . Look, look! She's even jealous." And caressing Virgília at length: "This angel never forgot her old Plácida. She's the very picture of her mother . . . Sit down, sir . . ."

"I can't stay."

"Are you going home?" Virgília asked. "We'll go together."

"I am."

"Get me my hat, Dona Plácida."

"Here it is."

Dona Plácida went to fetch a mirror and held it up before her. Virgília put on her hat, tied the ribbons, and arranged her hair as she spoke to her husband, who said nothing in reply. Our good old woman chattered away unstoppably; it was her way of hiding how she was shaking. Virgília, her first fright mastered, had regained her self-possession.

"There we are!" she said. "Goodbye, Dona Plácida; don't forget to visit, do you hear?"

The other woman promised that she would, and opened the door for them.

CHAPTER CV

EQUIVALENCE OF WINDOWS

Dona Plácida shut the door and collapsed into a chair. I immediately came out of the bedroom and took two steps on my way to tear Virgília away from her husband; that was what I said, and it was good that I did, because Dona Plácida held me back. At one time I came to the conclusion that I had said it only so that she would hold me back; but simple reflection will suffice to show that, after the ten minutes I had spent in the bedroom, the most genuine and heartfelt gesture could only have been that. This follows from the famous law of the equivalence of windows, which I had the satisfaction of discovering and formulating in Chapter LI. My conscience needed airing. The bedroom was a closed window; I opened another, with my move to go out, and took a breath.

CHAPTER CVI

A DANGEROUS GAME

I took a breath and sat down. Dona Plácida was thundering around the parlor, filling it with exclamations and lamentations. I listened without saying a thing; I reflected whether it wouldn't have been better to have shut Virgília in the bedroom and stayed in the parlor, but I soon saw that it would have been worse; it would have confirmed suspicions, the spark would hit the gunpowder, and there would be a bloody scene . . . Things were much better this way. But what was to come? What would happen at Virgília's house? Would her husband kill her? Beat her? Lock her away? Throw her out? These interrogations made their way slowly through my brain, just like the dark periods and commas that make their way across the field of vision of tired or ill eyes. They came and went, with their dry, tragic look, and I was unable to seize one of them and say: It's you, you and no other.

Suddenly I saw a black figure before me; it was Dona Plácida, who had gone in, put on her mantilla, and was offering to go to Lobo Neves's house. I reflected that it was dangerous, that he would be suspicious of such a hasty visit.

"Don't worry," she interrupted, "I'll know how to go about things. If he's at home, I won't go in."

She went out; I was left ruminating on the incident and its possible consequences. In the end, it struck me that I was playing a dangerous game, and I wondered if it wasn't time for me to get up and move along. I felt overcome with a longing for marriage, a desire to channel my life. Why not? My heart still had room to explore; I did not feel incapable of a chaste, severe, pure love. In the end, adventures are the torrential, vertiginous part of life, the exception; I had wearied of them; and, I can't say for certain, but I may have felt a prick of remorse. No sooner had I thought this, I let myself follow my imagination; I then saw myself married, with a winsome wife by my side, gazing on a babe sleeping in its nanny's lap, all of us far off along the green and shady grounds of a country home, and through the trees we could make out a sliver of sky that was blue, extraordinarily blue . . .

CHAPTER CVII

NOTE

"Nothing happened, but he suspects something; he is quite serious and won't say a thing; he's just gone out. He smiled just once, at Nhonhô, after scowling at him for a long time. He hasn't treated me badly, nor has he treated me well. I don't know what will happen; God willing, it will pass. Take caution, for now, great caution."

CHAPTER CVIII

WHICH IS NOT UNDERSTOOD

Herein lies the drama, here you have the tip of the ear of a Shakespearean tragedy.[1] That scrap of paper, scrawled in parts, crumpled by hands, was a document befitting analysis, something I will not do in this chapter, nor in the next, or perhaps anywhere in the rest of the book. Could I deprive the reader of the pleasure of noting for himself the coldness, the perspicacity, and the spirit of these few hastily written lines, and behind them the tempest in the other person's brain, the disguised rage, the despair that stifles itself and meditates, as it can only come out in mud, blood, or tears?

As for myself, if I should tell you that I read the note three or four times that day, believe it, because it's true; what's more, if I should tell you that I reread it the next day, before and after breakfast, you may believe it, as it is pure reality. But if I should tell you of the commotion I felt, you should feel free to doubt me, and mustn't accept my statement without proof. I was unable then, and remain unable still, to discern what I felt. It was fear, yet it was not fear; it was pity, yet it was not pity; it was vanity, yet it was not vanity; to wit, it was love without love, that is, a love without delirium; and all this came to a combination that was altogether complex and vague, something you will not understand, just as I failed to. Let us suppose that I said nothing at all.

THE PHILOSOPHER

It being known that I reread the letter before and after breakfast, one may deduce that I breakfasted, and all that remains to say is that this was one of the most sparing meals of my life: an egg, a slice of bread, a cup of tea. I did not forget this tiny detail; amidst so many important things which were obliterated, that breakfast was saved. The principal reason might have been precisely my misfortune; but it was not; the principal reason was the reflection I heard from Quincas Borba, who visited me that day. He told me that frugality was not necessary to understand Humanitism, much less to practice it; that this philosophy was easily reconciled with the pleasures of life, including the table, the theater, and love; and that, indeed, frugality might indicate a certain tendency toward asceticism, which was the fullest expression of human foolishness.

"Take Saint John," he went on. "He lived off grasshoppers in the desert, instead of peacefully growing fat in the city and starving out the Pharisees in the synagogue."

God spare me the task of telling Quincas Borba's story, which I heard in its entirety on that sad occasion: it was a long and complicated story, but an interesting one. And as long as I'm not telling the story, I will likewise excuse myself from describing his appearance, which was greatly changed from that which I had seen in the Passeio Público. I'll be silent; I'll say only that if a man is defined essentially not by his features but by his attire, then this was not Quincas Borba; he was a judge without a robe, a general without a uniform, a merchant without a deficit. I noted the perfection of his overcoat, the whiteness of his shirt, the cleanliness of his boots. His very voice, once hoarse, seemed restored to its old resonance. As for his gesticulation, while it had not lost the liveliness of old, it was no longer quite so wild, and obeyed a certain order. But I don't want to describe him. If I spoke, for example, of the gold stud at his breast, or of the quality of the leather of his boots, I would begin a description, which I will leave out for the sake of brevity. Content yourselves with the knowledge that the boots were patent leather. And the fact that he had inherited many thousands of milréis from an old uncle in Barbacena.

My spirit (allow me a childish comparison!), my spirit was, just then, like a sort of shuttlecock. Quincas Borba's story would give it a blow, and it rose; just as it was about to fall, Virgília's note would give it another blow, and it was thrown into the air once again; it began to sink, and the episode from the Passeio Público would meet it with a fresh blow, just as firm and powerful as the first. I don't believe I was born for complex situations. This pulling and pushing of opposite things unbalanced me; I felt an urge to wrap up Quincas Borba, Lobo Neves, and Virgília's note in a single philosophy and send them to Aristotle as a present. Nevertheless, our philosopher's narration was instructive; I wondered at the talent for observation with which he described the gestation and growth of vice, internal struggles, slow capitulations, and the creeping familiarity of the mire.

"Look here," he observed, "the first night I spent on the São Francisco steps, I slept as soundly as if they were the finest feather bed. Why? Because I moved gradually from a wooden bed to a pallet, from a room of my own to a jail cell, from a jail cell to the street . . ."

Finally, he wanted to explain his philosophy to me; I asked that he not.

"I'm quite preoccupied today and I wouldn't be able to follow you; come by later, I'm always at home."

Quincas Borba smiled slyly; perhaps he knew of my affair, but he said nothing more. He only added these parting words at the door:

"Come to Humanitism; it is the supreme shelter for the spirit, the eternal sea into which I dove to wrest the truth from its depths. The Greeks thought they'd pull the truth out of a well.[1] What a small-minded notion! A well! But that's precisely why they never found it. Greeks, sub-Greeks, anti-Greeks, a whole long line of men leaned over the well in hopes of seeing the truth emerge from it, and it was never there to begin with. They wore out ropes and pails; some of the more daring ones went down to the bottom and brought up a frog. I went straight to the sea. Come to Humanitism."

CHAPTER CX

31

One week later, Lobo Neves was named president of a province. I seized on the hope of a refusal, were the decree to come out on the 13th again; but the date was the 31st, and this simple transposition of the numerals eliminated their diabolical substance. How profound are the mainsprings of life!

THE WALL

As it is not my custom to disguise or hide anything, I will devote this page to the story of the wall. They were just about to set sail. As I walked into Dona Plácida's house, I saw a folded paper on the table; it was a note from Virgília saying that she would wait for me that night, in the back garden, without fail. It concluded: "The wall is low on the alley side."

I scowled in irritation. The letter seemed uncommonly daring, poorly thought out, even ridiculous. This wasn't just an invitation to scandal, it was begging for mockery to boot. I imagined myself climbing over the wall, however low and near the alley it might be; and, just as I was about to cross it, I saw myself pounced upon by an officer of the law and taken to jail. The wall is low! And what of it? Of course Virgília had no idea what she'd done; she might already have regretted it. I looked at the paper, which was wrinkled but inflexible. I felt an itch to tear it up into thirty thousand pieces and throw them to the wind as the last spoils of my adventure; but I drew back in time. Self-love, the indignity of the flight, the idea of fear . . .

There was nothing to do but go.

"Tell her I'll go."

"Where?" Dona Plácida asked.

"Where she said she'll be waiting for me."

"She didn't tell me anything."

"In this note."

Dona Plácida's eyes widened.

"But I found it this morning, in your drawer, and I thought that . . ."

I had a strange feeling. I reread the note, looked at it, and looked again; it was, in fact, an old note from Virgília, received at the start of our affair, arranging a meeting in the back garden, for which I had indeed climbed over the wall, a low, discreet wall. I tucked the paper away, and . . . I had a strange feeling.

CHAPTER CXII

PUBLIC OPINION

But it was written: that day was to be one of obscure incidents. A few hours later, I came across Lobo Neves on the Rua do Ouvidor; we spoke of the presidency and of politics. He seized on the first acquaintance who drifted by and left me, after many warm greetings. I recall that he was reserved, but struggling to disguise that reserve. It struck me then (and may the critics forgive me if this judgment should prove presumptuous!), it struck me that he was afraid—not of me, or himself, or the law, or his conscience; he was afraid of public opinion. I surmised that this anonymous, invisible court, in which each member both prosecutes and judges, was the check on Lobo Neves's free will. Perhaps he no longer loved his wife; his heart might have been cold to the indulgence of his latest actions. I believe (again, I must appeal to the goodwill of the critics!), I believe that he would be willing to break with his wife, as the reader must have broken off many personal relations; but public opinion—that opinion which would drag his life through every street, open up a painstaking inquiry into the case, gather each detail, precedent, inference, and piece of evidence, one by one, and relate them in idle sitting-room conversations, that fearsome public opinion, with its fascination for bedrooms—stood in the way of the dissolution of the family. At the same time, it made revenge impossible, for it would mean revealing all to the world. He could not show his resentment of me without seeking a marital separation; so he was forced to simulate his prior ignorance, as well as the same sentiments he had harbored then.

It pained him, I do believe; especially during those days,

from what I saw of him, it pained him greatly. But time (and this is another point on which I must beg the indulgence of thinking men!), time hardens sensibilities and obliterates the memory of things; one might suppose that the years would wear down the thorns, that distance from events would erase their contours, that a retrospective shadow of doubt would cover the nakedness of reality; in other words, that public opinion would come to occupy itself with other adventures. As the son grew, he would seek to satisfy his father's ambitions, and would be the heir to all his affections. That and public activity, prestige, and then old age, infirmity, decline, and death, a requiem, an obituary, and the book of life would be shut without a single page of bloodshed.

CHAPTER CXIII

SOLDER

The point, if there is any to the previous chapter, is that public opinion is a fine solder for domestic institutions. It is not impossible that I may expand on this idea before the book is out; but neither is it impossible that I may leave it as it is. One way or another, public opinion is a fine solder, in both the domestic realm and the political. Some bilious metaphysicians have gone to the extreme of calling it the simple product of foolish or mediocre minds; but it is evident that, even if such an extreme notion were not its own refutation, one has only to consider the salutary effects of public opinion to conclude that it is the highly sophisticated result of the flower of mankind—that is, of the majority.

CHAPTER CXIV

END OF A DIALOGUE

"Yes, tomorrow. Will you go to see us off?"

"Are you mad? That's impossible."

"Goodbye, then!"

"Goodbye!"

"Don't forget Dona Plácida. Go see her now and then. Poor thing! She went to say goodbye to us yesterday and cried her eyes out, saying I'd never see her again . . . She's a good soul, isn't she?"

"Certainly."

"If we should write one another, she'll receive the letters. I'll see you in . . ."

"Two years?"

"Of course not! He says it's just till the elections."

"Is that so? Well, we'll see each other soon, then. Look, they're watching us."

"Who?"

"Over there on the sofa. We have to separate."

"It pains me greatly."

"But we must; goodbye, Virgília!"

"I'll see you soon again. Goodbye!"

THE LUNCH

I did not see her off; but at the appointed hour I felt something that was neither pain nor pleasure, a mixture of relief and longing, mingled together in equal proportion. Reader, do not be irritated by this confession. I am well aware that in order to titillate your fancy, I ought to sink into tremendous despair, shed a few tears, and forgo lunch. It would be novelesque, but it would not be biographical. The pure reality is that I lunched, as I had on other days, succoring my heart with the memories of my adventure and my stomach with the delicacies of Monsieur Prudhon . . .

. . . Old men of my time, do you perchance remember that master chef at the Hotel Pharoux, a fellow who, according to the owner, had served at the famous Véry and Véfour in Paris, as well as at the palaces of Count Molé and the Duke de la Rochefoucauld? He was an illustrious figure. He came to Rio de Janeiro at the same time as the polka . . . The polka, M. Prudhon, the Tivoli, the Foreigners' Ball, the Casino, there you have some of the best recollections of that time; but the master's delicacies were the most splendid of them all.

Indeed they were, and on that morning it seemed that devil of a chef had guessed at our misfortune. Never had ingenuity and artifice smiled on him as they did then. What refined spices! What tender meats! What elegant forms! One ate with one's mouth, eyes, and nose. I didn't save the bill that day; I know it was costly. Ah, the pain! I needed to bury my love in magnificent fashion. There it went, away across the sea, in space and time, and I remained there at the end of the table, with my forty-odd years, so idle and so empty; I remained, never to see my love again, for even if she could return, as return she did, who would ever ask for the fragrance of morning when faced with the twilight of afternoon?

CHAPTER CXVI

PHILOSOPHY OF OLD PAPERS

I was left so sad by the end of the last chapter that I might have resolved not to write this one, rest a while, purge my spirit of the melancholy weighing on it, and continue later. But no, I don't want to waste time.

Virgília's departure gave me a taste of life as a widower. During the first days I shut myself up at home, spearing flies—like Domitian did, if Suetonius isn't lying[1]—but spearing them in a very particular way: with my eyes. I speared them one by one, tucked away in a spacious drawing room, stretched out in the hammock with an open book in my hands. That was all: nostalgia, ambitions, a bit of tedium, and a great deal of wandering daydreams. My uncle the priest died during this time, as did two cousins. I was not distraught; I took them to the cemetery as one might take money to the bank. What am I saying? As one might take letters to the post office: I sealed the letters, put them in the box, and entrusted the letter carrier with the task of delivering them to the recipient. It was around then that my niece Venância, Cotrim's daughter, was born. Some died, others were born; I was left to the flies.

At other times I grew agitated. I would go to my desk drawers, spill out old letters from friends, relatives, loves (even from Marcela), and open all of them, read them one by one, and reconstruct the past tense . . . Ignorant reader, if you fail to keep the letters of your youth, you will never come to know the philosophy of old papers; you will not savor the pleasure of seeing yourself, off in the half-light, sporting a tricorn hat, seven-league boots and an Assyrian beard, dancing to the sound of an Anacreontic panpipe. Keep the letters of your youth!

Or, if the tricorn hat isn't to your liking, I will avail myself of the words of an old seaman who frequented Cotrim's house; I will say that, should you keep the letters of your youth, you will find reason to "sing a yearning." It seems that our seamen refer in such a way to songs of the land, when sung on the high seas. As poetic expressions go, it is the saddest you can ask for.[2]

CHAPTER CXVII

HUMANITISM

Two forces, however, to be joined by a third, compelled me to return to my habitually bustling life: Sabina and Quincas Borba. My sister had advanced Nhã-loló's marital candidacy in truly forceful fashion. When I came to, the girl was practically in my arms. As for Quincas Borba, he finally explained Humanitism, the philosophical system designed to ruin all the rest.

"Humanitas," he said, "the principle of things, is nothing but man himself, divided across all other men. Humanitas has three stages: the *static*, preceding all creation; the *expansive*, the beginning of things; the *dispersive*, the appearance of man; and it will have yet another, the *contractive*, the absorption of man and things. *Expansion*, in beginning the universe, suggested to Humanitas the desire to enjoy it; hence the *dispersion*, which is nothing more than the personified multiplication of the original substance."

As this interpretation did not strike me as entirely clear, Quincas Borba expanded on it in greater depth, dwelling on its overarching lines. He explained to me that on one side Humanitism was connected to Brahmanism, in terms of the distribution of men across the various parts of the body of Humanitas; but that which in the Indian religion bore only a narrow theological and political meaning was, in Humanitism, the great law of personal value. Thus, to descend from the chest or the kidneys of Humanitas—that is, to be essentially *strong*—was not the same as descending from its hair or the tip of its nose. Hence the need to cultivate and temper one's muscles. Hercules was nothing but an early symbol of Humanitism. On this point, Quincas Borba pondered that paganism might have arrived at the truth had it not become belittled by the bawdier aspects of its myths. Nothing of the sort would happen to Humanitism. In this new church there are no facile adventures, nor pitfalls, nor sorrows, nor childish joys. Love, for example, is a priesthood; reproduction, a ritual. Since life is the greatest benefit the universe can bestow, and there is no beggar who does not prefer poverty to death (which is itself a delightful influx of Humanitas), it follows that the transmission of life, far from being an occasion for gallanting, is the supreme hour of a spiritual Mass. Hence there is truly only one misfortune in life: never being born.

"Imagine, for example, that I had never been born," Quincas Borba went on. "I would certainly not have the pleasure of speaking to you now, eating this potato, going to the theater . . . in a word, living. Note that I do not make man a simple vehicle for Humanitas; no, he is at the same time the vehicle, coachman, and passenger; he is Humanitas itself in miniature; hence the need to adore oneself. Would you like proof of the superiority of my system? Consider envy. There is no moralist, Greek or Turk, Christian or Muslim, who does not rail against the sentiment of envy. They are in perfect accord, from the fields of Edom to the heights of Tijuca. See here; leave off old prejudices, forget all the frayed rhetoric, and study envy, that subtle and noble sentiment. If each man is Humanitas in miniature, clearly no man is fundamentally opposed to another man, despite appearances to the contrary. Thus, for example, the hangman who executes a condemned man may arouse the vain lamentations of the poets; but concretely, this is Humanitas correcting in Humanitas an infraction of the law of Humanitas. I would say the same of an individual who disembowels another; this is a manifestation of the strength of Humanitas. Nothing stands in the way of his being disemboweled in turn (and there are examples of this). If you have understood well, then you will easily comprehend that envy is nothing but an admiration that struggles, and since struggle is the highest function of the human race, bellicose sentiments are those most suitable to its happiness. It follows then that envy is a virtue."

Why deny it? I was stupefied. The clarity of his explanation, the logic of his principles, the rigor of his deductions, all of it seemed supremely grand, and I had to suspend the conversation for a few minutes while I digested the new philosophy. Quincas Borba could barely hide his satisfaction at this triumph. There was a chicken wing on his plate, and he gnawed on it with philosophical serenity. I posed a few objections, flimsy ones, which he took little time to dismantle.

"To understand my system properly," he concluded, "one must never forget the universal principle, which is divided and epitomized in each man. Look: war, which seems a calamity, is a useful operation, which we might call Humanitas cracking its knuckles; hunger (at this he sucked philosophically on the chicken wing), hunger is a test to which Humanitas sets its very entrails. But I need no more demonstration of the sublimity of my system than this very chicken. It fed on corn, which was planted by an African—imported from Angola, let's say. That African was born, grew up, and was sold; a ship brought him here, a ship built from wood cut down in the forest by some ten or twelve men, borne on sails sewn by some eight or ten men, to say nothing of the rigging and other elements of the nautical apparatus. Thus, this chicken, which I have just had for lunch, is the result of a multitude of efforts and struggles, executed with the sole aim of checkmating my hunger."

Between the cheese and the coffee, Quincas Borba demonstrated to me that his system meant the destruction of pain. Pain, according to Humanitism, is an utter illusion. When a child is threatened with a stick, even before it is beaten, it closes its eyes and trembles; this *predisposition* is the foundation of an illusion, which is inherited and transmitted. Adopting the system is certainly not enough to do away with pain at once, but it is essential; the rest is the natural evolution of things. Once man is quite persuaded that he is Humanitas itself, he has only to turn his thoughts back to the original substance to ward off any painful sensation. The evolution is so profound, however, that it may easily take a few thousand years.

Some days later, Quincas Borba read to me his great masterwork. It spanned four large manuscript volumes, a hundred pages each, written in a small hand and peppered with Latin citations. The last volume was a political treatise founded on Humanitism; this was possibly the most tedious part of the system, albeit conceived with formidable logical rigor. If society were reorganized around his method, it would not eliminate war, insurrection, a simple beating, an anonymous knife blow, misery, hunger, or disease; but since these purported scourges were errors in comprehension, for they were nothing but external movements of the same inner substance, destined to have no influence on man beyond a break in the monotony of the universe, of course their existence would be no impediment to human happiness. Moreover, even if such scourges (a radically false notion at that) might eventually correspond to the narrow-minded concept of times past, this likewise would fail to destroy the system, and for two motives: 1st, because the substance of Humanitas holds the absolute power of creation, each individual ought to find it the greatest delight in the world to sacrifice himself to the principle from which he descends; and 2nd, because not even this would diminish the spiritual power of man over the earth, which was invented solely for his recreation, along with the stars, breezes, dates, and rhubarb. Pangloss, he told me as he closed the book, was not as foolish as Voltaire made him out to be.

CHAPTER CXVIII

THE THIRD FORCE

The third force calling me to the throng was the pleasure of shining in society and, above all, inaptitude for a solitary life. The multitude enticed me, applause courted me. If the idea of the plaster had presented itself to me then, who knows? I might not have died straightaway and fame would be mine. But the plaster did not come. What did was the desire to throw myself into something, with something, for something.[1]

CHAPTER CXIX

PARENTHESIS[1]

I would like to leave here, between parentheses, a half-dozen maxims of the many I composed around this time. They are the yawnings of boredom; they may serve as epigraphs to speeches that have nothing to say:

———

One can bear another man's bellyache patiently.

———

We kill time; time buries us.

———

A philosophizing coachman used to say that the pleasure of carriage rides would be scant if everyone rode in carriages.

———

Believe in yourself; but do not always doubt others.

———

It is incomprehensible that a Botocudo Indian should pierce his lip only to adorn it with a stick. This reflection is by a jeweler.

———

Don't be cross if your kindness is poorly repaid: better to fall from the clouds than from a third-story window.

CHAPTER CXX

COMPELLE INTRARE

"No, sir, like it or not, you'll have to marry now," Sabina said to me. "What a fine future! A childless bachelor."

Childless![1] The idea of having children gave me a start; the mysterious fluid swam through me once again. Yes, it behooved me to become a father. A bachelor's life might have certain advantages of its own, but they were tenuous and purchased at the price of solitude. Childless! No; impossible. I prepared myself to accept everything, even a connection to Damasceno. Childless! Since by then I placed great trust in Quincas Borba, I went to him and laid out my paternal stirrings. The philosopher was overjoyed as he listened; he declared that Humanitas was roiling in my breast; he encouraged me to marry; he reflected that these were a few more guests knocking at the door, et cetera. *Compelle intrare*, as Jesus said. And he did not leave me without first proving that the story in the Gospels was nothing more than a foretoken of Humanitism, wrongly interpreted by the priests.

CHAPTER CXXI

DOWNHILL

After three months' time, everything was going marvelously. The fluid, Sabina, the girl's eyes, and her father's desires were among so many other forces leading me to marriage. The memory of Virgília appeared from time to time at the door, and a black devil would thrust a mirror in my face, showing her off in the distance, dissolved into tears; but another devil would come, a pink one, with a mirror reflecting the image of Nhã-loló: tender, luminous, and angelic.

I'll say nothing of my years. I felt them not; what's more, I'll add that I had cast them aside one certain Sunday when I went to Mass at the chapel on Livramento Hill.[1] Since Damasceno lived in Cajueiros, I often went with his family to Mass. The hill was still bare of residences, save the old mansion atop it, where the chapel was. Well, one Sunday, as I was heading down with Nhã-loló on my arm, some phenomenon caused me to begin shedding two years here, four years there, then five a short while ahead, such that by the time I reached the bottom I was only twenty years old, just as sprightly as I had been then.

Now, if you would like to know under what circumstances the phenomenon occurred, you have only to read the chapter to the end. We were coming from Mass: she, her father, and I. Midway down the slope we came across a group of men. Damasceno, who was walking by our side, saw what it was and rushed ahead, overjoyed; we went after him. What we saw was this: men of all ages, sizes, and colors, some in shirtsleeves, others in jackets, others thrust into tattered overcoats; a range of postures, some squatting, others with their hands on their knees, the latter sitting on stones, the former leaning against a wall, all with their eyes fixed on the center, their souls leaning out of their pupils.

"What is it?" Nhã-loló asked me.

I motioned for her to be silent; I gently opened up a path, and all gave way, without a single one seeing me. Their eyes had been trussed to the center. It was a cockfight. I saw the two contenders, two cocks with sharp spurs, eyes of fire, and cutting beaks. Both shook their bloody crests; their breasts were scarlet and plucked clean, and fatigue was overcoming the both of them. But they fought on, their eyes locked, beak down, beak up, a blow from one, a blow from the other, trembling and furious. Nothing else existed for Damasceno; for him, the spectacle had blotted out the universe. In vain did I tell him that it was time for us to go down; he did not respond, he did not hear; he was given over to the duel. Cockfighting was one of his passions.

Just then, Nhã-loló tugged gently on my arm, saying that we should go. I accepted this counsel and headed down with her. I had said that the hill had no other houses back then; I had also told you that we were coming from Mass, and since I did not tell you that it was raining, the day was, of course, fair, with a delightful sun. And a strong one. So strong that I soon opened up the parasol, grasped it high up the handle, and turned it at such an angle as to add a page to the philosophy of Quincas Borba: Humanitas osculated Humanitas . . . And that was how the years went falling off as I came downhill.

We lingered a few minutes at the foot of the hill, awaiting Damasceno; he arrived soon thereafter, surrounded by the bettors and discussing the details of the fight. One of them, the stakeholder, was handing out ragged ten-tostão notes to the doubly gleeful winners. As for the cocks, they were under their respective owners' arms. One of them had his crest so mangled and bloodied that I believed him to be the loser; but I was mistaken—the loser had no crest whatsoever. Both had their beaks open, panting, bone-tired. The bettors, for their part, were contented, despite the heat of the fight; they sketched biographies of the contenders, recalling the feats of both. I walked on, discomfited; Nhã-loló, mortified.

CHAPTER CXXII

A VERY FINE INTENTION

What mortified Nhã-loló was her father. The ease with which he had fallen in with the bettors had thrown old habits and social affinities into relief, and Nhã-loló had come to fear that I might find him an unworthy father-in-law. The way she set herself apart was remarkable; she studied herself and she studied me. Elegant, refined life attracted her, principally because it struck her as the most reliable means by which to make us suit one another. Nhã-loló would observe, imitate, and infer; at the same time, she dedicated herself to masking her family's inferiority. On that day, however, her father manifested it so extravagantly that she was saddened to no end. I sought to distract her from the matter with jests and gentle witticisms; all in vain, for they no longer lifted her spirits. Her distress was so profound, her dejection so expressive, that I came to see in Nhã-loló the positive intention to separate her cause from that of her father in my eyes. This sentiment struck me as superiorly elevated; it was yet another affinity between us.

"There's nothing for it," I said to myself. "I must pluck this flower from the swamp."

THE REAL COTRIM

Despite my forty-odd years, I believed that I should not propose the marriage before first speaking with Cotrim, for I prized family harmony. He heard me out and responded gravely that he would not opine on the affairs of his relatives. He might be suspected of harboring some interest if he were to praise Nhã-loló's rare talents; he would thus be silent. What's more, though he was convinced that his niece bore a true passion for me, if she were to consult him he would counsel against the match. This was not out of any bad feeling; he appreciated my virtues and never tired of praising them, as was only fair; and as for Nhã-loló, he would never deny that she would make an excellent bride; but between there and counseling marriage lay an abyss.

"I wash my hands of it entirely," he concluded.

"But you said the other day that I should be married as soon as possible . . ."

"That's another matter. I do believe that marriage is indispensable, especially for those with political ambitions. You must know that in politics, bachelordom is a hindrance. But as for the bride, I can have no say, nor do I wish to, nor ought I, even if it were my place, which it is not. From what she has told me, it seems that Sabina overstepped herself, making certain confidences to you; but in any case she is not a blood relative of Nhã-loló's, as I am. Look . . . but no . . . I won't say that . . ."

"Say it."

"No; I won't say anything."

Cotrim's scruples may seem excessive to those unaware that

he possessed a ferociously honorable character. I myself treated him unfairly during the years after my father's estate was settled. I recognize now that he was a paragon. People accused him of avarice, and I believe they were right; but avarice is nothing more than the exaggeration of a virtue, and virtues should be like budgets: better a surplus than a deficit. Since he had a brusque way about him, he had enemies, and they went so far as to accuse him of savagery. The only thing they alleged on this score was that he often sent slaves to the Dungeon,[1] from which they would descend streaming with blood; but, apart from the fact that he only sent runaways and incorrigibles, it so happens that, having dealt for so long in the smuggling of slaves, he had become somewhat used to the slightly harsher treatment required by that sort of business, and one cannot honestly attribute to a man's original nature that which is the pure effect of social relations. The proof that Cotrim harbored pious sentiments was to be found in his love of his children and in the pain he suffered when Sara died a few months later; an irrefutable proof, say I, and hardly the only one. He was the treasurer of a fraternal order, and a member of several religious societies, even a perpetual brother[2] in one of them, which hardly fits with his reputation as a miser; although the truth is that this charity had its own benefits: the brotherhood (of which he had been a board member) had an oil portrait painted of him. He was not perfect, certainly; he had the fault of sending notes to the newspapers about this or that charitable act of his—a reprehensible fault, or at least not one to be lauded, I agree; but he excused himself by saying that good deeds were contagious when made public, an argument to which one cannot deny some weight. I truly believe (and in this I see his greatest merit) that he practiced these occasional charitable acts only with the aim of arousing the philanthropy of others; and if this was his intention, one must admit that publicity was a sine qua non. In short, he might have owed a few courtesies to some, but he didn't owe a cent to a single soul.

CHAPTER CXXIV

AN INTERLUDE

What lies between life and death? A short bridge. Nevertheless, if I were not to compose this chapter, the reader would
suffer a grave shock, one quite inimical to the effect of the
book. To jump from a portrait to an epitaph may be altogether
real and ordinary; the reader, however, only seeks refuge in a
book to escape from life. That is not to say that this reflection
is my own; I will say that there is a measure of truth in it, and
that, at the least, the form of it is picturesque. And I repeat: it
is not my own.[1]

CHAPTER CXXV

EPITAPH

HERE LIES

DONA EULÁLIA DAMASCENA DE BRITO

DEAD

AT NINETEEN YEARS OF AGE

PRAY FOR HER!

CHAPTER CXXVI

DISCONSOLATION

The epitaph says it all. Better that than narrating to you Nhã-loló's illness, her death, the despair of the family, the funeral. You are hereby informed that she died; and I will add that it was on the occasion of the first outbreak of yellow fever.[1] I shall say nothing more, except that I accompanied her to her final rest, and that I bade her farewell with sorrow, but without tears. I concluded that perhaps I had never truly loved her.

Behold the excesses to which ignorance may lead; I was somewhat hurt by the blindness of the epidemic, which, in killing left and right, also carried off a young lady who was to be my wife; I could not understand the need for the epidemic, much less for that particular death. I believe that it struck me as even more absurd than all the rest. But Quincas Borba explained to me that epidemics were useful for the species, albeit disastrous for a certain number of individuals; he had me observe that, as horrendous as the spectacle was, there was a considerable advantage: the survival of the greatest number. He even asked me if, amidst the general mourning, I didn't feel some secret delight in having escaped the clutches of the plague; but this question was so senseless that it was left unanswered.

Just as I have not told of her death, nor will I tell of the funeral Mass. Damasceno's sorrow was profound; the poor man seemed a ruin. Two weeks later, I visited him; he remained inconsolable, and said that the great pain with which God had punished him had been compounded by the pain inflicted on him by men. He said nothing more. Three weeks later he returned to the matter, and then confessed that, in the midst of this irreparable tragedy, he had yearned for the consolation of the presence of his friends. Twelve people, no more, and three-quarters of them Cotrim's friends, had accompanied his dear daughter's body to the grave. And he had sent out eighty invitations. I reflected that the losses were so widespread that this apparent disregard might be forgiven. Damasceno shook his head, incredulous and sad.

"Come now!" he moaned. "They've forsaken me."

Cotrim, who was also there:

"Those who truly care for you and us did come. The eighty would come out of formality; they would speak of the government's inertia, the druggists' panaceas, the price of houses, or of one another . . ."

Damasceno listened to him in silence, shook his head once more, and sighed:

"But if only they had come!"

CHAPTER CXXVII

FORMALITY

It is quite a great thing to have been endowed by heaven with a particle of wisdom, the gift of finding the relations between things, the ability to compare them, and the talent to draw conclusions about them! I held that psychic distinction; I still give thanks for it now, from the bottom of my tomb.

Indeed, an ordinary man who heard those last words of Damasceno's would not remember them when, some time later, he happened to look at a picture of six Turkish ladies. Well, I remembered them. These were six ladies of Constantinople—modern ladies—in their street garb, faces hidden, not with a thick fabric that would truly cover them, but with the slightest of veils, which made as if to reveal only the eyes, when it truly revealed the entire face. And I was amused by the cleverness of this Muslim coquettishness, which so hides the face—fulfilling its purpose—but fails to hide it—and thus exposes its beauty. Apparently there is nothing to connect the Turkish ladies to Damasceno; but if you are a profound and penetrating soul (and I very much doubt that you will deny me that), you will understand that in both cases, we are beholding the tip of the ear of a gentle but inflexible companion of man in society . . .

Sweet Formality, you are the great staff of life, the balm of the heart, the peacemaker between men, the bond between earth and heaven; you dry a father's tears, you win the indulgence of a Prophet. If pain is ever to abate, and a conscience ever to conform, to whom but you do they owe that tremendous gift? When esteem goes by with hat undoffed, it says nothing to the soul; but indifference, courting it with kind words, leaves a delightful impression. The reason is that, contrary to an old, absurd formula,[1] the letter does not kill; the letter gives life; the spirit is the object of controversy and doubt, interpretation, and thus struggles of life and death. Long live you, sweet Formality, in the name of Damasceno's peace and Mohammed's glory.

CHAPTER CXXVIII

IN THE CHAMBER

And mark well that I saw the Turkish picture two years after Damasceno's words, and I saw it in the Chamber of Deputies amidst a great hue and cry as a deputy discussed a report by the budget commission—I myself being a deputy as well. For those who have been reading along in this book, there is no need to play up my satisfaction; and for the rest it is equally useless. I was a deputy, and I saw the Turkish picture, leaning back in my chair between one colleague who was telling an anecdote and another who was sketching a portrait of the orator in pencil on the back of an envelope. The orator was Lobo Neves. The wave of life had carried us to the same beach, like two shipwrecked sailors' bottles; he contained his resentment, while I ought to have contained my remorse; and I employ this suspensive, dubitative, or conditional tense in order to convey that I in fact contained nothing at all, except for the ambition to be a minister.

CHAPTER CXXIX

NO REMORSE

I had no remorse. Had I the proper instruments, I would include a page of chemistry in this book, wherein I would decompose remorse down to its simplest elements with the aim of determining positively and conclusively why Achilles marches around Troy with his adversary's body and why Lady Macbeth marches around the room with her spot of blood. But just as I have no chemist's instruments, I had no remorse; I had a mind to be minister of state. If I must finish out this chapter, I will say that I would rather be neither Achilles nor Lady Macbeth; if forced to choose, I would prefer Achilles, rather go about in triumph with the body than bear the spot; that way, at least, one hears Priam's pleas and gains a handsome military and literary reputation. I did not hear Priam's pleas, but rather Lobo Neves's speech, and I had no remorse.

CHAPTER CXXX

TO BE INSERTED
INTO CHAPTER CXXIX

The first time I was able to speak to Virgília after the presidency was at a ball in 1855. She wore a magnificent dress of blue grogram, and bared the same shoulders of yesteryear to the light. This was not the bloom of her first youth—quite the contrary—but she was still beautiful, an autumnal beauty heightened by the evening. I recall that we spoke at length without alluding to anything of the past. Everything was understood. A glancing, vague turn of phrase, or a gaze, and nothing more. Soon thereafter, she left; I watched her go down the stairs, and, by I know not which phenomenon of cerebral ventriloquism (may the philologists pardon me for that barbarous construction), I murmured this profoundly retrospective remark:

"Magnificent!"

This chapter is to be inserted between the first and second sentences of Chapter CXXIX.

CHAPTER CXXXI

ON SLANDER

Just as I had finished saying that, through the aforementioned cerebro-ventriloquial process—expressing a mere opinion, mind you, not remorse—I felt someone's hand on my shoulder. I turned; it was an old friend, a naval officer, a jovial fellow with a bit of a brazen streak. He smiled wickedly, and said:

"You rogue! Reminiscing about the past, eh?"

"Long live the past!"

"I'm sure you've gotten your old position back."

"Push off, you rascal!" I said, threatening him with a finger.

I confess that this dialogue was indiscreet—principally the last retort. And it gives me even greater pleasure to confess it because women are the ones known for their indiscretion, and I do not wish to finish this book without duly correcting that notion of the human spirit. In terms of amorous adventures, I have found men who smiled or could only muster a cold, monosyllabic denial, et cetera, while their partners in the affair would give no quarter and would swear by the Gospels that it was all slander. The reason for this difference is that women (except in certain cases, such as the situation in Chapter CI) give themselves over to love—that is, Stendhal's passionate love, or the purely physical love of certain Roman ladies, for example, or women among the Polynesians, Laplanders, Kaffirs, and perhaps other civilized races as well; but men—I speak of men in cultured, elegant society—men yoke their vanity to the aforementioned sentiment. What's more (and I am referring here only to illicit encounters), when a woman loves another man, she feels that she is betraying a duty, and thus has to deceive with greater skill, refining her perfidy; while the man, feeling himself the cause of the infraction and the victor over another man, becomes legitimately proud, and soon moves on to a less harsh and less secret sentiment—that fine fatuousness that is the gleaming sweat given off by merit.

Whether my explanation is true or not, I am content to leave it written on this page, for the use of the ages, that women's indiscretion is a sham invented by men; in love, at least, they are veritable sepulchers. They are, however, often brought to ruin by clumsiness, or restlessness, or failing to resist gestures or gazes; and that is why a great lady and a fine spirit, the Queen of Navarre, once employed the following metaphor to say that every amorous adventure would be found out, sooner or later: "There is no little dog so well trained that it cannot be heard to bark."[1]

CHAPTER CXXXII

NOT TO BE TAKEN
SERIOUSLY

Upon quoting the words of the Queen of Navarre, it has occurred to me that around here, when a person sees another
who's out of sorts, he tends to ask: "Well, now, who's killed
your little dogs?" as if to say, "Who's put an end to your affairs, your secret adventures, etc." But this chapter isn't to be
taken seriously.

CHAPTER CXXXIII

HELVÉTIUS'S PRINCIPLE

We were at the point at which the naval officer had just extracted a confession from me about my affair with Virgília, and here I will correct Helvétius's principle[1]—or, rather, explain it. It was in my interest to remain silent; to confirm suspicions of an old affair would be to awaken some slumbering hatred, give rise to a scandal, or at the very least acquire a reputation as indiscreet. Such were my interests; and a superficial reading of Helvétius's principle would indicate that, accordingly, I ought to have fallen silent. But I have already presented the mainspring of masculine indiscretion; ahead of the interest posed by *safety*, there was another, that of *vanity*, which is more intimate and more immediate: the first was reflective, and supposed a preceding syllogism, while the second was spontaneous, instinctive, and sprang from the entrails; finally, the first had a remote effect, and the second, a direct one. Conclusion: Helvétius's principle held true in my case—the difference is that the interest in question was not apparent, but hidden.

CHAPTER CXXXIV

FIFTY YEARS

I have not told you yet—but I'll tell you now—that when Virgília went down the stairs and the naval officer touched me on the shoulder, I was fifty years old. My life itself, therefore, was heading down the stairs; or the best part of it, at least, a part full of pleasure, agitations, and frights—cloaked in deception and duplicity—but the best part of it, in the end, if we must speak in ordinary language. If, however, we employ another, more sublime language, then the best part was that which remained, as I will have the honor of telling you in the few pages left in this book.

Fifty years old! There was no need to confess it, really. You'll already have noticed that my style is no longer so nimble as in its first days. On that occasion, after my dialogue with the naval officer, who put on his cloak and left, I'll confess that I grew somewhat sad. I returned to the salon, where it occurred to me to dance a polka and be intoxicated by the lights, the flowers, the crystals, the pretty eyes, and the light hum of private conversations. And I do not regret it; I grew young again. But half an hour later, when I retired from the ball at four in the morning, what did I find in the back of my carriage? My fifty years. There they were, the stubborn things, neither numbed with cold nor stiff with rheumatism, but dozing away their weariness, rather anxious for a bed and repose. Then— behold just how far the imagination of a drowsy man can go— then I seemed to hear this, from a bat perched on the roof of the coach: Mr. Brás Cubas, your rejuvenation lay in the hall, in the crystals, the lights, the silks—that is, in others.

CHAPTER CXXXV

OBLIVION

And now I feel that if any lady has made it this far, she will close the book and never read the rest. For her, the only interesting part of my life, which was love, has been snuffed out. Fifty years old! Not yet infirmity, but no longer vigor. Let another ten come, and I shall understand what an Englishman once said; I will understand "what it is to find none who can remember my parents, and with what a face OBLIVION will look upon me."[1]

Let the name be printed in small capitals. OBLIVION! It is only right that all due honor be given to a figure so despised and so worthy, that tardy but unfailing guest. The lady who shone at the dawn of the current monarchy feels his presence, but it is all the more painful for she who flaunted her blooming charms under the administration of the Marquis of Paraná,[2] for her triumph is closer at hand, and she may be given to feeling that her rivals have stolen her carriage. If she is worthy of herself, she will not persist in trying to stir that lifeless or dying memory; she does not seek in today's gaze the same warmth of yesterday's, when those setting out on the march of life were others, their souls gay and their feet swift. *Tempora mutantur.* She understands the nature of the whirlwind, which carries off the leaves from the grove and the rags from the road, saving none and pitying none; and if she has a shred of philosophy in her, she will not envy, but rather grieve for those who have stolen her carriage, as they, too, will be helped to dismount by that unflagging footman OBLIVION. A spectacle put on to amuse the planet Saturn, which has been quite bored of late.

CHAPTER CXXXVI

USELESSNESS

But, either I am very much mistaken, or I have just written a useless chapter.

THE SHAKO

And then again, no; it sums up exactly what I reflected on the following day to Quincas Borba, to which I added that I felt dejected, and a thousand other sad things. But the philosopher, with his superior judgment, bellowed at me that I was slipping down the fatal slope of melancholy.

"My dear Brás Cubas, don't let yourself be overcome by these vapors. The deuce! You must be a man! Be strong! Fight! Win! Shine! Influence! Dominate! Fifty is the age for wisdom and government. Take heart, Brás Cubas; don't go soft. What have you to do with the passage from ruin to ruin, flower to flower? You must try to savor life; and know that the worst philosophy is that of the sniveler who lies on the riverbank to bemoan the never-ending flow of the waters. It is their business to never come to rest; come to terms with that law, and try to make the most of it."

The authority of a great philosopher is felt in the smallest things. Quincas Borba's words had the magic effect of shaking me out of my mental and moral torpor. Let's have at it; govern we will, it's high time. Until then, I had not intervened in the great debates. I had been courting a minister's position through bowing and scraping, teas, commissions, and votes; and the position had not come. I would have to seize the rostrum.

I started slowly. Three days later, during a discussion on the budget for the Ministry of Justice, I took the opportunity to ask the minister modestly if he didn't think it wise to reduce the size of the National Guard's shakos. The object of the question was not of a great scale, but even so, I demonstrated that it was not unworthy of the cogitations of a statesman; and

I cited Philopoemen, who ordered that his troops' bucklers be replaced with larger shields and their spears with heavier pikes, a fact that history did not find unbefitting the gravity of its pages. Our shakos were in need of a profound trimming, not only because they were inelegant but also because they were unhygienic. Out on parades, under the sun, the excessive heat they produced might prove fatal. Given that one of Hippocrates' precepts was to keep one's head cool, it seemed callous to force a citizen to risk his health and life, and hence the future of his family, out of purely sartorial considerations. The Chamber and the administration ought to recall that the National Guard was the bulwark of liberty and independence, and that citizens called to a service that was freely bestowed, habitual, and arduous were entitled to have their burden lessened by the establishment of a light and comfortable uniform. I added that the weight of the shako was casting citizens' heads down, and the nation needed men whose brows might rise, proud and serene, in the face of power; and I concluded with this idea: the weeping willow, which bends its branches toward the earth, grows in cemeteries; the palm, erect and steadfast, grows in the wilderness, in public squares, and in gardens.

The speech was variously received. As for its form, its bursts of eloquence, the literary and philosophical elements, the opinion was unanimous: they all told me that it was perfect, and that no one had ever pulled so many ideas out of a shako. But many judged the political part of it deplorable; some called it a parliamentary disaster; in the end, I got word that others already counted me in the ranks of the opposition, among them the oppositionists in the Chamber, who went so far as to insinuate that a motion of no confidence might be in order. I forcefully repudiated this interpretation, which was not merely erroneous, but also slanderous, my support for the cabinet being known to all; I added that the need to reduce the shako was not so great that it could not wait some years; and that in any case, I had reached a compromise on the extent of the cut, contenting myself with three-quarters of an inch, or even less; finally, even if my idea were not to be adopted, I was satisfied with simply having introduced it in debate.

THE POSTHUMOUS MEMOIRS OF BRÁS CUBAS

Quincas Borba, however, had no reservations.

"I am not a man of politics," he told me at supper; "I can't say whether you acted wisely or not; but I do know that you delivered an excellent speech."

And then he recalled the most striking parts, the beautiful images, the robust arguments, with the measured praise that so befits a great philosopher; then he took the issue to heart and impugned the shako with such force and lucidity that he wound up wholly convincing me of the danger it posed.

CHAPTER CXXXVIII

TO A CRITIC

My dear critic,

Some pages ago, upon saying that I was fifty years old, I added: "You'll already have noticed that my style is no longer so nimble as in its first days." You may find this incomprehensible, given my present state; but I would call your attention to the subtlety of my remark. I do not mean that I am older now than when I began the book. Death does not age one. What I do mean is that at every stage of the narration of my life, I experience the corresponding sensations. So help me God, I have to explain everything!

CHAPTER CXXXIX

OF HOW I DID NOT BECOME A MINISTER OF STATE

. . . .
. . . .

CHAPTER CXL

WHICH EXPLAINS
THE PREVIOUS

Some things are better said by falling silent; this is the case with the previous chapter. Those with dashed ambitions of their own may comprehend it. If the passion for power is the strongest of all, as some have said, then imagine my despair, pain, and dejection on the day I lost my seat in the Chamber of Deputies. All my hopes abandoned me; my political career was at an end. And mark that Quincas Borba, through philosophical inductions, concluded that my ambition was not a true passion for power but merely a whim, a desire to amuse myself. In his opinion, this sentiment, while not more profound, is much more bothersome, on par with women's love of lace and finery. Cromwells or Bonapartes, he added, those who positively burn with the passion for power, will get there by force, by hook or by crook. I did not share that sentiment; my sentiment, lacking their strength, lacked their certainty of result; hence my greater affliction, disenchantment, and sorrow. My sentiment, according to Humanitism . . .

"The devil with you and your Humanitism," I broke in. "I'm fed up with philosophies that get me nowhere."

The harshness of this interruption, given the stature of the philosopher, was as good as an affront; but he forgave the irritation with which I spoke to him. Coffee was brought in; it was one o'clock in the afternoon, and we were in my study, a handsome study overlooking the grounds, with good books and *objets d'art*, a Voltaire among them, a bronze Voltaire whose sarcastic smirk seemed all the sharper as he looked on me just then, the scoundrel; excellent chairs; outside there was the sun, a tremendous sun, which Quincas Borba—either poking fun or poetizing, I don't know—referred to as one of the ministers of nature; a cool breeze was blowing, and the sky was blue. In each window—there were three—there hung a cage with birds, chirruping a rustic opera. All bore the appearance of a conspiracy of things against man: and, though I was in *my* study, looking at *my* grounds, sitting in *my* chair, listening to *my* birds, next to *my* books, illuminated by *my* sun, none of it was enough to cure me of my longing for that other chair, which was not mine.[1]

CHAPTER CXLI

THE DOGS

"Well, what do you intend to do now?" Quincas Borba asked me, going to rest his empty coffee cup on a windowsill.

"I don't know; I'll hide my head in Tijuca; I'll flee from men. I'm ashamed, I'm disgusted. So many dreams, my dear Borba, so many dreams, and I'm nothing."

"Nothing!" Quincas Borba interrupted with a look of indignation.

To distract me, he invited me out, and we headed over toward Engenho Velho. We went on foot, philosophizing away. I shall never forget the good that walk did me. The words of that great man were a cordial of wisdom. He told me that I could not flee from combat; if the rostrum was closed to me, it was incumbent upon me to open a newspaper. He even used a less elevated expression, thus showing that philosophical language might fortify itself with the slang of the streets. Found a newspaper, he told me, and "bust up their little racket."

"A magnificent idea! I'll found a newspaper, I'll tear them apart, I'll . . ."

"Fight. Maybe you'll tear them apart, maybe you won't, what's essential is that you fight. To live is to fight. A life without struggle is a dead sea at the heart of the universal organism."

A bit farther on, we came across a dogfight, an incident with no significance to the eye of a common man. Quincas Borba had me stop and observe the dogs. There were two of them. He noted that nearby was a bone, the motive for the war, and further called my attention to the fact that the bone had no meat on it. A plain, bare bone. The dogs were biting one another, growling, with fury in their eyes . . . Quincas Borba put his walking-stick under his arm, seemingly in ecstasy.

"How beautiful it is!" he said from time to time.

I wanted to tear myself away, but I couldn't; he was rooted to the ground, and began walking again only when the fight ceased entirely and one of the dogs, bitten and defeated, went to take its hunger elsewhere. I noted that he was sincerely joyful, although he contained that joy, as befitted a great philosopher. He had me observe the beauty of the spectacle, recalled the object of the struggle, and concluded that the dogs were hungry; but the privation of sustenance meant nothing in the grand scope of philosophy. Nor did he neglect to mention that in some parts of the globe the spectacle is even grander: human creatures are the ones struggling with the dogs for bones and other, less appetizing morsels; a struggle that becomes infinitely more complicated, as man's intelligence enters into it, with all the wisdom he has accumulated over the ages, et cetera.

CHAPTER CXLII

THE SECRET REQUEST

"What a multitude of things there are in a minuet!"[1] as some-one once said. What a multitude of things there are in a dog-fight! But I was no servile or fearful disciple, loath to make a reasonable objection here or there. As we walked, I said that a doubt had arisen in my mind; the advantage to be had in fight-ing over food with dogs was not quite clear. He responded with exceptional gentleness:

"Fighting over it with other men is more logical, as the con-tenders are of the same condition, and the bone will simply go to the strongest. But why would the spectacle be any less grand were we to fight with dogs over a bone? There are those who voluntarily eat grasshoppers, like the Precursor, or worse, like Ezekiel;[2] it follows that bad things are edible; what remains to be seen is whether it is worthier for a man to fight for them out of a natural need or to prefer to do so in obedience to an exal-tation that is religious, and hence modifiable, whereas hunger is eternal, like life and like death."

We had reached the door of my house; I was given a letter and told that it had come from a lady. We went in, and Quin-cas Borba, with his philosopher's discretion, went off to read the spines of the books in one of the bookcases while I read the letter, which was from Virgília:

> My good friend,
> Dona Plácida is quite poorly. I beg of you to do
> something for her; she is living on Escadinhas Alley;

see if you can manage to place her in the Santa Casa
da Misericórdia.

Your sincere friend,

This was not Virgília's fine and correct hand, but a coarse, un-
even scrawl; the V of the signature was nothing more than a
scribble with no alphabetic intention, such that if the letter
were to come to light, it would be quite difficult to attribute its
authorship to her. I turned the paper over, and over again.
Poor Dona Plácida! But I had left her the five thousand milréis
from Botafogo Beach, and I could not understand how . . .

"You'll understand," said Quincas Borba, taking a book
from the shelf.

"What?" I asked, startled.

"You'll understand that I've only told you the truth. Pascal is
one of my spiritual grandfathers; and though my philosophy is
worth more than his, I cannot deny that he was a great man.
Now, what does he say on this page?" And, hat on head, walking-
stick under his arm, he pointed out the line with a finger. "What
does he say? He says that man has 'a great advantage over the rest
of the universe: he knows that he dies, while the universe knows
nothing of it.'³ You see? The man who fights over a bone with a
dog thus has a great advantage over it, that of knowing that he is
hungry; and this is what makes the struggle grand, as I was saying. 'He knows that he dies' is a profound expression; and yet I
believe that mine is profounder still: he knows that he is hungry.
For the fact of death, we might say, limits human understanding;
the awareness of extinction lasts but a brief moment and ends forevermore, while hunger has the advantage of returning and pro-
longing our conscious state. It seems to me (if there's no immodesty
in saying so) that Pascal's formula is inferior to mine, although it
does remain a great thought, and Pascal, a great man."

CHAPTER CXLIII

I WON'T GO

While he returned the book to the shelf, I reread the note. At supper, seeing that I spoke little, chewed endlessly without swallowing, and stared at the corner, the end of the table, a dish, a chair, or an invisible fly, he said:

"There's something wrong with you; am I right in guessing that it was the letter?"

"Yes."

Indeed, I was quite vexed, bothered by Virgília's request. I had given Dona Plácida five thousand milréis; I highly doubted that anyone could be more generous than I was, even close to it. Five thousand! And what had she done with them? She'd thrown them away, of course, squandered them on great parties, and now it was off to the Misericórdia, and I was to take her! A body may die anywhere at all. Besides, I didn't know if I remembered where this Escadinhas Alley was; but to judge by the name, it was probably some cramped, dark corner of the city.[1] I'd have to go there, be the object of the neighbors' attention, knock on doors, et cetera. What a nuisance! I won't go.

CHAPTER CXLIV

RELATIVE UTILITY

But night, that good counselor, reflected that in the name of courtesy I should obey the wishes of my former lady.

"Overdue bills must be paid all the sooner," I said to myself as I got up.

After breakfast I went to Dona Plácida's house; I found a bundle of bones wrapped in tatters, stretched out on an old, repulsive pallet, to which I handed over some money. The next day I had her moved to the Misericórdia, where she died a week later. That's not quite it: morning found her dead; she left life furtively, just as she had entered it. Once again I asked myself, as I had in Chapter LXXV, if it was for this that the sacristan at the See and the sweetmaker had brought Dona Plácida into the world, in a moment of particular good feeling. But I soon realized that were it not for Dona Plácida, my affair with Virgília might have been interrupted or broken off entirely in its full bloom; hence, that was what Dona Plácida's life was good for. A relative utility, I'll grant you that; but what the deuce is absolute in this world?

CHAPTER CXLV

SIMPLY REPEATING

As for the five thousand milréis, it's not worth recounting that a stonemason in the neighborhood pretended to be in love with Dona Plácida, managed to arouse her sentiments, or her vanity, and married her; and that after a few months he devised some business, sold all the bonds, and fled with the money. It's not worth it. It would be just the same as the story of Quincas Borba's dogs. Simply repeating a chapter.

CHAPTER CXLVI

THE PROSPECTUS

It was high time to found the newspaper. I drew up the prospectus, which was a political application of Humanitism; but
since Quincas Borba had yet to publish his book (which he
was perfecting year by year), we agreed to make no reference
to it. Quincas Borba requested only a signed, confidential declaration that certain new principles applied to politics had
been taken from his manuscript.

This was the cream of prospectuses; it promised to heal society, destroy abuses, and defend sound principles of liberty
and conservation; it appealed to commerce and agriculture; it
quoted Guizot and Ledru-Rollin; and it finished with this
threat, which Quincas Borba found small-minded and narrow: "The new doctrine which we profess must inevitably
overturn the present administration." I must confess that,
under the political circumstances, the prospectus seemed a
masterpiece to me. As for the threat at the end, which Quincas
Borba found small-minded, I demonstrated to him that it was
saturated with the purest Humanitism, as he himself would
confess some time later. Humanitism excluded nothing; Napoleon's wars and a scuffle between nanny goats were, according
to our doctrine, equally sublime, with the difference that Napoleon's soldiers knew it when they died, something that apparently does not happen with nanny goats. I was doing
nothing more than applying our philosophical formula to the
prevailing circumstances: Humanitas wished to substitute Humanitas for the welfare of Humanitas.

"My beloved disciple, my caliph," cried Quincas Borba,

with a note of tenderness that I had not heard in him before. "I may now say, as the great Mohammed did: were the sun and moon to be set against me, I would not abandon my ideas.[1] You must believe, my dear Brás Cubas, that this is the everlasting truth, older than worlds, which will outlive the ages."

CHAPTER CXLVII

FOOLISHNESS

Straightaway I sent a discreet note off to the press, saying that an opposition newspaper would likely begin printing in a few weeks' time, under the direction of Dr. Brás Cubas. Quincas Borba, to whom I read the note, took up the pen and, in a spirit of truly humanistic brotherhood, added the following after my name: "one of the most glorious members of the last Chamber."

The following day, Cotrim came by my house. He was somewhat disturbed but disguised it, striving to look calm, even cheery. He had seen the note in the paper and thought that he should, as a friend and relative, dissuade me from such a notion. It was an error, a fatal error. He explained that I would be placing myself in a difficult situation, and, one way or another, shutting the door to Parliament. Not only was this a positively admirable administration—about which I might very well disagree—but, moreover, it would certainly have a long life; what could I gain by indisposing it against me? Some of the ministers were fond of me; there might come a vacancy, and . . . I interrupted him then to say that I had meditated at length over the step I was to take, and I would not retreat an inch. I went so far as to suggest that he read the prospectus, but he refused forcefully, saying that he wanted to have not the slightest part in my foolishness.

"It's pure foolishness," he repeated. "Think for a few days, and you'll see that it's foolishness."

Sabina said the same thing that night at the theater. She left her daughter in the box with Cotrim and took me out into the corridor.

"Brother Brás, what are you doing?" she asked me, distressed. "Why on earth would you provoke the government for no reason, when you could . . ."

I explained that it would not befit me to beg for a chair in Parliament, and that my idea was to overturn the administration, for I thought it was no match for the challenges of the day—not to mention that it was out of line with a certain philosophical formula. I assured her that I would always employ a courteous, though forceful tone. Violence was not a seasoning that pleased my palate. Sabina tapped her fan on the tips of her fingers, shook her head, and returned to the matter, alternating between supplication and threats; I told her no, no, and no. Disabused of her hopes, she accused me of preferring the counsel of jealous strangers to hers and her husband's.

"Well, do as you see fit," she concluded. "We've done our duty."

She turned her back on me and returned to the box.

CHAPTER CXLVIII

THE INSOLUBLE PROBLEM

I published the newspaper. Twenty-four hours later, there appeared in other papers a declaration from Cotrim, the substance of which was that as he was not a member of any of the parties into which the nation was divided, he thought it expedient to make it clearly known that he had no influence or any part, direct or indirect, in the newspaper of his brother-in-law, Dr. Brás Cubas, whose ideas and political comportment he repudiated entirely. The current administration (as well as any other composed of equal talents, for that matter) seemed to him perfectly apt to promote the public good.

I could not believe my eyes. I rubbed them once, twice, and reread this extraordinary, inopportune, wholly enigmatic declaration. If he had nothing to do with the parties, then what was something as ordinary as the publication of a newspaper to him? Not every citizen who finds an administration good or bad takes it upon himself to make declarations of the sort in the press, nor is he obliged to. Cotrim's intruding on the matter was truly a mystery, and his personal aggression toward me not less so. Our relations had been plain and good-natured; I could think of no discord, no shadow, nothing after the reconciliation. On the contrary, my recollections were of nothing but kindnesses; for example, when I was a deputy, I was able to obtain contracts for him with the Navy Arsenal, contracts that he continued fulfilling with the greatest punctuality, and which, he had told me a few weeks earlier, might earn him some two hundred thousand milréis in another three years' time. Was the memory of such a kindness powerless to keep him from publicly affronting his brother-in-law? The reason for the declaration must have been quite compelling, leading him as it did to both intemperance and ingratitude; I confess that it posed an insoluble problem . . .

THEORY OF BENEFITS

. . . so insoluble that even Quincas Borba was unable to solve it, despite having studied it at length and with great good will.

"Good riddance!" he concluded; "not every problem is worth five minutes of attention."

As for the charge of ingratitude, Quincas Borba rejected it entirely, not on the grounds of its improbability, but as wholly absurd, for it did not follow the conclusions of a good humanistic philosophy.

"You cannot deny me one fact," he said, "which is that the pleasure of the benefiter is always greater than that of the beneficiary. What is a benefit? It is an act that causes some privation on the part of the beneficiary to cease. Once the essential effect is produced—that is, once the privation has indeed ceased— the organism returns to its previous state of indifference. Suppose you have tightened your waistband too far; to make the discomfort cease, you loosen it, breathe, savor an instant of pleasure, your organism returns to indifference, and you no longer think of your fingers, which carried out the act. Just as nothing lasts, so it is natural that memory should fade; it is no air plant, it needs soil in which to root. The expectation of other favors, of course, will always preserve the beneficiary's recollection of the first; but this fact, which is, incidentally, one of the most sublime that philosophy may have the opportunity to observe, can be explained by the memory of privation—or, to use another formula, by the privation that continues in memory, echoing that past pain and advising that an opportune remedy be kept at hand. I'll not deny that, even in the absence of such a thing, the memory of the kindness may at times persist, accompanied by a degree of affection; but these are true aberrations, with no value in the eyes of a philosopher."

"But," I replied, "if there is no reason for the memory of the kindness to last in the mind of he who receives it, there must be even less reason for it to linger with the bestower. I wish you would explain that point."

"One doesn't explain that which is evident by nature," retorted Quincas Borba; "but I'll say one thing more. The persistence of the benefit in the memory of he who practices it may be explained by the very nature of the benefit and its effects. First, there is a sentiment of a good deed, and by deduction the awareness that we are capable of good deeds; second, one enjoys the conviction that one is superior to another creature, superior in state and in means; and this is one of the most legitimately pleasing things for the human organism, according to the best opinions. Erasmus, who wrote a few good things in his *Praise of Folly*, called readers' attention to the beneficence with which two donkeys scratch one another.[1] Far be it from me to reject this observation of Erasmus's; but I will say what he did not, which is that if one of the donkeys scratches the other one better, he must have a special gleam of satisfaction in his eyes. Why does a pretty woman look in the mirror so often, if not because she finds herself to be pretty, and because this gives her a measure of superiority over a multitude of other, less pretty or positively ugly women? Conscience is the same; it contemplates itself frequently when it finds itself beautiful. Remorse is nothing but the grimace of a conscience that sees itself to be hideous. Do not forget that, since everything is a simple irradiation of Humanitas, both the benefit and its effects are perfectly admirable phenomena."

CHAPTER CL

ROTATION AND
TRANSLATION[1]

Each undertaking, affection, or age contains an entire cycle of
human life. The first issue of my newspaper filled my soul with
a vast dawn, crowned me with verdure, and gave me back the
gaiety of youth. Six months later the hour of old age struck,
and two weeks after that came death, which was furtive, just
as Dona Plácida's had been. On the day when morning found
the newspaper dead, I sighed like a man come from a long
journey. And so if I say that human life nourishes and gives
rise to other lives, which may be more or less fleeting, just as
the body feeds its parasites, I believe that I will not be saying
something entirely absurd. But rather than trust in a figure of
speech that may prove somewhat lacking in clarity and suit-
ability, I'll call upon an astronomical image: in his path around
the great mystery, man executes a dual maneuver of both rotation and translation; he has his days, which are as unequal as
those on Jupiter, and with them he makes up his year, which
may be more or less long.

Just as I was concluding my rotation, Lobo Neves was concluding his translation. He died with one foot on the ministe-
rial step. Word had it for a few weeks that he would be a
minister; and just as the rumor filled me with no end of irritation and envy, it is not impossible that the news of his death
may have brought me a measure of tranquility, relief, and a
minute or two of pleasure. Pleasure is a strong word, but it is
true; I swear to the ages that it is the purest truth.

I went to the funeral. In the mortuary chapel I found Virgília by the coffin, sobbing. When she lifted her head, I saw that
she was really crying. As the funeral procession headed out,

she embraced the coffin, distraught; she had to be removed from it and taken inside. I say to you that her tears were genuine. I went to the cemetery; and, if the truth be told, I could barely bring myself to speak; I had a stone in my throat, or on my conscience. At the cemetery, principally when I tossed my spadeful of lime over the coffin down in the grave, the dull thud of the lime gave me a passing but disagreeable shudder; and all that afternoon had the weight and color of lead; the cemetery, the black clothes . . .

CHAPTER CLI

PHILOSOPHY OF EPITAPHS

I left, moving away from the groups and pretending to read the epitaphs. I do like epitaphs; they are, among civilized folk, an expression of that secret, pious egotism that induces man to wrench from death at least a scrap of the shade that has passed on. Hence, perhaps, the inconsolable sorrow of those who have their dead in a pauper's grave; it seems to them that the anonymous rot seeps into their own souls.

CHAPTER CLII

VESPASIAN'S COIN

They had all gone; only my carriage awaited its master. I lit a cigar and distanced myself from the cemetery. I could not shake the funeral ceremony from my eyes, nor Virgília's sobbing from my ears. The sobbing, in particular, had the vague and mysterious sound of a problem. Virgília had betrayed her husband in all sincerity and was now weeping for him in all sincerity. There you have a difficult combination, which I struggled to make sense of along the whole route; at home, however, as I got out of my carriage, I suspected that the combination was not merely possible but even natural. Sweet Nature! The toll of pain is like Vespasian's coin;[1] it does not smell of its origin, and may be reaped from good as well as from evil. Morality may reprehend my accomplice; but that is of no consequence to you, implacable friend, so long as you receive your tears in a timely manner. Sweet, thrice sweet Nature!

CHAPTER CLIII

THE ALIENIST

I was beginning to grow plaintive, to which I preferred sleep. I slept, dreamt that I was a nabob, and awoke wanting to be one. It often pleased me to imagine these contrasts of religion, state, and creed. A few days earlier I had pondered the hypothesis of a social, religious, and political revolution that might transform the archbishop of Canterbury into a simple tax collector in Petrópolis, and I carried out lengthy calculations to determine whether the tax collector would eliminate the archbishop, or whether the archbishop would reject the tax collector, or what portion of an archbishop may lie within a tax collector, and what share of a tax collector may suit an archbishop, et cetera. Apparently insoluble questions, but in reality they are quite soluble, once one realizes that in a single archbishop there may actually be two archbishops: the one from the bull and the other one. It's settled, I'll be a nabob.

It was just a joke; I told it, however, to Quincas Borba, who looked at me with no little caution and pity, and subsequently had the graciousness to inform me that I was mad. I laughed at first; but the high conviction with which the philosopher spoke frightened me somewhat. My only objection against Quincas Borba's word was that I didn't feel mad, but since madmen do not normally have a different opinion of themselves, this objection was rendered worthless. Now, just see if there is any fundament to the popular belief that philosophers are indifferent to the smallest matters. The next day Quincas Borba sent an alienist to examine me. I knew him and was stricken with fear. He, however, behaved with the greatest delicacy and skill, bidding me farewell so gaily that I resolved to ask if he truly did not think me mad.

"No," he said, smiling, "few men have as much sense as you, sir."

"So then Quincas Borba was wrong?"

"Roundly so." And then: "Quite the contrary. If you are a friend to him . . . I do ask that you find some sort of diversion for him . . . something to . . ."

"Good heavens! Do you really think so? . . . A man of such spirit, a philosopher!"

"No matter. Madness may enter any house."

You may imagine my affliction. The alienist, seeing the effect of his words, recognized that I was indeed a friend of Quincas Borba's and attempted to diminish the gravity of his diagnosis. He noted that it might come to nothing, and even added that a little dash of lunacy, far from doing any harm, gave a certain spice to life. When I rejected this opinion, horrified, the alienist smiled and said something so extraordinary, so very extraordinary, that it merits nothing less than a chapter.

CHAPTER CLIV

THE SHIPS OF PIRAEUS

"You must recall," the alienist said to me, "that famous Athenian maniac who believed that all the ships docked at the port of Piraeus were his property. He was nothing but a poor wretch who might not even have had Diogenes' barrel to sleep in; but the imaginary possession of those ships was worth all the drachmas in Hellas to him. Now, within every one of us there is an Athenian maniac; and anyone who swears that he has never mentally owned at least two or three schooners is certainly lying."

"Even you?" I asked him.

"Even me."

"And me?"

"You as well; and your servant. Especially him, if that man beating the carpets at the window is your servant."

Indeed, one of my servants was beating the carpets as we spoke in the garden, off to the side. The alienist observed that he had thrown open all the windows some time ago, drawn the curtains, exposed the richly furnished drawing room so it might be seen from the outside, and concluded:

"This servant of yours has the Athenian's mania: he believes the ships are his, and that hour of illusion will give him the greatest happiness on earth."

CHAPTER CLV

A WARMHEARTED THOUGHT

"If the alienist is right," I said to myself, "there's no use pitying Quincas Borba; it's all a matter of degrees. Nevertheless, it is only right that I care for him and keep his brain free of maniacs from other localities."

CHAPTER CLVI

THE PRIDE OF SERVILITY

Quincas Borba disagreed with the alienist in relation to my servant.

"He might, metaphorically," said he, "attribute the Athenian's mania to your servant, but metaphors are neither ideas nor observations taken from nature. What your servant has is a noble sentiment perfectly in keeping with the laws of Humanitism: the pride of servility. His intention is to show that he is not just *anyone's* servant."

Then he called my attention to the coachmen at grand houses, whose bearing is haughtier than their masters'; to hotel servants, whose degree of solicitude follows the social position of each guest, et cetera. And he concluded that this was all the expression of that same delicate and noble sentiment—ample proof that man, even when blacking boots, can be sublime.

BRILLIANT PHASE

"You're the sublime one," I declared, throwing my arms around his neck.

Indeed, it was impossible to believe that such a profound man could ever succumb to madness; that was what I said after I embraced him, as I revealed the alienist's suspicions. I cannot describe the impression that this revelation had on him; I remember that he shuddered and grew very pale.

It was around then that I reconciled once again with Cotrim, never having understood the cause of our differences. The reconciliation was opportune, since solitude was weighing on me and life had become the worst of fatigues: namely, the fatigue of the idle. Soon thereafter he invited me to join a lay brotherhood, which I did not do without first consulting Quincas Borba:

"Go, if you wish," the latter told me, "but only temporarily. I'll see to adding a dogmatic and liturgical element to my philosophy. Humanitism will be a religion itself, the religion of the future, the only true one. Christianity is only good for women and beggars, and the other religions are no better: they all tend toward the same vulgarity or weakness. The Christian paradise is a worthy emulator of its Muslim counterpart; and as for Buddha's Nirvana, it's no more than a notion hatched by paralytics. You shall see what humanistic religion is. The final absorption, the *contractive* phase, is the reconstitution of substance, not its annihilation, et cetera. Go wherever you are called; but never forget that you are my caliph."

Now behold my modesty; I joined the Third Order of ***, served in a few positions there, and this was the most brilliant phase of my life. And yet I am silent; I'll say nothing, nothing of my services, what I did for the poor and the sick, nor the rewards I reaped, nothing, I'll say nothing whatsoever.

Social economy might have something to gain if I were to show how any external reward pales beside a subjective and immediate one; but that would mean breaking the silence that I swore to keep on this score. Moreover, phenomena of the conscience are not easily analyzed; if I were to speak of one, I would have to speak of all those that hang on it, and in the end I would write an entire chapter on psychology. I will simply declare that it was the most brilliant phase of my life. The tableaux were mournful; they had the monotony of misfortune, which is just as tedious as that of pleasure, and perhaps worse. But the joy that one gives to the souls of the ill and the poor is a reward of some value; and let no one say that it is negative, for only the beneficiaries receive it. No; I received it in reflected form, and even so, it was so very great that it gave me an excellent idea of myself.

TWO ENCOUNTERS

After a few years, three or four, I had tired of the charge and I left it, not without an important donation that earned me a portrait in the sacristy. I will not finish the chapter, however, without saying that I witnessed the death, in the Order's hospital, of—guess who? . . . the lovely Marcela; and I saw her die on the very day when, upon visiting a tenement house to give out alms, I found . . . now you won't be able to guess . . . I found the flower of the thicket, Eugênia, Dona Eusébia and Vilaça's daughter, just as lame as I had left her, and even sadder.

Upon recognizing me she grew pale and lowered her eyes; but it lasted only an instant. She quickly raised her head and gazed at me with great dignity. I understood that she would take no alms from my pocket, and I held out my hand to her as I would to the wife of a capitalist. She greeted me and then shut herself in her small room. I never saw her again; I heard no more about her life, whether her mother had died, or what misfortune had brought her to such misery. I do know that she remained lame and sad. It was with that profound impression that I arrived at the hospital, where Marcela had been admitted the day before, and where I saw her expire half an hour later, ugly, thin, decrepit . . .

CHAPTER CLIX

SEMIDEMENTIA

I understood then that I was old, and felt the need for some support; but Quincas Borba had set out six months earlier for Minas Gerais, taking with him the best of all philosophies. He returned four months later and came by my house one morning nearly in the state in which I had seen him in the Passeio Público. Now his gaze was transformed. He was demented. He told me that so as to perfect Humanitism, he had burned the whole manuscript and would begin again. The dogmatic part was completed, though unwritten; it was the true religion of the future.

"Do you swear by Humanitas?" he asked me.

"You know I do."

My voice could hardly escape my breast; and I had yet to discover the full, cruel truth. Quincas Borba was not only mad, but he also knew that he was mad, and this shred of consciousness, like a flickering lamp in the gloom, greatly aggravated the horror of the situation. He knew it, and was not vexed by the affliction; on the contrary, he told me that this was a test by Humanitas, which liked to entertain itself this way. He would recite long chapters of the book to me, and antiphons, and spiritual litanies; he went so far as to perform a sacred dance that he had invented for the ceremonies of Humanitism. The frightful charm with which he lifted and shook his legs was singularly fantastical. At other times he would sulk in a corner, his eyes staring, eyes in which from time to time there flashed a persistent beam of sanity, as doleful as a tear . . .

He died shortly thereafter, at my house, swearing endlessly that pain was an illusion and that Pangloss, poor slandered Dr. Pangloss, was not as foolish as Voltaire supposed.

CHAPTER CLX

ON NEGATIVES

Between Quincas Borba's death and mine, there came the events narrated in the first part of the book. Chief among them was the invention of the Brás Cubas Plaster, which died along with me, thanks to my illness. Divine plaster, you would have given me the first place among men, above wisdom and above wealth, for you were a genuine, heaven-sent inspiration. Chance decided against it; and that is why you all will remain hypochondriacs forevermore.

This last chapter is all negatives. I didn't attain fame with my plaster, I wasn't a minister, I was no caliph, and I never knew marriage. It is true that, alongside these lacks, I was granted the good fortune of not having to earn my bread with the sweat of my brow. What's more, I didn't suffer Dona Plácida's death, or Quincas Borba's semidementia. What with one thing and another, anyone might imagine that there was neither want nor surplus, and consequently that I came out even with life. And he would imagine wrongly; because, upon arriving at the other side of the veil, I found myself with a small sum, which is the final negative in this chapter of negatives: I had no children; I did not bequeath to any creature the legacy of our misery.

Notes

PROLOGUE TO THE FOURTH EDITION

1. The title *Memórias Póstumas de Brás Cubas* alludes to *Mémoires d'Outre-Tombe* (Memoirs from Beyond the Grave), by René de Chateaubriand (1768–1848), which were published in 1849–1850, after the author's death.
2. While Machado wrote this preface for the third edition in book form, it came to be considered the fourth edition overall; as the author indicates, the narrative was originally published in serial form in the *Revista Brazileira*.
3. João Capistrano de Abreu (1853–1927) was a historian best known for his *Capítulos de História Colonial*; he also wrote on one of Machado's great literary precursors, the novelist José de Alencar.
4. Antônio Joaquim de Macedo Soares (1838–1905) was a keen-eyed and prolific literary critic in mid-nineteenth-century Rio.
5. One might say that *Viagens na Minha Terra* (Travels in My Homeland) is Portugal's belated response to *Tristram Shandy*, whose author Brás also references here. In the book, readers follow João Baptista da Silva Leitão de Almeida Garrett (1799–1854)—better known by his last pair of surnames—on a thirteen-day journey from Lisbon to the provincial town of Santarém, a travelogue liberally interwoven with historical, cultural, and sentimental digressions. Almeida Garrett's narrative was first published in serial form starting in 1843, and would be released in two volumes in 1846.
6. Laurence Sterne (1713–1768) is often the first author evoked when readers of English try to place Machado de Assis. His *Life and Opinions of Tristram Shandy, Gentleman* (1759–1767) remains as gloriously unlike anything else in its time as the *Posthumous Memoirs*; over the course of nine volumes Tristram

does his best to narrate his roundly silly background and journey through life, getting so sidetracked that his own birth comes only in Volume III.

7. The young military officer Xavier de Maistre (1763–1852), confined to his room for six weeks as punishment for dueling, took advantage of his quarantine to write *A Journey Around My Room* (1794). In the slim volume, he explores each and every item in his cramped quarters as if they were the sights of a strange land, with plenty of time left over to spin out fanciful digressions. Several allusions made in Maistre's *Journey* also appear throughout the *Posthumous Memoirs*, such as the Athenian maniac in Chapter CLIV.

TO THE READER

1. Marie-Henri Beyle (1783–1842), the novelist who went by the pen name Stendhal, opened his 1822 treatise *Love* by announcing that he was writing for only a hundred readers, of whom he knew but a few. A few decades later, Machado de Assis would join that select book club; he references the book here, in the note to the reader, and will return to it in Chapter CXXXI when discussing various forms of love.

2. In the first edition, the list of authors included an additional name: "Sterne, or Lamb, or Xavier de Maistre . . ." The excised Lamb is Charles Lamb (1775–1834), the essayist perhaps best known for his humorous essays under the pen name Elia. The Brazilian critic Eugênio Gomes, who devoted an article to examining the alterations between the version of the novel published in installments in the *Revista Brazileira* and subsequent editions, explained the omission as follows: while Machado admired and drew on Lamb, his essays are not as formally inventive as Maistre's or Sterne's works, and hence should not be understood as characterizing a "free form."

3. In this choice I diverge from the other translators of the novel. William Grossman, E. Percy Ellis, and Gregory Rabassa uncharacteristically agree that Brás is offering the displeased reader a "snap of the/my finger[s]." *Piparote*, however, being defined in dictionaries both period and modern as a "fillip"—a blow with the finger braced against the ball of the thumb—seems to be a clearly distinguished action. The image that it has always evoked for me is that of a massive Brás Cubas dispatching the reader

with a blow from his fingernail, just as he disposes of the corpse of the unfortunate black butterfly in Chapter XXXI. Since "fillip" is a word that would give me pause, I opted for the more colloquial "flick," hoping that context makes it clear that this is not an obscene gesture.

CHAPTER I: THE DEMISE OF THE AUTHOR

1. In the novel as it appeared in the *Revista Brazileira*, this chapter opened with a quotation from *As You Like It* (c. 1599) by William Shakespeare (1564–1616): "I will chide no breather in the world but myself; against whom I know most faults" (III.2). The quote in English was followed by Machado's Portuguese-language translation. Eugênio Gomes noted that while the epigraph was eliminated, Machado took a liking to his own translation of "breather"—*fôlego vivo*, or living breath—and used it multiple times in subsequent compositions.

2. The distinction between *autor defunto* and *defunto autor* is not immediately evident, especially for first-time readers. While the noun normally precedes the adjective in Portuguese, this can be inverted for poetic effect without altering the meaning of the phrase. *Defunto autor,* grammatically, may look identical to *autor defunto*: dead author/dead author. Here, however, there is a difference, as signaled by the phrase "for whom the tomb was another cradle." The first case is the traditional sense of "deceased/late" to modify "author"; in the second, *defunto* is the noun and *autor* is the adjective. William Grossman thus rendered the phrase as follows—"I am a deceased writer not in the sense of one who has written and is now deceased, but in the sense of one who has died and is now writing"—which is clear but less compact. Machado uses a similar phrasal structure in the short story "Manuscrito de um Sacristão" (A Sacristan's Manuscript) published in *Histórias sem Data* (1884): a character introduces himself as a "sacristão filósofo" and then as a "filósofo sacristão." In the first case, *sacristan* is the noun and *philosopher* is the adjective, and in the second the *philosopher* is the noun and *sacristan* the adjective—one might translate it as "sacristan-philosopher" and "philosopher-sacristan."

3. Brás is favorably comparing his memoirs to the first five books of the Hebrew Bible, also known as the Pentateuch or the Torah.

4. Catumbi, then a rural refuge on the other side of a mountain range from aristocratic Laranjeiras, has since been fully incorporated

into the fabric of metropolitan Rio de Janeiro. Rio natives coming to the book today may have difficulty imagining Brás's stately country home overlooking what is now a highway-scarred valley and the Sambódromo, the arena where the samba schools parade during Carnival.

5. This would have been the equivalent of $150,000 in U.S. dollars at the time—a few million today, when adjusted for inflation. The currency unit that Brás references is the *conto*, which was the equivalent of one thousand milréis or a million réis; so as to give readers a sense of that scale, and since most prices in the novel are expressed in terms of contos and milréis, I have translated all references to contos in terms of thousands of milréis. This and all subsequent estimates of value are based on contemporary exchange rates and the Measuring Worth Project calculator. My thanks to William Summerhill for his help with these calculations.

6. Brás is referencing Act III, Scene 1, of *Hamlet*, the "To be or not to be" soliloquy, in which the prince speaks of "The undiscovered country from whose bourn / No traveler returns."

7. The passage beginning with "It's true . . ." and ending with "to show it" was added between the *Revista Brazileira* printing and the novel's first publication in book form, in 1881. When first inserted, the passage was slightly different: "It's true, she suffered more. I won't say she tore her hair with grief or let herself roll across the coffin in epileptic throes." Multiple critics attribute the subsequent alteration to Machado's queasiness about referencing an epileptic fit, since he suffered from the disorder himself.

8. The illustrious traveler in question was François-René Chateaubriand (1768–1848), who observed the scene in his *Itinéraire de Paris à Jérusalem* (1811) and remarked on the constancy of the storks' voyages over thousands of years, almost seeming an insult in contrast with the endless changeability of men's affairs—hence "the ruins and the ages" to which the birds are solemnly indifferent.

CHAPTER II: THE PLASTER

1. The text itself contains very few clues as to the composition of the miracle medicine that springs full-fledged into Brás's mind. An *emplastro* or *emplasto* is defined in Francisco Solano Con-

stância's 1836 Portuguese-language dictionary as a medicine of soft consistency applied to a cloth and placed over a wound. This corresponds closely to the *Oxford English Dictionary*'s definition for plaster ("a solid medicinal or emollient substance spread on a bandage or dressing and applied to the skin, often becoming adhesive at body temperature"); an additional meaning, making the term even more fitting, is "A healing or soothing measure; (now) *esp.* an ineffective or short-term remedy."

2. The Sphinx's warning—translated into English as "Decipher me or be devoured," or "Decipher me or I'll devour you"—has come into Portuguese as the ringing *decifra-me ou devoro-te*, which is very pleasingly rhymed. In my search for a canonical English translation of the phrase, I found that this particular formulation doesn't feature in most accounts of Oedipus's triumph, whereas the Portuguese saying—likely due to its chiming ring—has become much more widely used. William Grossman took his cue from the rhyme in the original and came up with "Decipher me or I devour thee," and I came to prefer this to an unrhymed solution.

3. In both English and Portuguese, the meaning of the word "hypochondria" has drifted from the sense of melancholy—derived from "hypochondrium," defined by the *Oxford English Dictionary* as the "liver, gall-bladder, spleen, etc., formerly supposed to be the seat of melancholy and 'vapours'"—and converged with "hypochondriasis," a nervous disorder where patients believe themselves afflicted by multiple diseases. While William Grossman translates the remedy as an "anti-melancholy plaster," I have followed E. Percy Ellis and Gregory Rabassa in maintaining a term with "hypochondria" at its root, wishing to maintain this suggestive etymology, with its convergence of real and imagined ailments.

4. The *tercio* was a Spanish infantry unit used mainly in the sixteenth and seventeenth centuries—so named because in theory they were one-third pikemen, one-third swordsmen, and one-third arquebusiers or musketeers—which was adopted by Portugal before the union of the Iberian crowns (1580–1640) and maintained through the reestablishment of Portuguese independence. The efficacy of this model waned over the course of the seventeenth century, and *terços* had been transitioned into other units by the end of the eighteenth century. Thus, the regiments were "old" by the time Brás was born in 1805; but they had ceased to be a force of much significance a full century earlier.

CHAPTER III: GENEALOGY

1. Unlike Spain, Portugal declined to allow universities to be established in its South American colony. This served to maintain intellectual homogeneity among the elites, as the upper crust whose sons would seek higher education sent them to universities in Portugal such as Coimbra. This would begin to change only after the Portuguese court, fleeing Napoleon, came to settle in Rio de Janeiro in 1808.

2. The title of Count da Cunha was created for António Álvares da Cunha (1700–1791), the first viceroy of Brazil to govern the colony from Rio, which he did from 1763 to 1767.

3. While Brás Cubas, the Portuguese explorer, governed the captaincy of São Vicente (one of the provinces that made up colonial Brazil), it was founded by Martim Afonso de Sousa. Cubas did, however, found the settlement of Santos in the 1540s.

CHAPTER IV: THE FIXED IDEA

1. Camillo Benso, Count of Cavour (1810–1861), was one of the great architects of Italian unification. He eventually served as prime minister of the country, but governed for not even three months before succumbing.

2. While Brás perished in 1869, he had evidently been keeping up with international affairs through the time of the earthly publication of his memoirs in the early 1880s. Otto von Bismarck (1815–1898), the first chancellor of the German Empire, had been serving in the position since 1871 and would leave it only in 1890, physically unscathed by the position but having fallen out of favor with Kaiser Wilhelm II.

3. "Pumpkinhead" is a reference to the pun in Seneca's Menippean satire *Apocolocyntosis (Divi) Claudii*, or the *Gourdification of the Divine Claudius*, which imagines the emperor's transformation into a squash.

4. The poet Brás references is Victor Hugo (1802–1885), with his accusatory 1833 play *Lucrèce Borgia*. The medieval historian Ferdinand Gregorovius (1821–1891) authored a study, *Lucrezia Borgia: A Chapter from the Morals of the Italian Renaissance* (1874), which sought to rescue its subject from accounts that depicted her as a "moral monster" accused of incest and murder. The introduction proclaims her "the most unfortunate woman

in modern history," either "because she was guilty of the most hideous crimes," or "because she has been unjustly condemned by the world to bear its curse." His avowed aim was to steer clear of both paeans and attacks: hence, neither a lily nor a swamp.

5. The Battle of Salamis, a decisive conflict in the Greco-Persian wars, was a naval clash in 480 BCE in which the outnumbered Greeks staved off Xerxes and won a crucial victory.

6. The Augsburg Confession, presented in 1530 to the emperor Charles V, comprises the twenty-eight articles of faith at the foundation of the Lutheran churches.

7. Oliver Cromwell (1599–1658), Lord Protector of the Commonwealth of England, oversaw several incarnations of Parliament before dissolving the body entirely in 1653.

CHAPTER V: IN WHICH A LADY BETRAYS HERSELF

1. A literal translation of the Portuguese title would be "In Which a Lady's Ear Appears." This appears to be a translation of the French expression *montrer le bout de l'oreille*—to show the tip of one's ear, meaning to show one's true colors or betray one's true feelings. The concept recurs several times in the novel. Here, the lady's behavior runs the risk of revealing an illicit affair: hence my translation.

2. According to Herodotus, the Macrobians were legendarily long-lived, a report that eventually made their name synonymous with longevity. A look at mid-nineteenth-century Brazilian newspapers reveals that cases of people reported to be stupendously old were often listed under the heading *Macróbios*.

3. After this sentence, in the novel as published in the *Revista Brazileira*, this followed: "A puff of air was thus to me what the grain of sand was to Cromwell." Machado is likely referencing the passage on Oliver Cromwell's death of a urinary infection in the *Pensées (Thoughts)*, by Blaise Pascal (1623–1662), translated here by the Reverend Edward Craig: "Cromwell was about to desolate all Christendom. The royal family had been ruined, and his own would have been completely established, but for a small grain of sand which entered the ureter. Even Rome was about to tremble before him; but when this atom of gravel, which elsewhere was as nothing, was placed in that spot, behold

he dies, his family is degraded, and the king restored!" Machado would reference the grain of sand again in his column in *A Semana* on December 2, 1894, comparing the tiny but destructive grain to the even more devastating bacterium responsible for the then ongoing yellow fever epidemic.

CHAPTER VI: *CHIMÈNE, QUI L'EÛT DIT? RODRIGUE, QUI L'EÛT CRU?*

1. This is a quote from *El Cid* (1637), Act III, Scene 4, by Pierre Corneille (1606–1684), although the dialogues are reversed and the second is made into a question. The original read: "Chimène: Rodrigue, qui l'eût cru . . . / Don Rodrigue: Chimène, qui l'eût dit . . ." In Richard Wilbur's translation: "Chimène: Rodrigue, who dreamt . . . ? / Don Rodrigue: Chimène, whoever thought . . . ?"

2. In Isaiah 38, King Hezekiah is "sick unto death," and God turns back the sun—as evidenced by the way its shadow falls on a sundial—to show that he has heard his prayer. The remedy provided to the monarch by the prophet Isaiah is, appropriately, translated as a "plaister" in the King James Version.

3. In the original Portuguese, Brás refers to Juventa or Juventas, the Roman name for the divinity identified with Hebe, cupbearer to the gods who served them the food and libations that fed their eternal life.

4. These are festivities surrounding the feast of Saint John the Baptist, on June 23–24, close to the winter solstice in the Southern Hemisphere. In Brazil, celebrations have come to stretch throughout the month, taking in the feasts dedicated to Saint Anthony (on the 13th) and Saint Peter (on the 29th).

5. The name of Virgília and Damião Lobo Neves's son, for example, is—to put it mildly—a problem. *Nhonhô* is the only name by which we know the character, and it is a diminutive derived from a culturally freighted term, *senhor*, meaning "sir" or "master." The same term is used in reference to Brás at multiple points in the novel; in those instances I have translated it as "master," "young master," or the like, and preserved the word where it designates Virgília's son.

6. The noun *bacharel*, still used in contemporary Portuguese, has no easy English equivalent. It means "one who has received a university degree"; while this is easy enough to convey, the

sociolinguistic stumbling block is that the term is often used in reference to those without any profession, or need to have a profession. Nhonhô may have a law degree, but it is highly unlikely that he practices law; hence, he is identified simply by the fact of his degree. The term *licenciado*, used in reference to the Coimbra graduate Luís Cubas in Chapter III—the first Cubas man who had the privilege of studying rather than working—functions similarly.

7. George-Louis Leclerc, the Count of Buffon (1707–1788), was best known for his vast *Natural History, General and Particular*, the publication of which spanned decades and some thirty-six volumes.

CHAPTER VII: THE DELIRIUM

1. In the *Iliad*, Achilles' horse Xanthos is temporarily granted the power of speech by Hera and foresees his rider's death. In the Bible (Numbers 22:28), Balaam's ass is given voice by the Lord and remonstrates with her master for the beatings she has received.

2. In the Bible, Job curses the *day* on which he was born, and the *night* on which he was conceived. Of previous translators of the novel, William Grossman and E. Percy Ellis correct Machado to have Job cursing the day he was born, whereas Gregory Rabassa maintains the error—as he once wrote, "I have always maintained that if Homer nodded in the Greek he should nod in English"—and I have followed suit.

3. The term *ventre* comes from the Latin *venter*, meaning belly or abdomen, and its principal meaning in Portuguese has come to be "womb." Hence, in his translation of the novel, William Grossman has the exhortation to "open your belly and devour me," whereas Gregory Rabassa has "open up your womb and digest me." E. Percy Ellis steers clear of the female abdomen altogether with "swallow me whole and digest me." I opted for "maw," since it originally meant belly or womb, but gives the sense of jaws or a yawning opening; the notion of a womb digesting something would seem to betray a shaky command of anatomy. The same word appears in Chapter XIX in a similar sense, with the *ventre* of the sea opening up to receive a body; the other translators maintain "belly" (Grossman), "jaws" (Ellis), and "womb" (Rabassa).

CHAPTER VIII: REASON VERSUS FOLLY

1. The quotation from *Tartuffe, or The Impostor, or The Hypocrite*, by Jean-Baptiste Poquelin (1622–1673), better known as Molière, has been condensed somewhat from the original—"*C'est à vous d'en sortir, vous qui parlez en maître. / La maison m'appartient, je le ferai connaître*"—albeit condensed into an alexandrine verse in French. Adapting from Henri van Laun's translation, we might express the quotation as "The house belongs to me, it is for you to get out." In the play these words are proffered by the titular hypocrite, Tartuffe; crucially, he is not the rightful owner of the house, but rather a puffed-up usurper. Hence the narrator's observation that Reason quoted Tartuffe, "and with greater reason" than he: in this case, the house is actually hers.

CHAPTER IX: TRANSITION

1. In the *Revista Brazileira* edition of the novel, the chapter ended here.

CHAPTER X: ON THAT DAY

1. The dobra and half-dobra were names given to a succession of Portuguese coins of varying values. In 1805, the exchange rate stood at approximately $1.20 per milréis, and a half-dobra was worth 6.4 milréis. Adjusted for inflation, two half-dobras would be a generous sum, something like a few hundred dollars today.
2. In the Brazilian Northeast, the Dutch occupied the city of Salvador from 1624 to 1625 and the region around Recife and Olinda, in Pernambuco, from 1630 to 1654. Much like the Dutch presence in New Amsterdam, this decades-long occupation would leave its mark on the city; and some Jews expelled after the fall of Dutch Recife would move on to the Manhattan settlement.

CHAPTER XI: THE CHILD IS FATHER OF THE MAN

1. The line "The Child is father of the Man" comes from "The Rainbow," also known as "My Heart Leaps Up," a poem published in 1807 by William Wordsworth (1770–1850).

2. In the 1880 and 1881 editions, the sentence appeared as follows: "Yes, my father adored me; he loved me with that meritless affection that is the simple, powerful impulse of the flesh, a love that reason neither defies nor governs."

3. Here, opening the next paragraph, was the following passage in the earliest published edition of the novel: "So good, so simple, my mother harbored at the bottom of her heart a shadow of melancholy, which I inherited, just as I inherited my father's fatuousness. She was given to melancholy; I think, however, that life exacerbated that which was a natural tendency. She had too much heart, a delicate sensibility, and was high-strung and sickly. One or the other of these qualities were combined, and alternated, in myself."

4. *Tanga*, which today designates a skimpy bathing-suit bottom in Brazil, is variously used in the period of the novel to refer to loincloths and a sort of cloth wrapped around the waist. One 1836 dictionary defines it specifically as "a piece of cloth with which slaves cover their private parts."

5. Tertullian was a Christian theologian who lived in the second and third centuries CE, best known for his *Apologeticus*, in which he defended Christians from Roman persecution. The Nicene Creed, so called because it was adopted in 325 CE by the Council of Nicaea, is a statement of faith accepted across multiple Christian churches, affirming the divinity of Jesus Christ and the Holy Spirit.

CHAPTER XII: AN EPISODE FROM 1814

1. By late 1805, Napoleon Bonaparte (1769–1821) had already become the first Emperor of France, crowned himself King of Italy, and would soon capture a number of Rhenish states. Before Brás was out of short pants, the emperor had invaded the Iberian Peninsula and driven the Braganças, the Portuguese royal family, into exile in Rio de Janeiro.

2. Bonaparte's first fall came in 1814, when a coalition of nations, having driven him out of Germany, took Paris and exiled the general to the island of Elba. He would escape from the island and rule for a brief period before being condemned to a definitive exile on the island of St. Helena in 1815.

3. Manuel Maria Barbosa du Bocage (1765–1805) was a Portuguese poet who fell afoul of the authorities over the subversive

content of his verses. Assuming that we believe Vilaça's bluster, he might have had a literary duel with the poet after Bocage's release from prison, which came in late 1798. The establishment known as Botequim do Nicola (today, Café Nicola) was founded in downtown Lisbon in the middle to late eighteenth century and became famous as a haunt of Bocage's, where he composed and delivered many a biting satirical poem.

4. The French-born aristocrat Marie Madeleine de Montmorency-Luxembourg (1778–1833) became the Duchess of Cadaval upon marrying Miguel Caetano Álvares Pereira de Melo (1765–1808). Vilaça presumably mentions the Duchess and not the Duke because the latter left his mark on history by being the sole fatality on the voyage that brought the Portuguese court to Brazil in 1808 (see note 4 to Chapter XIII).

5. Antônio José da Silva (1705–1739), known as "O Judeu" (or "The Jew"), was a satirical playwright born in Rio and executed by the Inquisition in Lisbon. His productions, while largely spoken, were referred to as "operas" because they contained musical components. The line that Vilaça quotes is drawn from a scene in *Anfitrião, ou Júpiter e Alcmena* (Amphitryon, or Jupiter and Alcmene), in which Jupiter, disguised as Alcmene's husband, Amphytrion, bids farewell to her after a night spent together. Later on, Brás references Jupiter/Zeus's propensity to disguise himself in order to seduce women, alluding to the stories of Leda and the swan, Danae and the shower of gold, and Europa and the bull.

CHAPTER XIII: A LEAP

1. *Compelle intrare* is a quotation from the parable of the banquet (Luke 14:23). In the King James Version: "And the lord said unto the servant, Go out into the highways and hedges, and compel *them* to come in, that my house may be filled."

2. Rua do Piolho, which translates into "Louse Street"—hence a fitting residence for a teacher with the surname Cockroach—was a real thoroughfare, named after a resident with that unattractive nickname. It remains in downtown Rio but has since changed its name to the less off-putting Rua da Carioca—*carioca* being the designation for natives of Rio, derived from the Carioca River, which fed a fountain just off the street in question.

3. In the *Revista Brazileira* edition of the novel, there follows: "Let us flee from this past, so remote, so blanketed, alas! with funerary crosses."

4. Unlike much of Latin America, Brazil went from being a colony to an empire in its own right. In 1808, the Portuguese court had been driven out of Lisbon by Napoleon and set up shop in Rio de Janeiro, shifting the center of power of the Portuguese crown westward across the ocean. When the monarchs were pressed to return in the following decade, King João VI went back to Portugal, but his son Pedro stayed and declared Brazil's independence on September 7, 1822, becoming Pedro I of Brazil.

CHAPTER XV: MARCELA

1. The translation of the idiomatic expression *Você é das Arábias!* is one of the points on which the critic and Machado scholar Raimundo Magalhães Júnior found fault with both William Grossman and E. Percy Ellis. The expression is defined in a contemporary idiom dictionary as follows: "said of an individual who is uncommon, singular, extraordinary and peerless, eccentric or unsurpassable." Grossman and Ellis interpreted it as "You are irresistible . . . I think you must have Arabian blood" and "You come straight out of the Arabian Nights!" respectively. Magalhães Júnior, pointing out that the expression isn't literal, suggested the translation "You are simply amazing." The idiom has become less common over the years, however, and I was loath to lose the reference to Arabia, which will be picked up on when Brás's mind wanders to Scheherazade a couple of chapters later. I wound up digging in the dictionary and dusting off the adjective "Arabian-night," which derives, of course, from the *Arabian Nights* but refers to things magical and wondrous in general.

2. In the narrative published in the *Revista Brazileira*, another chapter came between these two, titled *Commotion*. "Chapter XV moved me so greatly that I no longer have the heart to write Chapter XVI, which would be even more moving than the former; this page will be left to rest. The reader may close the book, recapitulate what he has read, or simply have the devil take both the author and his memoirs. For my part, I will turn the page and write . . ."

CHAPTER XVII: CONCERNING
THE TRAPEZE AND OTHER MATTERS

1. While it is difficult to account for inflation, purchasing power, and other factors over the centuries with any real precision, this would amount to at least a few hundred thousand dollars today.

2. As published in the *Revista Brazileira*, the sentence went as follows: "Marcela started slightly; her pupils blazed like those of a starving hawk; she raised up half of her body." Machado may have eliminated this metaphor out of a desire to avoid repeating an avian pupil—another appears in Chapter XX as Brás refers to his budding ambition.

CHAPTER XVIII: A VISION IN THE HALLWAY

1. In the collection of Middle Eastern folktales variously translated as *The Thousand and One Nights*, *One Thousand and One Nights*, or *The Arabian Nights*, one of the stories is of the barber's second brother, Bakbarah the Toothless. Bakbarah is walking along the street in Baghdad when he is presented with the opportunity to have an audience with a beautiful young lady, but advised that he must behave as mildly as possible and never contradict her. He is subsequently used as a plaything by the grand vizier's wife and her ladies, who slap him around, shave, paint, and perfume him to look like a woman, and force him to strip half naked, all for the promise of an amorous encounter that never materializes. Eventually, believing that he is pursuing the mistress of the house to her chambers, he runs down an alleyway and out onto the street, as Brás recalls, only to be beaten again by jeering onlookers.

2. The term *correeiro*, which first appeared in Chapter I, may be translated as saddler or beltmaker, one who works with leather. Here, William Grossman translated the term as "leather venders," E. Percy Ellis as "riff-raff," and Gregory Rabassa as "harness-makers." To go to the source: in G. S. Beaumont and Forster's translations of *The Thousand and One Nights*, the men who beat Bakbarah are "curriers." Burton and E. W. Lane translate them as "leather-sellers," N. J. Dawood as "merchants," and John Payne as "fell-mongers." The unfortunate lover's name is translated variously as El-Heddar, Al-Haddar the Babbler, Bec-bac, Bakbarah, and Backbarah the Toothless. Like previous

translators, I have opted to maintain Machado's spelling of the name.

CHAPTER XIX: ON BOARD

1. Eclogues are poems on a pastoral theme, generally structured as a dialogue.

CHAPTER XXI: THE MULETEER

1. Adjusted for inflation, this princely sum would be comfortably under $20 today.

CHAPTER XXII: RETURN TO RIO

1. A duodecimo, or a twelvemo, was a book in which the pages were folded so as to form twelve leaves, or twenty-four pages, the result being something closer to a pocket paperback than a folio.

CHAPTER XXIV: SHORT, BUT HAPPY

1. Through the 1881 edition, the sentence read as follows: "I plucked from all things the phraseology, the husk, and the ornamentation, which were for my spirit, vain and naked, what seashells and corpses' teeth are for the breast of a savage."

CHAPTER XXV: IN TIJUCA

1. Tijuca is a neighborhood in Rio de Janeiro's Zona Norte that shares a name with the mountainous national park abutting it. At the time of the novel it was a rural region dotted with country estates; in other narratives, many of Machado's newlyweds choose to spend their honeymoons up in the hills of Tijuca.

2. The quotation is from *As You Like It*, Act IV, Scene 1. To this observation by Jaques, Rosalind responds: "Why then, 'tis good to be a post."

3. Prudêncio describes the house as *roxa*, which in modern-day Portuguese means purple. The term derives from the French *roux* by way of the Latin *rufus*, or red; Francisco Solano Constâncio's 1836 dictionary defines *roxo* as either violet or flaming red. Contemporary usage indicates that the term drifted over time from red to purple, with *roxo* eventually overlapping with the then existing terms *cor de violeta* (violet) and *purpúreo* (purple). Given the impossibility of ascertaining the exact hue of the fictional house, I ultimately preferred "red"—after all, Dona Eusébia is seen as something of a scarlet woman.

CHAPTER XXVI: THE AUTHOR HESITATES

1. *"Arma virumque cano"*: these are the first lines of Virgil's *Aeneid*, rendered as "Arms and the man I sing" in Frederick Ahl's translation. The phrase has an additional resonance in the Portuguese-language canon, as it is echoed in the first line of Camões's *Lusiads*—*"As armas e os barões assinalados"*—or, in Sir Richard Burton's translation, "The feats of arms, and famed heroic host."

CHAPTER XXIX: THE VISIT

1. In the first and second editions, there followed: "Strictly speaking, his son had disembarked in that precise moment, wearing a linen top-coat, hands in his pockets. There was then, in my father's eyes, something of the old Cid; his soul had gathered all of its last sparks into a single flame." Eugênio Gomes saw this edit as yet another move to cut down on unnecessary name-dropping, with the removal of the reference to *El Cid*; one might add that the image of the dying sparks being gathered into a single flame will be repeated in Chapter XLIV.

CHAPTER XXXI: THE BLACK BUTTERFLY

1. In the *Revista Brazileira* edition of the novel, we find another clause after this one. In English, the full sentence would read: "The gentle way in which it began moving its wings, once settled, had a sneering air, a sort of Mephistophelian mockery, that greatly displeased me." Once again, as mentioned in the preceding note,

Machado eliminates a literary reference, with the additional effect of diminishing the apparent malice of the doomed butterfly.

2. In the earliest version of the novel, as it appeared in the *Revista Brasileira*, the paragraph ended with the following observation: "This may not be the true interpretation, but it is certainly the most plausible."

CHAPTER XXXIII: BLESSED ARE THEY THAT GO NOT DOWN

1. "Tartuffism" is a reference to Tartuffe, the title character in Molière's 1664 play; by extension, the term designates false pretenders to virtue. In *Zur Genealogie der Moral*, Friedrich Nietzsche (1844–1900) uses the term "Tartüfferie," rendered in Portuguese as *tartufice*; this was translated at least once into English as "Pecksniffianism," in a cross-literary reference to Seth Pecksniff, the moralizing and hypocritical Dickens character.

CHAPTER XXXIV: TO A SENSITIVE SOUL

1. As if a reference to Diana's immaculate thigh in a passage about crippled legs weren't bad enough, the word for "thigh" in Portuguese (*coxa*) is the same as the feminine form of the adjective for "crippled" (*coxo*).

CHAPTER XXXVI: ON THE SUBJECT OF BOOTS

1. In a parting shot at the defenseless Eugênia, Brás's hypothetical audience doesn't literally boo, but rather stamps its feet in disapproval (the verb is *patear*, from the word *pata*, foot or paw).

CHAPTER XLV: NOTES

1. In the 1880 edition, the chapter ended as follows: "These, apparently items in a simple inventory, were notes that I had taken for an extremely succulent chapter, in which I proved that the earth should continue to spin around the sun, for the reasons that: a) nature only

invented death to give life to certain industries—undertaking, coachmaking, printing, the mortuary industry, and others which she wisely foresaw; and b) once these industries should die, in the absence of human death, it would not be improbable for their respective industrialists to die, which would be the same thing in the end. But all these are notes for a chapter that I will not write."

CHAPTER XLIX: THE TIP OF THE NOSE

1. In *Candide, or Optimism*, by François-Marie Arouet, or Voltaire (1694–1778), Dr. Pangloss is a character whose philosophy is a parody of Leibnizian optimism; in the face of successive and increasingly grotesque catastrophes, he insists that all is for the best and that he and his fellow characters are living in the best of all possible worlds.

CHAPTER L: VIRGÍLIA, MARRIED

1. The reign of Pedro I—the First Reign—lasted from Independence Day on September 7, 1822, to April 7, 1831, when the emperor abdicated in favor of his son, still a child. There followed a period known as the Regency, which lasted until the fourteen-year-old heir took the throne on July 23, 1840, inaugurating the (second) reign of Pedro II. Given the time frame, a lady who had graced balls during the tenure of both monarchs would have had to maintain her charms for a full decade at the very least.

2. Dante Alighieri's *Inferno* tells the story of Francesca da Rimini and Paolo Malatesta in Canto V. Francesca was married to Paolo's brother Gianciotto, or Giovanni the Lame, and is said to have fallen in love with her brother-in-law while they both read the story of the affair between Lancelot and Guinevere. The book is Francesca's undoing not only in that it opens the door to temptation, but also in the sense that it leads to a double punishment: murder at the hands of Gianciotto and an eternity in Hell.

CHAPTER LI: MINE!

1. The phrase *"vi, claramente visto"* is a quote from the 1572 epic poem the *Lusiads*, by Luís de Camões (c. 1524–1580), in a

passage describing St. Elmo's fire—"I saw, and clearly saw, the living Light / which sailor-people hold their Patron-saint," in Sir Richard Burton's translation.

CHAPTER LII: THE MYSTERIOUS PARCEL

1. In the earliest version of the novel, Brás was afraid of finding green, or unripe guavas; Machado, no doubt realizing that this was hardly the most humiliating outcome, made them rot in the final version.
2. Between Brazil's independence and the 1840s, the value of the milréis relative to the dollar had fallen by half; still, Brás's find would be the equivalent of tens of thousands of dollars today.
3. William Grossman, E. Percy Ellis, and Gregory Rabassa all translate this term—*lenço de tabaco*—as "pouch" or "packet" of tobacco. The term *lenço* (handkerchief), however, suggests something slightly different and slightly less savory, and led me to the discovery of the late sartorial institution of the snuff handkerchief. Those given to using snuff, inhalable tobacco, would either sneeze or wipe their noses after a vigorous whiff; and the resulting brown stains meant that one would reserve a specific piece of cloth for the purpose. Useful, certainly, but not the sort of thing that it would ruin one's day to lose.

CHAPTER LIII: . . . .

1. In the first published version, we read: "trembling with fear, since it came at the garden gate, in full view of the stars—of Othello's chaste stars." The quotation is from Act V, Scene 2, of Shakespeare's play, in Othello's soliloquy just before he murders Desdemona.

CHAPTER LVII: FATE

1. As it appeared in the *Revista Brazileira*, the chapter was titled: "In Which the Author, Finding No Name for This Chapter, Limits Himself to Writing It."
2. In Dante's *Divine Comedy*, this verse refers not to two souls in Purgatory, but to the poet himself and a soul he speaks to, that

of the illustrator and illuminator Oderisi da Gubbio. In Dorothy Leigh Sayers's translation: "step for step, like oxen in the yoke."

3. In the earliest version of the novel, after "Poor Fate!" the passage went as follows: "Are you still alive, my old man? How I long to tug on your beard! The last time I saw you was in some melodrama; you were sonorous, nearly in perfect meter, falling from the lips of the hero into the ears of the heroine. Then, I can't recall whether I saw you running by in commemorative speeches or in the verses of a funeral mass; but you were surely changed, old man: you were stumbling, wrinkled, worn to tatters. Where are you now, great solicitor of human affairs? Perhaps off creating a new skin, another face, other manners, a different name, and perhaps you may come to fall from the lips of the hero into the ears of the heroine once again . . . Now I can't remember where I was . . . Ah! Down the devious byways. Well, I charged fate with the task of guiding me down them. And I said to myself that things were in God's hands."

CHAPTER LIX: AN ENCOUNTER

1. Father Manuel Bernardes (1644–1710) was a Portuguese priest and writer. In his book *Os Últimos Fins do Homem* (1728) we find the phrase *"trage ao bizarro"* (bizarre garb) in reference to nuns who, despite their vows of chastity, poverty, and obedience, dressed up in extravagant clothes.

2. Brás rather rudely dates the man's ragged clothes to the period of the Babylonian Captivity, in which the Jews were exiled to Babylon in the seventh and sixth centuries BCE.

3. Legend has it that Albrecht Gessler, a Habsburg bailiff in the Swiss canton of Uri, put his hat on a pole in the town square and forced passersby to bow to it. William Tell refused, and the bailiff, aware of the man's fame as a marksman, promptly challenged him to split an apple set on his son's head.

4. In the first edition, this section onward was a chapter on its own, titled "Five Milréis."

5. The eighteenth-century church of São Francisco de Paula still stands in downtown Rio, on the square that bears its name. An examination of the flight of steps out front—which do not appear to have been altered since Brás's time, judging from period images—reveals that they are far too narrow for a grown man to sleep on, however skeletal. Conclude from that what you may.

6. In 1842–1843, the value of one milréis, or a thousand réis, was roughly half that of one dollar; adjusted by the U.S. Consumer Price Index, $2.50 then might be close to a hundred dollars today. By the same method, the porridge that Quincas mentions, hypothetically priced at two *vinténs*, or forty réis, might go for less than one of today's dollars.

7. The Latin phrase, traditionally translated into English as "In this sign thou shalt conquer," refers to a vision of a cross that appeared to the emperor Constantine (272–337) before a decisive battle, emblazoned with the motto in Greek. After this vision and his victory, the emperor converted to Christianity.

CHAPTER LXIII: LET'S RUN AWAY!

1. Augusta Candiani (1820–1890) was an Italian opera singer who had a successful career in Brazil. Her admirers were so passionate that, after one performance of *Norma*, they famously unhitched her carriage and pulled it themselves. In an 1877 newspaper column, Machado de Assis confessed that in his youth, he had been one of the prima donna's "temporary horses."

CHAPTER LXVIII: THE WHIP

1. Valongo is the name of the quay where slaves were brought into Rio starting in 1811, and also the market where they were sold, which was declared illegal on November 7, 1831 (not that this precluded a robust smuggling industry). During the decades when it was officially active, the wharf received hundreds of thousands of enslaved Africans, a significant portion of the approximately four million brought to Brazil. In Chapter XLVII, Brás indicates that his affair with Virgília begins in 1842; in the following year, 1843, the notorious quay would be covered over by the Cais da Imperatriz, built specially to receive Teresa Cristina of the Two Sicilies, the bride-to-be of Emperor Pedro II. Recent excavations in Rio's downtown have revealed the two layers, with the large, even stones of the empress's landing giving way to the haphazard cobblestones of the slave wharf.

2. In the *Revista Brazileira* version of the novel, Brás refers to Prudêncio as a *patife* (villain) instead of a *maroto* (rascal).

CHAPTER LXIX: A DASH OF LUNACY

1. Born in modern-day Uzbekistan, Tamerlane, or Timur (1336–1405), was a conqueror who referred to himself as the "Sword of Islam" and founded the vast Timurid Empire.

CHAPTER LXXI: THE FLAW IN THE BOOK

1. In the novel's first and second editions, the chapter ended as follows: "The air you breathe is muddied, dear leaves. The sun that lights you, though it belongs to all, is a dull, poor one, the sun of cemeteries and Carnival."

CHAPTER LXXIII: REFRESHMENTS

1. This chapter was originally titled "O *Lunch*" (The Lunch), with the English term amended to "luncheon" after the second edition. In the preface to his translation of the novel, William Grossman justifies altering the chapter title in translation with the argument that "luncheon" meant "afternoon snack" to Machado and his public. The English word "lunch" has indeed been preserved in modern Portuguese as *lanche*, which means a snack (or a sandwich, in São Paulo). So as not to cause confusion, I have opted to change the term but translate it as "refreshments," which has less of an informal air than "snack" in twenty-first-century English.

CHAPTER LXXIV: THE STORY OF DONA PLÁCIDA

1. The *tostão* was the equivalent of 100 réis; *dez tostões*, which is how Dona Plácida's monthly wage is reported, was how people commonly referred to one milréis. Since this is one of the few occurrences of *tostão* in the novel, I opted to translate this currency unit in such a way as to highlight its relative (lack of) value.

CHAPTER LXXVII: RENDEZVOUS

1. The Portuguese here is treacherously ambiguous: *"Era claro que me enganara"* can mean either "It was clear that I had been mistaken" or "It was clear that she had deceived me."

CHAPTER LXXVIII: THE PRESIDENCY

1. Colonial Brazil was divided into fourteen hereditary captaincies, subsequently administered by governors-general; under the Brazilian Empire, the territory would be organized in a number of provinces, later dubbed states under the Republic. Hence, while Lobo Neves's appointment would be roughly equivalent to that of a governor in the United States, I have opted to directly translate the term "president of the province," as the term "governor" was used prior to the Empire and following it, but not during this period.

CHAPTER LXXIX: COMPROMISE

1. In the earliest edition of the novel, the chapter ended as follows: "On this score I am reminded of a naturalist—I can't remember which, but some naturalist—from whom I read this curious observation: 'Cats do not caress us, they caress themselves on us.' I see that I was striking a cat's compromise." The "naturalist" he is quoting is actually the eighteenth-century French writer Antoine de Rivarol (1753–1801), who expressed it as: *"Le chat ne nous caresse pas, il se caresse à nous."* The chapter's original title, accordingly, was "Cat's Compromise."

CHAPTER LXXXII: A MATTER OF BOTANY

1. This is a reference to a poem by the Portuguese writer Almeida Garrett, titled precisely "As Pegas de Sintra" (The Magpies of Sintra), in which the author describes how King João I was caught by the queen in the act of kissing a lady-in-waiting, and his flustered justification was overheard and gleefully repeated by the magpies around the palace.

CHAPTER LXXXIII: 13

1. In the novel as published in the *Revista Brazileira*, after this sentence, the chapter ended as follows: "And so we stayed. Men's superstition must be good for something, after all."

CHAPTER LXXXIV: THE CONFLICT

1. On the eve of battle, the Greek general Pelopidas (c. 410–364 BCE) dreamt that the gods had demanded the sacrifice of a red-haired virgin. As his subordinates were debating the proposition, a filly with a fiery red mane ran through the camp and was chosen to stand in for a human woman.

CHAPTER LXXXV: THE MOUNTAINTOP

1. Brás again references the collection of folktales known as *The Arabian Nights* or *The Thousand and One Nights*. The stories are woven together with the following thread: The sultan Shahryar, having found his first wife unfaithful to him, has her executed and decides to marry a new virgin every night and execute each the next morning. Scheherazade, the vizier's daughter, volunteers for the post. She tells a new story every night, but leaves off just before the story's end as dawn is breaking so that the sultan will spare her.

CHAPTER XCI: AN EXTRAORDINARY LETTER

1. Quincas Borba is quoting from Act I, Scene 2, of *The Barber of Seville*, by Pierre-Augustin Beaumarchais (1732–1799), which was first performed in 1775. Figaro is speaking to Count Almaviva, who comments on how sleek and fat the barber has become. In David Coward's translation, the barber responds: "Heigh-ho, your Lordship, it's the poverty that does it."

CHAPTER XCII: AN EXTRAORDINARY MAN

1. Though Damasceno refers to it as a "revolution," 1831 saw no armed conflict, but rather a series of political clashes between

liberal Brazilians opposed to Pedro I's conservative cabinet and his hard-line approach, and Brazilian-based Portuguese loyal to the emperor. On April 7, Pedro finally abdicated in favor of his five-year-old son, leaving for Europe shortly thereafter. A series of regents governed the country before the heir was able to take the throne.

2. The saying from "other parts" is a reference to the observation by Nicolas Chamfort (1741–1794) that France was an absolute monarchy tempered by songs. By this he meant that, faced with a salvo of taxes under Cardinal Mazarin, the French people responded with the few weapons at their disposal—satirical rhymes hence known as "Mazarinades."

3. After the Slave Trade Act of 1807, England had taken the lead in opposing the continued dealing of slaves. While Brazil had officially banned the slave trade in 1831, with a law declaring that all slaves brought into the country would become free on arrival, it was solemnly ignored in practice. This gap between law and enforcement would give rise to the Portuguese expression *para inglês ver*—for the English to see—which refers to something that is merely for show and not to be taken seriously. If Brás, as Baroness X indicates, is around forty, then the narration has reached late 1845, by which point Parliament had passed the Aberdeen Act, giving the Royal Navy the power to stop and search Brazilian ships. The law provoked outrage; the definitive abolition of the slave trade—via Brazilian legislation—would not come until five years later.

4. Lest the reader raise an eyebrow at this intimacy: one of the most popular dances of the period was the quadrille, in which couples line up opposite one another.

5. The town of Praia Grande would eventually become the modern-day city of Niterói, which lies across Guanabara Bay from Rio de Janeiro.

CHAPTER XCV: THE FLOWERS OF YESTERYEAR

1. This plaintive question seems to echo the refrain of "Ballade des Dames du Temps Jadis," by François Villon (1431–1463). In Dante Gabriel Rossetti's translation, the poet asks, "Where are the snows of yesteryear?"

CHAPTER XCVIII: TAKEN OUT

1. The reference is to Blaise Pascal's *Pensées*. In W. F. Trotter's translation, the fragment in question reads: "Man is neither angel nor brute, and the unfortunate thing is that he who would act the angel acts the brute."

CHAPTER CVIII: WHICH IS NOT UNDERSTOOD

1. See Chapter V for the first reference to the "tip of the ear" metaphor. I would have liked to use "tragic tip of a Shakespearean iceberg" here, but the iceberg-related phrase is a post-*Titanic* coinage, after which the public was all too aware of the relationship between the visible portion of an iceberg and its true bulk.

CHAPTER CIX: THE PHILOSOPHER

1. This is a reference to the motto *Veritas in puteo*, or "Truth lies in a well," indicating the difficulty or effort involved in dredging up the truth of things, which Diogenes attributes to Democritus. R. D. Hicks, however, in his version of Diogenes' *Lives of Eminent Philosophers*, indicates that the original Greek would better be rendered as "Truth lies in an abyss."

CHAPTER CXVI: PHILOSOPHY OF OLD PAPERS

1. On the Emperor Domitian (51–96), Suetonius writes in his *Lives of the Twelve Caesars*: "At the beginning of his reign he used to spend hours in seclusion every day, doing nothing but catch flies and stab them with a keenly-sharpened stylus. Consequently when someone once asked whether anyone was in there with Caesar, Vibius Crispus made the witty reply: 'Not even a fly.'"

2. In the *Revista Brazileira* edition, the chapter ended with the following additional lines: "For that matter, that very same old seaman used to confess his age (past fifty) with this equally seafaring phrase: 'How old am I, sir? I'm halfway to land.' Finally, he used the term 'admiral's night' for a night of high and fine

recreation. Who on earth teaches rhetoric to sailors?" The phrase "admiral's night" would eventually baptize one of Machado's short stories, in which, incidentally, a dejected character is described with the same phrase: *"meio caminho para terra"* (halfway to land).

CHAPTER CXVIII: THE THIRD FORCE

1. The chapter was originally as follows: "The third force (See the first line of the previous chapter), the third force calling me to the throng was my impatience to shine in society, and, above all, my inability to live alone. The multitude attracted me, applause courted me; galas, tumults, and drumbeats were all great objects of seduction. If the idea for the plaster had presented itself to me then, who knows? I might not have died straightaway and I would be famous. But the plaster did not come. What did come was the desire to throw myself into something, for something. Tout notre mal vient de ne pouvoir être seuls. [All of our misfortunes proceed from an inability to be alone.] This maxim by La Bruyère always struck me as utter nonsense. There is no doubt that sociability is men's chief virtue, while the second is curiosity, the third is punctuality in payments, the fourth is military valor, and so on." The eliminated reference is to the philosopher Jean de La Bruyère (1645–1696), with a quotation from his 1688 book *Characters*.

CHAPTER CXIX: PARENTHESIS

1. In the first version of the chapter, it was both lengthier and actually enclosed by parentheses, as follows: "(Is there any critical soul so perverse that she might attribute my opinion on La Bruyère to an envy of his maxims? I will blunt this blow from the outset by transcribing a few of those which I composed around that time, and which I tore up shortly thereafter, finding them unworthy of printing. I wrote them during a period when the yellow flower of Chapter XXV had opened again; they were yawnings of tedium. See for yourselves:)"

CHAPTER CXX: *COMPELLE INTRARE*

1. In the earliest version of the novel, this sentence was followed by the phrase: "Here came the secret sting."

CHAPTER CXXI: DOWNHILL

1. Machado de Assis spent his childhood on Livramento Hill, in Rio's port zone; his parents were married and he was baptized in the Livramento chapel.

CHAPTER CXXIII: THE REAL COTRIM

1. Calabouço, or Dungeon, was the name given to several institutions in Rio used for imprisoning runaway slaves, slaves accused of crimes, or those sent by their masters to be punished by the State. This time in Brás's life marked the high-water mark in terms of the sheer number of slaves in the city of Rio—nearly 80,000 were recorded in the 1849 census (out of a population of just over 200,000).
2. *Irmão remido* was a designation in such associations, reserved for members who paid high lump fees and were thus freed of any further financial obligations.

CHAPTER CXXIV: AN INTERLUDE

1. In the novel as it appeared in the *Revista Brazileira*, the chapter closed as follows: "Let it stand as an interlude, and on this score, let us tell an anecdote. This was back in the time of my parliamentary life; there were five of us; we were speaking of all sorts of things, and the conversation happened to touch upon business with Río de la Plata. Then, one said: 'The government should never forget that money is the backbone of war.' To which I responded that no, the backbone of war was good soldiers. One of my listeners scratched his nose, another consulted his watch, the third drummed on his knee, the fourth took a few strides around the room, and the fifth was me. But I continued speaking, and reflected that this entirely worthy idea was not mine, but rather Machiavelli's; this circumstance led the first to

cease scratching his nose, the second to cease consulting his watch, the third to cease drumming on his knee, and the fourth to cease striding; and all surrounded me and asked me to repeat the saying, and I did, and they were beside themselves, and nodded their heads in approval, savoring it and learning it by heart. Which I esteemed greatly, as I have always loved worthy ideas. But let us go to the epitaph."

CHAPTER CXXVI: DISCONSOLATION

1. The first outbreak of yellow fever in Brazil began at the end of 1849. The disease disproportionately affected the more European sectors of the population, as they had the least resistance to it. The scourge thus threatened to upset the balance of power in a city with a considerable population of enslaved people (see note 1, on the Calabouço, or Dungeon, in Chapter CXXIII). The racial disparity in the fatalities was so great that one story attributed the plague to the fact that white parishioners had refused to carry a statue of St. Benedict on their shoulders in a religious procession, and that the black saint sent the disease in revenge.

CHAPTER CXXVII: FORMALITY

1. This is a reference to II Corinthians 3:4–6, where we read in the King James Version that "God . . . hath made us able ministers of the new testament; not of the letter, but of the spirit: for the letter killeth, but the spirit giveth life."

CHAPTER CXXXI: ON SLANDER

1. In George Saintsbury's translation of the *Heptaméron*, a collection of short stories written by Margaret, Queen of Navarre (1492–1549), the Duchess of Burgundy delivers the following verbal blow to her niece, the Lady du Vergier: "There is no love so secret that it is not known, and no little dog so well broken in and trained that it cannot be heard to bark."

CHAPTER CXXXIII: HELVÉTIUS'S PRINCIPLE

1. The French philosopher Helvétius (1715–1771) wrote that the great driving force behind life is self-interest, born of the love of pleasure and fear of pain, which shapes our judgment, our actions, and our affections. While Brás announces that he will correct this theory, he ultimately confirms it in his actions, merely adjusting the terms to fit the philosopher's formulation.

CHAPTER CXXXV: OBLIVION

1. The reference is to Browne's *Christian Morals*, which Machado almost certainly took from the opening of Charles Lamb's essay "My Relations." It goes as follows: "I am arrived at that point of life at which a man may account it a blessing, as it is a singularity, if he have either of his parents surviving. I have not that felicity—and sometimes think feelingly of a passage in Browne's Christian Morals, where he speaks of a man that hath lived sixty or seventy years in the world. 'In such a compass of time,' he says, 'a man may have a close apprehension what it is to be forgotten, when he hath lived to find none who could remember his father, or scarcely the friends of his youth, and may sensibly see with what a face in no long time OBLIVION will look upon himself.'" In my translation, since the quotation is abbreviated and somewhat altered, I simply attempted to echo the language of Browne.

2. Honório Hermeto Carneiro Leão (1801–1856), the Marquis of Paraná, led the imperial cabinet from 1851 until his death. Since Brás would have turned fifty in late 1855, we can surmise that this hypothetical lady would have peaked just a few years earlier. This is one of multiple comments making it abundantly clear how swiftly women's beauty was seen to fade (see note 1 to Chapter L).

CHAPTER CXL: WHICH EXPLAINS THE PREVIOUS

1. In the *Revista Brazileira*, a short chapter followed this, titled "If I Ever . . . ," which read: "If I ever write another book, I will tell

of my life in Parliament. Not now; I haven't enough time, and I am profoundly vexed."

CHAPTER CXLII: THE SECRET REQUEST

1. The "someone" in question is François Marcel (d. 1759), the dancing-master, as portrayed in Helvétius's essay "The Mind Relatively to Society," in *De l'Esprit* (1758). This is the relevant passage, from the first English translation: "However frivolous an art may appear, yet it is susceptible of infinite combinations. When Marcel, with his hand placed on his forehead, his eyes fixed, his body without motion, and in the attitude of profound meditation, on seeing a young lady dance, cries out, What variety in a minuet! doubtless, this dancing-master then perceived in the manner of bending, rising, and performing the steps, elegancies invisible to common eyes; and there his exclamation is no farther ridiculous than in the too great importance it places on trifles."

2. While St. John the Baptist ate grasshoppers in the desert—this is Quincas Borba's second disdainful reference to the fact—Ezekiel is ordered by God to eat a scroll and obeys, finding it "as honey for sweetness."

3. This passage from Blaise Pascal's *Pensées* is slightly altered in Quincas Borba's paraphrasing; in W. F. Trotter's translation, which William Grossman quotes in *Epitaph of a Small Winner*, it goes as follows: "But were the universe to crush him, man would still be more noble than that which has slain him, because he knows that he dies, and that the universe has the better of him. The universe knows nothing of this." The paraphrase thus eliminates man's knowledge of the superiority of the universe. Given the distance between Pascal's phrasing and Quincas Borba's somewhat plainer speech, I opted to translate straight from the Portuguese.

CHAPTER CXLIII: I WON'T GO

1. While Brás puzzles despairingly over the location of the Beco das Escadinhas, Machado knew perfectly well where it was; the street, whose name translates to Narrow-Stairs Alley, was one of the routes leading up Livramento Hill, where the author was

born. Another Beco das Escadinhas could be found in the nearby port neighborhood of Saúde.

CHAPTER CXLVI: THE PROSPECTUS

1. This appears to be an adaptation of a quote from Charles Mills's 1817 *History of Muhammedanism*, which Machado had in his library in French translation. In the English: "Though the sun were set against me on my right hand, and the moon on my left, I would not swerve from my course."

CHAPTER CXLIX: THEORY OF BENEFITS

1. Desiderius Erasmus (1466–1536), in *In Praise of Folly*, takes the adage *Mutuum muli scabunt*, or "One mule scratches another," to comment: "What shows such willingness to please as the way mules scratch each other?"

CHAPTER CL: ROTATION AND TRANSLATION

1. Here, translation is not what is allowing you to read this book, but rather the Euclidean process by which an object moves through space. Inter-language translation and spatial translation are not homonyms in Portuguese (they are *tradução* and *translação*, respectively), but it seems fitting that they should be disorientingly blended here, in a book translated through time and across languages.

CHAPTER CLII: VESPASIAN'S COIN

1. In Suetonius's telling, the emperor Vespasian (9–79) imposed a tax on public toilets. When his son Titus complained about the indignity of the practice, the emperor held up a gold coin and asked if the smell of it offended the younger man's nose. Upon hearing that it didn't, Vespasian said, "Yet it comes from urine." This interaction reportedly gave rise to the maxim *Pecunia non olet*—money doesn't stink.